The Hardy Boys Casefiles ™

Books in THE HARDY BOYS CASEFILES ™ Series

11 Brother Against Brother
12 Perfect Getaway
13 The Borgia Dagger
14 Too Many Traitors
15 Blood Relations
16 Line of Fire
17 The Number File
18 A Killing in the Market
19 Nightmare in Angel City
20 Witness to Murder
21 Street Spies
22 Double Exposure
23 Disaster for Hire
24 Scene of the Crime
25 The Borderline Case
26 Trouble in the Pipeline
27 Nowhere to Run
28 Countdown to Terror
29 Thick as Thieves
30 The Deadliest Dare
31 Without a Trace
32 Blood Money
33 Collision Course
34 Final Cut
35 The Dead Season
36 Running on Empty
37 Danger Zone
38 Diplomatic Deceit
39 Flesh and Blood
40 Fright Wave

41 Highway Robbery
42 The Last Laugh
43 Strategic Moves
44 Castle Fear
45 In Self Defense
46 Foul Play
47 Flight into Danger
48 Rock 'n' Revenge
49 Dirty Deeds
50 Power Play
51 Choke Hold
52 Uncivil War
53 Web of Horror
54 Deep Trouble
55 Beyond The Law
56 Height of Danger
57 Terror on Track
58 Spiked!
59 Open Season
60 Deadfall
61 Grave Danger
62 Final Gambit
63 Cold Sweat
64 Endangered Species
65 No Mercy
66 The Phoenix Equation
67 Lethal Cargo
68 Rough Riding
69 Mayhem in Motion
70 Rigged for Revenge

The Hardy Boys Casefiles ™

Franklin W Dixon

Witness to Murder
Street Spies
Double Exposure

AN ARCHWAY PAPERBACK
Published by SIMON & SCHUSTER
New York London Toronto Sydney Tokyo Singapore

WITNESS TO MURDER, STREET SPIES and
DOUBLE EXPOSURE were first published in Great
Britain by Simon & Schuster Ltd in 1992
First published together in this combined edition
in 1996 by Simon & Schuster Ltd
A Viacom Company

Simon & Schuster Ltd
West Garden Place
Kendal Street
London W2 2AQ

The Hardy Boys, Aa Archway Paperback
and colophon are registered trademarks
of Simon & Schuster Inc.

Simon & Schuster of Australia Pty Ltd
Sydney

A CIP catalogue record for this book is
available from the British Library
ISBN 0-671-00478-6

Printed and bound in Great Britain by
Caledonian International Book Manufacturing Ltd,
Glasgow

WITNESS TO MURDER

Chapter

1

"Now, THERE'S SOMETHING to die for." Joe Hardy's blue eyes sparkled as he looked down the aisle of the restaurant.

"A pepperoni pizza?" his older brother Frank joked. But he knew Joe was looking at the waitress, and she was worth a look.

Ever since nineteen-year-old Annie Shea had started working at Mr. Pizza, plenty of guys had tried to get her to go out with them. But Joe Hardy was the only one who had caught her interest.

Girls always liked Joe Hardy. Six feet tall, blond, well-built, seventeen-year-old Joe attracted girls the way a magnet attracts iron filings.

His brother Frank also caused girls to turn and stare. But Frank Hardy had a steady girl—Callie

Shaw—and he wasn't interested in anyone else.

Joe smiled at Frank. "Can you believe I'm going out with Annie, big brother? Eat your heart out. When I'm around, she can't even see you."

"Maybe she just prefers children," Frank said, and grinned slyly. He took every opportunity to remind Joe that he was a year younger. "Sure you can handle a gorgeous woman of nineteen, Joe?"

"I'm trying, I'm trying." Joe returned his brother's grin.

Annie Shea *was* stunning. She was tall, had a great figure, and looked wide-eyed and innocent, as if she didn't know that all the guys in Mr. Pizza were looking at her. When she caught Joe's eye, she broke into a smile that reached up to her dazzling hazel eyes. Her coppery hair billowed about her shoulders as she approached the boys with their order.

She set the special pizza on the small warming lamp. Then she served a slice to each of the boys while continuing to smile at Joe as if there were no one else in the room.

"I hope I'm the only one you smile at." Joe reached for Annie's hand, but she was too fast for him. She spun around with a laugh and scurried back to the kitchen, ignoring Frank completely.

Frank was glad to see his brother so happy. Joe

looked as if he were really in love, for the first time since Iola Morton's death.

Before he could shut it out, a flash of memory sent Frank back to the explosion. An explosion caused by a terrorist bomb placed in the boys' car. The death trap had been set for the Hardys, but Iola had accidentally walked into it—and died in their place. Frank thought of the grim days following the incident, the days when Joe hadn't uttered a word. His brother had become a stranger, full of cold, hard rage and guilt.

"Hey, Frank." Joe waved his hand in front of Frank's eyes. "Don't take it so hard. I'll give you some of my tips on women if you want. You're never too old to learn new tricks."

Frank took a sip of his soda, swallowing the lump that had formed in his throat. "What do you know about Annie, Joe? This pizza job's temporary, right?" He watched Joe deliberately wrap strings of cheese over the tip of his slice of pizza.

"I told you already," Joe said, obviously annoyed. "She comes from out of state. She had a bad experience with an old boyfriend, and her family didn't amount to much." He stopped his staccato delivery and raised his shoulders once.

"But that's all over now," he finally said. "She came to Bayport to make a new start. She likes to hear about my detective work. She even said she'd like to try being a detective. Nothing wrong with that, is there?'' Joe had put an end to the discussion. Frank knew that his brother wasn't going to share any more right then.

He also knew Joe resented being grilled about anything, especially a girl he obviously wanted Frank to like. But Frank didn't feel comfortable with Annie. When she was around, his antennae went up. Something about the girl felt wrong.

Frank tried to ignore these feelings. He was a man of logic, a man of facts. But there it was—he just didn't trust her. Probably he needed a rest. Probably they both needed a rest. Ever since that incident with Iola, he and Joe had been involved in one case after another.

Joe, especially, had gone about their cases with a passion and intensity that sometimes worried Frank. He'd be glad to see his brother relaxed and happy again, Frank thought as he watched Annie toss a wave at Joe from across the room. Joe was concentrating on his pizza and didn't see her, so Frank waved back for him. But Annie frowned and quickly turned away when she noticed Frank.

Frank reached for a slice of pizza and tried to concentrate on the food.

Mr. Pizza, located in the Bayport mall, was always busy, and that day every booth was jammed. But even through the drone of voices and the clatter and thud of dishes, Frank heard the pay phone near the door jingle. A guy at the nearest table answered it. Frank watched as the guy put a hand on Annie's arm to stop her.

For a moment she stood still, with a puzzled look on her face. Then she delivered the order she was carrying and returned to answer the phone. Turning her back on the crowd, she cupped the palm of one hand over her ear and held the phone to the other.

"Now, *that's* popular," Frank said.

"What is?" Joe had his back to the pay phone.

"Getting calls on the pay phone where you work, especially at lunchtime." Frank nodded in Annie's direction.

Joe turned around. "Strange. Annie doesn't know anyone in Bayport. She lives alone."

Annie appeared to be arguing with someone on the other end of the line. The longer she talked, the more agitated she became. Finally she hung up and stood rigid for a moment, her shoulders hunched over, her fingers pressed to her forehead.

Spinning around, she started toward the Hardys' table. Her dead white face was in stark contrast to her flaming hair. For a second, Frank caught a glint of excitement—but then all he saw was fear, filling Annie's beautiful hazel eyes.

Joe half rose from his chair. "Something must be wrong," he said, his eyes narrowing as Annie hurried to their table.

"Joe, you have to help me." Annie sounded desperate.

Joe stood up and took the girl's arm. "What's wrong, Annie?"

"Wait here until I tell Tony I'm taking off." She started to remove her apron but stopped to address Joe again. "Say you'll help me."

"Sure, Annie. We'll help," Frank assured her.

Annie's eyes flitted to Frank and then immediately back to Joe. She grasped Joe's hand and leaned in toward him. Despite her obvious fear, there was something like excitement in her eyes. "Just you, Joe, please." Her voice was a frantic whisper. "Please!" Tossing her apron on Joe's chair, she strode to the order counter.

Tony Prito, the manager of Mr. Pizza and one of the Hardys' best friends, tried to tell Annie that it wasn't a great time to take off, but she wouldn't listen. She pushed past him and dashed into the kitchen. She returned with a black purse slung over her shoulder and rushed to the front of the restaurant.

Joe motioned Frank to sit back down. "Stay here, Frank. I know you don't like Annie. If she needs help, *I'll* help her."

Joe dashed out of the restaurant, following in Annie's wake. Frank was left, openmouthed and surprised at his brother's attitude.

Joe had to hustle to catch up to Annie, who was halfway to the mall's outdoor parking lot.

"Annie, wait up. You have to tell me what's going on. I can't help you if I don't know what kind of trouble you're in."

Annie whirled around and took hold of both of Joe's arms, staring at him with shining eyes. "Joe, you'll think I'm awful."

"No, I won't, Annie. Tell me. Who was that on the phone?"

"Phil Sidler."

Joe's hands clenched into fists. "The creep who—"

"An old boyfriend. Now that I've met you, Joe—well—Phil was the worst mistake I've ever made in my life."

"That doesn't matter now, Annie—"

Annie kept holding tight to Joe's arms, as if he offered the security she needed. "Yes, it does, Joe. He's here. Phil found out where I'm working. He says he's coming to get me, and take me away with him."

Before Joe could object, she continued with greater insistence. "I didn't tell you that he's insanely jealous. He'd fight a guy if I even looked at him because he was so possessive. I—I can't take it, Joe. It's starting all over again, and I don't know what to do."

Joe took Annie in his arms and smoothed her soft hair. "Annie, please don't worry. I'll protect you from this creep."

"Take me home, Joe, will you? Oh, my

7

clothes," she said, snapping her fingers. "I'm not thinking straight. You get the van while I go back inside. I left my clothes. I can't let Phil find me. I just can't!"

Joe took off to get the van. He'd take Annie home, then come back for Frank. Frank would be mad, but Joe didn't care. His big brother was getting altogether too critical lately, acting as if he had to take care of Joe. As if Joe couldn't think for himself, or choose a girlfriend. When Frank started telling Joe who to go out with, he needed to cool his heels. Joe smiled at the idea.

Slipping his key into the lock on the driver's side, he was about to step into the van when he heard Annie scream—quite nearby. "Joe, help me!"

He spun around and saw a sleazy-looking blond guy holding Annie. It looked as if she were shouting at him. All at once she jerked loose, turned, and dashed back toward the mall. The guy lunged out, grabbed a handful of blouse, and pulled Annie behind a row of cars.

Annie screamed again. "Joe, help!"

"Help, Joe, help me!" She sounded like the voice in the recurring nightmare that so often robbed him of sleep. It was Iola's voice, calling out to him from a roaring ball of fire as the car exploded.

Joe clenched his teeth so tightly that he could feel his jaw muscles jump.

But this wasn't Iola screaming for him. It was Annie. *Annie* needed help!

After jumping into the van, he twisted the key and the motor roared to life. He backed up, screeched to a stop, swung around, and headed for the two figures. He would pull Annie into the van and take off before her attacker could follow them.

Ahead, Joe could see Annie twisting to get away from the blond, skinny man. He had her by the arm, but Annie was strong and quick. She slipped from his grasp and stepped toward the oncoming van. The man threw himself forward and got one arm wrapped around her waist.

Bending over, she kicked back and caught his shin with the heel of her shoe. He held on, and the momentum of her kick sent them both reeling backward, out of sight between two cars.

"Joe!" Annie screamed.

As Joe started to slam the brake down, the man flew out from between the cars—right into the hood of the van.

Joe finished stomping the brake. The van bucked, and Joe flew forward, his forehead violently hitting the windshield. Through the glass, for one split second, Joe was face-to-face with the man and his grotesque expression of surprise.

Then a sickening thump sounded as the man's body was tossed into the air as if it weighed no more than a rag doll.

Chapter

2

"I THINK SOMEONE was killed!"

"That new girl who works here." Two people coming into Mr. Pizza were buzzing with excitement.

Frank sat for a second, immobilized. Killed—someone was killed? Annie—something had happened to Annie. Or *Joe*. Leaping to his feet, Frank slammed his chair onto the floor and dashed outside, pushing people out of his way.

In the parking lot the light atop an ambulance slowly revolved, throwing regular flashes of red light onto the crowd of curious onlookers. Moving closer, Frank saw the Hardys' black van at the center of the confusion.

"Joe!" he shouted. Frank pressed through bodies until he was close enough to spot his brother. He caught his breath and forced himself to speak normally. "That's my brother," Frank explained to an officer who was holding him back.

Joe Hardy was standing dazed beside the van, cupping a cold compress to his forehead. Two police officers were talking to him. One of them was Officer Con Riley, a friend of the Hardys. His expression was intense and professional as he questioned Joe.

Scanning the scene quickly, Frank saw two paramedics loading a body onto a gurney. Annie Shea, practically hysterical, was standing nearby with a policewoman on one side and a policeman on the other.

"Joe, what happened?" Frank asked quietly, nodding a hello at Con Riley.

"I-I'm not sure." Joe slumped against the fender of the van, continuing to hold the compress to his forehead. He took a deep breath and tried to answer Frank's question.

"Annie screamed for help. Just as I got to her, that guy—she says his name is Phil—flew right in front of the van." Joe grabbed Frank's arm. His eyes pleaded for help. "Frank, I couldn't stop in time. I couldn't help hitting him. Is he—all right?"

Con Riley shook his head grimly. "He's dead, Joe. I'm afraid you're going to have to come to the station. We'll need to go over the whole story."

"Annie?" Joe started toward the girl, but Frank grabbed his arm.

"She's all right, Joe, but I think she's on the verge of hysterics. Let the officers help her. They're trained to deal with this sort of thing."

Frank didn't want Joe going to Annie. Joe was in big trouble, and Frank couldn't help thinking that it was Annie Shea who had gotten him into it, accidentally or not.

There was nothing to be gained by staying at the scene. The police took the van—and Joe—to the Bayport police station. Frank went with them, taking advantage of the time Joe spent filling out forms to call his father.

"I think you'd better come down, Dad," Frank said. "Joe's going to need you."

"I couldn't stop, Frank, he just jumped out in front of me." Joe repeated this as he and Frank waited for Joe to be questioned. "I didn't mean to kill him. I was trying to help Annie."

"I know that, Joe." Frank put his arm on Joe's shoulder. He knew how his brother must feel.

"When Annie called for help, Frank"—Joe hesitated—"I, for a second, thought it was Iola. I saw Iola in the fire again, begging me to help her—"

"Joe." Frank gripped his brother's arm. "Try to get ahold of yourself. Someone will be in any minute to question you. Try to reconstruct what happened out there.''

To help Joe gain control, Frank went over the incidents with him, making him cover every detail up to the time of the impact.

"Joe Hardy?" A woman in a uniform entered the room where Joe and Frank were waiting. "I'm Officer O'Hara."

"Hello," Frank said, standing and holding out his hand to ease the tension in the room. "I'm Frank Hardy and this is my brother, Joe." Joe stood also. "I don't think we've met before."

"I've just joined the Bayport force," she informed them, ignoring Frank's hand and taking a chair. "Please be seated."

Officer O'Hara was an attractive woman in her early thirties, with blond hair, which she wore pulled back from her face. She studied Joe intently for a moment, saying nothing.

"I'd like to hear your version of this . . . 'accident,' Mr. Hardy," she finally said in a very businesslike manner.

Frank didn't like the clipped way Officer O'Hara said the word *accident*. Did she question Joe's innocence?

Joe repeated the story Frank had by now committed to memory. Frank listened for anything in Joe's testimony that might suggest a deliberate act on his brother's part. There was nothing. What had Annie told the officers? Obviously she was now in a similar room, being questioned as Joe was.

"Ms. Shea says she screamed for your help, Joe." Officer O'Hara glanced at her notes. "She states that she and Phil Sidler were arguing just before his—death." Again the pause. Officer O'Hara was painting a picture of the scene that Frank didn't like. Something was on her mind.

"Annie was afraid of him," Joe explained. "She'd just told me he wanted to take her away with him, that he was insanely jealous. She had moved to Bayport to get away from this guy." Joe tightened one hand around the arm of the chair and rubbed his forehead again.

"But she had been romantically involved with Phil Sidler in the past?"

"I guess so. She called him her old boyfriend. What difference does it make? She was terrified of him." Joe seemed to be losing patience. "Ask my brother. She came to our table scared. She wanted me to take her home."

Frank nodded yes. "She seemed terrified. But what does this have to do with Phil running in front of Joe?" Frank was ready to ask some questions himself.

Officer O'Hara ignored him. "Annie is confused over exactly what happened out there, Mr. Hardy. But she did tell us that she's gone out with you. That she's crazy about you, and that you appear to care for her. What we're wonder-

14

ing, Mr. Hardy, is whether you considered Phil Sidler a rival for Annie Shea's attentions? Maybe you were jealous, too."

She cleared her throat before carefully wording the accusation. "Maybe you saw an opportunity to get rid of this rival and call it an accident."

Joe's mouth dropped open. He looked at the officer in total amazement. "I—I—" Standing, he straightened his shoulders, but his hands were trembling. "That's just not true. You can't believe it is."

Officer O'Hara studied her notes as if trying to make a decision. "I don't know what to believe, Mr. Hardy."

Joe was sure of only one thing right then. He would never have killed Phil Sidler intentionally.

Joe and Frank spent a lot of time chasing and apprehending dangerous criminals, but both brothers hated violence. And Joe knew he could never kill or even lash out at anyone because of jealousy.

Frank stood up and faced Officer O'Hara. "Don't say anything else, Joe," he advised his brother. "You don't have to answer her questions. I've called Dad. He'll be here any minute. I think we may want to call his lawyer."

"Probably a good idea, boys." Officer O'Hara took a deep breath and stood up also. "Since I plan to book Joe Hardy on suspicion of vehicular homicide."

Chapter
3

THE BOYS REMAINED in the small room where Joe had been questioned. Joe was still in shock at being accused of deliberately killing Phil Sidler.

The whole afternoon had been like a bad dream, he was thinking. First, his girl was attacked by some creep from her past. Then when he went to the rescue—Joe killed him. It was an accident, but now the cops . . . Wake up, he said to himself angrily. This is no time to lose it!

Frank spent the same waiting time mulling over the facts in Joe's case. But there were too many things he didn't know, too many pieces of the puzzle that he didn't have. He couldn't draw any conclusions.

Fenton Hardy soon arrived, acting more like a worried father than a famous detective. He had

16

asked the family lawyer to meet them at the station. The lawyer advised Joe to say nothing more about the accident and worked on getting Joe released quickly.

Finally, the door to the interrogation room opened, and Fenton Hardy poked his head in. "Let's go, boys, Joe's out on bail. What do you say? Home?"

"I can't go until I know Annie is all right," Joe said to his father.

"I'll check on her and take her home if she needs a ride," Frank offered. "She's in no danger now, and she'll probably just want to rest."

Joe started to protest, but his father interrupted. "That would be best, son. We need to talk." He turned to Frank. "The police have finished checking out the van. It's in the rear parking lot."

Reluctantly, Joe left with his father out the back door, and Frank went to search for Annie. He found her in the small waiting room near the front desk, where Officer Riley was standing and talking on the phone.

Annie looked up. "Where's Joe?"

"I'll take you home if you need a ride, Annie. Joe is going with our dad. She free?" Frank mouthed silently to Officer Riley through the open door.

The officer nodded, and Frank led Annie out to the van.

After giving Frank her address, Annie said no more. She withdrew into herself and hunched her shoulders up close to her ears and pressed her body against the passenger door. Frank didn't exist for her.

"Annie," Frank said finally as he swung the car around to head toward Annie's neighborhood. He wanted to talk about the accident, but he felt awkward. Annie had always tried so hard to avoid him. "If you and Phil were struggling and you pushed Phil away, so he fell in front of the van, then it was an accident. You can't be blamed, and Joe would be cleared."

Annie said nothing, continuing to stare out her window.

"You know they've accused Joe of killing Phil, don't you?" Frank said a little louder to the back of the girl's head.

"What happened out there, Annie? What did you tell the police that made them suspect Joe of vehicular homicide?" Frank had raised his voice and was biting off each word now. He hoped to scare Annie into revealing something that hadn't come out so far.

"I—I'm not sure, Frank," she said in a sleepy voice. Slowly she turned her head until she was looking out the windshield. She still wouldn't look at Frank. "Phil knew Joe was coming. He tried to get away, I guess. He ran the wrong way."

"Why would he try to get away from you, or Joe for that matter? A guy who'd fight anyone who looked at you doesn't sound like someone who'd run from a confrontation."

"I don't know. All I know is he stepped in front of the van."

"If you told the police that, why don't they believe Joe? Why have they booked him?"

"How am I supposed to know what the cops are thinking?" Annie said, her gaze concentrated on the side window again.

Frank wanted to probe deeper, but he kept silent. Annie was probably still in shock. Maybe she'd remember more later.

She lived in the worst section of Bayport, where the buildings were old and jammed together. Rents were cheap there, of course, and Frank figured it was the best Annie could afford.

"You can let me out here." Annie was unbuckling her seat belt as Frank slowed, looking for the number. She cut off the offer that Frank started to make of seeing her to her door. "I'm fine."

Frank shrugged and stopped the van. If Joe was going to get any help from Annie, he was going to have to question her himself.

That night Frank slept restlessly. He rose early to find Joe slumped in a chair in the den, staring blankly at an early-morning TV show with the sound off.

"Did you sleep at all, Joe?" Joe shook his head, almost as if to clear it. Frank turned off the TV. "Let's get some breakfast. Maybe we'll both feel better."

"I've gone over and over it, Frank. I keep seeing Phil Sidler, flying out and landing in front of the van. His eyes, Frank. He keeps staring at me. Right through me. It's spooky." Joe shut his eyes and exhaled in one loud burst as if he could force the picture from his mind.

"Joe—"

"I know only one thing for sure, Frank. It *was* an accident."

"We both know that, Joe, but it seems we're going to have to prove it. I'm heading over to the police station this morning. I want to go over the evidence."

"I'm coming, too." Joe stood up and followed Frank into the kitchen. Absently he plugged in the coffee maker.

"It's better if you stay here, Joe. I think they'll talk more if you're not there. I want to see the coroner's report and Annie's testimony."

"Annie," Joe muttered. "I have to see Annie."

"Not now. Wait till I know what she said." Frank used a no-nonsense tone of voice.

Joe tapped on the countertop with a spoon, then dropped it so that it danced across the smooth surface and clattered onto the floor. After he picked it up, he paced the long, rectangular space.

Frank took out a skillet, eggs, and butter and went about preparing breakfast. He knew one thing for certain—hunger wouldn't improve Joe's state of mind.

"Look, I promise I'll report back as soon as I can," Frank said as he dished up a plateful of scrambled eggs to set in front of Joe with a glass of orange juice. "Now sit down and eat. I can't have you starving."

Frank's first stop was at police headquarters to talk with Con Riley. Fortunately; Officer O'Hara wasn't on duty. Frank didn't know for certain that she'd try to stop his investigation, but he did feel more comfortable with her absent.

"Con." Frank spoke openly to his friend. "I need some help. You know Joe didn't murder Phil Sidler."

"I'd have my doubts," Con Riley agreed, tugging at his chin. "What kind of help, Frank? This isn't my case, you know."

"Just let me see the police notes, Con. Annie's testimony, the coroner's report."

"Well," Con Riley said hesitantly. He glanced around. No other police officers were in the room at the moment. Frank shrugged and gave him an encouraging smile. Con sighed. "I was planning to look them over again myself," he said in a low voice. "I guess if you leaned over my shoulder and caught a quick glimpse, it wouldn't hurt."

Con pulled Joe's file. He spread the papers over the counter, and together he and Frank went over everything.

"Look here, Con." Frank pointed at the coroner's report. "This states that Phil Sidler died of a blow to the head, a probable skull fracture."

"They've scheduled an autopsy," Con told Frank. "Something else might show up."

"Multiple fractures—" Frank went on. "And an opinion that the fatal blow to the head was caused by the bumper clipping Phil's head."

"Makes sense."

"No, it doesn't, Con." Frank shook his head. "Joe remembers seeing Phil over the hood of the van. He's having nightmares about eyes staring at him." Frank jumped up, spread his arms, and leaned into the counter, facing Con. "It's not possible. If he's lying against the hood of the van, there's no way a bumper can hit him on the head."

"How about when he rolls off? He could've got clipped when he fell."

"He approached the car at an angle—from the side—so he'd probably slide off that way. He'd fall clear of the bumper—I think." Frank added the "I think" so it didn't sound as if he were telling Con his job. Frank thought so fast and so logically that most people couldn't keep up with him. He riffled through the rest of the papers at great speed.

Annie's testimony wasn't much help. When asked if she thought Joe could have stopped and not hit Phil, Annie had answered that she couldn't really see.

"I'll tell you, Frank, Joe's in a tight spot," Con said seriously, stacking the police notes back together and placing them in the file folder.

"He shouldn't be, Con," Frank said. "There's something strange going on here. Did the police find out anything about Phil Sidler? Search his car? Find out where he was staying?"

"We found a hotel key in his pocket. And an officer went to his hotel. Not much there." Con showed Phil's few belongings to Frank.

A sports bag held a change of socks and underwear. Phil hadn't planned on staying in Bayport long. There was a wadded-up jacket in the bag and a sports magazine also. Phil's billfold contained almost a hundred dollars in crumpled bills, a driver's license—giving his age as twenty-five—and a picture of Annie. The snapshot was slightly out of focus, but it was Annie smiling at the camera.

The number for the pay phone at Mr. Pizza was scribbled on the back of a matchbook cover from the Bayport Downtowner. Frank knew the hotel; it was in the same poor part of town where Annie lived.

23

"Is this what led you to Phil's hotel?" Frank asked Con, holding up the matchbook cover.

"Yep. He'd registered there three days ago."

"Not yesterday?" Frank added a visit to the hotel to his list of places to investigate.

"See for yourself, Frank." Con grinned as he packed up Phil's gear.

"I plan to. Thanks, Con. Joe and I appreciate your help."

"Luck to you, Frank."

Frank glanced at his watch. In the confusion of the events of the day before and that morning, he almost forgot that he'd told Callie he'd take her to lunch. He called to ask her to meet him at Mr. Pizza at twelve.

Mr. Pizza didn't open until 11:45. Frank parked near the service entrance and slipped in through the back door.

The room was heavy with the smell of yeast and green peppers cooking. Frank found his friend Tony Prito in the storeroom, lifting down a restaurant-size can of tomato sauce. Although Tony was the restaurant's manager, he did most of the initial preparations in the kitchen and carefully supervised the chefs.

"Frank, good to see you," Tony said when he looked up and saw his friend. "I heard about the accident. How's Joe?"

"Not too good." Frank filled Tony in.

"That's ridiculous," Tony said, slamming

down the sauce. "Joe would never kill anyone because he was jealous."

"I don't think he had time to get jealous," Frank pointed out. "He'd never even met this Phil Sidler. Listen, Tony, could you give me some background on Annie? I want to know everything you know about her."

"That won't take long, Frank. I don't know much. She needed the job. I needed help. She seemed okay, so I hired her."

"Where had she worked before?" Frank asked.

"She said she had no past restaurant experience, but who cared? How much experience does it take to carry a pizza to a table? Now, if she would have been cooking . . ." Tony smiled.

"Did she seem different yesterday or the day before when she came to work, Tony?" Frank asked.

Tony thought about that while he opened a cardboard barrel of flour. "Well, Annie wasn't a chatterer, didn't say much at all. Last couple of days, though, she talked a blue streak."

"About what?"

"Nothing in particular. You know how girls can yap on and on about nothing at all. She had the other girls laughing a couple of times. Probably doesn't mean anything, but I noticed it."

"Thanks, Tony." Frank turned to leave.

Tony stopped him with his voice. "Let me know if there's anything I can do for Joe."

"Will do." Frank headed out to the restaurant through the kitchen.

Callie was waiting for him in the entryway. "I don't know why I put up with you, Frank. You invite me out to lunch at twelve and then aren't here on time. We could have made it for a later time."

"Hi to you, too, Callie," Frank said. "You're a patient woman. Listen, do you mind if we eat someplace else? I can't face pizza today."

"Sure, Frank. But what's wrong? We eat here so often, I thought you liked only pizza."

Frank filled Callie in as they got seated at a sandwich bar in a corner of the mall's eating area.

"Joe's been accused of murder?" Callie's face registered her astonishment. "How can that be? When did this happen?"

"Yesterday. You must not have seen the news last night or today's paper. The *Bayport News* made a big deal out of the son of Fenton Hardy being involved in a vehicular homicide."

Frank gave Callie the rest of the details as they ate. "There's something wrong here, Callie. I'd like to know what Annie really saw."

"You're being kind of hard on Annie, Frank," Callie answered. "You may not like her, but you have to give her the benefit of the doubt. I think you're trying to make a mystery where none exists. What Joe needs is a decent lawyer, not a detective looking for motives that aren't there."

"Yeah, I keep telling myself that. Maybe I need a vacation." Frank smiled at the pretty blond girl sitting opposite him. He watched as she echoed his smile by lifting the edges of her mouth in a slow grin that spread infectiously up to her understanding eyes. Callie was the world's most patient and understanding friend. Frank felt lucky that she put up with him.

"Listen, Callie," he said, polishing off a hamburger. "I've got some more ground to cover. Will you forgive me if I run?"

"Don't I always?" Callie said, deciding at the last minute to make it a joke.

Frank smiled and sketched a quick wave as he dashed out. Maybe he *was* inventing this case, but he was determined to check out every angle for Joe's sake. Callie was right in saying a good lawyer could get Joe off, but Frank didn't want Joe to be left dealing with another guilt trip. Frank didn't even know what he was looking for at this point, but he was going to investigate every detail.

The Bayport Downtowner was once in the heart of Bayport, but the center of the city's activities had moved. The neighborhood had been left to change with the times. Trouble was, it hadn't changed for the better.

Half the fluorescent tubes in the fixture in the entrance of the cheap hotel were broken. The windowpane in the main door was cracked, and the door itself stuck when Frank tugged on it.

Behind the counter a clerk nodded sleepily in the dusty air of the lobby, air that had trapped stale cigar smoke. Two elderly men sat in a lobby off the entryway, watching a game show on TV.

"Ahem." Frank cleared his throat to alert the clerk that he had a potential customer.

"Oh, hello. Want a room?" The man behind the desk was past retirement age, and Frank figured he'd taken the job to have something to do. The salary couldn't be much.

"Can you tell me what room Phil Sidler is in?" Frank asked for starters.

"Unfortunately, Mr. Sidler doesn't reside here anymore." The clerk flashed a toothless grin.

"Okay, what room did he have when he did live here?" Frank found he didn't have his usual patience with people.

"Won't do me any good to tell you. Police have it sealed off. Why do you want to know? Was Sidler a friend of yours? Police might want to talk to you." The old man wasn't dumb.

"A friend of mine thought she left her purse in his room. I said I'd get it back for her." It was a clumsy story but the best Frank could come up with on the spur of the moment.

"Cops took everything." The man relented for

28

a moment as he added, "Two-oh-nine, second floor, corner. But you'd better try the police station, sonny." The clerk, tired of acting important, walked over to the small lobby full of faded easy chairs and joined the two men watching the game show.

Frank hesitated. The clerk really didn't seem to care if he went up for a look. He glanced around to make sure no one was watching, then quietly he took the stairs two at a time. Upstairs, Frank read the police notice on Phil's room and turned the knob once. The door was locked.

Disappointed, he slipped back downstairs and out the building. He stood on the sidewalk for a moment, looking up at the grimy facade of the hotel.

Suddenly Frank realized that the rusty fire escape must be right outside the corner room. He found a couple of wooden crates left in a nearby alley. He piled the crates up in a shaky tower beneath the fire escape and climbed it. He was almost able to reach the bottom rung of the ladder, which hung down from the second-floor landing.

As Frank jumped up to grab the ladder, the crates collapsed with a loud crash. For a moment he swung helplessly in empty space, one hand clutching the metal rung, waiting for someone to come out to see what was going on. But no one bothered.

Instead, the rusty ladder began slowly to ease down under his weight until Frank could climb it up to Phil's window. His sneakers muffled his footsteps, but the metal creaked and rattled with each step and once even banged against the building.

Standing outside what he was sure had to be Phil's room, Frank glanced about before trying the window. A matchbook cover was wedged into the space between the metal railing and the building. Two cigarette butts had been ground out on the railing. Frank could imagine someone leaning against the building, smoking and absentmindedly pushing the cardboard cover into the small space.

The advertisement on the match cover was for a bar in New York City. It might mean nothing, it might have been left there long ago, but Frank stuck it into his pants pocket to investigate at a later time.

The window to Phil's room was unlocked and open, two or three inches. So much for sealed rooms, Frank thought. But after raising the window and stepping into the room, Frank knew that the police weren't the only ones to have been there.

He quickly closed the venetian blinds so no one could see him in the room. The place was a shambles. Chairs had been overturned; upholstery had been slit; the mattress was in shreds.

Someone had done a very thorough job searching Phil Sidler's room.

Frank was reaching for the light switch to have a better look when he heard the click of the door lock. He started to whirl around to hide, but there was no time to move. The doorknob turned. Frank's only impression was that the man who entered was tall.

"What the—" the man cried. His reactions were lightning fast. He raised his arm to deliver a blow.

Before Frank could reach out to protect himself, he was sent spinning into gaping blackness.

Chapter
4

FRANK HAD DUCKED so that the blow only glanced off his skull. But it did momentarily make him black out—enough to keep him from identifying the man later. All he knew was that the man was very tall—and agile. Shaking his head once, Frank looked around and saw he was alone. He staggered out into the hallway and recovered enough to weave down the stairs.

Out on the street he looked both ways. An elderly woman was making her way slowly toward the corner of the block. A tomcat, scarred from many battles, looked back at him before rolling his back once and moving on. But no tall man. The man had been unbelievably quick. He had reacted to seeing Frank in the room in a fraction of a second. Who was he?

Frank knew it wasn't logical that he was the same person who had ransacked the room earlier. The search had been thorough enough not to be continued or repeated. And how did the man get into Phil's room? It seemed that he had a key. Had Phil been accompanied to Bayport?

The hotel clerk had disappeared, so Frank didn't bother to find and question him about the stranger. He'd probably gone out for coffee, Frank decided. Tight security in this place.

There was no way of knowing where the tall man had gone, why he had been there in the first place, or whether he might return. But Frank didn't want to leave without checking out Phil's room. He might not get a second chance.

Frank gently probed the spot on his head where he'd been hit. He could feel an egg forming, but at least he wasn't bleeding. He decided to take one more chance.

He slipped back up the stairs and into Phil's room. This time it remained empty. Frank searched for a few minutes. Nothing. It was pure luck that Frank had turned up that matchbook cover on the fire escape. Of course, it could have belonged to a previous occupant. The month had been dry, so the condition of the cover would have remained the same for several weeks.

After climbing down the fire escape—just in case the hotel clerk had returned to his post—

Frank got in the van and headed for home. He needed to talk to his father and Joe.

"Where's Dad?" asked Frank, striding into the den.

Joe was slumped in a chair, dully watching an old movie on television. Mr. Hardy had insisted that Joe stay in the house because he was only out on bail. Fenton Hardy knew Joe could get in trouble and then the police would have no choice but to lock him up.

"He left for the police station right after he told me not to leave the house for the tenth time." Joe followed Frank into the kitchen. "What did you find out, Frank? And where have you been?"

"Police station. Nothing new." Frank debated whether or not to tell Joe about the incident in Phil's room but chose to keep it to himself in case Joe decided to investigate.

"Well, I've had it with sitting around, Frank. I've got to find out where Annie is and whether she's okay." He started to pace the kitchen. "I've been calling her place all day and there's no answer."

"I can see you've been worried," Frank said, staring into the open refrigerator. "No milk, no ice cream. Where's the chocolate cake Aunt Gertrude made yesterday?"

Joe grinned, almost like his old self. "That'll teach you to leave me here alone."

"You ate the whole thing?" Frank muttered, not believing it. "It's only four-thirty."

"Frank, give me my keys to the van. I'll stop at a bakery on the way back from checking on Annie." Joe's grin vanished.

Frank had used Joe's keys when they had driven to the police station after the accident. He had conveniently kept them. Just telling Joe to stay at home would never work for long—no matter who gave the order. While Joe might not directly disobey his father, he had always made up creative excuses for "forgetting."

"I'll go with you," Frank said. "Let me go to the station and talk to Dad, then I'll come right back and we'll find Annie."

"Stop treating me like a kid, Frank." Joe tried to stick his hand into Frank's pocket, and the two scuffled.

"Boys!" Gertrude Hardy, the Hardys' aunt and baker of the consumed chocolate cake, appeared in the doorway. "Every time I think the two of you have grown up, I find you acting like children. If you want to wrestle, please go outside."

Frank grinned at the scolding. It was good to see his aunt back to her old self. One of the boys' cases had revolved around their aunt's being falsely accused of murder. Frank suddenly realized that now a second member of the Hardy household was in the same circumstances. He glanced at Joe, who was staring longingly out the window as if he were jailed.

"I hope you're going to start dinner early, Aunt Gertrude," said Frank. "I'm starved, and this human garbage disposal has emptied the kitchen in one afternoon."

"I'll start supper soon. Oh, by the way, your father called. He said to tell you that neither of you is to leave the house until he comes home. He wants to talk to both of you."

Frank was glad to have his father back up his opinion—for the eleventh time—that Joe should stay put. He exchanged a glance with his brother and checked his pocket for Joe's car keys, then settled for an apple to hold him till dinner. He went up to his room to think.

Dinner was quiet, with each member of the Hardy family caught up in his or her own thoughts. Finally Mrs. Hardy spoke. "Fenton, what's the latest on Joe's case?"

Mr. Hardy looked at both Joe and Frank. Frank got the idea his father didn't want to discuss this matter at the dinner table.

"Officer O'Hara is unbendable," Mr. Hardy said, pushing away his half-eaten dinner. "I think my 'unofficial connection' to the department is hurting you, Joe. I'm sorry. She doesn't want anyone to think she's playing favorites by letting you off easily."

Aunt Gertrude frowned, then harumphed.

"Surely no one else down there thinks our Joe could run over someone deliberately."

"Women," Joe scoffed, unable to resist baiting his aunt. "Why the Bayport Police Department thought they had to hire a woman is beyond me."

Joe's mock-chauvinistic attitude set everyone laughing. It was a relief. This was one family that needed a laugh.

Aunt Gertrude, who had argued equal rights for women for years, pretended to be offended by Joe's remarks. "Are you saying that women don't make good detectives?"

Joe grinned and helped himself to Aunt Gertrude's apple pie. "I think they make better cooks."

"I refuse to contribute to this discussion on any grounds I can come up with." Fenton Hardy smiled, filled his coffee cup, and headed for his study.

While Joe started in on the pie, Frank excused himself and followed his father. "I checked out Phil Sidler's hotel room, Dad." Frank told his father what had happened there.

The fact that Phil's room had been searched and that someone wanted his identity kept secret told Frank there was more going on in the case than a simple automobile accident.

His father confirmed his opinion, and then tried to stop Frank's investigation.

"Frank, I got some more information late this

afternoon. The police checked out Phil Sidler. He's a strong suspect in a recent diamond robbery in New York. The robbery looked like it was related to a number of similar crimes around the state. There's a strong connection to one gang.''

"Then they think Phil Sidler was a member of this gang?" Frank gingerly rubbed the back of his head where the lump was now perfectly formed.

"Yes, and, Frank—" Fenton Hardy got up from his desk and walked over to the window, looking out. He was silent for a while.

"What is it, Dad?" Frank asked, breaking the quiet.

Mr. Hardy swung around and walked back to face Frank. "The New York district attorney's office is claiming that Annie Shea might also be part of this gang. I think O'Hara believes that Annie got Joe involved."

Chapter
5

"THAT'S CRAZY," FRANK SAID, getting to his feet. "What's with that woman? How could she possibly think Joe's a thief!"

"Calm down, Frank. She doesn't know Joe. And our getting angry at her won't help him any. Although I have to admit that I had the same reaction at the station."

"I didn't tell Joe about going to Phil's room and about it being searched. I don't like keeping secrets from him. Do you think we should tell him about Annie?"

"I don't know, Frank. I guess we both know what he'd say."

"Let's sleep on it, Dad." Frank headed for his room. "A thief *and* a murderer!" he muttered. "Perfectly dumb."

39

In the morning, when he and Joe were eating their late breakfast, Frank decided to tell Joe everything. After all, Joe had everything at stake, and Frank was beginning to feel that he needed his partner to help him.

"Joe, I have some bad news," Frank said, buttering his toast and spreading Aunt Gertrude's homemade strawberry jam on top.

"Shoot. I'm getting used to it." Joe polished off a second glass of milk.

"The police on the Sidler case suspect Phil of being part of a recent diamond heist. It seems he might have been part of a gang."

"So I found a criminal for them. Maybe now they'll thank me instead of accusing me of murder." Joe's tone of voice suggested his depression had turned to anger.

"Joe . . ." Frank hesitated. There was only one way to tell Joe this—straight. "Joe, the cops have heard from the New York DA's office. They think Annie might be part of the gang."

Joe stared at Frank in disbelief. "You'll think up anything to get at Annie, won't you, Frank? I know you don't like her, but I never thought you'd say anything like this."

"I didn't make it up, Joe. Call Dad. Call the police department. Talk to Con," he said quietly and evenly.

"I'll do better than that." Joe pushed away

40

from the table. "I'll ask Annie. She'll tell me the truth."

"I'm going with you to look for her, Joe."

"Not if you're going to accuse her of being a crook."

"Joe, I don't know what's going on here any more than you do. I have no idea if Annie is guilty or innocent. I'm just telling you what Dad told me. But I don't want you to be alone. I don't want anything to happen so O'Hara will have an excuse to lock you up."

Joe studied Frank's face. Finally he said, "Okay, big brother, looks like I'm stuck with you. Let's go."

The Hardys first drove to Mr. Pizza to see if Annie would be coming in that day. Joe's face was grim as they approached the back door.

"Hey, Tony," Joe said as they walked into the kitchen, where Tony Prito was dumping flour in a large bowl to make dough. "Annie around?"

"Joe, sorry about your troubles," Tony said, greeting the Hardys after turning on the mixer. "Let's move away from the noise," he said, and strolled over to a corner. "Annie won't be in today. But, well, she was here earlier. She sneaked in during the night and slept in the back room."

"She *slept* here last night?" Joe didn't know what to make of this news. "Why?"

"This morning when I found her she asked me

not to tell you. But under the circumstances, I think you should know. She's scared, Joe, really scared.'' Tony crossed back to the mixer to check on the dough.

"But—but Phil Sidler is dead. What is she afraid of now?'' Joe drummed his fingers on a countertop. "Where was she going when she left here?'' he asked.

"Don't know.'' Tony raised his voice to be heard over the whir of the machine. "I guess she went back to where she's staying. She asked for her pay this morning and quit her job—''

"Let's go, Frank,'' Joe said, cutting off Tony.

They dashed to the van and took off for Annie's apartment. "Let me see Annie alone, Frank?'' Joe asked as Frank snugged up to the curb.

"Sorry, pal. I'm going in with you.'' Frank thought of Phil's room, and he had a bad feeling about this one.

Joe shrugged and bolted. Frank followed as soon as he had pocketed the keys.

Inside, the old apartment building was even worse than it looked on the outside. The stairway was dark—all the bulbs were broken or burned out. The institutional green paint was peeling, and the combined odors of stale cooking grease and damp turned the boys' stomachs.

Joe referred to the row of mailboxes in the entryway before taking the stairs two at a time to the third floor. The creak of each step accented the soft thud of Joe's sneakers hitting the treads.

Right behind him, Frank snatched at Joe's arm when they reached the third floor. "Joe, wait. Whoever searched Phil's apartment may have done the same to Annie's. Or maybe he's doing it now. If we go busting in there—"

Joe shrugged off Frank's grasp. "You're right. If they've hurt Annie, I'll . . ." Clenching his teeth, Joe forced himself to slow down. The boys crept slowly along, looking in both directions.

The door to the first apartment in the third-floor hall was ajar. Joe glanced in. A small child with huge brown eyes peered up at him. Frank stepped around to see what Joe was looking at. He smiled.

"Cammie, shut that door and get in here," a shrill voice sounded. But the child only stuck her thumb in her mouth and continued to stare at Frank, who waved.

He moved back to glance over the banister, viewing the entire stairway. They'd seen no one but the child, and everything seemed normal enough. Somewhere, the muffled sound of a blaring television set spewed out a game show, the announcer's voice probably describing dozens of wonderful prizes.

Joe pointed to the last door in the hallway. Quietly they made their way down to it. Each took a position on either side of the door. Joe started to knock, but at his touch the door creaked open.

"Annie? What—" Joe called out. He pushed the door back and stepped into the room, Frank acting as his shadow.

The room was in the same condition as the one in the Bayport Downtowner. Chairs were overturned, the upholstery ripped open, dirty cotton stuffing was strewn beside them, looking like the spilled guts from a corpse. One wall of the room had been turned into a makeshift kitchen; pots and pans now spilled out in front of it.

Almost soundlessly Joe headed for a room off to the left. He swung the door open.

The bedroom was in a similar state. Blankets had been tossed to the floor in a heap. The mattress had been slashed and gutted like the chairs. Drawers were piled on the floor, their contents dumped out. Annie's clothing had been tossed everywhere. A red sweater hung limply from the mirror like a flag on a windless day.

Joe, out of patience and no longer cautious, shouted out frantically. "Annie! You here?" He pushed open the door to the tiny bathroom and glanced at the tub. He was almost afraid to look.

No one. It was empty. What Joe feared most had happened. Annie was gone!

Chapter

6

"WHERE IS SHE?" Joe groaned and leaned against the bathroom doorframe.

Frank could hear the pain in his brother's voice, but there was little he could do to comfort him. "I don't know, Joe, but when I went to take a look at Sidler's room in the Bayport Downtowner, it looked just like this."

"Why didn't you tell me last night?" Joe asked. "You knew Annie was in danger. We could have come and gotten her."

"I wasn't thinking straight, Joe. Sorry, but I guess I thought she'd be fine." Frank leaned in to touch his brother's arm. "Joe—"

"Leave me alone." Joe knocked Frank's hand away.

"Joe, Annie may have left town. She may have

45

run away. She drew her pay, quit her job. That means she must have had a plan."

"She wouldn't have left town without telling me, Frank." Joe's voice pleaded that she hadn't. "I know she wouldn't."

"Let's search the building." Frank gave Joe new hope.

"I know she said there's storage in the basement. She put her suitcases down there. But she would have to take them if she'd left." With restored purpose, Joe took off into the hall and down the stairs to check out the basement.

Frank took the time to stop at the open door they'd passed. He knocked and looked down at the child, who smiled up at him.

"Cammie— Who?" A tired-looking woman snatched up her child. "Who are you? Get out of here."

"Sorry, ma'am. The door was open. I wanted to ask if you heard anything unusual last night or this morning. Or if you've seen the red-haired woman who lives on this floor."

"I didn't hear anything. I didn't see anything, or anyone, either. We mind our own business here. Now, get out."

Frank backed away from the door and left the woman scolding her daughter for opening it in the first place. Bounding down the stairs, he caught up with Joe, who had just checked out the first floor.

"The basement's this way," Joe said, leading Frank to a door at the end of the hall.

The light Joe flicked on at the top of the stairs didn't help much. The stairwell was dim, and the stairs were dusty. If anyone in the building was in charge of maintenance, he or she took the job lightly. Frank stepped in front of Joe and started down slowly, one step at a time.

Frank doubted that whoever searched Annie's room would think to check the storage area, but it paid to proceed cautiously. He knew that Joe wanted to throw caution aside and burst into the basement.

The basement was empty. Joe's face was grim. "I think that's probably a storage room over there," he said loudly, his voice bouncing off the concrete walls.

Just as they reached the storage room and were inspecting the padlock on the door, they were surprised by a voice behind them. "Joe?" The whisper seemed like a shout in the cool quiet.

"Annie!" Joe turned and ran to her as she stepped out of a nearby closet. He caught her just as she started to collapse.

"Joe, I was so afraid I'd never see you again," Annie said faintly.

"You know better than that. I'm just glad I thought about the basement. What are you doing here?"

"Hoping you'd find me!" Annie burst into tears.

Joe reassured Annie that he was there to help her.

Frank sighed. Although glad Annie had been found, he couldn't help wishing they could put her on a bus with a ticket to someplace far away. Whatever trouble Annie had gotten herself into now directly involved Joe.

"What happened, Annie?" Frank asked, questioning the girl. "Who searched your room?"

"I don't know, Frank." Annie stepped from the safety of Joe's arms. She blew her nose on a tissue Joe provided. The tears on her face streaked the dirt and dust she had collected in her hiding place, and even Frank felt protective. She looked as vulnerable as a young child.

"I came back from Tony's this morning," Annie continued, "and walked in on a guy trashing my room. I'd never seen him before, but obviously he'd been there for a while. Obviously you saw it." Annie choked back another sob. "Joe, he tried to kill me! I ran. I've been here, hiding, ever since."

"He tried to kill you?" Frank questioned. "Did he have a gun—a knife? What did he look like? Can you describe him?"

"It all happened so fast. I—I don't know."

"Someone searched your room and threatened

to kill you, Annie. You must remember something. Think. Did he have a gun?"

"No." Annie threw a glance at Joe that seemed to say, "Make your brother leave me alone." She was sending out a signal loud and clear—damsel in distress, damsel in distress.

"Frank, cool it. You don't have to come on like a tough cop. Annie's had a bad scare. Let's go so she can clean up. We'll get a soda and talk like civilized people."

Frank ignored Joe. "We'll get out of here in a minute. Annie, did he pull a knife on you?" He returned his attention to the girl.

"I—I don't think so."

"How did he try to kill you? Did he grab you, try to strangle you?" Frank asked.

"Frank, I was scared." Annie was getting angry at him and his tone of voice. "I— Maybe he didn't try to kill me, but I thought he was going to. He pushed me aside and ran when I walked in on him."

"Now we're getting somewhere," Frank said, glancing at Joe. "What did the man look like, Annie?"

"I don't know. He—he was tall. Really tall."

And quick, Frank added to himself. That is, if it was the same guy who startled him in Phil's room. It wasn't much to go on, but it was something. Whoever had been looking for Phil obviously knew that Annie had some connection to him.

At this point, though, there was only one thing that Frank was perfectly certain of. Whatever was going on, Annie *was* scared. Frank had seen pure fear before, and recognized it now in the girl's eyes. Maybe he had been too hard on her with his questions. After all, he hadn't noticed anything when he was surprised by what seemed to be the same attacker. Anyway, no matter how much he wished Joe wasn't involved with her—he was. And now, so was Frank. They had to help her.

"Annie, I think you should know that the police suspect that Phil Sidler was a thief." Frank realized he might be telling Annie something she already knew. "In fact, he's been connected to a gang of jewel thieves that has been active in the New York area for some time. Now, we think that because you knew Phil, and someone knows you knew him, you may be in very real danger."

"What should I do, Frank?" Annie clung to Joe's hand. "I'm scared to death." She turned wide eyes on Frank. "You'll help me, won't you?" She looked lost and childlike.

"You know we will, Annie."

"I don't know anything about Phil Sidler," Annie said. "I mean, not recently."

"When was the last time you saw him?" Joe

asked. Frank was glad to hear Joe switch to a more businesslike tone.

"I—I can't remember." Annie frowned. "I did visit his mother before I came to Bayport. That would have been, let's see, just over a month ago."

"When had his mother last seen him?" Frank asked as he led the way back upstairs to Annie's apartment.

"She said she hadn't seen him in a long time, but she made me read a letter that Phil had written to her." Annie paused as if wondering whether or not to go on. "She—well, she always wanted Phil and me to stay together. She was urging me to go find Phil."

"Did you look at the address on the letter? Where was Phil when he wrote it?" Frank continued to press for information.

"I glanced at it, since his mother kept insisting I look at it. I think it was a Hundred-eleventh or -twelfth Street, something like that. In New York City."

"It's not much to go on. But I found a matchbook cover outside Phil's apartment. It came from a bar on Amsterdam Avenue, way uptown. I think I'm going to take a little trip to the city. And I think, Annie, that I'd better share with you all the information I have so far."

"I'm going, too, Frank," Joe answered. "Anything we find out will help Annie. Obviously someone thinks she knows something, and she's involved whether she wants to be or not."

"I'm not staying here alone," Annie protested. "I'll go also. Besides," she added shyly, with a hint of the old sparkle in her eyes, "you know I always wanted to watch you detectives in action."

"Okay," Joe agreed. "Get your stuff ready. I'll run down for your suitcases. You're not staying here anymore."

They waited until Annie washed up, changed into a skirt and heels, and threw her stuff into the bags, which they tossed in the back of the van. After pulling into a fast-food place, they ordered hamburgers, fries, and sodas, which they ate on the way to the city.

The trio sat quietly as Frank maneuvered through the traffic on the streets of the Upper West Side of Manhattan.

Finding the bar was easy, and Frank luckily got a parking spot nearby. It was nearly five o'clock, the time the bar started to fill with customers. It was small and shabby, and the bartender was especially friendly.

"Hiya, folks. Welcome to Norm's. Long time no see, A—"

"Are you Norm?" Annie cut off the greeting and laughed. "Sorry to bother you, Norm, but we just need some information. My friends are looking for a guy named Phil Sidler. Lived around here, we think."

None of Annie's earlier fear showed in this exchange. She stepped easily into the role of private investigator. She seemed to have a natural talent for the work. "Tall, blond, wore his hair in long sideburns. Big nose, so thin if he turned sideways you might miss him," she joked.

The bartender grinned, eyeing Annie curiously. "Good description. What's this information worth to you?"

Annie dug in her purse and pulled out a twenty. She casually tucked it into the glass closest to her as she perched on a bar stool.

"Last time I saw him, he called the Riverview Apartments home." Norm continued to arrange beer mugs in neat rows, all the time keeping a cheerful smile on his face. "Two blocks west of here, on a Hundred and twelfth."

"Thanks, Norm—if you're Norm." Annie smiled and rejoined the Hardys, who had watched the exchange with astonishment. "Not bad, huh?" she whispered to Joe.

"You're hired," said Joe, putting his arm around Annie and escorting her out onto the street. "Our agency could use a woman." He grinned at Annie as if the two of them were alone, and Annie looked relieved that she had done well in spite of her nervousness.

Meanwhile, Frank was deep in thought. Had

he imagined it, or had the bartender recognized Annie as they entered the bar? He glanced at the smiling, wholesome-looking girl, beaming under Joe's affectionate praise. Surely Frank was wrong. Why would a nice nineteen-year-old girl be known in a dive like that?

Frank erased the thought from his mind. He had too many other things to worry about now.

Even though the Riverview Apartments were just two blocks from Norm's bar, they moved the van and parked beside the curb outside the red-brick building. If there was any view of the river from the building, it would be from the roof, Frank thought, on a clear day. They approached the entrance but stopped at the bottom of the three steps.

"How do we get in?" Joe looked at the wrought-iron gate in front of the entrance door. Each needed a key.

"Up to you, Annie." Frank and Joe quickly disappeared around the corner to watch Annie.

She waited a couple of minutes, until an overweight, matronly woman started toward the building, then she took a deep breath and stepped into the role as if she were made for it. Quickly Annie rummaged through her purse. "I've done it again," she said, scolding herself as the woman approached the door of the building. "Phil will kill me if I've lost it."

"Left your key inside, did you?" The woman

asked, eyeing Annie suspiciously. "You young people are so careless these days."

"Oh, thank goodness." Annie looked at the woman with relief, ignoring her doubtful gaze. "At least I can wait for Phil in the hall instead of on the doorstep." She chattered on, charming the woman, and finally entered the building with her. Annie even held her groceries while she opened the two doors into the Riverview Apartments.

"Pretty good member of our team, huh, Frank?" Joe said as the Hardys approached the door moments later. Annie held the front door open, and they slipped through.

"Apartment Seventeen, top floor," Annie whispered. "His name is still on the box."

The Hardys, trusting Annie's skills by now, pushed the button for the small, rickety elevator and rode up in silence.

"Oh!" Annie stepped backward right into Joe and gasped as the door to 17 swung open. It was not locked. Inside, the picture was the same— someone had been there, too.

They made a quick search, but expected to find nothing. Annie stood in the middle of the one tiny dark room the whole time, glancing over her shoulder and twisting the ring on her finger nervously.

"Let's get out of here, guys. I don't like this." After seeing this new evidence, Annie was no longer pleased to be playing detective.

Frank didn't like it, either, but he wanted to search thoroughly, anyway. He didn't know what he expected to find.

Once again there was nothing. Whoever was employed in the search-and-destroy division of this operation was skilled and thorough.

"Okay, let's go," he said, and led the way back to the elevator.

Out on the sidewalk in front of the building, they all gratefully breathed in the fresh air. Annie walked toward the van ahead of the brothers, anxious to be safe inside the vehicle. As she was passing a limousine parked at the curb, both passenger doors opened.

Before either of the Hardys could react, two men dressed entirely in black leaped out and grabbed Annie, who barely had time to let out one short scream.

The men wrestled Annie into the car and roared away.

Chapter

7

"No!" SHOUTED JOE.

"Let's go after them," Frank yelled, heading for the van. "Keep your eye on that car."

The Hardys dashed for their van, and Frank had the engine roaring before Joe fastened his seat belt.

Frank followed the limo easily, racing through yellow lights and weaving in and out of traffic. But near a group of warehouses a red light stopped them. Frank had been so intent on chasing the limo that he didn't notice it until it was too late. It was then that he heard the scream of a siren and saw a red flashing light appear in his rearview mirror.

"Ignore them," Joe urged. "We'll lose Annie." He sat forward in his seat as if he could help Frank drive faster.

Frank heaved a sigh. "I can't, Joe. Keep an eye on the limo as long as possible." Frank pulled the van to the curb and waited for the ticket that was certain to follow.

When Frank stopped, Joe jerked open his door and hit the sidewalk running. One of the police officers called out to him, but he ignored the man's shouts. He sprinted after the limo for two blocks, watching it pull farther and farther away. Annie, he thought determinedly, I can't lose you now.

The black car slowed at an intersection, and just as Joe thought he might catch up, it turned right and disappeared. Joe pounded the concrete even harder until he reached the corner where the limo had turned. There was an empty lot on one side, an old building surrounded by a high fence on the other, and directly in front of him a ramp that led to underground parking.

Joe's lungs burned as his breath came in ragged spurts, and his legs, with the oxygen depleted, felt heavy as lead. He glanced around, knowing the limo hadn't gone farther. It had to have gone down the ramp.

Cautiously he slipped into the cool darkness that led under a building. The light was dim, but as soon as Joe's eyes adjusted, he saw only a few cars in a neat row. Was the building abandoned?

No black limo. This was impossible. The limo couldn't just vanish.

"Okay," snapped the officer, with his hand ready on the butt of his gun as Frank rolled down the window. "Out of the van—with your hands up. Let's hear your excuse for running a red light, and in your pal's case, escaping to avoid arrest."

"Officer, I know this is going to sound wild . . ." Frank began, obediently climbing out of the car. Obviously, Joe's running off had alerted the cops to trouble. The officer's partner stood on the passenger side of the van—his hand also ready to draw his revolver—speaking into a two-way radio.

"We're chasing a black limousine. Two guys jumped out and kidnapped a friend of ours." Frank tried to sound convincing. "A girl. Please believe me. This is urgent."

The officer grinned. "Well, I haven't heard *that* story before. Good, kid, real good. Let's see your license. Officer Nolan, check the registration," he added to his partner. "Is it in the glove compartment?" he asked.

Frank nodded and handed his license over. "I swear it's true, sir," he continued. "Can you just check it out? Then I'll take the ticket. The van is mine."

"In a minute, kid. Before I do anything I'm

going to search the van—with your permission, of course—for any illegal substances.''

"Papers check out, Officer Delgado," Nolan said. "I'm going after his buddy. He must have had some reason to run." He took off in the direction that Joe had run.

"Check out the black limo while you're at it, Nolan," Delgado called sarcastically. "I'll keep an eye on this one."

"Will do," Officer Nolan called back.

Delgado checked out the van and then took Frank's license and walked slowly back to the patrol car with it.

Frank climbed back in the van and pounded the door once, letting out his frustration. It took way too long to write a ticket, he thought, looking for Joe or Nolan.

Finally Officer Delgado returned. "Your license is good and no tickets lately." The man seemed surprised, as if he had expected Frank to have a record. "Sign here." He shoved a clipboard through Frank's window along with a ballpoint pen.

Frank looked it over. This was going to cost him, and his dad would be furious, but even worse was not knowing where Joe was. He scribbled his name and handed back the clipboard.

"Your father's Fenton Hardy?" the officer asked.

"Yes, sir," Frank said with no further comment. His dad was a former New York City detective, but Frank would never have mentioned his father's name or connections under these circumstances.

"He's not going to like this, I'd guess."

"No, sir. May I go now?" Frank was poised, ready to turn the key in the ignition.

"Let's see what my partner and your friend found." Delgado pointed out Nolan and Joe, who were just returning.

Nolan caught Delgado's eye and shook his head a couple of times. Joe, who was staring straight ahead, had a disgusted look on his face.

Delgado grinned. "Black limo? Life-or-death matter? Good try, Hardy," he said, and patted Frank's door once. "You're free, kid."

Frank turned then to Joe, who'd crawled into the passenger seat. "Did you lose it?"

"The limo turned right and vanished, Frank." Joe bit his lip, looking grim.

"Vanished? You sure?"

"Sure I'm sure. It wasn't that far ahead of me. There's an empty lot on one side, a fence around an old building on the other. I checked every car in this underground lot that it had to have turned into. Nothing."

"Let's check it out again." Frank drove the two blocks.

The underground lot was posted PRIVATE, NO

PARKING, VIOLATORS WILL BE TOWED. Frank pulled onto the ramp despite the warnings. He wanted to see for himself.

"Let's look around again, Joe. It's our only lead. We can't give up."

"I'm not giving up," Joe said. "A car that big doesn't just disappear."

"It could have taken off by now," Frank said, calmly assessing the situation.

Either that or the black limo *had* disappeared into thin air. There was no clue of any kind. The boys even checked the walls for a button to a hidden panel, but they found nothing.

After driving back up the ramp, the Hardys carefully searched the area within a two-block radius. Nothing. Feeling dejected, they headed back to the underground parking lot and down the ramp. One more look-see, they decided.

They'd lost Annie to who knows who or what. They hopped out their doors—neither wanted to give up. Joe walked around the front of the van to join his brother.

"When are you going to call it quits, boys?" a man said, moving up on them from the rear of the van.

The Hardys spun around to face two men all in black. They wore black ski masks over their faces with only their eyes and mouths showing. But it wasn't the men's appearances that held the Hardys' attention.

It was the pair of Browning 9mm automatic pistols that they had aimed at the brothers' hearts.

Chapter

8

FRANK AND JOE barely had time to exchange a glance before they were grabbed and had their hands securely tied behind their backs and blindfolds knotted into place across their eyes.

"What have you done with Annie?" Joe demanded. He and Frank stumbled as they were prodded to move blindly forward.

"Ain't that sweet, Clive? The kid's worried about his girlfriend."

"If you've hurt her . . ." Joe's threat died out as he realized there was nothing he could do at the moment.

"What'll you do about it? You gonna be a hero?" The thug laughed. "We got us a Prince Charming, Clive."

"Shut up, Hodge. Just move along."

Frank was trying to memorize by smell and sound where they were being taken. They didn't walk far before they entered an elevator. A strong chemical smell, not unlike that of shoe polish, permeated the space.

The smell disappeared the minute they left the elevator. There was a deep carpet underfoot now, and they were being led down what seemed to be a long hall.

"Good evening, boys," a voice greeted them just before their blindfolds were removed. "I'm sorry to inconvenience you, but you'll soon appreciate the reason for this secrecy."

Frank blinked twice to focus his eyes. Then he looked around, amazed. The men who had grabbed them were now wearing mirrored sunglasses instead of their ski masks.

The office they were in was decorated only in black and white. Walls were stark white, broken up randomly by a series of black and white abstract paintings. The carpet at their feet, deep and luxurious, was slightly off-white. The desktop in front of them looked as if it were fashioned from one solid piece of pure black marble.

And behind the desk, leaning back casually in a large office chair, sat a tall man. His long legs were crossed at the ankles and were resting on the marble top as if he were attending a casual meeting. He wore a finely tailored black business suit. His hair had been recently styled, but the boys couldn't see his eyes; they were hidden behind mirrored sunglasses.

And he wore diamonds. Many diamonds. On his right pinkie finger, on top of a thin, white leather glove, he sported an enormous, many-faceted diamond ring. A small diamond sparkled in the lobe of one of his ears. And the finishing touch was a diamond stickpin pushed jauntily into his black tie. Frank was no expert, but it hardly took a jeweler to appraise the stone in that ring. If the diamond was real, it had to be worth at least a million.

The man's tone as he greeted them was that of a polite host at a party. He smiled. But his smile was as cold and hard as the diamond in his tie. And his gloved hands he kept to himself, the fingers interlocked and resting on his outstretched legs.

"Who are you?" asked Joe, shrugging off the hands that still held him. "Where's Annie?"

"I'm right here, Joe." Annie's voice came from behind them as a third man pushed her forward.

"Are you all right, Annie?" Joe started to move to her, but strong hands kept him where he was.

"I—I guess so," Annie stammered.

On the desk in front of the head man, Frank recognized the black purse that Annie had kept clutched to her. Its contents were spilled out across a white blotter. Frank's quick eye inventoried the contents, and he was surprised to find that Annie had been hiding a secret.

She was in possession of a gun. Why would a girl who was a waitress in a pizza joint need to be armed?

"What do you want with us?" Joe asked, growing more impatient.

The man smiled again, perfect white teeth glittering in his wide mouth. "Forgive me for not making the introductions. My name is Cutter, Mr. Cutter. You are Frank and Joe Hardy, are you not?"

"How do you know that?" Joe asked.

Cutter chuckled. "I don't bring in visitors without knowing their identities."

"Do you always tie up and blindfold your guests?" asked Frank, trying to decide how much danger they were in.

"Untie them," Cutter commanded, gracefully lowering his legs to the floor. "It was merely a precaution. But on to the business at hand." He pushed the contents of Annie's purse—minus the gun—back into the bag. Annie stepped forward to claim it, anger in her movements.

The man slowly smiled at her. And then he quickly relaxed the gesture of friendliness and tightened his lips into a straight line. "Where are the diamonds, Annie? Phil double-crossed me, but I know you can't be that foolish."

Frank and Joe stared at the tall red-haired girl beside them, waiting for her answer.

"I don't know what you're talking about," she protested. "I've told you . . ."

"You were good friends with Phil Sidler—"

Annie cut him off. "A while ago. I'm not responsible for what he was involved in now. So bringing me here is a waste of time."

Frank couldn't tell if Annie was bluffing or not. But he had spent enough time with her that day to know that she was a fairly competent actress. Was she acting now?

Cutter sat forward, his impatience growing. "So far, I have treated you as my guest, Annie, you and your friends here. I'm a patient man, but I have been known to lose my patience. At which point I have ways of getting the information I need."

"She told you she knew nothing," said Joe, stepping toward Cutter's desk.

At Cutter's signal, the three henchmen moved forward to take Annie's, Frank's, and Joe's arms once again. "You impress me as intelligent young people—if a bit reckless. In my experience, young people never have all the money they'd like. I'm in a very lucrative business, and good help is hard to find. I'll tell you what I'm going to do."

He paused for effect, looking at each of his prisoners. "I can guarantee you each a more-than-generous salary, and a bonus for each job well done. I would, of course, expect Annie to return the items in her possession that belong to me. This would indicate her willingness to join me. I'll give you time to think over my offer." Cutter stood up then and indicated with a turn of his head that Joe, Frank, and Annie were to be escorted from his office.

The gun between Frank's shoulder blades kept him from protesting or trying to get away. The trio was led down a hall and shoved into another room. The lock clicked behind them.

The room was a small gym, fitted with weight machines, a stationary bike, a rowing machine, and mirrors.

Frank looked around. "Nothing like the Y, is it?" he said, making an attempt at humor. "Listen, Annie, whatever you're mixed up in, it's time to level with us. Obviously we're on the same side for the moment." He gave her a searching look. When she didn't answer, he said, "I think you'd better start by explaining why you were carrying a gun."

"Wouldn't you—if you were me?" Annie exploded angrily. Then she reined in her fury. "I was scared," she said. "When that man attacked me in my own apartment—of course I wanted to defend myself." Her hazel eyes pleaded with Frank to understand. "The gun is my father's," she said. "I took it when I left home. He was—

well, he was pretty abusive, and I was afraid he might go crazy and come after me with it when he found out I was gone. I decided to keep it when I got to Bayport—just in case. I was on my own, after all."

She glanced at Joe, whose level gaze had never left her. "I never would have used it," she said weakly, trying to smile at him.

"What about you and Phil?" Frank demanded.

Annie released a deep breath. "I'll tell you the same thing I told Cutter. I have no idea what Phil Sidler was involved in now. My bad luck was that I cared for him. I met him when I was in high school. I was just a kid."

It wasn't as if Annie was an old lady now. Frank wasn't sure he believed her, but he had no choice but to let the matter drop.

"Okay, here's the way I figure it." He leaned back against the saddle of the bicycle. "Cutter's behind all the jewel robberies in the area for the last several months, maybe longer. Obviously he specializes in diamonds. Phil Sidler double-crossed him, and because Phil contacted Annie, Cutter now thinks Annie has the diamonds or knows where they are." Frank held up a hand, palm out, to stop Annie from protesting again.

"He thinks cutting us in is the easiest way to get the diamonds back," added Joe, relieved that Frank wasn't dumping on Annie anymore. "Right now we've got two choices. We can pretend to join them. Or we can try to get out of here."

Frank looked around. There were no windows; it looked as if the door they came in was the only way back out.

"Would you trust Cutter?" asked Annie. "I don't think he'd cut us in on his business."

"I didn't say we'd trust him. Only pretend to join him." Frank checked each piece of equipment. "Do you think he was the guy in your apartment, Annie?"

"I don't know. But I think I'd have remembered the way he was dressed."

"He might wear civvies when he's out of here," Joe said, looking around at the well-appointed gym. Unable to resist, he jabbed at a punching bag hanging from the ceiling in a corner of the room.

"Annie, I can't blame you for not being able to describe the man in your room," Frank said. "I only got a glimpse of the guy who stunned me at Phil's. But he was tall, and quick. Like he worked out every day. I think it could have been Cutter."

"If Cutter has all these thugs working for him, Frank, it makes more sense for him to send them to do his dirty work," Joe argued logically.

"You're right." Frank silently ran through their options. "I don't think we can pretend to go along with Cutter's offer. I think we'd better try

71

to break out. I just don't trust him. I think we'll do better taking action on our own."

"I agree." Joe looked around. "This should do the job." He lifted the dumbbell from the bench press after removing several weights. "Not that I can't lift that much." Joe grinned at Annie. "But it's unwieldy when it's that heavy. This should be just about right." He tossed the bell slightly.

Frank was catching on to Joe's plan. "Wonder how long they'll leave us here? We could get a pretty good workout. I've been short of time lately." He sat down, adjusted the cable beside him, and pushed the hand grips of the weight machine forward, pressing fifty pounds.

"You admit you're turning into a ninety-eight-pound weakling?" Joe kidded.

"How can you two mess around at a time like this?" Annie complained. "These guys'll kill us if we don't cooperate." She slumped down on the floor beside the rowing machine.

"They could," Joe agreed, walking close to the door with the dumbbell.

"They won't kill you, Annie. They think you have some information they need. But you might wish they would kill you." Frank joined Joe at the door.

"Leave her alone, Frank," Joe said to his brother. "We need to concentrate on getting out of here. Call them, Annie. I'm tired of waiting."

Annie went over to the door and leaned her ear

against it. Then she knocked. "You win, guys," she said into the crack where the door met the frame. "I'll tell you everything."

No answer. It seemed as though there was no one outside the door. But a click signaled that someone *had* been waiting for Annie's reply. The door was swung open slowly, and a gun was thrust into the room.

"Okay, come on out. It didn't take you long to make up your minds." Cutter grinned, and Frank, right behind Annie, could see her mirrored in his sunglasses.

Frank then went into action. In a single motion he shoved Annie past Cutter with his left hand, and with his right delivered a single karate chop to the man's gun hand. Joe was right behind him.

"Here, catch," said Joe, tossing the dumbbell to the second man.

The thug's automatic reaction was to raise his hands to deflect the weight. As he did so, Joe grabbed his gun arm, twisting it so that he released the Browning as the dumbbell fell to the floor. Before the two knew what had hit them, they had been disarmed and locked into their own prison.

"At least they'll have something to do," Joe quipped. "I thought they were grossly out of condition, didn't you, Frank?"

The hall ran both ways, but instinct sent the boys in the direction from which they'd come.

The carpet muffled their footsteps as they hurried to the elevator. Inside the huge cage, the three stood silently gritting their teeth, their patience stretched thin by the slowness of the descent.

The door opened into the parking garage, and the trio started to dash out, Joe's hand around Annie's arm.

They stopped abruptly. Frank knew right then—without a doubt—that the tall man who'd knocked him out at Phil's was not Cutter.

Because here, blocking the entrance to the elevator, had to be his playmate from the hotel. This man was six-six, at least. As Frank watched, the tall man grabbed both Annie and Joe. He raised a revolver and held it steady. It was pointed straight at Annie's head.

Chapter

9

"ALL RIGHT, KIDS," the man said coolly. "It's time for some answers. We'll talk in your van. Move." He pointed the way with his gun, and when they didn't move fast enough, he nudged Joe forward by ramming the barrel into his spine.

"Ahhh!" Joe's breath rushed out in one burst, and he fell forward from the waist. Frank whirled around, his hands raised, ready to strike. But the tall man was too fast for him and kept his gun level and trained on both Frank and Joe.

Annie took a step back out of the man's line of sight. Before Joe could say, "Make your move, Annie," she had done so. Pulling her arm back to maximum power, Annie smashed the tall man just behind the ear with the heel of her hand. He was out cold.

Frank and Joe must have been wearing identical looks of astonishment, because Annie answered their question before it was asked. "I learned karate in junior high. I was a brown belt when I was fifteen."

"Good work," Frank said, meaning it.

"We're out of here!" Joe said, and reached out for Annie's arm. It was an unnecessary action, since she was ready to move before he was.

In the van, with the engine roaring, Joe advised Frank to head for home. "We need someplace to plan our next move and hide Annie."

"I think it's obvious that a lot of people know who we are. So they probably know where we live. I don't think we should go home; we'll only put Mom and Aunt Gertrude in danger."

"Do you have a better idea?" Joe snapped. "We've got to find someplace safe for Annie."

"I don't want to put your family in danger," she said defensively. "Frank thinks I've put them in enough already. If you'll drop me at the bus station in Bayport, I can disappear on my own."

"No way," Joe said, throwing Frank an annoyed glance. "I can't do that. We'll hide you someplace. Don't worry. If you aren't involved, you'll be free to live anyplace you like."

Frank noticed that Joe had said "if." Had he done some thinking about Annie? One thing was clear to anyone: she had gotten rid of the tall man unbelievably fast and efficiently. Also, she didn't

76

seem to be as frightened as she had been earlier. Frank wondered why she had ever felt scared at all with a gun in her purse and a karate chop like the one she used on the tall man.

Frank changed his mind and headed for home.

After Frank discussed the case with his father, Fenton Hardy was of two opinions. Yes, he thought it was risky business bringing Annie into the Hardy home. But he agreed with Joe that it was more risky to leave her out on the street alone.

"Even though Joe is only in this mess because of her, Frank," Mr. Hardy said, "we are involved. *And* she is the key witness to Joe's accident."

Frank moved on to another subject. "Do you have any ideas about who this mysterious Cutter might be?"

"Just waiting for you to ask." Fenton Hardy got up and went to his file cabinet and flipped through several drawers as he went back half a dozen years. "Here it is."

"You know him?" Frank asked excitedly.

"Daniel Cutter was a small-time safecracker until he proved that he could open any safe. His reputation grew. The Cutter, they started to call him. Everyone wanted him to work for them. But he got careless or ran out of luck about ten years ago. A gas tank from an acetylene torch exploded in his face."

"The glasses . . ." Frank mused. "And the gloves. It must be the same guy. But he's working on a new nickname now. He's into jewelry heists. Diamond Dan Cutter would suit him. I estimated he was wearing over a million dollars' worth of stones."

Fenton Hardy nodded distractedly, his mind obviously moving in new directions. "Maybe he didn't really know who you were even though he knew your names. You were only Annie's companions to him." Fenton Hardy closed the file drawer and wandered back to his desk. "It's impossible to trace diamonds after they've been cut, recut, or reset. Our only hope is if you can take us back to the gang's hideout."

"Finding the building is a snap, but I don't know the secret to get up to the apartment. I know you don't just get on the elevator."

"Sorry, Frank, but I don't like it. I'm going to have to turn all this information over to the police. I don't want you to go back there alone. Okay?"

Frank met his father's eyes and slowly nodded. "Okay. I agree. I'm going to talk to Joe now."

"Tell him the police want to see him in the morning. The more he cooperates, the better it looks. I don't want him doing anything reckless. You and Annie can go with him. They might want to ask you some more questions after I speak with them."

"Sure, Dad." Frank headed for the kitchen, the first place in the Hardy house to look for Joe.

Joe had helped Annie get settled in the guest room and then gone back to the kitchen to polish off the food they'd picked up at a deli. He sat at the kitchen table, drinking a glass of milk and eating a ham and swiss on rye.

"Joe, I've done some thinking." Frank pulled out a pad of paper from behind the kitchen phone. "Look at this."

Joe was interested in Frank's time schedule until he found out that all the events involved only Annie.

"Annie gets the phone call from Phil, which we witnessed," Frank said, beginning his list of facts. "According to her, that was the first time she'd heard from Phil in ages. Right?"

"What are you getting at, Frank?"

"Hold on. Try to think for a minute, and don't just act on your feelings for Annie." Frank sat down beside Joe.

Joe grumbled but kept listening.

"The next several hours we all spent at the police station. I took Annie home, but we know she spent that night at Mr. Pizza in the storeroom, right?"

"What are you getting at?" Joe asked again.

"Either she got the gun out of storage after she was attacked, as she said, or she could have had it in her purse all along—before Phil called her on the phone." Frank stared at his brother but Joe only looked at the last of his sandwich. Frank continued.

"I think that Annie already had the gun, Joe, that she'd seen Phil or heard from him before that phone call. We know he checked in at the hotel two days earlier. Now, she was scared of someone—even after Phil was dead. That was why she spent the night at Mr. Pizza." He took a deep breath. "I think that someone was Cutter and his men. She knew he'd be looking for her."

"I don't want to hear any more of these crazy ideas, Frank." Joe stood up.

"I'm afraid my 'crazy ideas' are right on target this time. Or if not, you tell me why *both* Cutter and the tall man think Annie has the diamonds. Doesn't that strike you as strange, Joe? Face it, Annie isn't telling us the whole story. She's not only a girl dealing with a jealous boyfriend, she's a stranger with a gun and a mean karate chop—"

"If you're trying to convince me Annie's a jewel thief, forget it. I admit that everything doesn't fall into place, but Annie Shea is not a crook."

"You're not thinking, Joe."

"Yes. I am. And what's more, I've decided

that Annie isn't staying in Bayport a minute longer. I'm going to take her someplace safe."

"Where? Dad wants us all to go down to the Bayport police station tomorrow, to tell them about everything that's happened. They specifically want to see you at ten o'clock. And then we'll probably have to talk to New York cops— since we were taken by Cutter and his goons there."

"I'm taking Annie upstate, Frank. That's it. Once I get her safely hidden away, I can work on the case and talk to the police."

"Joe, not being available to the police tomorrow morning is like admitting you're guilty. They'll think you skipped out on your bail. Dad could get in big trouble, too."

"Hold on, Frank." Joe started to move to the kitchen door. "I'll be back before they know I'm gone."

"I'm not going to let you go, Joe." Frank stepped in front of his brother.

Joe laughed. "You're not going to *let* me go? Out of my way, Frank. Please, get out of my way."

Frank faced him and realized what he knew all along—it would be impossible to stop his brother once he made up his mind to go.

"If you screw up, Joe, don't expect me to cover for you," Frank said to his back.

"I won't, Frank. I promise. And I *will* be back on time." Joe patted his brother on the shoulder and took off.

Frank banged his fist on the counter in frustration as Joe Hardy disappeared up the stairs.

Chapter

10

JOE KNOCKED AT Annie's door. "Annie, you asleep?"

"No, Joe. Come on in. What's wrong?" Annie sat on the side of her bed, still dressed, her suitcases unopened. "I've been trying to figure out what to do. I've already caused too much trouble."

"I have a plan, Annie. I'm glad you haven't unpacked anything. We're leaving here."

"Where are we going?" Annie stood up and slipped on her shoes.

"I have a friend who has a cabin upstate. There are a couple of small motels in the area. I'm going to take you up there and hide you out in a motel until this mess gets worked out. Then I'll come back for you."

Annie stared at Joe. "Joe, I told you I'll just leave town, disappear."

"No, Annie. Trust me. If you lay low for a few days, I can crack this case. But I can't if I'm worrying about you."

"I can take care of myself," said Annie.

"I did notice that," Joe said with admiration in his voice. "But something might come up that even you can't handle."

Annie's eyes held his for a moment and she said nothing. "This is Frank's idea, isn't it?" she said finally. "To get me away from you."

"Frank wants you to stay," Joe insisted. "He's—he's concerned about you."

Annie laughed bitterly. "He's never liked me," she said. "Maybe it's because I'm not like Callie. I don't have parents who take care of me and have money and—"

"Annie," Joe interrupted, taking her hand. "Who cares what Frank thinks? I like you—a lot. And *I* want you to be safe."

At his words, Annie's troubled face cleared, and she smiled gratefully at Joe. "I guess that's why you're the Hardy I decided on," she teased, and gave him a happy kiss on the cheek.

It was around eleven when Joe and Annie climbed into the van and pulled away from the house.

"You hungry, Annie?" Joe asked.

She smiled ironically. "No, but I bet you are."

The first fast-food place they came to, they ordered and then ate as they drove along the highway. It's good being alone with Annie, Joe thought as he checked the rearview mirror and switched to the fast lane. Inside the van they were safe, in a warm and cozy cocoon far from the problems of the world.

With Annie so quiet Joe had time to do some serious thinking. He didn't like there being tension between Frank and him, but he knew that Annie was right when she said Frank had never liked her. And now Frank was doubly suspicious of her. It was also true that there were some facts about the case that just didn't add up. Maybe it was time to ask some questions.

"Annie, you asleep?" She turned to look at him and gently shook her head. "Can we talk?" This time she nodded. "That day in Mr. Pizza, when you got the phone call from Phil, that wasn't the first time you'd heard from him lately, was it?" Joe glanced over at her, curled up so sweetly in the seat beside him.

She hesitated but finally spoke. "No. Phil called me a few days earlier from New York. He wanted me to come to the city to see him. He said he'd hit the big time, and he wanted another chance with me."

"What did you tell him?"

"That I wanted nothing to do with him. Believe

me, Joe, I was through with Phil Sidler. I was afraid of him.''

"But what happened? He wouldn't take no for an answer?''

"He said he was coming to talk to me. I begged him not to. I told him it wouldn't do any good, that I wouldn't see him.'' Annie twisted the ring on her right hand. "He wanted to know if there was anyone else.''

"What did you tell him?''

"I knew he'd be jealous, Joe. If I mentioned another guy, he'd have a fit. So I lied. I told him no, but that I still didn't want to see him. He called again when he got to Bayport. He said he was coming to Mr. Pizza to get me. He said I'd change my mind when I heard about all the money he'd made.''

"You think he was talking about the diamonds? That he'd double-crossed Cutter for the stones?''

"I don't know. I didn't ask where he'd gotten the money. He was always involved in some crazy get-rich scheme that only made him poorer. Joe.'' Annie reached out in the dark and put her hand on Joe's arm. "You believe me, don't you? I never knew how nice a guy could be until I met you. I'd never do anything to hurt you.'' In the beams from an oncoming car Annie's face was suddenly brightly lit, and Joe's heart did a flip-flop when he glanced at her gorgeous hazel eyes.

Annie snuggled closer to him. And Joe could

smell her cologne and shampoo as her hair softly brushed his cheek.

Joe hadn't thought he could ever care for anyone after Iola had been killed. But he had started feeling good about Annie. Now the accident had come between them. And he was beginning to have doubts about Annie's story. Some of it didn't add up.

His mind whirled with unanswered questions as he drove through the dark night. He glanced into the rearview mirror every few minutes to make sure they weren't being followed.

"Wake up, Annie." Joe gently roused the girl an hour later. "We're almost there."

"I wasn't asleep." Annie yawned. "I was thinking."

"About me?" Joe teased.

"I wish I'd met you years ago."

"Years ago I was just a kid," Joe had to admit.

"You're no old man now." Annie laughed. She looked out the window. "Why are we driving on these back streets?" She glanced into the sideview mirror, suddenly alert.

Joe had pulled off the highway at the exit for Allendale. He'd driven around the gray and deserted streets several times before heading for the motel he remembered. He didn't want to alarm Annie, but he was being realistic.

"I want to be sure no one's following us."

"You think they would? You think Cutter's

men could have been watching your house?"
Annie's voice rose in alarm.

"Calm down, Annie. I said I was just being
careful. No one's followed us. I've been watching
all the way from Bayport."

"And I thought your mind was on me." Annie
tried to smile, but Joe could see that she was still
tense.

Pulling into the parking lot for the small motel,
Joe managed a laugh. "Holiday Hideout." He
read the name of the motel. "Like the sound of
that?"

"It's hard to think of this as a holiday," Annie
answered solemnly, looking at the neon vacancy
sign.

They had to ring the bell to wake someone up
so they could register. A woman unlocked the
door. She was tying a bathrobe around her ample
waist, her hair in rollers, her eyes heavy with
sleep as she came out to greet them.

"Do you have a room left?" asked Joe.

The proprietor eyed the two of them, then
smiled when she noticed Annie twisting her ring.
Joe saw that she'd switched it to her left hand,
and she was looking at him with dreamy eyes. He
felt his face heat up.. The woman laughed. "I can
always spot honeymooners. I'll bet you two
eloped, didn't you?" She reached under the desk
and fumbled for the guest register. "I guess you'll

only want the one night, won't you? Going on to Niagara Falls?"

Joe didn't know what to say. Honeymooners wouldn't choose to spend a week at the Holiday Hideout.

"We don't have much money, Mrs.—" Annie was asking for the woman's name.

"Booth. Edith Booth."

"Mrs. Booth. We can't go far. So we thought we'd find someplace clean and inexpensive and then take some day trips. I understand there are lakes near here where we can picnic."

"Why, sure. In the morning I'll give you a map and point out the places of interest. I understand starting out broke. Why, me and Earl, that's my husband, didn't have two quarters to rub together when we got married. But if you love each other—"

"Could I pay three nights in advance?" Joe interrupted the woman, who sounded as if she'd go on forever now that she'd decided to be friendly. "Then we'll see if we want to stay longer."

"That'd be fine." Edith Booth handed the pen to Joe.

He hesitated and glanced at Annie, who took his arm and smiled up at him. "Want me to write it, Joe?"

"No." Joe quickly scribbled Mr. and Mrs. Joe Hardy. This was getting ridiculous, he thought.

He paid cash and, after getting the key, hustled Annie out.

She burst into laughter the minute they got into the van to drive the short distance to the room. "Oh, Joe, you should have seen your face when I pretended we were married."

"Why did you do it, Annie?" he grumbled as he moved the van to Unit 10, the farthest from the office and the street, dark and shadowed except for the small light over the door. Mrs. Booth wanted them to have privacy.

"It was fun, Joe. But how will I explain it when she sees me alone tomorrow, though?"

"You can say we had our first fight and I left you because you're so conniving. Here's some money, Annie. I'll try to call every day." At least Annie's little game had made her forget about being afraid. Joe was glad for that.

He walked Annie to her room. "I hate to leave you here alone. Some husband, huh?" he teased.

"I'll be fine, Joe," Annie assured him. "My suitcase." She hurried back to the van. "I still think I should have left Bayport alone, though. I don't have much money, but if you'd have lent me some—what you're spending for the motel—I'd have paid you back when I got another job."

"I want you to be able to stay in Bayport, Annie." Joe pulled her close. "Frank and I will get to the bottom of this mess. Then you can go back to work and we'll take up where we left off—Mrs. Hardy." Joe laughed.

"Very touching," said a deep voice from the shadows. The tall man, the one Annie had so neatly disposed of, moved forward into the light. The single overhead bulb reflected off the gun that he had shoved into the small of Annie's back.

"You couldn't have followed us!" Joe said, frustrated. He had taken every precaution. How had this man materialized out of the shadows just after they arrived?

"I'll take those diamonds, Annie. Back away and don't try anything," he said to Joe. "Not if you want to see this girl alive in the morning."

Chapter

11

"I DON'T HAVE any diamonds," Annie snapped.

"But you know where they are. I'll bet on it."
The tall man pushed on Annie's shoulder so she
was facing him now. There was no doubt that he
was in control. "My instincts are never wrong."

"Are you a friend of Phil's?" Annie asked.

Joe studied this man who was so persistent and
sure of himself. He didn't look like he'd be a
friend of Phil Sidler's. Tall, middle-aged, graying
slightly at the temples, he might have been a
college professor or a businessman.

Maybe he had found out about the robbery and
decided this was an easy way to make his fortune.
Or maybe he headed a rival gang and the two
were fighting over this haul. That was it, Joe
decided. The guy had to be a rival of Cutter's.

Joe was trying to identify his slight accent, although he wasn't sure what good that would do.

"Who are you?" Joe insisted.

"A concerned party." The man pointed toward the van with the gun. When Annie didn't move right away, he gave her a quick shove with the flat of his hand.

Joe had no choice but to climb back into the van with Annie. The tall man settled himself in the seat behind Joe and Annie so he could keep the gun trained on her.

"Back to Bayport, Joe," he instructed. "I'll leave my rental car here."

So he'd been watching the house and he'd followed them the whole way. Joe felt like an incompetent beginner. How had the guy done it? And how did he know where they lived? They had left him unconscious in that parking garage in New York City.

Joe glanced at his gas gauge. It was approaching empty. Good. What would this man be able to do with a car out of gas on the highway in the middle of the night?

"What good will it do us to return to Bayport?" Joe asked, trying to get the guy to talk. Maybe he'd let something slip.

"We're going on a little treasure hunt with Annie planning the itinerary. Someone has three million dollars' worth of diamonds, and I want them."

"Three million?" Joe whistled. No wonder the thieves were so insistent.

"Three million?" Annie echoed.

"It doesn't take that many diamonds if they're quality ones. They could be hidden in a very small space." Joe decided that the tall man knew what he was talking about.

"You think Phil Sidler had them? That he really did double-cross Cutter and his men?" Joe asked.

The man relaxed back into his seat. He seemed willing to talk, but Joe noticed that he kept the gun leveled at Annie. "Phil did have them at first," he said. "But they weren't in his hotel at Bayport or in his apartment in New York. We're still looking for them. Logic tells me that Phil either gave them to Annie or that he told her where they were hidden."

"How many times do I have to tell people I have no idea what's going on here?" Annie protested. "Phil told me nothing, and I certainly don't have three million dollars' worth of diamonds or I wouldn't be here."

"If Phil had told Annie anything, she'd have told the police," said Joe. "Wouldn't you, Annie?"

"Of course I would." Annie turned her head and stared out her window.

Joe was not so sure. Three million dollars would tempt almost anyone, he thought. He was at a point where he didn't know what to believe, so he concentrated on driving. Until he thought of a plan, he wasn't in control of the situation anyway.

"Of course, it is possible that the hiding place of the jewels died with Phil," the man in the backseat said.

"Who *are* you?" Joe asked again. "You're not in Cutter's gang. You're not a friend of Phil's. What's your connection with all this? Are you part of a tour group? Did you miss your bus?"

The man smiled. He seemed pleased by Joe's defiance. "Let's just say that I'm trying to return the diamonds to their rightful owner."

"And who is that?" Joe turned slightly, only to see the gun raised and aimed at him.

This time there was no answer. They drove a few miles in silence and then, "Slow down, Joe. Drive the minimum speed for a few miles."

Joe sighed, resigning himself to following orders until he was in a position to disarm their passenger. He slowed the van to forty miles an hour, a mere crawl on the turnpike. There was no traffic on the highway now. The clock in the van read two A.M.

"Can I turn on the radio?" Joe asked with some sarcasm in his voice.

"Forget it," the man barked.

Glancing in the rearview mirror, Joe noticed a single pair of lights behind the van. He wondered why the car wasn't passing. No one drove forty on the turnpike—not even little old ladies.

"Speed up," came the voice from behind him. "Drive about five miles over the speed limit but no more. We don't need the highway patrol pulling us over."

Joe pressed his foot down on the accelerator and sped up. As he guessed it would, the car behind them kept pace.

"Just as I thought," the tall man said, looking worried. "Trouble."

Annie looked in the sideview mirror. All she could see were a pair of headlights. "It's Cutter," she said. "Hurry, Joe. Don't let him get me again. He threatened me before. If he catches me again, he'll kill me, Joe. I know he will.

"Annie." She was practically hysterical. "Stay calm, Annie. I won't let them get you."

In compliance with the tall man's orders, he continued slowing down and speeding up, sometimes placing his foot on the brake abruptly. As the cat-and-mouse game continued, Joe tried to relieve his impatience by reviewing the situation.

He'd made a mistake bringing Annie upstate. Both of them could have been safe in the Hardys' home right then. Now it looked as if Joe might be responsible for her death—and possibly his own. If Cutter's men were following, they'd be playing hardball this time. There'd be no easy escape.

Had their escape earlier been a farce, anyway?

Had Cutter let them go, planning to tail them until Annie led him to the diamonds? Joe realized with a sudden shock that he now believed she had the jewels. He must be tired. The only thing he knew for sure was that they wouldn't stop at anything to regain that fortune.

The next time Joe slowed down, the car behind them pulled up beside the van. The driver tried to force Joe off the road. But Joe swung left onto the shoulder, then swerved hard to the right and speeded up, leaving the other car behind.

"Any suggestions?" Joe asked, sarcasm in his voice. "You're in charge of this little game."

"I hadn't planned on Cutter's following us," the man answered.

Joe was tensed for action as he sped off into the tunnel of light that his headlights cut into the dark. He pulled into the passing lane and drove faster.

"One of them has a gun, Joe!" Annie screamed. The car had pulled up beside them on her side. "An Uzi. He's going to shoot."

Joe didn't think the guy would shoot Annie if he believed she knew where the diamonds were. But better not take chances. Flicking a switch, he brought bulletproof panels down to cover all of the windows. Now Joe could use the van almost as a tank. He slowed, then glanced into the other lane. Speeding up, he left the smaller car far behind.

Now the only thing he had to worry about was their shooting out his tires.

Annie said, glancing at Joe, "I'm starting to believe maybe you *can* take care of us."

Deftly weaving from lane to lane so the guys behind him couldn't get a clear shot at his tires, Joe became aware of every muscle in his body. He hungered for action, a real confrontation to end this chase. But instead he called up his powers of patience.

He knew that eventually the state police would have to pull him over. The way he was driving he *had* to attract attention—at least that was what he was hoping. And when the police did stop him, the car behind them wouldn't stick around. But with the kind of luck Joe was having lately, the trooper on duty would be taking a coffee break. Not much action in the wee hours of the morning.

Joe pressed his speed higher and higher, continuing to weave back and forth. He guessed the guys pursuing them weren't going to shoot because they would have gotten off a couple of rounds already. They didn't want to risk Annie in an accident.

"Good idea, Joe," the voice behind him commented. "Attracting the state police is smart. In fact, the police do seem to be the perfect answer here. Take the next exit."

The man had to be bluffing. He couldn't really want the law to stop them. But Joe decided that the tall man must have figured that if their action got Cutter's men off their tail, he was all for it.

"Hang on," he said to Annie. He needn't have bothered. She was clutching the door in a death grip.

Joe braked and took the off ramp at a speed that sent the van careening dangerously. Without stopping, he made a right-hand turn that led eventually onto the main street of a small town. The small car fell behind.

The streets of the town were brightly lit but devoid of people. One all-night gas station was closed up tight. But they were in luck. A policeman sat in his patrol car in the parking lot of a local café. Probably he had been dozing or listening to his radio, but he came to life when Joe shot by.

Light swirling, siren screaming, he pulled out after the van. Gratefully Joe pulled up to the curb, flipping a switch to roll the window shields down. He'd take the ticket gladly. He was happy, though, that Frank had been driving in New York City. Both the Hardys' driving records were getting badly tarnished by this case.

"Tell him you want to go to the station. Say you have an incident to report. And don't try getting away—either of you," their passenger growled.

Before Joe could react to the stranger's surprising behavior, the policeman was at his window.

"Out for a little drive, are you?" he asked as Joe rolled his window down and handed him his license.

"Sir, I can explain. There was an incident on the highway that I need to report. A car tried to run us off the road. My friend here and I felt we were in danger."

"Please help us," Annie added in a voice that was still filled with fear.

The officer looked at Joe's license, then handed it back slowly. "All right. But this had better be good. Third street, turn left, second building on the right, back entrance. I'll be right behind you, so don't try any funny stuff."

"No, sir," said Joe, and groaned with relief after the officer turned away. He'd tried all the funny stuff he knew earlier.

"Very good, Joe. You sounded very much like a law-abiding citizen. And our friends have stopped following us."

Right, Joe thought, and the first person to be reported to the police will be you. If he played his cards right, they'd be rid of both opponents in a couple of minutes. But Joe wondered why the tall man was being so cooperative. Why was he going along to the station? Didn't he know Joe would turn him in?

The station was empty except for one dispatcher and one clerk, a woman in uniform at the front desk. Joe and Annie headed for the desk, followed by the police officer and the tall man.

The tall man had pocketed his gun as they got out of the car and seemed to have forgotten that he and Annie were there. After Joe arrived at the front desk with Annie, he noticed that their kidnapper had stopped the officer to talk with him in private. After a brief conversation, the two headed down the corridor and into a room; the door quickly closed behind them.

"Miss," Joe said to the officer at the desk. "That man in there with the patrolman, he's armed and has been holding us captive."

She looked at Joe as if he were hallucinating but picked up the phone and punched in an extension.

"I see. Thank you," she said after reporting Joe's accusation and listening a moment. "You're to wait here," she instructed Joe and Annie. "Sit down anywhere. It'll be a few minutes."

Joe felt as if he were being left out, and he felt he had every right to know what was happening. Also he discovered he was exhausted. He'd give anything to wake up and discover he'd been dreaming the whole incident. He followed Annie to a group of chairs, but instead of sitting down, he headed past them toward the closed door where the officer and the tall man had disappeared.

"Sir, I'll have to ask you to be seated." The policewoman's sharp voice stopped Joe.

"But—"

"Those are my orders. I suggest you comply."

Joe sat and crossed his legs at the ankles. Nervously he tapped one foot up and down in a frantic rhythm. Annie sat flipping through the pages of a magazine, as though she were casually waiting for an appointment. Only a slight tremor in her hand revealed her anxiety and fatigue.

"What do you think's going on, Joe?" she whispered to him finally.

"I have no idea. And I don't like not knowing. We've been here over half an hour."

Finally Joe returned to the desk to demand some information. "Officer." He had to speak to get her attention. She acted as if he were invisible.

"Yes?" She walked over to the counter where Joe was standing and fuming.

"I'd like to see the man who came in here with us."

"What man?" the woman asked as if she'd never seen Joe before.

"When the officer brought us in, there was a very tall man with us. He was over six-six. I'd like to see him, Officer Lloyd," Joe said, reading the woman's name tag.

"I'm sorry, there's no one here of that description."

"But—I came in with him." No tall man? Joe couldn't believe it. "At least let me talk to the officer who brought us in."

"He's not here, either. He went out to answer a call."

"He's gone?" What was going on? "Look, Officer. I was brought in here for a traffic violation. You can't keep me all night. Just give me my ticket and I'll leave."

"Oh, I'm sorry, sir. Didn't anyone tell you? You're free to go. I have no information about a violation. It must have been dropped."

Joe was too stunned to move for several seconds. Finally he did spin around and stride back to Annie.

"Come on, we're getting out of here."

"What's going on? Where's the tall man?"

"I have no idea, but I'm not going to argue with anyone because I'm not getting a ticket. This is bizarre."

Annie didn't question the reason for their freedom. "I'm exhausted, Joe. Can we go back to your place? I felt safe there."

"My plan exactly. So far we've gotten no-where—fast. And I have an appointment at ten in the morning—this morning."

Outside the station the sky was beginning to lighten. Before they got in the van, Joe checked it over carefully but found no evidence of tampering. Also there was no sign of the man who'd held them captive on the wild ride down the highway. It was as if he had never existed, and the incident had never happened.

He glanced around the small, quiet town, but it seemed empty. No one had started leaving for work yet; no joggers were pounding the streets. There was no sign of the car that had followed them.

"Who was that man?" Annie asked out loud. "And where did he go? I don't understand why he keeps appearing and disappearing."

"I'd like to know what story he told the police," Joe said. "But right now, I'm starving. It's almost light. We can at least have breakfast before we go."

Joe pulled the van in front of the café that now was open. The aromas of freshly brewed coffee and bacon frying greeted them when they entered. "I'll take a number one and a number four," Joe told the waitress at the counter, and handed the menu to Annie. "To go."

"Are you sure that'll be enough, Joe?" Annie smiled. "I'm not sharing. I'm starving, too." She gave the waitress her order.

They each drank a cup of coffee while they waited, and Joe ate two sweet rolls. Then he handed the bag to Annie and paid for the food. A couple of sleepy men wandered in as they walked out. Joe glanced in all directions, then climbed into the van. He felt almost relaxed as he swung onto the highway. Now was the time to ask Annie some serious questions.

"I must say, Joe Hardy," Annie started before he had a chance, "spending the night with you is not boring."

Joe didn't laugh, and Annie looked over to see why.

"Sorry, Annie. I've got some bad news—the excitement may not be over." Joe's two big breakfasts turned to lead in his stomach. "We may have lost the mysterious stranger, but I don't think we've lost Cutter."

Annie stared into the sideview mirror, her face slowly turning into a mask of pure terror. "No, Joe! We can't let them get us. I know them! They'll force me to talk and then they'll kill me!"

Chapter

12

JOE SPED UP in a desperate attempt to get away, but the car behind them was determined not to lose its quarry again. Pulling alongside Joe, the chase car kept pace with Joe.

"Joe, they're pointing Uzis at us!" Annie screamed, and ducked down in her seat.

Joe again flicked the switch that brought down the bulletproof shields. The round of bullets hitting the van spurred him on. The bullets were obviously being aimed at the van's tires now. The men must have decided to chance killing Annie for the opportunity to talk to her. Surviving this assault, Joe decided, would be a matter of blind luck.

"We're dead, Joe." Annie was crumpled up in the seat beside Joe.

"Hang on, Annie. I can lose them—I promise. I know the area. My dad used to bring us fishing around here."

Joe swung off the expressway. The car chasing them sped by, brakes squealing. Almost immediately after the exit ramp, Joe took a narrow dirt road that led to a thickly forested plot of land. The road, a one-lane rutted path, wound upward, and the van bounced and skidded until Joe was forced to slow down.

The road became narrower and steeper until it leveled out and headed downhill. It was on the downhill side that the van began to cough.

"What the—" Joe glared at all the gauges. What he saw made his heart sink. "Oh, no!"

"What's wrong?" Annie asked.

"We're out of gas." Joe grinned sheepishly.

"Out of gas? Joe, you're kidding. How could you run out of gas?"

"Easy. I had a lot on my mind." He looked around quickly, his mind clicking now. As the van coasted to a stop, he maneuvered it off the road. "Come on, we're bailing out."

"Joe, there's no place to go."

"Sure there is." He turned off the ignition. Deep forest surrounded them. After jumping out, Joe locked the van. He had no choice but to leave it. Cutter's car had no doubt made a U-turn by now and was headed in their direction. The van wasn't hidden completely, but someone would have to know where to look to see it.

Joe reached for Annie's hand, and within seconds they were in the forest, hidden by trees and brush. The birds immediately grew silent, aware of the intrusion. But a squirrel overhead scolded, complaining about the visitors.

The ground crunched with each step because of the carpet of leaves underfoot. To Joe they sounded like a couple of bears crashing about, and there was no way to be quiet. Any minute Cutter's thugs could catch up and hone in on them.

Annie wobbled along beside him. It was all she could do to keep upright. Joe looked at her shoes. She still had on the high heels.

"Take them off," he advised.

"It would be even slower going. I can't run barefoot."

"Why don't girls wear sensible shoes?"

"I didn't know we were going for a hike in the woods," Annie complained.

Joe clutched Annie's hand tightly and slowed down. He was looking for a clearing not too far from where they'd left the van. Just past the clearing there was a small fishing cabin he and his father had rented some years earlier. If they could find the cabin, if it was still there, they could take refuge, or at least stop and assess their situation.

"I'm sorry, Joe." Annie's breath came in short bursts. "I can't go much farther without resting. If they followed us—"

"They would have caught up by now, Annie." Joe tried to reassure her. He felt sure they were being followed, but he didn't know how far behind Cutter's men were, or how good they were at tracking. There were several ways he and Annie could have headed from the van. With any luck, the men could have taken a wrong trail or split up, leaving the odds better for Joe.

Joe swore at himself under his breath. He was a fool, stupid and careless—an amateur. How could he run out of gas. They'd had a head start when the chase car had flown past the exit. Maybe he and Annie could have gotten across the dirt road to the state highway, then pulled into one of the little towns over there and hidden out. Any number of small roads crisscrossed these wooded hills, and Joe knew most of them. Sometimes, bored with fishing, he and Frank had ridden dirt bikes for miles.

But he couldn't dwell on what might have been. He needed a plan for escaping Cutter's men now. And if he could successfully overpower them, how could he and Annie get back to town? Cutter's car. That was it. Ambush them and take their car.

"Annie." Joe pulled her into a small clearing and behind an outcropping of rocks. "I've got a plan. We're going to stop and wait for them. You stay here. I'm going to see if I can find another place to hide."

"Joe, don't leave me alone," Annie pleaded.

"I'm not leaving. Get back behind those rocks and keep your eyes open. And keep that karate chop ready."

Hunched down, Joe ran for a thick tree. He paused, listened, heard nothing. Maybe they weren't being followed. A short distance away a small stream bubbled and slid over rocks. A thrush sang in sweet, melodious tones. Joe was pleased to hear it, since its presence meant no one was disturbing the bird.

Circling back the way they'd come, careful to plant his feet on grass or rocks rather than dry leaves, he listened. Nothing.

He was on the verge of deciding that he and Annie were alone when a scream pierced the air. At the same time a shot rang out.

"Annie!" he yelled, and dashed back to where he'd left her.

She had been struggling with a man, and was just throwing him to the ground when Joe reached her.

The man rolled over, jumped up, and whirled at Joe's approach. Annie was reaching for a rock to hit him on the head when three men crashed out of the woods behind her and shouted, "Hold it—right there."

One man had an Uzi pointed straight at Annie. Another trained his weapon on Joe. The third lowered his gun and picked up the .44 Magnum his partner had dropped when he'd fallen to the ground.

"What's the matter, Clive?" the thug with the machine gun said. "Can't handle a little girl?"

"This is no ordinary girl, pal. Take my word for it. You tie her up." He grabbed Annie's arms. She struggled, her eyes pleading with Joe to help her.

Before Joe could move, two of the other men slammed him to the ground. Twisting loose, Joe rolled and kicked upward, catching one man in the stomach. Even so, his two attackers finally managed to pin him facedown. Then Joe felt a small circle of cold steel against his neck.

"We have orders not to kill you, kid, but we might just forget. So lie still."

"You could say it was an accident," the man called Hodge gasped. He'd helped wrestle Joe to the ground and was nursing a bruised solar plexus. "Your gun went off in a struggle."

"Please, don't kill him!" Annie demanded. "You've got me. Let him go."

"Let him go, lady? You've got to be kidding."

Joe's fear for Annie forced him to make one more try for freedom. If he could get the machine gun . . . Twisting out from under the man who held him captive, Joe kept low, then hacked at his wrist with a powerful blow. The gun flew from the man's hand, but just as Joe closed his hand around the weapon, the butt of a gun slammed into his head from behind. Through a burst of stars, Joe heard Annie scream. Then he toppled onto the forest floor.

It was hours later when sunlight streamed into the clearing, warming Joe's stiff body. His temples pulsed in a wave of pain. His head felt as if it were filled with lead pellets. He managed to focus his eyes, but he could move neither his arms nor legs. Both were tied securely behind him. Slowly, Joe forced himself to raise his head as the world around him flashed and wavered like a gruesome light show. Pain and fear struck his gut like a lightning bolt.

The fear was not for himself. It was for Annie. Cutter's thugs were gone, and they had taken the girl with them.

Joe had failed to protect her—and for Annie his failure meant certain death.

Chapter

13

A BLUE JAY shrilled overhead as if laughing at Joe's predicament. Two squirrels chattered, chasing each other down the bark of a nearby tree. Each sound made his headache worse.

Yet Joe couldn't lie there suffering. That wasn't doing him or Annie any good. He used the pain like a whip to bring himself to a state of alertness and to remain conscious.

Slowly Joe rocked from side to side, trying to gain the momentum he needed to turn over. The movement only twisted the ropes tighter, making them cut into his wrists and ankles. Finally, he flipped over onto his back, biting his lip to keep from crying out as the ropes cut deeper into his already raw skin.

He managed to sit up and look around. He saw

nothing that he might use to cut through the cords. He was no longer near the rocks where Annie had hidden, but near the creek now.

If his memory served him correctly, there were rocks clustered all up and down the stream bed. He used to climb on the rocks years ago.

Fatigue threatened to eliminate the surge of adrenaline he'd mustered by turning over. Annie's in trouble, he reminded himself. And it's my fault. How long had he been unconscious? Not too long, he thought, since the sun was still low in the east. There was a chance to find her if he could get out of there soon.

He debated whether or not it would be faster to roll or scoot down to the stream. Scooting won since it was the less painful of the two. But twice he lost his balance and rolled when he would have preferred to move in the slower manner.

Finally he reached his goal. There were plenty of sharp edges in the jumble of rock piles beside the stream, left there by some long-ago shift in the mountainous terrain.

Joe's mouth was so parched he could scarcely swallow, and the water teased him. It was so near, yet he couldn't reach it. He had to get loose first. Again he endured the agony as he lifted his hands behind his back to the edge of a rock and began to slide the rope back and forth.

It took less time than he'd anticipated once he

got a rhythm going. The granite was razor sharp where a piece had broken away long ago.

When he felt his bonds release, he gave a sigh of relief. Quickly he brought his arms, stiff and sore, around to his ankles to untie the cord there. He rolled to the creek, drank deeply, then ducked his head into the cold water to clear his cobwebby brain.

His muscles screamed as he stood, but he insisted that his legs move until he reached the road.

The van was still hidden beside the small dirt road, but it was useless to Joe. There were flares in a toolbox in the back, but no one was likely to be driving by so early in the day. Joe checked his watch, but it was crushed and broken. Apparently, he had smashed it during the fight with Cutter's men. Joe took off on foot for the highway.

He was sweating profusely from the pace he'd maintained when he came in sight of the highway. Never had morning rush-hour traffic looked so good. One, it suggested that it was not so late as Joe had feared. Two, with all these people out there, someone had to pick him up.

Or would they? He must look awful. That was it. He'd play on looking awful. Taking a handkerchief from his pocket, miraculously still white, he dabbed it in the fresh blood on his wrists that were rubbed raw enough to bleed. Then he tied it around his head. Stepping back off the road, he searched until he found a dead limb of sufficient length and strength to fashion into a crutch.

He climbed the embankment to the expressway and went into his act. Placing the crook of the limb under his armpit, he limped in an exaggerated manner, using the limb to partially support himself. Then he turned and stuck out his thumb.

No one stopped. While he didn't blame them—he rarely picked up hitchhikers—he thought surely they could see that he had been injured.

Suppressing the desire to either run out into the road and wave someone down or scream at the cars whizzing by, he continued to wave and thumb for a ride.

Finally a station wagon did pull over just ahead of him.

"Have a problem, young man?" To Joe's surprise, his rescuer was an elderly woman. She sat ramrod straight in the driver's seat, her white hair piled high on her head.

"Yes, ma'am. I wrecked my car back on that dirt road." He motioned toward the woods. "Hit a rock in the road as I came over a hill. I need to get some help."

"Get in, young man. You must have been driving awfully fast to have gotten hurt that badly. I'll bet you weren't wearing your seat belt, were you? You young people think nothing bad can ever happen to you."

Lady, Joe said to himself, you'd never believe how many bad things I've seen.

He grinned sheepishly at her. "Well, I guess I was being a little careless. I was thinking about the good fishing back there in those streams. I really appreciate your stopping. I was afraid no one was going to pull over."

"Normally I wouldn't. I never pick up hitchhikers. Most of them are jailbirds. But you look like my brother Homer's grandson, Peter Hobbs. You don't know Peter, do you?"

"No, ma'am." They continued driving and talking for another hour. Joe couldn't believe he was sitting there making small talk with this woman. But at least she was driving the speed limit, and by some rare bit of luck she was headed to Bayport also.

"Decided to go live in the city, he did," she said, picking up the thread of conversation she had dropped an hour earlier. "Said he could get a job in New York. Don't know why anyone'd want to live in the city, though. Peter took a job as a policeman," the old woman continued. "Don't know why anyone would want to be a policeman."

Police! Joe groaned. His appointment with the Bayport police.

"Are you hurting?" the woman asked when she heard Joe's groan. "Should I take you to a hospital?"

"No, ma'am. I'll be all right. I just remembered something. What time is it?"

"Near nine o'clock. I've got plenty of time. My dentist appointment's at ten right here in Bayport, and then I thought I'd do some shopping at the Bayport mall. Maybe take in a movie. Not too many movies I like to see these days, but I do like a good cry or a love story."

"I don't suppose you'd have time to drop me at High Street and Elm, would you, ma'am?" Joe interrupted gently.

"Why, that's very near my dentist. Maybe your luck is changing." The woman laughed softly, and a pleased look came onto her face.

Joe certainly needed a change in luck. "Yes, ma'am, I hope so. I'm lucky you weren't afraid to pick me up."

"That's right," she agreed, and slowed up to pull up against the curb. "This close enough to where you need to go?"

"Sure is, ma'am." Joe unlatched the car door. "And thanks again."

"You're welcome. Maybe you should see a doctor."

"I will." Joe slammed the door and waved. He limped until she drove out of sight, then tossed his crutch into a nearby trash basket and sprinted home.

With any more of the luck his rescuer mentioned he could get home, shower, call a cab, and get to the police station in plenty of time. What he had to decide before he got there was how much of this story to tell Officer O'Hara. Would she believe any of it? Could the police find Annie any sooner than he could?

Nearing the Hardy home, Joe pulled up short. His luck must have run out. Stopping on a lawn two doors from his house, he stared.

A police car was parking in front of his place. It looked like Officer O'Hara in the driver's seat. What had happened to bring her here instead of waiting for Joe at the station? And what would she do when she found Joe gone?

Chapter

14

FRANK HARDY STOOD in the doorway of his house trying to make a decision. He knew Joe wasn't home, and he didn't know how long he could cover for him.

"Good morning, Officer O'Hara. Officer Riley," he said, trying to be pleasant. It was good Con was there; maybe he could defuse any unpleasantness. "What brings you here so early?"

"This is not a social call, Mr. Hardy." Officer O'Hara was all business. "I suspect you know that. I'm here to see your brother."

"He had a bad night." Frank stalled, wondering where Joe could be. He knew that his taking off with Annie was a bad idea. But his appointment with the police wasn't until ten. "I knew his appointment wasn't until ten so I didn't wake him. Is something wrong?"

"That's what I'm here to find out. We got a call at the station telling us Joe had left town. Was he skipping out on his bail?"

"Who told you that?" Frank asked.

"The call was anonymous. But I decided it was worth following up." Officer O'Hara was growing impatient.

"Joe is innocent, Officer O'Hara, and he's cooperated with you from the beginning. Why would he have any reason to skip out?"

"That's what I want to find out."

Frank took the risk of being blunt even though he didn't want to annoy Officer O'Hara any further. She already believed that Joe was a murderer.

"Excuse me for saying so, Officer, but I think your time could be better spent finding the people who are really responsible for Phil Sidler's death. The jewel thieves. It's obvious there's a connection there."

"Are you telling me how to do my job now?" O'Hara started past Frank into the foyer.

Officer Con Riley followed her in with an apologetic shrug and a rueful smile for Frank. Frank read the gestures to say he'd better produce Joe and satisfy the young officer's curiosity.

"Do you have a search warrant, Officer

O'Hara?'' Frank asked, politely but firmly blocking her entry into the living room.

"Do I need one, Mr. Hardy?" O'Hara asked back.

Frank finally gave in and sighed. He'd protected Joe as long as he could. "Joe's room is upstairs." He followed O'Hara, however, prepared to keep talking.

Officer O'Hara marched briskly up the stairway and down the hall. She knocked sharply on the door Frank indicated and smiled grimly when she got no answer. Twisting the knob, she strode in. Frank was shocked to see Joe's bed a jumble of blankets and the spread in a pile on the floor.

He didn't even try to hide a relieved grin as the bathroom door opened.

"Officer O'Hara," Joe Hardy said, his face a picture of surprised innocence. "I thought my appointment was at ten. Get anxious to see me?" Joe's timing was perfect, his entrance suspiciously well planned. He strolled in from his bathroom, wrapped only in a long towel, hair wet and tousled. He was perfectly decent, but he wasn't dressed for greeting guests. He held another towel to hide his scraped wrists.

Officer O'Hara stepped back, completely flustered. "Oh—I—" she stammered. Then she regained her composure. "Excuse me, Mr. Hardy, there was no answer to my knock on your door, and I had been led to believe—"

"Believe what, Officer?" Joe grinned, pretending to be unaware of the woman's embarrassment. "That I'd forgotten my appointment with you? I was just getting ready."

"Fine, Mr. Hardy. I'll wait while you finish dressing and give you a ride." Officer O'Hara spun around quickly and left the room, followed by a greatly amused Con Riley. He didn't say anything to Joe or Frank, but he didn't have to.

"Joe, where have you been?" asked Frank when he was alone with his brother. He had enjoyed Joe's act so much that he had trouble sounding angry.

"Frank, listen, I'm going to talk fast." Joe turned immediately serious. "The van is on that little dirt road we used to take when we went fishing with Dad. North of here about an hour."

For the first time Frank noticed the abrasions on Joe's wrists. He stepped forward, taking Joe's hand. "What happened? You need to see a doctor."

"There isn't time. I'll pour some antiseptic over them when I'm dressed. Our elusive tall man forced Annie and me to return to Bayport, but Cutter's men caught up to us before we could get here. They've taken Annie, Frank. We've got to help her."

"I had to swear to Dad I wouldn't go back to Cutter's hideout. Not without New York City cops. He's going to contact some of his old buddies on the force today and set everything in motion.''

"Then I'll have to go alone, Frank. Annie's life is in danger now—not later.''

"Tell the Bayport police the whole story, Joe,'' Frank urged.

"Getting Annie out of there is my number-one priority, Frank, but you know as well as I do that we've got to find the diamonds—to connect Phil to the robberies. And to clear Annie and then me. I want you go get the van. Take a can of gas.''

"You ran out of *gas?*'' asked Frank.

"I don't want to hear it, Frank. Just go get the van.'' Joe rummaged through a drawer.

"I have a better idea.'' Frank paced the floor while Joe dressed. "I'll send a tow truck for the van, and we'll borrow Callie's car. It'd take too much time to go out and get the van right now.''

"I will report Annie missing, and I won't interfere with the NYPD, but I think it's up to us to find her. Dad would understand that.''

Back in the bathroom Joe poured some hydrogen peroxide over his wrists, wincing as the antiseptic bubbled and fizzed in the scrapes and cuts. He shrugged off the bandages that Frank pulled from the medicine cabinet. "Don't need them. Pick me up at the station in half an hour.'' Joe ran down the stairs.

Frank used Joe's extension phone to make his calls.

"Of course you can borrow my car, Frank," said Callie when he reached her. "But I'm going along. I'm tired of never seeing you."

"This may be dangerous, Callie. I don't want you along."

"I don't care what you want, Frank. I can drive. You may need me. I won't go inside, but I'll keep the engine running."

Frank knew better than to argue with Callie when she was in that mood. Besides, she might be right. They could need her if they had to make a quick getaway. Cutter's men and the tall man, whoever he was, knew the van. They wouldn't be looking for Callie's car.

Callie picked Frank up and they drove to the police station. Joe was already pacing the sidewalk outside.

"Rehash of the whole case," he explained as he hopped in the back seat of Callie's little green car. "That's all they wanted to do. Waste of time. They didn't even want to hear what happened yesterday. I told them I hadn't been able to locate Annie, but they weren't concerned."

"I guess even they're convinced she's part of the gang," Frank said. "But they can't do anything until they get some hard evidence against her."

While Frank wanted Annie safe, he did remind Joe that Annie, if involved, had gotten herself into this mess.

125

"Ready for a little trip to New York City, Callie?" asked Frank as they hopped into the car.

"Filled the tank before I picked you up. You navigate." She spun efficiently out of the lot and headed for the expressway.

"I'm glad you remembered to get gas," said Frank, looking at Joe and hoping to get a smile. But Joe stared into the distance as though he hadn't heard what Frank said.

Frank and Joe reviewed all they knew about the case on the way to the city, but what they arrived at was that they had no concrete evidence that would convict Cutter. And that the identity of the tall man was still a mystery. His involvement in the case seemed to be independent of the police or the jewel thieves.

"Find a space or double-park, Callie," Frank instructed as they entered the underground lot that held the key to Cutter's hideout. "Head the car for the exit and wait. We might need to get out of here fast."

"If we ever get inside." Joe seemed less optimistic than Frank about finding the secret for getting upstairs to Cutter's secret apartment.

Facing the solid concrete wall, Frank and Joe didn't know where to start looking. Somewhere there was a hidden panel, a button, or switch, that brought down and opened an elevator large enough for a car. The limo seemed to have disappeared into thin air, so that had to be the explanation.

The wall was cold to the touch and rough-textured. Frank patted, punched, searched, having started at the middle and headed right. Joe, beside him, moved to the left, fingering the solid wall in the same manner.

In a matter of minutes, they met back in the center where they'd started. "Nothing," both agreed.

"There has to be someplace we haven't touched, some combination," Joe said. He pounded the wall with his fist in frustration.

"That's a fairly astute assumption, boys," a voice behind them said.

"What—you—" Joe and Frank swung around as one. They had been too intent on the wall to realize they were being watched.

"What a nice surprise to find you here, Joe." The tall man, looking weary and dressed in very rumpled clothing, leaned casually on a green Chevy—one of the only cars in the garage.

His smile was casual, almost gentle.

But the 9mm Beretta in his hand was all business.

Chapter
15

"YOU BOYS ARE in good company," the tall man continued. "I couldn't find the combination to get inside, either. My real hope was that one of Cutter's men would come down and show it to me."

"What do you mean? You left us there in that police station," said Joe. "What did you tell them, anyway?"

"I asked them to stall you for as long as possible, thinking that if Cutter's men thought you'd reported them to the police, they'd give up on you—for then. I showed my credentials to the officer and explained the situation. It didn't work, though. By the time I got a ride from one of the officers back to my car and returned, I saw Cutter's thugs follow you out of town."

"If you're so all-seeing, Mr. Wise Guy, I guess you saw them tie me up and leave with Annie."

"I didn't know you weren't in their car. I just saw the car pull off the road and then return. I assumed you were in the car with Annie. I followed them back to the city, but unfortunately I lost them in traffic on the way back. By the time I got here, they'd done their disappearing act."

Joe started to lunge for the man, but Frank stopped him. "Settle down, Joe. We don't have time to fight with someone who might be on the same side we are. Why don't you put your gun away, whoever you are. Admit it—you haven't gotten any further than we have. At least we've been inside this place."

"True. And you did leave in one piece. Luck, maybe."

"Who *are* you?" Joe was willing to talk only if he knew who he was talking to. "You showed the police something convincing. Why don't you try your credentials out on us?"

The tall man slipped his gun into a shoulder holster inside his suit jacket. Then he held out his hand. "Brookshier. Selden Brookshier. CSO."

Frank shook hands, but Joe ignored the man's friendly gesture. "CSO?" Frank asked.

"Central Selling Organization—out of London. Diamonds. That last shipment was ours, and we frown on people killing our couriers and helping themselves to our property. This sight never arrived."

"Sight?" Frank questioned. "I thought we were looking for diamonds."

"A sight is a package of rough diamonds purchased by one of our clients, usually a dealer or a diamond cutter," Selden Brookshier explained. "The value of a parcel averages about a million dollars. This one happened to be worth three times that."

"Do the Bayport police know you're here?" Frank asked. "Are you working with them?" That must have been how Brookshier walked into Phil's room. He'd stopped at the police station and picked up a key.

"Yes, but as you've seen, I try to keep a very low profile. The fewer people who know who I am, the better. We don't like any publicity about our shipments. The more people who know about them, the more likely we are to become targets for thieves. We suspect someone on the inside told Phil Sidler—who at the time worked for Cutter—of this delivery. A woman who worked for the dealer."

"Annie?" Frank said.

"Exactly. She handled the correspondence and plane tickets. She knew her employer had viewed the stones, sent the check for them to London, and was expecting them. She wouldn't know the exact delivery time, since we don't say, but all that took on her part was a little patience."

"You're guessing." Joe didn't want to hear that Annie was involved in the robbery. "Do you have any evidence that Annie was involved?"

"No more evidence than we have against Cutter, but it all adds up. We attribute half or more of the jewelry jobs in this state to Cutter and his gang. We've caught people who work for him, but never Cutter or any of the higher-ups. We've never gotten enough evidence on Cutter that we thought would stick. Annie and Phil may have done us a favor in the long run, but neither may live to be thanked. I doubt if anyone lives to brag about double-crossing Cutter."

"We've got to get Annie out," said Joe, suddenly realizing that time might be running out for his friend.

"Come on." Frank returned to searching the rough concrete wall, starting to feel a sense of frustration knowing that they were near Cutter's hideout.

"Of course!" Frank said suddenly. "We should have been using our eyes instead of our sense of touch. Look here." He pointed to what might be mistaken as a grease spot on the gray wall.

Pressing on the spot started the sound of whirring, grinding, and purring. Slowly, large double doors, wide enough for a car to drive through, opened before them. The trio hopped inside and looked over the selection panel. "Any suggestions?" asked Frank.

"Start with One," Joe suggested. "We don't have to get off if it's wrong."

The elevator was painfully slow. Frank hoped some signal upstairs wasn't tipping off a guard that they were coming.

A *ping* sounded for Floor One, and the doors ground open to reveal another small parking garage. The black limousine sat directly in front of the elevator doors, ready to move out when needed.

Angrily, Joe punched Three. "It makes sense that Cutter would live on top."

But when the door opened on Floor Three, they saw immediately that this choice was wrong. Avocado green indoor-outdoor carpet led away from the elevator. Frank clearly remembered a plush, cream-colored pile—the luxurious surroundings that Daniel Cutter cultivated.

"I don't believe it." Joe pounded on the elevator wall as the doors slid closed, and Frank pushed the button labeled Two.

It was evidence of Cutter's faith in his ingenious hideaway that there was no guard in the hall on Floor Two. Frank, Joe, and Selden Brookshier moved silently into the hall, looked both ways, and headed down the hall to the right. A murmur of voices floated out the second door they came to. Frank motioned to Joe, who slid in front of the doorway. The threesome poised to listen.

"I knew you'd come to your senses, Annie." It was Cutter's voice, cold, sinister, mocking. "Too bad you held out for so long. Wouldn't it have been easier on you to have just led us to the diamonds without all this fuss?"

"You slime." Annie's voice was shaky, but angry still.

"Greedy people never win, Annie. Your share of the three million would have been generous, and with Phil out of the way, you could have had a percentage of his cut. You took care of him for us, so you earned it. He was scum. I usually don't hire such lowlifes, but I was careless this time.

"You're a strong and beautiful woman, Annie Shea. Not only could you have parlayed your cut into a bigger bankroll, but you could have kept working for us. The pay goes up with every successful job. Who knows, with your looks and polish, I might have taken a special interest in you."

"Over my dead body," Annie said with steel in her voice.

Cutter laughed. "Yes, you make it easy for me to believe that."

Frank kept one eye on Joe. He had been known to make some impulsive moves in the past, and Frank knew his emotions were involved here.

Anger at Cutter and his men wouldn't help Joe think rationally.

Annie spoke again. "Phil Sidler reminded me of one thing, Cutter. No one in this world can be trusted. I'll take *you* to the diamonds. By now, I'd think you might have some qualms about trusting any of your hoodlums with three million dollars."

There was a moment of silence. "You may have a point there, young lady, but you realize I've created this sanctuary for one reason. The world was never that kind to me. Here I am surrounded by everything I desire. Comfortable settings, excellent food—I have a chef I brought from Belgium, remarkable man. Some of the works of art—you no doubt haven't had time to enjoy them—would cause heart palpitations to any museum curator. I have a theater, a pool, a gym. Anything I desire is brought to me. Why should I go out into polluted air, traffic—the real world?"

"Because you want those diamonds. And those are my conditions," Annie answered.

"I hardly think you are in any position to dictate the conditions, Annie. But I admire your guts. As I said, it's a shame—"

"I'm willing to die before I tell you," Annie said, her voice getting stronger.

Joe crossed back to Frank. "She's on our side, Frank, I know she is. No matter what you've

heard. She's getting Cutter out of here for us."
Joe's voice was the slightest whisper, but Frank
signaled for absolute silence.

"Novel idea." Cutter paused, no doubt to think
about Annie's ultimatum. "I haven't been outside
for years. Perhaps I should see if it's still as bad
as I remember."

There was a long pause before Cutter added,
"Oh, and, Annie, if you don't deliver this time,
only one of us will come back alive."

Chapter

16

BROOKSHIER SQUEEZED FRANK'S arm and tapped Joe on the shoulder. He motioned in the direction of the elevator. Joe shook his head. Brookshier insisted. Frank caught on. They had to get off this floor before Cutter made his move. They had no hope of capturing the gang on their own turf. They were outmanned and unarmed except for Brookshier's Beretta.

In addition, if Annie did have the diamonds and could persuade Cutter to go with her to where she'd hidden them, they could catch him with the evidence they needed to put him away for years. Put him in an equally isolated environment, but one where he might miss his little luxuries.

In the elevator Frank punched Ground Floor and willed the huge cage to move so they could escape ahead of Cutter's gang. Cutter would certainly bring along adequate protection for his venture into the real world.

"She's getting him out. Good for her." Brookshier slammed his fist on the palm of his left hand. "She's going to lead him to the diamonds, and we'll be right there with them."

Joe, Frank, and Brookshier dashed from the elevator the minute it opened. They crowded into Callie's car.

"What happened?" Callie asked. She had the engine running the minute she saw the trio head for her.

"Shut off the car," ordered Joe, "and get down. But be ready to move out when we tell you."

"Annie's inside," Frank explained, hunched in the front seat beside Callie. "She told them she has the diamonds, but she's talked Cutter into going with her to get them."

"They should be right behind us." Joe and Brookshier were tucked into the backseat.

In no time the elevator door rumbled open and the sleek, black limo purred, its engine barely humming. As it sped up the ramp into the New York City street, Callie flicked on the ignition. Her car sprang to life and she pulled out, pursuing them.

"Maybe you'd better keep low," she said to her passengers. "If anyone is watching out the back, they'll never suspect that I'm following them."

"Good thinking, Callie." Frank smiled at her from his slumped-down position. "You do come in handy sometimes."

"When this is over, Frank Hardy, you're treating me to the best dinner in Bayport. It's not every day I risk my life for you."

Her smile was warm, and Frank knew she liked being in on the action. "It's a deal, Callie."

The limo drove the speed limit, smoothly and skillfully negotiating the city streets and pulling onto the expressway.

"Hey, we're heading for Bayport," Joe said, peeking out the back window.

"I knew it," said Brookshier. "I knew Annie had the diamonds or knew where they were hidden, and I had a feeling they were in Bayport."

"What would Annie Shea do with three million dollars' worth of diamonds?" asked Callie. "I sure wouldn't know what to do with them. You can't spend diamonds."

"She may not have planned beyond taking them." Brookshier wiggled, trying to get comfortable in the small, narrow backseat. His tall frame didn't fold up easily. "You have to have the kind of connections Cutter obviously has to convert them to cash."

"I wouldn't trust anyone if I had them," Callie said. "If you don't know where to sell them, you might as well not steal them. Annie is pretty naïve."

Joe said nothing. Everyone in the car—except for him—seemed to have accepted the fact that Annie was a thief.

Callie had no trouble following the limo all the way into Bayport, and apparently no one in the dark vehicle suspected that she was tailing them. "Look, guys. We're headed for the Bayport mall."

Frank sat up cautiously. "They're pulling up to the delivery door of Mr. Pizza. I wish there were some way to warn Tony to clear out his kitchen and the restaurant. We don't want anyone hurt."

"I'll go in the front door," offered Callie.

"Call the police while you're there, Callie," Frank instructed. "Ask for Officer O'Hara or Con Riley. Tell them to get over here on the double. We don't want to give Cutter a chance to escape now that we have him with evidence. Better tell them to find our dad, too."

"I don't want Annie hurt," Joe said in a low voice. "Whatever she's done, there must be an explanation."

Frank hated to say that if Annie had stolen the diamonds there couldn't be any way to justify it—and there was still the unsolved mystery of Phil Sidler's death. Cutter's words came to Frank:

"Thanks for getting rid of Phil Sidler for us, Annie." What did that mean?

Callie parked as close as she dared to the limo. Quickly her passengers slid out. Then she drove around to the front of the mall before the others got inside.

Frank, Joe, and Brookshier watched as Cutter, dressed as he'd been when they'd seen him, including his diamond ring, stepped from the black car, flanked by two of his bodyguards. He looked around cautiously, probably feeling very vulnerable away from his sanctuary. Another man gripped Annie's arm, as if they thought her plan might be to escape from them here instead of leading them to the diamonds.

Tony Prito had obviously locked the storeroom door that day. "But look, Annie has a key," said Joe.

Sure enough, Annie had searched through her purse, then lifted out a key and prepared to slip it into the lock. She dropped the key, and as she bent to retrieve it, she made her move. Chopping across her guard's neck with one hand, she grabbed his gun and leaped forward. She took Cutter by the arm and spun him around, shoving the gun in his back. No one had suspected she'd make such a move, and they were all caught off guard.

For a moment Joe and Frank, along with Brookshier, stood frozen, watching. But as Annie

140

inched toward the storeroom door with Cutter as hostage, Joe leaped forward, running for the pair.

"Good work, Annie. I knew you had a plan."

Taking one of Cutter's bodyguards by surprise, Joe twisted him around and kicked the gun from his hand. Frank, never one to hang back when Joe made a move, disarmed the other man in a similar way.

Annie's face, bruised and swollen from the beating she'd taken, registered surprise, but not for long. "I should have trusted you more, Joe," she said, smiling gratefully at him. "I thought you'd stopped looking for me. Let's get these crooks packaged up nicely, and then call the authorities." Whipping out a scarf from her purse, Annie started to tie Cutter's hands behind his back.

"You're a fool, Annie," Cutter growled. "You think they'll let you go, even if you turn me in? Get the diamonds and we'll leave together. I'll show you a life you never even dreamed possible." Cutter's sunglasses had fallen to the ground during his scuffle with Annie. His eyes glared out evilly from the scars on his face.

Annie laughed. "What's that, Cutter? Locked up in your ivory tower? No thanks. I like beaches and sun and tropical waters too much to live like a recluse."

Joe and Frank slipped the belts off their pants to make sure Cutter's two bodyguards were bound and didn't go anyplace until the police arrived.

Brookshier checked out the man Annie had karate-chopped. He was still out cold. "The diamonds, Annie. Where are they?" That was his main concern. He'd let the police deal with the crooks. "We'll need them as evidence against Cutter. With them and your testimony, we'll put him away for a long time."

Annie smiled and backed closer to the storeroom door of Mr. Pizza, still holding the gun. "What are they worth to you? I kind of liked knowing I held a fortune in my hand." Slipping the key she had retrieved from the step into the lock, she swung open the door and paused in the doorway.

"We might be able to make a deal for you, Annie," said Brookshier. "Or maybe the reward for returning stolen goods will pay for a good lawyer. You were instrumental in capturing Cutter. That should count for something. We've been after him for some time."

"Don't listen to him, Annie," Cutter growled. "He won't get you any deal. There's still time for us to leave together."

Annie's eyes, sparkling with excitement, met Joe's disillusioned gaze. For a moment, as their eyes met, the girl's tough demeanor wavered, her triumphant smile faltered. She frowned at Joe and looked away.

"Give me the gun, Annie." Frank stepped closer to the red-haired girl. "Joe and I will help you all we can."

"I wish I could trust you, Frank. I know you mean well." For the first time Annie almost smiled at Frank. She held the gun comfortably, the cold steel no stranger to the palm of her hand.

"You have to trust someone, Annie." Joe inched closer.

"All right, Joe." She looked him full in the face now. She seemed to have made up her mind about something. "You. You reach into that barrel of flour." Annie motioned Joe past her and into the storeroom. She stayed in the doorway, her gun on Frank and Brookshier. "That's right, that one. The bag is buried near the bottom." She laughed. "I didn't want some pizza customer thinking they'd won the prize in a box of Cracker Jacks."

Joe leaned over and sifted his fingers deeper and deeper into the cardboard barrel of flour. Finally he stood up, having retrieved a small cloth sack with a drawstring at the top. He came back to Annie and, opening it, took out a handful of uncut diamonds, most of which were the size of a kid's marbles.

Frank whistled. One of the uncut gems was as large as the one in Cutter's ring. It was probably worth a million by itself. But Brookshier was right. Where would Annie have fenced a marble sack full of shiny rocks?

He looked at Brookshier, whose eyes were on the diamonds, the "sight" he was being paid to recover.

Joe, who stood closest to Annie, was too mesmerized by the gems to think for a moment. And before Frank could decide what to do, Annie called the next shot.

"Thanks, Joe." She snatched the bag as soon as Joe tumbled the rocks back into it and pulled the opening shut. At the same time the gun in her hand pushed into the small of Joe's back. "And if you don't mind, I'll need you for a little longer."

With those words she pulled Joe backward toward the door into the pizza restaurant. The problem of turning the stolen diamonds into cash didn't seem to matter to her.

She had the hostage she needed to escape.

Chapter

17

"ANNIE, DON'T DO this," Joe pleaded. "You trapped Cutter for us. That'll go a long way toward getting you a lighter sentence. You might even get probation."

"You really don't understand, do you, Joe?"

"I understand that I liked you, Annie. I can't believe you're doing this." Joe pulled away from Annie and leaned on a counter in the deserted pizza storeroom. He didn't think Annie would actually shoot him.

She kept her gun pointed at him, however. "I'm sorry it had to be you I'm taking hostage, Joe. But I certainly don't want to take Cutter with me to Rio. I lured him here because I wanted him and his men out of my way."

A sadness invaded Joe's whole being. Boy, he

thought bitterly, I really know how to choose 'em.

Maybe Annie sensed his feelings. "I'm sorry, Joe," she said again. "But you have to understand—this is my one chance to make it big. You don't know what it's like to grow up poor. I saw the home you were raised in. I know your type. You're the kind of guy who would never even look at me in high school because I was from the wrong side of town."

"This is not the way out, Annie. Even if you got to Rio and sold the diamonds, what would your life be like always running? Sooner or later you'd be caught."

Annie laughed a derisive laugh. The bright smile Joe liked so much had deserted her face now, leaving a bitter, hard expression he had never seen before. "Who cares? At least I'd have a good life until then."

"You could start over right here." Joe moved toward Annie.

"Stay away from me, Joe. I don't want to have to hurt you." Annie waved the gun. "But I will if you don't cooperate."

"Don't you care for me at all, Annie?" Joe asked. He needed to know that he hadn't been taken in totally by this beautiful girl. He needed to know that her optimism and courage, all the qualities he'd seen in her, were real, not lies she had fed him. And that her affection for him wasn't an act she'd put on to cover up what she was doing.

Annie stared at Joe for a minute. "Of course I do, Joe. I like you a lot. If—if things had been different . . ." Annie took a deep breath. "But they aren't." If Annie's toughness was an act, it was a good one. Her voice hardened, and she motioned for Joe to step in front of her. She was ready to make her move.

"Annie, when we got here, Callie went to call the police. They'll have the entire place surrounded by now. There's no possibility of your getting away." Joe made one more attempt at talking sense into Annie, into persuading her to give herself up.

"I'm sure the police, your father, Frank—all the people who are out there, Joe—value your life. They'll let me go since you'll be with me."

Joe shrugged and tried to harden his heart toward Annie. He needed to concentrate on getting away from her with neither of them getting hurt. In spite of everything, he couldn't stand to see Annie killed or injured. Silently he settled on a simple plan that he hoped would work.

The pizza restaurant was empty when they entered it. Callie and Tony had silently cleared everyone from the place. As they moved around tables and toward the front door, Annie clutched Joe's arm tighter and kept her gun jammed into his side. Slowly they inched their way toward the parking lot.

"How are you going to get to the airport, Annie?" Joe asked. If he could keep her talking, he might distract her easier.

"You're going to drive me, Joe. It'll be my last ride in your van."

"The van's out in the woods still. We'll have to borrow a car." Joe said whatever came into his head as he tensed himself for what was coming.

"Whatever you say, Joe. You know, you could go with me."

"No, Annie. I can't. It wouldn't work. I'll help you get away if I have to, but I won't go with you." Joe kept talking.

"Joe, are you all right?" Frank called as Joe and Annie stepped outside the mall into the parking lot.

The lot was full of police officers and spectators, although the police officers were trying to keep the onlookers pushed back. Fenton Hardy stood beside Frank, the two of them watching, wondering what to do.

"I'm fine, Frank," Joe called loudly, trying to act casual and put the police at ease. "I'm taking the Nova to help Annie get to the airport, but wait for me before you go to dinner, Frank. I'm practically *faint* with hunger."

Frank's eyes widened for a second as he realized that Joe was trying to send him a message. He shouted back, "That figures. Will do." And he smiled, a little nervously. Whatever Joe had planned, his smile said, Frank would try to play along.

"Shut up, Joe," Annie said, poking him with the barrel of her gun and glancing at the policemen. "You're making me nervous. I'm sure you don't want me nervous with this gun in your back and my finger on the trigger."

Joe stopped talking, but when they were as close to Frank as they were going to get, he made his move. Suddenly he melted into a dead faint at Annie's feet.

At the same time, he rolled into her, pushing her backward and off balance. Her finger squeezed the trigger of the gun she held, but since her gun was pointed into the air, the shot zipped off harmlessly.

Frank was ready. He sprinted toward the pair. But just as he reached for Annie's gun, she regained her balance and took a step back, giving herself a split second in which to shoot.

As Frank's momentum propelled him forward toward the weapon, he looked up at Annie. Tense and trembling, she had the gun aimed at Frank's chest and her finger on the trigger. Her eyes met Frank's. In that instant he knew that no matter how much Annie wanted the diamonds and her freedom, she couldn't shoot the gun.

"Annie," Joe said off to the side. When she turned to him, Frank quickly chopped at her arm and she dropped the weapon. Then it was only a matter of Joe and Frank holding on to her, not an easy task, since she fought like a wild woman.

Officer O'Hara closed in with handcuffs. With her arms pinned, Annie finally realized she had lost.

It was a quiet foursome who stood at the police station after all the formalities had been taken care of. Cutter and his men were behind bars. Annie had surrendered the diamonds, and they would be handed over to Selden Brookshier, who would return them to the manufacturer who had ordered them.

Brookshier thanked the Hardys for their help on the case and apologized for treating them so roughly.

"We must avoid publicity in these cases, you understand," he said again, trying to justify his methods. "That's why I had to hit and run from the start. It's vital that not too many people know that millions of dollars' worth of diamonds are delivered all over the country every day. As far as Annie goes—well, you see I had to scare her to get her to lead me to the jewels."

Officer O'Hara made her way to where Callie, Frank, Joe, and Fenton Hardy stood. "Joe," she said with some difficulty, "I guess I owe you an apology." She put out her hand. Joe took it with no hard feelings. "Before I met you and your brother, I had the idea that teenagers couldn't be trusted. I guess I'd better revise my thinking."

"What about the charges against Joe?" Fenton Hardy asked.

"They've all been dropped," Officer O'Hara said. "Annie finally told us the whole story, clearing Joe. Phil Sidler was already dead when Annie pushed him in front of the van Joe was driving."

"Annie killed him?" Frank said in an astonished voice. He had figured out that Annie pushed Phil, but not that she'd killed him first.

"She had a gun in her purse," O'Hara explained. "She hit him in the back of the head with it. Then she pushed him so it would look like Joe ran over him."

"Those staring eyes." Joe's face, already grim, showed even greater grief. Although he was glad to hear the charges against him were dropped, he didn't want to hear that Annie was a murderer.

"I think she may have even planned it, Joe," Officer O'Hara said. "She definitely meant from the beginning to set you up. She's a regular Black Widow. I'm arresting her for first-degree murder."

Joe shook his head in utter disbelief, but said nothing.

"Joe, she asked if she could see you again," Officer O'Hara said. "It's all right with me if you want to see her."

Joe hesitated. Then he shook his head slowly again. "No—I don't want to see her."

"I think this case is finished," said Frank, taking Joe's arm. "Let's get out of here, Joe."

Frank steered Joe toward the front door of the police station after taking the car keys that Callie slipped into his hand. He smiled at her gratefully, knowing she understood that he and Joe needed time alone.

In the lot they climbed into the car and sat quietly for a minute. Joe stared into space, utterly exhausted.

"Want something to eat, little brother?" Frank asked, starting the engine.

"It's funny," Joe said in a quiet voice. "I really am hungry. But I don't want pizza."

"Fine, pizza it's not. I'll surprise you."

"I may never eat pizza again. And remind me of one thing, Frank." Joe looked out the window at the growing darkness. "Not even to *look* at the waitress."

Joe spoke in a flippant manner, but Frank knew the remark covered a lot of pain. He also knew the pain would stay with Joe for a long time.

"Good idea, partner. We need to keep our minds on business anyway. And food. How does this sound: double cheeseburgers, fries, extra-creamy chocolate malts?"

"Mind-boggling." Joe smiled wearily.

STREET SPIES

Chapter

1

"WE'RE BEING FOLLOWED," Joe Hardy whispered over the hum of the elevator.

His brother Frank glanced around. Except for them, the elevator was empty. "Followed? By whom?" he asked.

"By my stomach." Joe put a hand to his midsection. "Feels like it's about five floors below us."

The high-speed elevator slowed to a stop. The Hardys were on the twentieth floor of the Empire Towers Hotel, just south of Central Park, in Midtown Manhattan. As the door opened, Frank looked in both directions, then stepped off the elevator and turned to the right.

"The room is this way," he said, taking a hotel key from his pocket and checking the number against the sign on the wall. "Dad said he'd meet us here at one o'clock. He didn't have time to explain on the phone, but said he'd give us the details when he gets here."

Joe followed Frank down the hall, a long tunnel of carpet and ceiling lined on either side with featureless doors. "Here it is," Frank said, putting the key into the lock.

As Frank turned the key, the door swung open. At the far end of the hotel room the curtains were pulled back, and the view was breathtaking. Stretching almost to the horizon in a green patchwork of lawn and trees and silver water, lay Central Park.

"We have about ten minutes," said Frank, checking his watch and settling into a chair near the window. His lean, six-foot-one-inch frame filled most of it easily.

Joe—burlier and built more like a football player—flopped down onto the bed near the door, closed his eyes and wondered why they were there. He and Frank had been trout fishing in Maine—catching their limit every day—when their father, Fenton Hardy, had called and asked them to meet him in New York. Whatever it was, it'd better be good, Joe thought, remembering the way that last trout had tasted, grilled over the coals of a campfire.

Nevertheless, Joe grinned in anticipation. Whatever his dad was up to, it was likely to be interesting and probably dangerous, to boot. Fenton Hardy had been a detective for the New York City Police Department for years but had quit to handle private cases that intrigued him. In some of those investigations he had involved Joe and Frank. Joe grinned again, remembering the time . . .

But Joe didn't get to finish the thought. There was a light knock at the door and then the sound of a key turning.

"Dad?" Joe asked, jumping up. "Come on in—it's open."

Fenton Hardy stepped into the room, followed by a tall, stern-looking man in an expensive suit and glasses.

"Frank, Joe," Mr. Hardy said, "I'd like you to meet Charles Chilton."

Frank stood up and extended his hand eagerly. "President of World-Wide Technologies?" he asked.

"Yes. I am," Mr. Chilton said with a note of surprise as he shook Frank's hand.

"I'm Joe Hardy," Joe said, shaking Mr. Chilton's hand. He threw Frank a quick, curious glance.

"Mr. Chilton's one of my heroes," Frank said in answer to his brother's unspoken question. "A few years back he started a little electronics business in his garage. Now it's a world leader in

3

miniaturized transmitters and receivers. I've used a lot of his stuff, and it's really super."

Fenton Hardy went to the window and stood looking out, his hands in his pockets. After a minute he turned, his face serious. "Mr. Chilton's got a problem," he said. "A new competitor, MUX, Incorporated, has been flooding the market with products designed by World-Wide Technologies."

"You mean they're stealing WWT's designs?" asked Joe. He whistled. "That could mean a load of money for someone."

"Not to mention the disaster it could mean for World-Wide," Fenton Hardy said. He sat down in a chair and motioned to Mr. Chilton to sit down, too. "I've just finished a complete security analysis of World-Wide Technologies," he went on. "I'm convinced that there's a leak. Protection from outside interference is top-notch. That's why I'm sure somebody *inside* the company is pirating designs for MUX."

"So that's why we're meeting in a hotel room," Frank interjected, brushing a hand through his brown hair. "If it's an inside job, you never know who you can trust."

Mr. Chilton smiled. "You were right, Fenton. These boys of yours are sharp." He turned to Frank and Joe. "Unfortunately, developing new gadgets means that we have to transport plans from our midtown office to our lab downtown.

4

Then we have to return the prototypes—the first working models of the new devices—back to our midtown office for marketing. It's complicated, but we feel it's worth our being in New York because of the international business we drum up here. It seems as if the designs are being stolen as we move them around."

"How do you transmit them?" Frank asked.

Mr. Chilton smiled again, more thinly. "It's ironic, in a way. We're world leaders in electronic communications, and yet we've found that the fastest way to transmit these designs in New York City is by bicycle."

"By bicycle?" Frank and Joe asked in unison.

"Not even over a modem?" Joe asked.

"No," Frank answered. "It would probably be too easy to tap the line. Right?" Mr. Chilton nodded.

"Now, this is where you come in," Fenton Hardy said. "The prototypes are carried by bicycle messenger. A firm called SpeedWay Messenger Service handles the job. We suspect that the spy inside the company—whoever he is—uses the messenger service to make the actual transfers. Since nothing appears to be tampered with when it finally arrives at either end, our guess is that the contents are unwrapped, photographed, then carefully rewrapped and sent on their way."

"So you want us to apply for jobs with this messenger service?" Joe asked, grinning. This wouldn't be a bad assignment. Hot-dogging through rush-hour traffic on a bike could be a real adventure—*if* he lived to tell about it.

"Right again," Mr. Hardy said. "Getting jobs should be easy. The turnover in messengers is pretty high." He gave Joe a worried look. "Riding a bicycle in New York is a high-risk business. I hope you'll be careful."

Joe nodded. "Why don't you just switch messenger companies?" he asked.

"Because we have to identify the source *inside* World-Wide," Mr. Chilton said. "If we don't, the spy will just set up a similar operation as soon as things quiet down. Whoever's selling these designs won't be discouraged just because we make things a little difficult for him."

Frank nodded. "So when do we start?"

Joe smiled, hearing the eagerness in his brother's voice. Obviously, this was a case that *both* of them were interested in.

"As soon as possible. Tomorrow morning, if you can. Messengers provide their own bikes. You'll probably need to find used ones to avoid attracting attention. And you'll have to work independently, for the same reason."

Frank Hardy glanced at Mr. Chilton, who had stood up and was jingling the coins in his pocket, obviously impatient to move on. "SpeedWay runs shifts around the clock," he said, "so one of you can be backup while the other's on the

6

job. This hotel room can be our command post. You boys can bunk here, too.

"If you need anything electronic," Mr. Chilton added, "let me know. I can probably get whatever you need—spying devices, transmitters—state of the art."

"We drove the van down from Bayport," Frank said. "It already has most of the equipment we need." He looked around. "All we'll need here is the phone."

Mr. Chilton turned to leave. "I hope you can find our spy, whoever he is," he said. "He's hitting us where we're most vulnerable—our new designs. We can't survive in this situation much longer."

Early the next morning Frank and Joe drove their van to a spot on Front Street, a block or two south of the South Street Seaport, and parked at the curb. Crammed with surveillance and communications equipment, a portable crime lab and a computer, the van was their mobile base of operations.

The afternoon before Joe and Frank had gone shopping for used ten-speeds. The two they'd found in a seedy-looking pawnshop on Second Avenue wouldn't win a beauty contest, but after Joe had spent the evening conditioning them, he was sure they'd perform.

They'd located the rest of their gear in an army

7

surplus shop—a field jacket for Joe, with a triangular armored-division patch on the shoulder with a picture of a cobra that read "Death from Above." For Frank, a navy turtleneck and a blue denim jacket.

In the same place they'd found cycling gloves and nylon bags that would serve as messenger bags.

As Joe unloaded his bike from the van, he was glad for the warmth of his newly acquired field jacket—the breeze off the East River was chilly. He could feel the unfamiliar miniature transmitter taped to his chest under his field jacket.

"Are you tuned in?" he asked Frank. He lowered his chin and spoke into his collar. "Can you read me?"

In the back of the van, Frank pulled on the headset. "Loud and clear," he said, turning some dials on the radio equipment in front of him. "Give me a call in a block or two so we can test it for distance. When you get your first assignment, let me know where you're headed and I'll see if I can actually tail you through traffic."

Joe pulled on his cycling gloves and gave Frank a quick thumbs-up as he rode off down Front Street. Although the nearby Seaport area had been renovated, the buildings right here were pretty run-down. Joe wrinkled his nose as he passed a fish warehouse. A man in a canvas apron

8

was pushing a cart piled high with fish along the sidewalk, a few gulls squawking overhead.

"Sure stinks around here," Joe said, glancing around to make sure that nobody was looking. They'd probably think he was talking to himself. "Just passed the fish warehouse," he added in explanation, raising his voice so that Frank could hear him over the roar of the cars on the elevated highway to his left along the river. It would probably have been better to have two-way communication so that he could hear Frank as well as talk to him. Maybe they could get that from Mr. Chilton later.

Next door to the warehouse was a taxi garage, and the building across the street bore a neon sign that announced "Punch's Gym." Next to that was an auto parts store, and beside that was Pete's Bar and Grill. Joe consulted a piece of paper with an address and turned the next corner.

SpeedWay Messenger Service was located in an old red brick building just off Front Street.

A small but noisy group of young men in their teens and early twenties were gathered in front. A black youth was sitting on his bike talking and laughing with a boy whose stringy blond hair hung limply from under a ratty watchcap. A kid with dark sunglasses and some Hispanics were lounging on the steps that led up to the office door.

Joe coasted up to the curb and swung his leg

over his bike, expertly stepping off before it stopped. He turned to the nearest kid, a tall, lanky black guy standing at the foot of the steps. A shapeless felt hat was jammed down over his half-closed eyes.

"Hey, man," Joe said casually, "I hear they're looking for messengers. That right?"

The youth nodded, coolly surveying Joe and his bike. "Hey, Gus," he shouted over his shoulder, "looks like we've got a live one." Turning back to Joe, he added, "You gotta talk to the man inside."

Joe walked his bike up to the wall and leaned it against the brick. Then he climbed the short flight of steps, followed by the black messenger, to the stark and almost empty office.

On one wall was a big chalkboard, obviously a dispatch board, with names written down one side in grease pencil: Lightfoot, Apollo, Slim, Wipe-Out, Gypsy. There was a desk in front of the board. A short, round-shouldered man sat behind the desk. He didn't seem much over thirty, but his face was drawn and pale and his brown hair was thin. He gave Joe a hard look.

"Yeah?" he grunted.

"I'm Joe Kincaid," Joe responded, offering his hand. "I'm looking for a job as a messenger."

The man ignored Joe's hand. "Are you fast?" he snapped.

"Sure, I'm fast," Joe said confidently. "I rode

10

bikes for years when I was a kid. But then I graduated to motorcycles." He grinned at the man and at the black guy, who was leaning in the doorway, listening. "As a matter of fact, I got pretty good at racing. Even won a few tough ones."

"Well, New York ain't kid stuff, and it ain't no motorcycle joy ride, either. I can vouch for that." The man shifted in his seat so that one leg stuck out from behind the desk. Joe noticed that he was wearing a leg brace and that a well-used wooden cane was leaning against the wall behind his chair. The man picked up a pencil. "How well do you know the city?"

"Well enough," Joe said a little defensively. It hadn't occurred to him that he might not get the job. The interview was beginning to feel like the third degree.

"No skin off my nose if you don't," the man said. "There's no free lunch around here. You get paid by the trip, not by the hour." He half hoisted himself out of his chair. "Lightfoot!" he barked at the guy in the door. "This one thinks he's hot. Check him out!"

By the time Joe got back outside, Lightfoot was already straddling his bike, a gleaming new Italian racing model that looked as if it must have cost at least six months' pay. Lightfoot jerked his head toward Joe's bike, and Joe got on, feeling a little uncertain. Joe had thought he'd just have to walk in the door and get his first assignment. What had he gotten himself into?

"Okay, Hot Dog, we'll check you out by racing around the block," Lightfoot said, grinning cockily. He pulled his felt hat even lower over his eyes and took a pair of black gloves out of his hip pocket. He nodded down the street. "We start that way. First one back here wins."

A kid in a black leather jacket raised a hand. "Hey, Lightfoot, aren't you going to tell him about the shortcut?"

Lightfoot glared at the kid, then tried to look casual. "Oh, yeah, the shortcut." He jerked his thumb over his shoulder. "There's an alley back there, around the corner. 'Course, if you want, you can go all the way around the block." He coasted into position at the curb.

"On your mark, get set, go!" someone shouted, and they were off.

In the back of the van a couple of blocks away, Frank smiled to himself as he adjusted his headset, picturing the start of the race. He wondered how Joe was feeling. This was one time his brother might have bitten off more than he could chew.

"Come on, Hot Dog, take him!" somebody yelled. Hot Dog? It was a perfect name for Joe.

Frank leaned forward eagerly, hunched over his receiver, trying to imagine what was happening on the other end of the radio connection.

For what seemed a long time, he could hear only jumbled street noises—whistles, horns, the roar of passing trucks—together with the whir of tires and the muffled panting of Joe's heavy breathing as he pumped harder and harder. If Frank knew Joe, he was giving it everything he had. More than anything in the world, Joe hated to lose.

Suddenly Frank heard the sound of skidding tires and a sharp, gasping, "Oh, no!" Then his ears were filled with a metallic crash and a solid, bone-crunching thud.

It was the sound of a bike and rider totally wiping out!

Chapter
2

THERE WAS DEAD silence on the receiver, then a low, faint groan.

In the van Frank pulled his headset closer to his ears and turned up the volume. What was going on? Had Joe been hit by a truck? Had he crashed headlong into something? Frank's first impulse was to jump out and find his brother, but he forced himself to remain still.

"Joe," he muttered through clenched teeth, even though he knew his brother couldn't hear him. "Joe, are you all right?"

Suddenly Frank's ears were filled with hoarse, raucous laughter.

"Sorry about that, Hot Dog," came Lightfoot's raspy voice. "Guess I forgot to tell you about that loading dock at the end of the alley.

That's what you get for being in the lead.'' More laughter, several voices together this time.

Then there was a grunt, and Frank heard Joe say sarcastically, "Yeah, Lightfoot, I'll *bet* you're sorry."

Frank relaxed a little. Joe's pride would be scraped a little raw, but he sounded okay. Something about Lightfoot's tone of voice, though, made him uneasy. It sounded almost sinister. Had this been an initiation—the kind of thing a street gang does when somebody new tries to break into the group? Or were the messengers on to them?

Back in the alley, Joe picked himself up from the asphalt, feeling his ribs and wondering if he hadn't cracked one or two. Dazed, he just stared at his bike. There wasn't any real damage—only the handlebars had been twisted out of alignment. He swallowed the anger he felt at Lightfoot for the potentially deadly joke he had played on him. Joe had hit the brakes just in time to avoid racing full speed into a loading dock at the end of the alley.

"Hey, Hot Dog!" Joe looked up. A half-dozen messengers were clustered around him. A thin white kid in dark glasses, jeans, and a T-shirt stepped forward to help Joe twist the handlebars back into shape. "They call me Slim," he offered, when the handlebars were straight. He took off his dark glasses and grinned at Joe as the knot of messengers began to break apart.

"Congratulations, man. You passed. You were way ahead of him, too. That doesn't happen very often."

"I passed?" Joe was still slightly dazed and more than a little mad.

"Yeah, it's a trick they play on all the new guys," Slim explained. "They race them into this blind alley, and the ones who come out in one piece get hired." He put his glasses back on before adding, "Personally, I don't think it's such a great idea."

"That makes two of us," Joe growled. He felt for the mike, wondering if it was still working. Frank had undoubtedly heard the crash—but had he heard anything else? Did he know that Joe was okay?

Slim gestured. "Come on. Let's get your name on the board in the dispatch office."

Wheeling his bike, Joe followed Slim through a back door and down a long hallway, past a storage room and into the office where he had applied for the job minutes before.

Activity had picked up. There were four or five messengers sitting at one end of the room, two of them playing cards, the others sprawled on the floor listening to rock music on a portable radio. Behind them was a row of wooden cubbyholes filled with messenger bags and personal gear. In the corner was an old sofa and table with a hot plate and coffee pot.

At the other end of the room the man with the leg brace had a telephone glued to one ear, and he was beckoning impatiently to one of the messengers. The kid ran up to the desk and the man thrust a piece of paper at him and snapped, "Get going!" As the messenger disappeared out the door, the man stood up and wrote an address beside the messenger's name on the dispatch board.

"Say, Gus," Slim called out over the noise of the radio, "how about putting Hot Dog's name up?"

Without a word, Gus wrote "Hot Dog" at the bottom of the list and sat down again. He picked up some personnel forms and thrust them at Joe.

"I guess you've already met Gus Ireland," Slim said as they walked to the sofa.

"Yeah," Joe replied. He sat down and started to fill out the forms. "Does he hate the whole world or is it just me?"

"Oh, Gus isn't so bad," Slim said with a grin. "He used to be one of the best riders on the street. Then a cabbie plowed into him at Broadway and Fulton, and he nearly lost his leg. Now he's stuck behind a desk. I think it's soured him."

Across the room, the two guys had stopped playing cards and were talking intently in the

17

corner. One of them glanced suspiciously at Joe, and they both stopped talking abruptly. Joe wondered why.

"That's Apollo and Wipe-Out," Slim said. "They've been in the business longer than the rest of us. There's not an address in the city that they can't find—blindfolded."

Before Joe could answer, a pretty girl walked in from the street. She was wearing fatigue pants and an oversize jacket with the sleeves rolled up, and her short red hair was brushed back from her large green eyes. Joe caught himself staring at her. "Who's she?" he asked curiously.

"Name's Gypsy," Slim replied. "She's only been here a couple of months, but she seems to be working out okay. She's weird, though. Keeps to herself, won't talk to anybody. Word has it she's moonlighting with another messenger company. She's already made enough to buy herself a new bike, and she was flashing some big bucks around here the other day."

Joe made a mental note to find out more about Gypsy. A new bike, big bucks—could she be making that money working for MUX? He picked up the forms he'd just filled out and took them to Gus's desk, where the dispatcher was just putting the phone down.

He glanced up at Joe. "Okay, Hot Dog," he said, "time to earn your pay. You've got a pickup in the financial district."

18

Joe took the work order Gus waved at him and headed for the front door. As he reached it, he turned back toward Slim. "Hey, thanks," he said.

"Sure thing." Slim shrugged. "Good luck."

Joe wheeled his bike down the front steps. "On my way to Chase Manhattan Plaza," he said out loud, hoping Frank could still hear him.

Joe was amazed at how easy it was for somebody on a bike—somebody who was willing to take chances—to cut through New York City traffic.

At the first intersection, he wanted to dismount and cross with the light, but he could see the cross-street traffic was snarled up so he rode across it without stopping. When the columns of bumper-to-bumper traffic traveling beside him ground to a stop, he threaded his way between two rows of cars all the way to the next light. He got a jump on the light, turned left on Water Street, and was off at the head of the column, pedaling south.

Then, out of the corner of his eye, he caught a glimpse of the Hardys' black van swinging into the lane behind him. Good, he thought to himself. Frank was on his way, so the radio must still be working.

"Hey, Frank, can you hear me?" he said. "If you can, give me a beep." A second later he was rewarded with the familiar sound of the van's horn honking amid all the other traffic noise. "So far, so good." Joe pedaled harder.

At the next corner Joe dodged between the lines of stalled traffic, slipping into the intersection as the light turned green. With a burst of energy, he rapidly pulled away from the lumbering buses and delivery trucks, pushing himself to top speed. But the van was stuck behind a bus.

Joe had driven in New York traffic often, but never on a bike. In the van he never got the *feel* of the traffic the way he did on the bike—and he didn't have the freedom, either. Joe felt wonderful that he was moving faster than anything around him. It was hard for him to remember that he was on a job, and that there could be real danger involved. This was *fun*—and he was getting paid for it, too!

In less time than he thought possible, Joe was locking his bike to a parking meter outside a sixty-five-story, glass-and-steel building. He didn't see a sign of Frank. He grinned, picturing his brother still stuck behind that bus. He rode the express elevator to his pickup on the thirty-eighth floor, where a smiling secretary handed him a brown envelope. Then back down the elevator, into the plaza, and onto his bike.

"I'm headed for West Broadway and Chambers," he said out loud for Frank's benefit, and pedaled off again. After he delivered the envelope, he stopped at a pay phone in a drugstore and dialed the number of the mobile phone in the van.

"Yeah, what is it?" Frank said. Joe could hear the frustration in his voice.

"It's me," Joe said. "How's the radio working? You picking me up okay?"

"No, I lost you when I got stuck in traffic. Too many buildings between us. Also, I don't think I'll be able to hear a thing when you go inside."

"We have two other problems," Joe said. "We need two-way communication. The guy in the van needs to be able to contact the guy on the bike. And we've got to figure out a way to track other bikes without actually following them."

"Right," Frank said. "A van can't keep up with all those bikes, running all over the place. We've got to come up with something. Radar? No, that won't work. It's only line-of-sight. Listen, Joe, maybe Mr. Chilton can some up with something. How about meeting near WWT's offices at noon?"

"I'll be there," Joe promised, and hung up. Then, with a sense of anticipation, he dialed SpeedWay's number. If he didn't have to meet Frank until noon, he might as well do another job. This messenger stuff was great.

At noon Joe coasted off Fifteenth Street into Stuyvesant Park, scattering a flock of gray-winged pigeons picking up crumbs from the side-

21

walk. On one side of the park there were a couple of red brick buildings that gave the small square the look of a New England village green. The benches were filled with people eating their lunches, reading newspapers, or taking naps in the sun.

In front of the peg-legged bronze statue of Peter Stuyvesant, Joe saw Frank, his army surplus messenger bag at his side. The two of them bought a couple of hot dogs from a vendor and found a bench in the corner of the small park.

"Did you get the equipment you were after?" Joe asked, wolfing his food.

Frank nodded. "Chilton sent down some great stuff," he said. He opened his bag and handed Joe a headset with a single earphone. It looked exactly like the portable radios people wore.

"With this," Frank said, "you can always stay tuned to your favorite station—me. With two-way communication, we can keep in touch better." He reached into his bag again and pulled out a round, palm-size metal container. "We also have a supply of miniaturized transmitters. They're perfect for this job. Each of them has a unique signal."

"That'll tell us *who* we're tracking," Joe said as he turned one of the transmitters over in his hand. "But it won't tell us *where*."

"That's where Chilton really shines," said Frank, grinning. "We'll be able to receive each bike's signal over a special set in the van that tracks the messengers on a computerized display." Frank's grin got a little wider. "The man promised us state of the art, and . . ."

Joe gave his brother a high-five as he finished the sentence. "And he delivers!" Joe looked closer at the small black sphere. "But how do I attach these things to the bikes? It's not like I can toss them into the backseat."

"They're magnetized," Frank said. "You can stick them on anything metal."

Joe nodded knowingly. "Like the metal plate under a bicycle seat."

"Yeah. With these gadgets, one of us gets his exercise biking all over Manhattan, while the other tunes in on likely suspects."

"Great," Joe said, putting the headset on and stuffing half a dozen small transmitters into his bag. "I need to get back to SpeedWay before I'm missed." He flashed Frank a grin. "Stay tuned— fun and games coming up."

The ride back to SpeedWay was uneventful until the last few blocks. Just south of the Seaport a yellow taxi raced past him, its right front tire splashing through a muddy puddle. A long wave arched directly in front of Joe and he plowed right through it. He was still dripping when he arrived at the office. The chair behind Gus's desk was empty.

Slim looked up from the corner where he was

playing checkers with Wipe-Out. "Hey, Hot Dog! Taking showers on company time?"

Joe made a face. "Anywhere I can dry off?"

Slim pointed to a door beside Gus's desk. "Washroom's in there."

Joe ducked inside. As he reached for the paper towels on the wall, he heard Gus's voice through the flimsy plywood wall that partitioned the washroom from the storage room. It sounded as though Gus didn't want to be overheard. Joe pulled off his headset so he could hear better.

"Look, Lightfoot," he was saying, "World-Wide says the heat's on. There's gonna be an investigation, some private eye asking questions, poking his nose into things. One wrong move and the good times will disappear."

Lightfoot mumbled something that Joe couldn't hear. Whatever it was, it seemed to make Gus furious. Joe heard Gus's cane whistle through the air and land with a loud clang as it hit something metal.

"Don't tell me you ain't got a lot to lose," Gus growled angrily. "Don't forget—you're in on this, too. One tiny foul-up and I'll make sure you're the first one in jail!"

24

Chapter

3

QUICKLY JOE PULLED down a couple of paper towels, dried himself, and repositioned his headset. He opened the door and peered out.

Everything looked normal. Gus was sliding into his chair, and Lightfoot, looking shaken, had joined Slim and Wipe-Out. No one paid any attention as Joe came out of the washroom and went out the door. Still wearing his bag, he squatted beside his bike, inspecting the spokes.

"I'm getting ready to 'decorate' one of the bikes, Frank," he said out loud, making sure there was nobody around to hear him.

"Roger," Frank said. His voice was loud and clear in Joe's ear. "Which one?"

"Lightfoot's. Did you pick up any of that touching little conversation inside?"

"Negative."

"It looks like Lightfoot's our guy," Joe said. "And Gus, too." He'd spotted the shiny ten-speed that Lightfoot had used in the race that morning, chained to the steps. Checking in both directions to make sure the coast was clear, he walked over to the bike, pretending to admire it. Taking a transmitter out of his bag and palming it, he reached under the seat as if he were testing it. The transmitter clicked into place against the metal seat plate.

Just at that moment Lightfoot came barreling out of the office and down the steps. He stopped short when he saw Joe standing by his bike.

Joe grinned carelessly. "Hey, man, that's a nice pair of wheels you've got there."

Lightfoot began to unlock his bike. "Keep your hands off this bike, if you know what's good for you." He was obviously in a bad mood. "What're you hanging around it for?"

"I'll bet you could have beaten me easily this morning," Joe said, trying to shift Lightfoot's attention. "You just let me take the lead so I'd make the turn into that blind alley."

"You catch on real fast." Lightfoot sneered. He pulled his gloves out of his hip pocket and put them on. Without another word, he swung a long leg over his bike and pedaled off.

Joe took a deep breath. "That's one," he said, dropping his chin to his chest.

"Roger," Frank said. "I'm tracking."

"Keep close watch on him," Joe said. He straightened up and walked back to his bike.

Late that afternoon Frank opened the rear doors of the van. Checking in both directions, he lifted his bike out of the back, closed and locked the doors, and pedaled south. A few minutes later he was parking his bike in front of SpeedWay. After having listened to Joe's transmissions most of the day, Frank felt as if he'd been there before.

The few messengers standing around didn't give Frank a second glance. Gus was behind his desk, bent over a stack of paperwork.

"Excuse me," Frank said to him, "are you the dispatcher?"

"Yeah," Gus growled. "What do you want?"

"My name is Frank Dodd. I heard you're hiring messengers."

Gus studied Frank's army-surplus sweater, ragged blue jeans and worn tennis shoes. "When was the last time you held a job?" he asked.

"I'm working my way through school," Frank said. "New York University. I'd like to ride your night shift."

Gus eyed him suspiciously, then leaned back and lit a cigarette. "Yeah. Well, we're always hiring messengers. They come and they go here." He grinned. "College types mostly go. They're soft—work's too tough for 'em."

27

"Look," Frank said, "I've worked for a delivery service before. I know this city like my mom's kitchen."

Gus gave him another close look. Then he seemed to make up his mind and became brisk and businesslike. "Night messengers are hard to find, so I'll give you a try. Bruce is the night dispatcher. He comes on in half an hour—you can be *his* problem. You work until midnight. Then we close. Here. Fill out these forms."

Frank picked up the personnel forms Gus pushed at him and retreated to a table across the room to fill them in. At least he didn't have to go through the ritual of the race, he thought.

When Frank finished and looked up, he saw that Gus was no longer watching him. At that moment, a slender guy with light brown hair came in. Even though it was dusk outside, he was still wearing sunglasses. Frank suspected it was Slim. The guy crossed the room, spoke briefly with Gus, then headed for Frank.

"Hi," Slim said. He held out his hand. "They call me Slim around here."

Frank nodded and shook Slim's hand. "Frank Dodd."

"Gus says he's decided to call you Doc," Slim said with a grin. "Says you're working your way through NYU."

"That's right," Frank said. He leaned forward and lowered his voice. "Actually, I'm getting a degree in business administration. I need to study a small business for a management course I'm taking—but don't tell Gus."

Slim nodded. "Got you," he said. "That's how we do things around here—we keep our eyes open and our mouths shut." Frank couldn't see Slim's eyes through his dark glasses. He wondered what Slim was trying to tell him.

There was no time to find out. Half a dozen calls came in in the next ten minutes, and both Frank and Slim were sent out to maneuver their bikes through Manhattan. Before Frank knew it, his shift was over and it was time to meet with Joe and his dad.

Frank ducked into a small midtown café well after dark. In a booth near the rear, he saw his father talking to Joe. Frank walked up to the booth quickly.

Fenton Hardy spoke to him. "Joe was just filling me in on the interesting conversation he overheard at SpeedWay's this afternoon."

Joe slid over to make room for Frank. "Gus was chewing Lightfoot out," he explained. "He said somebody at World-Wide had told him there was an investigation going on. Too bad he didn't say who his source was. We'd have this case all wrapped up."

"Still, it looks like you've identified two key suspects," Mr. Hardy said. He sipped his coffee. "It stands to reason that the dispatcher has to be involved. A messenger doesn't get to choose his pickups and deliveries.''

"Right," Frank agreed. "But identifying Gus and Lightfoot doesn't buy us much. We've got to figure out how they operate. And we need to know who *their* contact is, and whether there are other messengers involved.''

Mr. Hardy nodded. "If there are more messengers involved, our chances of identifying the contact will be increased. One of them is bound to get sloppy.''

"I've been wondering about that kid Slim," Frank said. "He seems to be on very good terms with Gus. *And* he's a little too friendly with new messengers.''

"There's a girl named Gypsy, too," Joe added. "She's only been there two months, but she's already made enough for a new bike. According to Slim, she was flashing big money around. And she keeps to herself. That would make sense, if she were sent to do the job by the contact at World-Wide.''

"Yeah, but that's Slim talking," Frank reminded Joe. "If Slim is involved, and he suspects you, he could be trying to throw you off the track.''

"Why would he suspect me?" Joe asked.

"It sounds like SpeedWay is a close-knit organization," Mr. Hardy said. "They may suspect anybody new. Besides, they're on their guard because they've been warned."

"Well, then," Joe replied, "it's a good thing there are two of us. They probably won't be looking for *two* undercover investigators."

"You probably should bug Slim's and Gypsy's bikes," Mr. Hardy said. "But it sounds like you two have made real headway today."

Frank looked up as the waitress arrived with three of the largest Reuben sandwiches he had ever seen. "Real headway?" he said, making a face. "Joe did, maybe. I spent most of my day stuck behind a bus."

Joe reported for work the next morning in a gray drizzle. When Slim arrived, Joe made a mental note of which bike he rode and then headed inside to check in.

Later in the day, Gus was scowling into the phone. "The regular messenger ain't back yet," he was saying. "Okay, okay, I understand." He listened a minute, then looked up and caught Joe's eye. "I gotcha," he snapped into the phone. He slammed down the receiver and waved at Joe. "Here's one for you, Hot Dog. Package pickup at Lexington and Fiftieth. The mailroom's in the basement. Hit it!"

Joe raised his eyebrows as he swung around and started toward the door. Lexington and Fiftieth? That was close to where . . . He glanced

31

down at the address on the work order Gus had handed him and almost froze in midstride. The name Gus had written down was *World-Wide Technologies!*

Twenty minutes later Joe was locking his bike in front of the Hawthorne Building, across Lexington from the imposing Waldorf-Astoria hotel. On the way he had tried to raise Frank on his transmitter, but there'd been no answer. He tried once more, without success, then shouldered through the double doors, heading for the elevators at the back of the lobby. He pulled his headset off and pressed the B button.

Joe stepped into the basement corridor. To his right was a counter running along the wall. As he approached, he noticed a girl with her head bent low over the counter. Her hair was long and dark, and swung across her shoulders just like— The memory hit him hard—*like Iola's*.

But he knew all too well it couldn't be Iola. His girlfriend had been killed by a terrorist bomb over a year ago.

The girl must have heard him coming. She looked up with a smile and then a nervous giggle. "You look like you've seen a ghost," she said. "May I help you?"

Joe tried to regain his composure. Now that he looked at the girl, he had to admit that she didn't really resemble Iola—except that she was very good-looking. Her nose had a cute tilt, and her dark eyes were large and expressive.

"Uh, yeah, maybe you can help," he said. "I'm looking for the mailroom."

"You've found it," the girl replied, giving him a curious look. "Welcome to the dungeon of World-Wide Technologies, Inc." She glanced at his messenger's bag. "You're from SpeedWay? You must be new. I haven't seen you before."

"Just started yesterday," Joe replied, still staring at her. Her lashes were unbelievably long. "A summer job to pay for school. I'm Joe Har—" Joe stopped, catching himself just in time. "Kincaid," he amended.

The girl didn't seem to notice his slip. She was putting a package on the counter. "I'm Tiffany Chilton, Mail Clerk and Keeper of the Inner Sanctum," she said. "Glad to meet you."

At the mention of her name Joe did a double take. Chilton? Was she any relation to Charles Chilton? "How'd you get stuck down here?" he asked, trying to sound casual.

"You won't believe this, but the president of this company is my father." Tiffany's pretty lips twisted sarcastically. "Charles Chilton," she said, "who *marooned* me down here in this stupid basement, away from all the action." She noticed Joe's intent look and frowned. "Do you know him?"

Joe thought quickly. "Not really," he said. "I

was working as an electronics technician before I got laid off, and we had some WWT equipment."

Tiffany managed an uninterested nod.

"So how come you're stuck down here, with the grunts?"

Tiffany shrugged angrily. "I told him I wanted to work this summer—maybe as his assistant. But Daddy's got this idea that starting from the bottom up will teach me the business." Her face darkened in a bitter scowl. "I guess I ought to know by now that as far as Charles Chilton is concerned, there's only one way to do things—the old-fashioned way."

Just then the phone rang. Before Tiffany could answer it Joe said, "How about that package?"

"Oh, yes," she said, handing him the small package she'd pulled out from under the counter. It was securely bound with strapping tape and stamped Highly Confidential. The phone rang again, and she reached for it. "It goes to Lower Manhattan," she said. "Off West Broadway, a few blocks up from the World Trade Center."

Joe looked at the address. And then he looked again, scarcely believing his eyes. The package Tiffany had given him was addressed to MUX, Incorporated! Was Mr. Chilton's own daughter the thief he was after?

Chapter

4

TIFFANY SPOKE INTO the phone and then put it down. She smiled at Joe, who was still staring at the package. "Think you can find the place?"

"Huh? Oh, yeah, sure," Joe mumbled. He looked up and managed to smile back. "Check you later."

Minutes later Joe was outside unlocking his bike. "Mayday, Frank!" he said into his hidden transmitter.

There was a pause. Then his headset responded. "Right, Joe. What's up?"

A man standing nearby turned to stare curiously at Joe, who seemed to be muttering to himself. Joe ducked his head, talking into his collar. "Hang onto your headset. I just picked up a package from World-Wide, courtesy of Tiffany

Chilton—Chilton's daughter, who's working in the mailroom. And unless I miss my guess, she's got a fair-size grudge against her father.'' He swung a leg over his bike and bumped off the curb, swinging across traffic.

"A grudge?" Frank asked. "Tell me more."

"Later. This package she gave me—" He paused, swerving to miss a street vendor. "It's addressed to MUX."

Joe grinned as he heard Frank whistle. "Hold on. Dad's here," Frank said. "I'm switching on the speaker." Then Joe heard Frank say, "Dad, you've got to hear this. Joe's got a package from Chilton's daughter, addressed to MUX!"

"Listen, you guys," Joe said urgently, "we've got to find out what's in it, and we don't have a lot of time."

"What do you think it is, Joe? Drawings, documents?" The voice belonged to Fenton Hardy.

"Wrong shape for that," Joe said. "It's a small squarish package—light."

"We'll meet you on the way to MUX and have a look," Frank said.

"But I don't know how we'll find out what's inside. The way it's taped, any tampering would be spotted."

"We'll have to take that chance," Frank said. "Maybe I can slip a razor blade under the tape and pry enough up to let the contents slip out.

36

I've been doing it with Christmas presents for years."

Fenton laughed. "Anyway, we haven't got much choice," he agreed.

There was a pause. "How about meeting us in front of the Houseman Building?" Frank said. "You know, the one that looks like a palace. We'll find a place to park in that block or the next one."

Joe made good time. He was almost to the rendezvous, pedaling hard, when another bike pulled alongside.

"Feel like racing, Hot Dog?"

Joe turned quickly. It was Slim, his messenger's bag slung over his shoulder. "Hi, Slim," he said loudly, hoping that Frank was picking up the conversation. "Headed back to the office?"

Slim shook his head. "Nope. Got a pickup down on Wall Street. Want some company?"

Great, Joe thought blackly. Just what I need. A tail. It suddenly occurred to him that if Frank's suspicions about Slim were right, Slim might be supervising this delivery.

"Sure," Joe replied casually. "Anybody else around? Maybe we can convoy."

Just then Joe saw the van turn onto the street a block ahead. He was almost at the rendezvous. Joe gritted his teeth. Would Frank show himself to Slim and blow both their covers? The van stopped at a light.

"I see we have a problem," Frank said in Joe's headset. Joe breathed a sigh of relief. At least Frank was on top of the situation.

"Listen carefully," Frank continued. "Dad's driving. At the next corner he'll make a right turn and cut you off. You raise a ruckus, and he'll jump out and pick a fight with both of you. While he's got Slim's attention, you drop the package through the window onto the seat. I'll put it back when I'm done with it, and you can pick it up. Got it?" He paused. "If you read me, tell Slim that you hope the sun comes out."

Joe turned to Slim as they rode through the next intersection. "You know, Slim," he said fervently, "I sure hope the sun comes out." And I sure hope that Dad knows how to time that right turn, he added to himself. If he doesn't, I'll know how a mashed potato feels.

Half a block later Joe came up behind the van as if to pass on the inside. Slim was a couple of lengths behind. As they reached the corner, the van turned abruptly, hitting Joe's bike lightly and forcing him to the curb. With a shout of rage, Joe slapped his palm against the side of the van.

"Hey, stupid!" he shouted. "Why don't you watch where you're going?"

The van braked. Seconds later Fenton Hardy came around the front, his hands clenched into fists. Slim had skidded to a stop just behind Joe.

"You crazy kid," Mr. Hardy shouted. "Don't

you know better than to pass on the inside? There's a law against that, you know. I ought to call the cops!"

"Crazy kid?" Joe shouted, stepping up to challenge him. "Where'd *you* learn to drive? A demolition derby?"

"You never signaled your turn," Slim interjected, glaring at Mr. Hardy. "Go ahead, call the cops, pal. See who gets the ticket."

As Slim was talking to Fenton Hardy, Joe saw his chance. With a fluid motion, he drew the package out of the messenger bag and keeping his body between Slim and the van, dropped the package behind him through the open window.

"Who asked you to butt in?" Mr. Hardy was advancing on Slim. A curious crowd was gathering on the sidewalk. "You bike jockeys are a menace to public safety. The cops ought to dump you all in the East River."

Somebody on the sidewalk yelled, "You tell 'em, fella! Those bikes are a hazard!"

"You're asking for it, old man," Slim said, starting to get off his bike.

"Come on, punk," Mr. Hardy said, stalling for time. "Put your muscle where your mouth is."

Slim, enraged, walked toward Mr. Hardy, his fist cocked. Joe looked nervously at his father, but Mr. Hardy seemed to have everything under control. While his face maintained the cocky arrogance of a street brawler, his cool eyes darted calculatingly toward the van.

"Hold on, Slim," Joe said forcefully, putting out a restraining hand. He glanced around at the hostile crowd. While some onlookers appeared to be angered by Mr. Hardy's belligerence, most were eager to see a reckless bicycle messenger get his due. Joe was beginning to feel like a guest at a lynching. "Let's cool it," he said.

Slim looked toward the crowd. "Yeah, I see what you mean, man." He sounded intimidated. "This could be a bad scene."

Joe turned to his father. "Look, mister, let's forget it. The cops are gonna be on both of us soon."

Mr. Hardy hesitated, then looked critically at Joe. "I guess we can call it even."

The three relaxed, and Joe squatted down, pretending to check out his bike. "Looks okay to me, Slim," Joe said. "Listen, why don't you go on? No point in both of us being late with our runs. I can handle it from here."

"You sure?" Slim said, glancing nervously at Mr. Hardy and the crowd.

Joe nodded. "See you later." He and Mr. Hardy watched Slim pedal out of sight as the crowd broke up.

Frank climbed out of the van and handed Joe the package, perfectly rewrapped.

"Maybe you should go into show business,"

Joe said to his father, tucking the package back into his bag and mounting his bike. " 'Put your muscle where your mouth is!' Whew!" Mr. Hardy laughed as he and Frank climbed back into the van and started the engine.

"Okay," Joe said into his transmitter, as he started off. "So what *is* in the package?"

"Some sort of circuit board," Frank said. "From what I could see, it didn't look like a production model, so it's probably a prototype. You can look at it later and tell me what you think."

"Look at it later?" Joe asked. He slowed to avoid a pedestrian. "But I've got to hand it over to somebody at MUX in a few minutes."

"True," Frank said. There was a nod of satisfaction in his voice. "But I took some nice closeups with the video camera. We've got it on tape!"

The address on the package led Joe into a run-down neighborhood only a few blocks east of the docks of the Hudson River. The street was lined with seedy little shops and empty stores, some of which had been converted into warehouse space. He came to the street number that matched the address on the package. The building looked empty.

Joe knocked on the front door. No answer. He pounded with his fist. After a minute he heard someone move inside. Slowly the door opened, and the expressionless, hostile face of an Asian man stared out at him.

"Is this MUX, Incorporated?" Joe asked. He couldn't imagine a legitimate corporation doing business here. "I've got a package to deliver to this address."

Without a word, the man reached for the package. He inspected it carefully, then began to shut the door.

"Hey, wait a minute," Joe said, putting his foot in the door. "You have to sign for that." He held out a clipboard. "Do you work for MUX?"

The door opened. The man grabbed the clipboard and scribbled a signature on it, then thrust it back. The door closed with a bang.

Joe studied the signature for a minute. It was totally unreadable. He got back on his bike and rode off, his head spinning with questions. Who was the strange character he'd just delivered the package to? Why would an up-and-coming corporation like MUX do business in a place like this? And why would a girl like Tiffany Chilton send a package to a major competitor?

Joe was brought out of his reverie by a voice.

"What's happening, dude?" demanded Lightfoot, who had pulled up beside him. Joe was almost back at SpeedWay. "You look like you're lost in the clouds."

Joe grinned back without replying. Was this another escort?

Suddenly a scream came from behind them. "Stop him! He's got my purse."

Joe turned to see a young kid running through the crowd, his left hand clutching a bright red purse, the broken strap fluttering behind him. "Want to nail that guy?" he asked Lightfoot.

"Why not?" Lightfoot kicked off.

As Joe pumped after him, Lightfoot swerved around pedestrians, hopped a curb, whipped right past the purse snatcher, and turned to cut him off.

That's when he—and Joe—realized what was in the punk's *right* hand.

The thief hadn't torn the purse strap loose, he'd *cut* it.

And now he was pointing the knife at Lightfoot!

Chapter

5

Joe could see sunlight gleaming on the knife blade as he came flying up. There was only one thing he could do. Joe turned slightly to come in on the guy's side.

The guy glanced over when he heard Joe coming up. But he was still only half turned as Joe rammed into him.

Joe and his bike parted company, but Joe was ready for that. He even managed to land on his feet.

The punk wasn't ready at all. He slammed into the pavement, his knife clattering as it fell from his hand. Joe quickly kicked it into a storm sewer, then retrieved the handbag.

The punk tried to get up, but Joe loomed over

him. "If you know what's good for you, stay down there."

Pushing through the gathering crowd, the owner of the purse darted forward. "Thanks for saving— Hey, Joe Hardy! 'Crimebusting' as usual, I see."

Horrified, Joe looked into a familiar face— Sally Gray. Of all the times to meet someone from Bayport! "I'm not Joe Hardy," he told her. "My name's Kincaid." He was all too aware of Lightfoot staring at his back.

"What's going on?" Sally demanded. She lowered her voice a little. "Are you on a case?"

Joe shot her a look, pleading with her to shut up. Then he heard a police siren. Several people had gone into the street to flag the patrol car down.

Lightfoot looked nervous. "Hey, man," he said, "cops and I don't get along. You want to be a hero, *you* sit on this guy." He hopped on his bicycle and was gone.

"Come on, Joe," Sally said as the police came up. "Are you undercover or something?"

Joe sighed. "I *was*."

He gave a statement to the police, who took the purse snatcher away. Then Joe headed for SpeedWay. As he pulled up at the office, he noticed all the messengers gathered out front. They looked as if they were waiting for someone. Were they waiting for him?

"Hey, Gus," somebody called, "he's back."

"Kincaid!" Gus shouted angrily from behind his desk. "Get over here!"

Joe went over to the desk. The rest followed him into the room and stood silently ringing the walls. Gypsy came in and stood by the door, all by herself.

"Slim says you were in an accident," Gus snapped. "Why didn't you report it immediately?"

"Well, it wasn't much of an accident," Joe mumbled. "I mean, I didn't think—"

"That's right!" Gus snapped. "You *didn't* think! First thing you do when you have an accident is report it. There're all kinds of assorted jerks looking to file a lawsuit if a bike so much as brushes them."

"He made up for it, though," Lightfoot said. "Hot Dog caught a purse snatcher. He's a real concerned citizen."

"Shut up!" Gus glared from Lightfoot to Joe.

Joe swallowed. Was Gus mad enough to fire him? "Listen," he said, "I'm sorry. I—"

But Gus ignored him. "That goes for the rest of you, too," he snarled at the other messengers. "I'm firing the next jerk who has an accident and doesn't report it *pronto*. And it'd better be the other guy's fault, too. Don't you read the newspapers? The mayor says messenger bikes are a hazard. If we give him half a chance, he'll run us off the streets and we'll all be out of a job. So keep your noses clean.''

Apollo grunted. ''How're we going to make a dime if we don't keep moving?'' he said in a voice too low for Gus to hear. ''We get paid by the trip—and peanuts, at that. If we can't cut a few corners, we might as well walk.''

''If you're smart, you'll make it,'' Joe heard Lightfoot say quietly to Apollo. ''So why don't you get smart?''

Apollo was glaring at Lightfoot. ''How many times I got to tell you, man? I don't go for your kind of action!''

Joe noticed that Gypsy was listening to Lightfoot with a thoughtful look on her face. When she caught Joe watching her, she turned away.

Gus slammed his hand on the desk. ''Everybody got the message?'' he barked. ''Back to work, all of you!''

Joe started down the steps. Now, while everybody was inside, might be a good chance to bug those other bikes.

Frank drove into the parking garage behind World-Wide Technologies and pulled into the second-floor space Mr. Chilton had directed him to use. After the accident a half-hour earlier, Fenton Hardy had called Chilton to tell him they'd intercepted a piece of World-Wide hardware and needed to identify it.

"There he is," Mr. Hardy said as Mr. Chilton got out of the elevator and moved toward them. He was accompanied by a tall woman in a gray suit.

"It's going to be a tight fit for four of us in here," Frank said, opening the van door.

"This is Louise Trent," Mr. Chilton said. "She's our chief designer. She knows more about our products than anyone else. Louise, these gentlemen are investigating the thefts. They want you to identify a piece of hardware."

After everybody had squeezed into the van, Frank squatted in front of the VCR and inserted the tape he'd made. Seconds later the screen was filled with the image of something that looked like a circuit board. A hand moved the board, revealing the component from several angles.

Ms. Trent sucked in her breath sharply. "That's the prototype of our new M twenty-seven board," she said. She turned on Frank, her voice sharp. "Where did you get this video?"

Frank threw an uneasy look at his father. Fenton Hardy spoke slowly, deliberately. "We can't reveal our source without harming our investigation. We have a strong suspect. But there are special problems in revealing this person's identity until we're absolutely sure."

Frank looked at Mr. Chilton, wondering what

he'd say if he knew that the suspect was his own daughter.

Mr. Chilton's voice was tight. "Are you implying that this person is in a position of trust at World-Wide?"

Mr. Hardy nodded.

"I'm very close to all my top people," Mr. Chilton said, his jaw working. "They're just like members of my family. I can't believe one of them would betray me." He swallowed. "Yes, you're right. Don't tell me until you're sure."

"What we really wanted to know," Frank said, "is whether this component is critical. That is, that this wasn't just a case of somebody picking up a free sample." He turned to Ms. Trent. "You're sure of your identification?"

Ms. Trent nodded. "Of course I'm sure. I designed it. See that?" She pointed to a dark rectangle in the upper corner of the screen. That's the Z twenty-seven thirteen chip. I'd know it anywhere."

"Then this single component could cost you a lot of business if the wrong people got hold of it."

"That's right," Mr. Chilton said. "What's valuable here is the *design*. The components are all off the shelf—you can buy them at the corner electronics store." He tapped the screen. "But if they have this, they can set up a production line in a week and beat us to the market. And they

49

can undersell us, if they have cheap labor. Then we'd be in real trouble.''

Frank and his father looked at each other. Mr. Chilton intercepted the look and nodded at Ms. Trent. "Thanks, Louise," he said. "That's all."

When the chief designer had gone, Mr. Hardy turned to Mr. Chilton. "I know that our primary objective is to identify the spy," he said. "But shouldn't we also try to legally force MUX out of this line of business?"

"I wish we could. But that's what's so frustrating. We don't know a thing about them. They came out of nowhere."

"What does M-U-X stand for?" Mr. Hardy asked.

"Maybe it's not an acronym," Frank suggested. "Isn't the word *mux* an abbreviation for the word *multiplexer?*"

Mr. Hardy looked puzzled. "What's that?"

"It's a communications switching device," Mr. Chilton said.

"A network controller," Frank added thoughtfully. *Network controller*. It sounded like a name that might have several meanings.

Mr. Chilton shook his head. "The corporation's a mystery," he said. "Even our marketing people can't tell us a thing about it."

Mr. Hardy snapped his fingers. "I know somebody who can," he said. "He's a stockbroker who's made a fortune finding skeletons in corporate closets. Frank can go talk to him and find out what *he* knows about MUX."

Maxwell Harris was an owlish-looking little man with wire-rimmed glasses. As Frank walked up behind him, he was staring intently at a video monitor on the desk in his Wall Street office. On a wall screen above his head, a ribbon of stock prices unrolled.

"Mr. Harris," Frank said. "I'm Frank Hardy."

"Oh, yes," the little man replied, without looking up from the screen. "Be with you in a minute." Several number displays flashed on the screen in rapid succession. A look of satisfaction appeared on Maxwell Harris's face. He cleared the screen and turned to Frank.

"Your father said you're after some background information." He gave Frank a curious look. "Something about industrial espionage."

Frank nodded. "The suspect company's name is MUX, Inc. It may have a storefront operation on the Lower West Side. But that's all we know."

"Mm-m-m." Mr. Harris seemed lost in thought. "Ah, yes, MUX. The new competitor in the electronics industry that's giving the domestic guys fits." He frowned. "I don't recall seeing MUX traded publicly. Why don't I look into it and give you a call? Where can I reach you?"

Frank gave him the van's mobile phone number. "We're in kind of a hurry, sir," Frank said hesitantly. He had hoped to walk out with at least a mailing address. "You think I could wait until—"

"These things take time, son," he interrupted. "Even with our computer system it could take up to an hour. I'll call you the minute I find something. Oh, and give your father my regards. He got me out of a tough spot last year—some phony inside trading charges. I won't forget him."

Frank nodded, thanked Harris, and turned to go. As he looked back, he saw that the little man was again engrossed in his screen.

Back in the van and out in traffic, Frank chided himself for being so impatient. If he didn't watch it he'd start acting as impulsively as Joe. Thinking of Joe, he realized he'd better check in with him.

But that was unsuccessful, too. Joe must be inside somewhere. Frank turned on the screen he'd mounted below the dash to check on Lightfoot. He'd programmed the grid of Manhattan streets on the screen. A quick glance revealed Lightfoot's blip—but it was stationary. He was at SpeedWay.

Just then the van's phone buzzed. To Frank's surprise, it was Maxwell Harris.

"I wasn't expecting to hear from you so soon," Frank said, negotiating a left turn. "Do you have something?"

"Yes," Mr. Harris said. "Well, yes and no. What I have is a very suspicious nothing.

"That corporation you asked about—MUX?" Harris continued briskly. "This may sound strange, but there's no such company!"

Chapter

6

"WHAT DO YOU mean?" Frank snapped impatiently. "If MUX doesn't exist, who's making all
that money?"

"MUX doesn't exist," Mr. Harris snapped
back, clearly annoyed with having to explain, "as
a conventional business organization. I checked
everything and only found a web of shadowy
transactions—all shielded by front companies.
The stock isn't traded over-the-counter, so the
company's privately owned."

"Can't you get an address, then?" Frank
asked.

"It isn't incorporated in New York, New Jer-
sey, Delaware, or the other states I checked. It
doesn't even have a federal tax number."

"How does it do business, then?"

"Same story," Mr. Harris said. "It's puzzling. Most of the company's business is transacted through a post-office box in lower Manhattan. Its finances are funneled through off-shore banks in the Caribbean and in Panama."

"What about production facilities?"

"None in this country. Its products are shipped through Taiwan from other countries on the Pacific Rim. The company uses a local advertising agency. It pays on time, and the checks don't bounce. It doesn't even have a phone number." He paused. "This corporation is like those quasars out in space you read about. There's an incredible amount of energy coming from somewhere, but when you look into the center there's nothing there."

"Like a phantom network controller," Frank said to himself. "Of course. Mux!"

"Sorry there isn't more," Mr. Harris said.

"Thanks. You've been a big help," Frank said. After saying goodbye to Mr. Harris, he tried again to reach Joe. This time he was successful.

"What's up?" Joe asked.

"How about a pow-wow?" Frank said. "I've got some info to pass along to you and Dad."

"I'm off in fifteen minutes. The hotel?"

"I'll get Dad," Frank said. "Over and out."

Half an hour later the three Hardys were in the hotel room overlooking Central Park. Frank filled them in on his conversation with Maxwell Harris.

"I've got two views on this case," Frank said, propping his feet up on the coffee table. "The first is that I've got it almost solved." He grinned bleakly. "The second is that we haven't scratched the surface."

"From what Harris told you," Mr. Hardy said, stretched full-length on the bed, "I suspect this goes a lot further than the espionage at World-Wide." He shook his head. "If all you've got to hide is a nickel-and-dime operation, you don't go to the trouble of covering your tracks the way these people have."

Joe was standing by the window, his hands in his pockets. "What's bothering me," he said abruptly, "is what happens if our covers get blown. That business this afternoon—when Sally yelled out my name in front of Lightfoot—has me edgy. And when I was bugging Slim's and Gypsy's bikes this afternoon, I couldn't shake the feeling that I was being watched."

Mr. Hardy nodded. "Watch yourselves. This operation might be just the tip of a criminal iceberg. Things could get dangerous."

Frank clasped his hands behind his head. "Meanwhile, we've still got a prime suspect inside World-Wide. What are we going to do about her?"

Joe swiveled around. "We don't know that Tiffany's involved," Joe said. "Just because she gave me the package doesn't mean she knew what was in it."

"I'm with Joe," Mr. Hardy said. "Even if she did, it's not likely that she's the only one at World-Wide involved."

Joe nodded his head vigorously. "That's right. She's stuck in the mailroom—how would she get hold of a prototype? Maybe somebody's trying to frame her."

Mr. Hardy frowned at his son. "I'm not sure you aren't letting your feelings get in the way." He thought for a minute. "But if she's being framed, your cover may already be blown."

"I don't follow you," Joe said.

"If somebody at World-Wide knows or suspects who you are, maybe he arranged for you to pick up the package in order to implicate Tiffany."

"And the motive?" Joe asked slowly.

"Maybe he's hoping that Chilton will either assume the thefts were caused by a rebellious daughter, or he'll put a stop to the investigation because Tiffany is involved."

Joe looked out the window. "Well, either way, I guess it's up to me to find out the truth."

Frank nodded and looked at his watch. "It's almost time for my shift. We need to know if anyone else at SpeedWay is involved—and I've got an idea how to do it."

* * *

Frank checked in shortly before five. Business was brisk that evening, but all of his runs were routine. When he got back about eleven, Bruce, the night dispatcher, was alone.

"Busy night, huh?" Frank asked.

Bruce rubbed his ear. "I've been on the phone since five." He glanced up at the clock. "Mind watching the joint while I get a sandwich? One of the other guys should be back shortly if you need a messenger."

"Sure," Frank said. What luck, he told himself. As soon as Bruce was out the door, he went to the dispatch board. As usual, it hadn't been erased for a day or two, and he began to decode Gus's scribbles.

Each row had a rider's name on it, his trips listed from left to right in each row. For each trip, the pickup and delivery addresses were listed, together with the time of pickup and delivery. Some of the addresses—those must be the regulars, Frank thought—were identified with abbreviations.

Frank quickly scanned the board. Suddenly he spotted something that rang a bell—HQWWT. Headquarters, World-Wide Technologies! With a start, he noticed that most of the WWT pickups were listed in Lightfoot's row. And Lightfoot *always* made the pickup when the delivery went to another one of WWT's New York offices.

Ah-ha! Frank thought. There it was—practically *proof* that Lightfoot was involved in this scam! At a glance, it looked as if Lightfoot's trip times were pretty long. There was only one logical explanation. He must be stopping somewhere along the way.

But it would take some serious study to confirm that guess. Frank reached into his bag and pulled out a small camera. Quickly he moved the desk light so that it brightened the board. Casting a furtive glance at the door, he aimed the camera at the board and clicked the shutter.

Just then there was a noise in the hallway. Frank jumped, startled, and the camera clattered to the floor. "Get away from there, you spy!" cried a voice loud enough to wake the dead.

Chapter
7

FRANK SPUN AROUND. An attractive young girl with short red hair was staring at him from the shadows of the hallway. It could only be Gypsy. But what was *she* doing there? According to Joe, she worked the day shift.

"What are you doing, selling this to the competition?" the girl demanded.

Frank put on his most winning smile. "I'm Frank Dodd," he said. He picked the camera up and shoved it back in his bag with a prayer that he'd managed to get a clear shot. He'd planned to take more than one, for insurance, but that idea was blown. "I'm new here," he added. "I don't think we've met."

She gave him a stony glare. "I asked what you

were doing with that camera? What is this, some secret investigation?"

Secret investigation? Was she on to him? Frank sat down on the corner of Gus's desk and grinned disarmingly. "No. I was just photographing the schedule board. What are you doing here so late?"

Gypsy was studying him with an intent look. "I've got it," she said wryly. "We've had all kinds, but you're the first photographer. The title of that one is what, 'Schedule Board at Midnight'?"

Frank relaxed a little. It didn't seem as if she were on to him. But she hadn't explained why she was hanging around so late at night, and she hadn't given her name.

"Actually," he said, "I'm a business student. I've got to do this class project on making business more efficient. So I decided to try to figure out how to optimize the run schedules." He grinned again. "Too bad you caught me. I didn't want Gus or Bruce to hear about it. I thought I'd work something out and surprise them."

"Oh, yeah. *Now* I know who you are," Gypsy said, her frown yielding to a smile. "You're the one everybody calls Doc. They say you're real smart—but weird. Always asking questions."

Frank shrugged. "How're you going to find out anything if you don't ask?" he responded offhandedly.

With her green eyes and red hair, Gypsy was really very pretty, in an unconventional way. She held herself with confidence, as if she'd tested herself in some pretty tough situations and had come out on top. But Frank still hadn't found out what she was doing at the office an hour before closing time. Had she been spying on him?

"You must be Gypsy," Frank said. "I thought you worked the day shift."

"I do." She went to the coffeepot and poured herself a cup. "But Gus told me that Bruce was shorthanded, so I asked to work a double shift this week. I need the money."

"Don't you get tired?" Frank said. Working extra shifts—was *that* how she'd gotten the money that had impressed Slim?

"Sometimes," Gypsy said with a shrug, stirring sugar into her coffee. "It's no big deal." Her glance was enigmatic. "That's the thing with you college types."

"Oh, yeah?"

She sipped her coffee. "Always thinking about the way things ought to be, not how they really are." A bitter matter-of-fact tone came into her voice. "You think the people who own this operation will give a hoot about your optimized schedules? Messengers are a dime a dozen—they need more, they hire more. If you don't like pedaling your legs off, you're replaced. This job doesn't come with employee benefits, Doc."

Bruce appeared at the door with a Styrofoam cup of steaming coffee and a paper plate with a wedge of tired-looking pie.

"Phone ring?" he inquired, settling himself in his chair and attacking his pie.

"Nope." Frank waited to see whether Gypsy would inform on him. To his relief, she kept quiet—at least for now.

Frank stretched and hoisted himself stiffly off the desk. His shift was over. He was in good shape, but he'd probably ridden thirty miles that night and his legs were tired. "Guess I'll call it a night," he said, checking his watch. It didn't look like anything was going to develop in the half-hour before closing, and he wanted to drop the film off at a one-hour photo place on his way back to the hotel. There was an all-night developer in Times Square. He looked at Gypsy. "Which way are you going? Want some company?"

She shook her head. "I think I'll hang around," she replied, picking up a newspaper. "Might make a dollar or two." She hesitated, then smiled conspiratorially. "See you later."

"Yeah," Frank said, picking up his messenger bag. He felt a twinge of gratitude for her silence. He would have liked to find out more about Gypsy. But there was no time now. He lifted his hand.

"See you," he said.

*   *   *

The next morning was cool and clear, and Joe's breath came out as a heavy mist as he pedaled back to SpeedWay. He had just finished a series of runs and was already hungry for lunch.

In front of SpeedWay, Slim and Apollo were hunched on the steps. Joe nodded to them and went inside.

A few minutes later, while Joe was pouring himself a cup of coffee, Gus called Lightfoot over for an assignment. Lightfoot listened, nodded, and left. Gus got up, hobbling painfully, and scribbled the trip entry on the dispatch board. Joe squinted, but he couldn't make it out.

Joe made himself wait a full minute before he edged over to Gus's desk. He had to see what was on the board without arousing Gus's suspicions.

"How's business this morning?" he asked casually.

"Still slow," Gus said. The phone rang and he picked it up. "SpeedWay," he barked. He swiveled in his chair, his back to Joe. Quickly, Joe scanned the board, finding Gus's last entry.

There it was. The origin was HQWWT, and the destination was World-Wide's lab, near Wall Street. This could be the break they'd been waiting for!

"Right," Gus said into the phone. "A messenger will be there pronto." He banged down the receiver, scribbled a note and address on a work order, and handed it to Joe. "Rush job," he commanded. "Go!"

Joe started out the door, reading the address. Bad news—it was on the Upper West Side. He couldn't follow Lightfoot. He stood for a second on the front steps.

"Well, brother, this one's all yours," he muttered into his mike.

"What's up?" Frank said in his headset.

"Lightfoot's on his way to World-Wide headquarters," Joe said as he headed for his bike. "He's got a delivery to the lab in Lower Manhattan. Afraid you're on your own. I've got a pickup on the Upper West Side."

"Roger," Frank said. There was a pause. "I've got him on the screen. Oh, and Joe?"

"Yeah?" Joe asked, getting on his bike.

Frank's voice held a note of deep satisfaction. "I've just studied the film I shot last night. It looks good for my theory. I'd bet anything that somewhere along the way, Lightfoot's making a side trip. Even accounting for traffic snarls, his runs are longer than they need to be by about fifteen minutes."

"Right," Joe said, pulling out into the street. "Now all we have to do is catch him in the act."

"Roger," Frank said. "Stay tuned for further developments." Frank waited for a clear spot and eased the van into the morning traffic. He knew that following Lightfoot was going to be tough.

Below the dash, the computer screen glowed green as Lightfoot's blip moved slowly north on the Manhattan grid that he'd overlaid on the screen. It didn't look like Lightfoot was in a hurry. After the pickup, of course, he'd head downtown.

Frank maneuvered the van around a stalled delivery truck, figuring that his best chance was to park the van on Lexington just south of World-Wide and take off ahead of Lightfoot when he came out. If he kept one eye on the screen and stayed *ahead* of Lightfoot's blip, he might have a chance. Frank knew from experience that if he tried to follow, he'd lose him at the first traffic light.

For several minutes, the blip on Frank's screen was stationary in front of World-Wide's office. Then it started to move south. Frank pulled out ahead of it. Lightfoot biked down Lexington for a couple of dozen blocks with Frank a block or two ahead. Another dozen blocks later, Frank slowed and let Lightfoot close on him until he could see him in the rearview mirror.

Suddenly Lightfoot leaned to the left and turned down a side street toward a section of old tenements and run-down brownstones.

"How's it going?" Joe asked through the dashboard speaker. "Has Lightfoot made the hand-over yet?"

"I think it's coming up," Frank said into the

mike. "He's in the East Village, which definitely *isn't* on the route."

Frank glanced to his left. Unfortunately, the cross street coming up was one way to the right. Past the intersection, he edged the van sharply to the left in front of a large delivery truck. The blast of its horn made his ears ring, but he pushed the accelerator to the floor and squealed left around the next corner, keeping one eye on the computer screen.

Lightfoot's blip had slowed. Still with his foot to the floor, Frank made another left and then, a couple of blocks later, a right. As he turned, the blip disappeared in the block just ahead. Frank muttered something unintelligible and slammed his fist on the dash in frustration.

"Say what?" Joe asked. "I didn't copy."

"He's gone," Frank said, looking around. "Disappeared." Except for the garbage truck making its pickups and a late-model cream-colored van nosed into an alley beside a vacant brick building, the street was empty. No signs of Lightfoot.

Suddenly Frank noticed a weak blip. He was almost on top of it. "No, wait," Frank said. "Something's showing on the screen, very faint. He must have taken his bike inside somewhere."

"Stay with it," Joe said encouragingly.

"Yeah," Frank said. He cruised slowly up the block, searching the buildings for any sign of movement. Of course, he could always park on the street and wait for Lightfoot to come out again. But by then the damage would have been done. The *important* character—the guy who was photographing the package—would have gotten away.

And then Frank saw it. A movement between the van and the building, in the alley. He glanced over his right shoulder as he passed it.

He punched the brake, sliding to a stop. "Joe," he shouted. "We finally got a break. Lightfoot just climbed into a van down here—bag, bike, and all. This could be it, brother."

Frank pulled into an empty lot just down the street from where he'd spotted Lightfoot. He backed the Hardys' van behind a dumpster, so it would be less obvious to passing traffic.

"I think we've struck pay dirt," Frank said. "Unless I'm dead wrong, right this minute somebody inside that van is photographing the contents of Lightfoot's package."

"Nice trick," Joe replied. "Now what?"

"No way I can break into that tin can. So I wait," Frank said. "And then I tail." A few minutes later the van went down the street, heading west. "Here we go," Frank said, and eased his van out from behind the dumpster, letting the other van have a half-block lead. From under the seat, he picked up a small pair of binoculars and read the van's license number. He could see the back of a head—Lightfoot?—through the rear window.

Ahead of him, the van turned right. Two blocks later, it double-parked beside the cars that lined the curb, its hazard lights flashing. The back doors opened. Lightfoot stepped out, bike in one hand. In the van, a stocky figure in coveralls pulled the doors closed behind him.

"There's Lightfoot," Frank reported to Joe, as the messenger mounted his bike with a graceful movement and headed out. "Looks like he's on his way to the branch office." The van's hazard lights went off and it pulled into traffic.

"And the van?"

"I'm staying with it," Frank said, making a right turn behind the van. "I've got the license number. I'm going to call Dad and have him check it out. Talk to you later." He switched off the radio and punched the buttons on the van's mobile phone, keeping one eye on the cream-colored vehicle in front of him. He heard the phone in the hotel room ringing.

Without warning there was movement to his right. A large delivery truck pulled out with maddening slowness, blocking his path. Frank leaned on the horn and started to swerve to the left, but a yellow taxi was coming head-on at him in the other lane.

He yanked the wheel back and hit the brakes.

When Fenton Hardy answered the hotel phone he was greeted with the sounds of screeching tires, then a sickening thud.

"Frank?" he yelled into the receiver, but no one answered.

Chapter

8

THE HARDYS' VAN had stopped inches short of the delivery truck. Frank was thrown forward, his stomach slammed against the steering wheel. The blow knocked the wind out of him.

Frank looked up and watched the vehicle ahead of him make a right turn. He could see that the street ahead was clear—the cream-colored van had disappeared.

Frank regained his breath and groaned. "Lost it."

"Frank?" Mr. Hardy demanded. "Is that you?"

"Yeah, it's me," Frank said with a sigh. "Listen, Dad, I need you to check a registration. Late-model cream-colored van. License number ACQ one fifty."

71

"Got it," Mr. Hardy said. "What's the story?"

"I was tailing it just now," Frank said. "A delivery truck cut me off, and I barely avoided a smash-up. Lost the other van." Quickly, he told Fenton about Lightfoot.

"Sounds like a good lead," Mr. Hardy said when he'd heard Frank's story and was reassured that Frank was okay. "I'll call you back as soon as I have a fix on it."

Frank stopped for the light, then turned left. He might as well see if he could pick up Lightfoot's signal again as the messenger returned from the branch office.

Meanwhile, Joe had returned to SpeedWay and asked Gus for the afternoon off. He'd prepared a couple of excuses in case Gus seemed reluctant, but the dispatcher only shrugged.

"Yeah, go on," he growled. "There's plenty who want to work, if you don't." He looked up. "Hey, Gypsy, Hot Dog's cutting out. You're taking his place in the rotation."

Several blocks later, Joe raised Frank on the radio. "I'm headed to World-Wide for a talk with Tiffany," he said. "How'd you make out with the van?"

"Lost it," Frank said disgustedly. "Dad's tracking the license. I'll let you know when I hear. What's your line with Tiffany?"

Joe grinned. "What do you think? I'm going to ask her out. In fact, if she weren't involved in the

72

case, I would have done it already." The truth was, Joe knew, that he liked Tiffany, and it wasn't just because she reminded him of Iola. Tiffany was special in her own way.

"Watch it, Joe," Frank said. "We're not on vacation, you know."

"Well, you know what they say," Joe joked, appreciatively eyeing three pretty girls clustered on the corner. "All work and no play . . ."

"Yeah, well better a dull boy than a dead detective, right, brother?" Joe sobered as he thought of Frank's warning. He did need to be careful here. All signs pointed to the probability that Tiffany was seriously involved in the case.

Tiffany was standing at the counter of the mailroom window, leafing through a stack of invoices. As Joe moved toward her, he noticed that she was surprised to see him, but her smile wasn't forced. It seemed warm and very genuine.

"Hi, Joe," she said. "I wasn't expecting any deliveries this afternoon. Have you got something for us?"

"Well, actually," Joe said, looking down at his fingernails, "I was just passing by on a return run. I thought I'd stop and say hello—thought maybe you'd like to go out for a soda or something."

"Spending your school money?" Tiffany teased with a grin. "You're a nice guy, Joe. I'd love to, but I can't right now. I just got back from an early lunch." A shadow crossed her face. "And my boss—my dad, that is—frowns on long lunches. He's been known to fire people who weren't back in an hour."

Joe grinned. "Such dedication ought to go rewarded," he said promptly. "How about dinner?"

The shadow darkened. "I can't, Joe. I have to work late tonight to get out a mailing." She sighed heavily and Joe leaned forward.

"Troubles?" he asked gently.

"Trouble in big doses," Tiffany said. She half turned away. "But I'm sure you're not interested in family stuff."

Joe reached for her hand. "But I *am* interested," he said. "I'd like to hear what's bothering you." It was true. He *was* genuinely interested. Why did her mouth tighten whenever she talked about her father? Was she angry because he wouldn't give her a better job in the company? Or was there something deeper?

Tiffany looked down at their hands, but she didn't try to pull her fingers away. "It's my father," she said, her voice so low he could hardly hear her. "Sometimes I almost think he hates me!"

Joe blinked. "Hates you? Why?"

"Because of the way I . . ." She paused and then looked up, pulling her hand away. She

74

pushed her hair back from her eyes in a gesture Iola had used. Tears welled up in her eyes. "It's because of the way I look," she said.

"But you're beautiful!" Joe exclaimed disbelievingly. "Why would he be angry about *that?*"

Tiffany blushed and lowered her eyes. "I look like my mother," she explained. "He hates her. He'd do anything to hurt her—anything." She swallowed hard. "She left him two years ago. Sometimes I think he goes out of his way to hurt *me*—like putting me down here all by myself— just to get even with her."

Joe frowned. He was thinking of the Mr. Chilton he had met, tall, suave, stern. Then he looked around at the bare, bleak workroom. Could Tiffany be right?

Or maybe Tiffany's tears were only an act to get his sympathy. There was no way to be sure.

Tiffany straightened her shoulders. "Thanks for listening," she said sheepishly, wiping her eyes with the back of her hand. "I guess I shouldn't have told you, but sometimes I— Well, sometimes it's too much."

Joe nodded sympathetically. Maybe logic worked for Frank, but instinct told Joe where the truth lay. He'd bet his last penny that she wasn't the kind of person to turn to crime for revenge. "Listen, Tiffany, anytime you want to talk, just let me know," he said.

75

Tiffany looked at him. "You really mean that, don't you?" she said.

Joe nodded. Then his eye fell on something sitting on the corner of Tiffany's desk. He leaned over the counter and picked it up. It was a small circuit board, a type he'd never seen before, but there was something about its configuration that . . .

Then it clicked. This was the same circuit board that Frank had shown him on the video last night in the hotel room—the one that had been in the package Tiffany had given him to deliver to MUX! He glanced in the upper corner, and there it was. A tiny rectangular chip with the number Z2713 stamped on it.

"What do you use this gadget for?" Joe asked, trying to make his question sound casual.

Tiffany blinked. "It was on my desk when I came back from lunch," she said. "I thought someone meant for me to ship it to one of the other offices, but no instructions came with it. I—"

The phone on Tiffany's desk rang. She picked it up.

"Mailroom. Tiffany speaking."

For a moment Joe didn't pay any attention to Tiffany's conversation. He was intent on the circuit board in his hand.

Then he became aware that there *wasn't* any telephone conversation. He looked up. Tiffany had gone rigid, her eyes wide, her face drained of color.

"Who are you?" she demanded in a whisper. "Tell me! Who *are* you?"

From where he stood, Joe heard the distinct click that meant the connection had been broken. For a moment more Tiffany stood silent. Then she started to breathe quickly, almost gasping for air.

"What is it, Tiffany?" he asked. "What's wrong?"

Tiffany's eyes were wide with shock. "I don't believe it!" she choked. "I'm being black-mailed!"

Chapter

9

"BLACKMAILED!" JOE BURST out. "Who was that on the phone?"

Tiffany sagged into a chair. "I don't know," she said.

Joe's mind raced, the questions coming fast. First he had to know if he was being set up, or if the call was real. "Was it a man or a woman?" he asked.

"I couldn't tell," Tiffany repeated. "The voice sounded like an echo, like it was in a cave or something." Her voice broke. She looked scared. "Whoever it was said I'm in real big trouble."

"What kind of trouble?" Joe asked. He studied her. He'd *swear* this wasn't an act. She was genuinely frightened.

Tiffany hesitated, as though wondering why she should tell him.

"You need help," Joe said urgently. "I can help you."

Tiffany hesitated. Then she shrugged. "Things can't get any worse," she said. "It's that thing you've got in your hand." She pointed at the circuit board Joe was still holding. "It's top secret. The voice on the phone said that they've been pirating stuff like that. Sending it to the competition—out of *this* mailroom! And if I don't cooperate with them, they'll make it look like I'm the one who's been doing it!"

"What do they want?" Joe asked. "Did they give you any instructions?"

Tiffany buried her face in her hands. "No, nothing," she said. "The voice said there'd be orders for me later."

She dropped her hands and looked up at Joe, tears staining her cheeks. "What am I going to do, Joe? My father will *kill* me if he thinks I've been helping his competition!" She shook her head, dazed. "I can't believe this is happening. Maybe it's some kind of joke."

"I don't think so," Joe told her. He wanted to say more, but he wasn't sure how far he should go. If this was some kind of trap, he could blow their whole investigation by spilling too much. But if the blackmail call *was* genuine, Tiffany needed his help. He had to get some answers, and he had to get them fast.

"Tell you what," Joe said, handing back the circuit board, "do you have someplace to lock this up? Someplace where nobody can get at it?"

"Yes," Tiffany said. "Over there." She indicated a small floor safe.

"Lock it up," Joe instructed her. "I'm going to talk to a friend. Maybe he can help. Give me the number here, and I'll call you later this afternoon." He grinned at her. "In the meantime, stay cool. We'll come out of this okay."

Outside, Joe pulled his headset out of his messenger bag and put it on, trying to look nonchalant. But when he bent over to unlock his bike and speak into his microphone, his voice was urgent. "Frank, do you read me? Frank, come in."

There was a crackle of static. "Roger, copy clear," came the reply. "Got a problem?"

"I need to talk to you and Dad as soon as possible. Where are you?"

"I just tracked Lightfoot on a delivery from World-Wide's Wall Street office up to Midtown," Frank reported. "The run was clean—no sidetrips. I just talked to Dad. He's at World-Wide's testing center. He checked out the van's license plate. It's leased—to MUX."

"How about getting together at Rollo's, up by

Lincoln Center?'' Joe asked. "You know, the sidewalk café?''

"Sounds good," Frank said. "I'll call Dad. Barring traffic problems, we should be able to be there in less than a half-hour."

"Roger," Joe replied. "Out." He coasted his bike out onto the street and merged into the traffic heading west.

As he got to Eighth Avenue, his bike jolted across a manhole cover that hadn't been replaced tightly. Joe looked back to check out his tire, then frowned. A pair of red wires were dangling from behind his seat.

That's weird, he thought. When he'd bought the bike and tried out the headlight, he'd noticed that the wires that led to the generator were blue. He hadn't seen any *red* wires. Joe sat up straight and thrust his fingers under the seat where the wires disappeared. His frown deepened. He could feel a small metal cylinder embedded in something that felt like damp putty.

Just ahead of him, the traffic light turned red, and he realized the purpose of the wires!

Without a second thought, Joe swung his left leg over the handlebars and leapt off the bike. He somersaulted into the crosswalk as his riderless bike rolled to the middle of the intersection, where the traffic had momentarily cleared.

Then a deafening roar echoed through the intersection, and Joe saw his bike disintegrate into shards of metal fragments. He got to his knees and scrambled to the curb, his head spinning. The front wheel of his bike had been blown free and was bouncing across the street. As he watched, it hit the curb and sailed away in a graceful arc.

Dazed as he was, ears still ringing from the explosion, Joe only vaguely noticed the cream-colored van that suddenly sped up and drove through the intersection. Taxis and cars began to edge around the fragments of his bike that lay in the middle of the street. Behind him, a small knot of curious shoppers and pedestrians watched.

A police car screeched to a stop across the street, siren wailing, lights flashing. Spectators on that corner pointed in Joe's direction and the patrol car whipped across the intersection and pulled up a few feet in front of Joe.

Both doors flew open. A tough-looking woman officer with revolver drawn jumped out of the passenger side and crouched down, using the door as a shield. The driver, a burly cop with a .357 Magnum in his fist, stepped to the front of the car. Both guns were leveled directly at Joe.

"Freeze, kid," the male cop snapped. "One move and you're history."

Chapter
10

JOE LOOKED BLANKLY at the cops and guns. "Freeze?" he repeated, dazed. "What for?"

"Don't get cute with us," the officer growled. He pulled Joe's headset off and took him by the arm, dragging him to his feet and pushing him toward the wall of the building on the corner. "Lean into the building, hands up, legs spread."

Joe did as he was ordered while the officer deftly searched him. "What's this all about?" he asked, hoping he could stop the cop before he came to the microphone. "Look, officer, whatever you're thinking, you're wrong. I was just making a run when all of a sudden the bike—"

"Save it," the officer ordered. His fingers closed on the mike taped to Joe's chest. He pulled Joe's shirt open and yanked the mike free. "See

83

this?'' he said, turning to the woman. "This guy's got to be one of the nuts we're after.''

The woman officer snapped a pair of cuffs on Joe's wrists and turned him around.

"But I don't understand," Joe said loudly, wondering if Frank was picking up any of the conversation. "What do you think I've done?''

"Save it," the woman said sharply. "We know you were after the mayor with that bomb on your bike.''

"After the mayor?'' Joe repeated. He wasn't sure he'd heard right.

"Come on," the male officer snapped, "you think we're stupid? The mayor's just down the block, talking to a group of small business owners who are bent out of shape because you messengers keep running down people in front of their shops.''

"And you think," Joe mumbled, "that I was going to ride a bike with a bomb on it into the mayor's meeting?'' He shook his head, trying to clear it.

"You said it," the woman officer said calmly. "We got word that you guys were going to make trouble today. The mike is proof that you're in contact with somebody else.'' She took Joe's arm and began to walk him toward the squad car. "Unless you've got a better story, kid, you're going to the precinct to tell us who masterminded this stunt.''

Joe planted his feet on the pavement. What story could he give them? That he, a seventeen-year-old high school kid, was actually working as a private detective? That he just *happened* to be disguised as a bicycle messenger? What lousy luck.

If they took him down to the station house, he could forget about the next couple of hours—maybe the rest of the day. He couldn't afford the time away from the case. He had to help Tiffany!

"Listen," he said urgently, "I've got to talk to the chief of police."

The woman's mouth dropped open. "To Chief Peterson?" she asked.

The burly cop barked a short, hard laugh. "This one's really a wacko," he said. He gave Joe a push. "Come on, stop stalling."

Joe took a deep breath. It was now or never, he knew. "My name is Joe Hardy," he said, speaking slowly and deliberately. "I'm working as a detective undercover. My brother and I helped Chief Peterson solve that epidemic extortion case last year." If he could talk directly to Samuel Peterson, his father's ex-partner, the chief would get him out of this jam in a hurry.

The burly cop took the woman by the sleeve. "How'd he find out about that extortion scheme?" he asked in a low voice. "They hushed that up tight, didn't they?"

The woman shrugged. "The kid sounds looney-tunes to me, but maybe we'd better check it out, just in case."

The officer pushed Joe toward the car. "Into the backseat," he said roughly.

As Joe got into the car, the woman officer slid into the front seat and picked up the microphone. "This is car seven twenty-one," she said. "We have apprehended a suspect. He says his name is Joe Hardy. Claims to be an undercover agent. Wants to talk to Chief Peterson."

There was a long pause as she listened to the static voice of headquarters.

"No, I'm not crazy," the woman said. There was another burst of static. "Yes, I know. But this kid does have some confidential information about a big case last year. We thought we'd better check it out. I'll stand by."

Joe sat back in the seat, watching through the wire screen that separated the front of the squad car from the rear. The two officers sat in front, talking. Several minutes later the radio crackled into life again.

"Samuel Peterson," a commanding voice said.

The burly officer reached for the mike. "Right, Chief. I mean, sir." He swallowed and his Adam's apple bobbed nervously. "Sorry to bother you, but we've got a kid in custody who claims to know you. His name's Joe Hardy. His bike blew up about a block from the mayor's anti-bike messenger meeting, and he's carrying some kind of transmitter. We think he may have been trying to nail the mayor himself."

There was a pause. "What does this kid look like?" the chief asked.

"Late teens. Six feet, blond hair, football-player type."

"Let me talk to him."

"He can hear you," the officer said, turning to Joe. "We've got him in the back."

"What's your father's name?"

The officer stuck the mike against the screen in front of Joe and pressed the transmit button.

"Fenton Hardy," Joe said loudly. "He was your partner years ago. You worked with us on the epidemic plot last year."

The officers looked at each other.

"Okay, that's good enough for me," the chief said. "He's who he claims to be. And he's clean. Let him go. If he needs any assistance, let him have it."

"But, sir . . ." the officer began, then hesitated.

"Yes, what is it?"

"What do we tell the press? It was a big explosion."

"Don't worry about them. I'll clear it. Oh, and, Joe, when this is over, I want a full report."

Joe leaned forward as the cop held the mike up. "Yes, sir," he said emphatically.

"Peterson out," the chief said.

The officers exchanged glances again. Then the

woman shrugged, got out, opened the back door, and unlocked Joe's handcuffs.

"Sorry," she said gruffly, "but you know how it is. We've had threats on the mayor's life." She reached into the front seat and handed Joe his headset and microphone. "Can we give you a hand?"

"How about a lift up to Lincoln Center?" Joe asked, glancing at the remains of the bike, still in the middle of the intersection. An officer was there now, directing traffic.

"You've got it," the driver said and turned on the flashing light. Carefully, he backed the car around. The traffic officer stopped the cross-street traffic and waved them through. As Joe looked back, he saw an armored truck pull up, and members of the city's bomb disposal squad began to collect the pieces of what had once been his bicycle.

"Hey, that was high drama," Frank said when Joe slid into his seat at one of the outdoor tables in front of Rollo's. "You had us on the edge of our seats for a while. The whole thing sounded like one of those TV cop movies."

"You picked it up?" Joe asked.

"Until the cop pulled off your mike." His father grinned, relieved. "Sounds like you're twice lucky. First, to be alive, and second, not to be in jail. How'd you talk your way out of there?"

The waiter brought cheeseburgers and fries as Joe filled them in on what had happened that afternoon, beginning with the phone call Tiffany had received.

"This is a whole different ball game," Mr. Hardy said, when Joe was finished. "And I'm afraid you're out of it, Joe."

"No way!" Joe shot back. "Tiffany needs my help! I'm not letting her down."

"Look, Joe," Frank said, "your cover's obviously been blown—no pun intended." He reached for the mustard. "While you were talking to Tiffany, somebody was stuffing your bike with plastic explosive."

"Right," Mr. Hardy said. "All of a sudden we're in the big league, and the other team's playing for keeps."

"Well, I'm sure that Tiffany isn't on their team," Joe said flatly. "Nobody's that good an actress. Besides, she didn't know I was coming over, so the blackmail bit wasn't staged." He paused, thinking. "Remember that cream-colored van?"

Frank sighed. "Of course."

"I saw one that matched your description racing through the intersection right after the blast. I'll bet the driver spotted me going into World-Wide, rigged the bomb, and then hung around to watch the fireworks."

There was a long pause at the table. Finally

Fenton Hardy frowned. "If what you say about Tiffany is true," he said, "then she's in as much danger as you."

Joe took a deep breath. His father was right. "I've got to warn her!" he said, pushing away his cheeseburger.

"Is that a good idea?" Frank asked.

"Good idea or not, I'm doing it, anyway," Joe said. He got up, went to a pay phone and, referring to the piece of paper Tiffany had given him, punched the number. The phone at the other end was picked up on the second ring.

"Hello!" Tiffany's voice was shrill, almost out of control.

"Listen, Tiffany, it's Joe." Joe hoped his voice sounded reassuring. "I think we can help."

"Oh, Joe." Tiffany drew in a shuddery breath. "Where are you? I need you—now!"

"What's wrong?"

"That person—the one who phoned earlier—called again. He ordered me to go upstairs to a vacant office and pick up a package. Lightfoot's supposed to come for it."

Joe took a deep breath. Things were happening fast. "Did you get the package?"

"I got it." Tiffany sniffed. It sounded as if she was trying not to cry. "But it wasn't sealed, and I . . . I opened it. It's on my desk right now."

"Good girl!" Joe exclaimed. "What's in it?"

"It looks like a radio, with a lot of knobs and dials and things." She paused. "What'll I do?"

"Wrap it back up," Joe said calmly. "When Lightfoot shows up, give it to him. He'll never get wherever he's going. We'll cut him off."

"We?" Tiffany asked. "We, who?"

"My brother, my father, and I," Joe said. "I don't have time to explain the whole thing right now, but we're working for your father."

"You're working for my *father?* You lousy—"

"It's okay, Tiffany." Joe tried to calm her. "Trust me." He grimaced and held the receiver away from his ear for ten seconds. When her anger died down he spoke again, more seriously. "Listen, as soon as Lightfoot leaves, give me a call." He gave her the number of the van's mobile phone, said goodbye, and rushed back to the table.

"Come on you guys," he said excitedly. "The spy just passed Tiffany a radio unit of some kind. She's supposed to give it to Lightfoot. We've got to intercept him. If we catch him red-handed, maybe we can get him to spill what he knows!"

"Hold on a minute, son," Mr. Hardy said. "You're not leaving here without a better plan. You know how tough it is to tail a bike with a van in traffic."

"Dad's right," Frank said. "Why don't I take my bike and go after him?"

"Okay," Joe said. He reached into his pocket

91

and pulled out one of the two transmitters he had left. "Take this," he said, tossing it to Frank. "I'll track the two of you in the van."

Mr. Hardy stood up. "Mr. Chilton has to be briefed. It's not going to be easy. I'll be at the hotel—keep in touch."

Minutes later Joe was in the van. He switched on the radio, then the computer screen. At that second the mobile phone buzzed.

Joe picked it up. "Tiffany?"

"Yes, Joe. Lightfoot just left with the package."

Joe eyed the green monitor. There was Lightfoot's blip, in front of World-Wide. It started to move, heading north. He checked Frank's blip. He was heading south.

"Good girl, Tiff," Joe said. "We'll get him!" He hung up and pulled out onto the street.

"Joe, do you have anything yet?" It was Frank's voice on the radio.

"Yeah. Tiffany just called. Lightfoot's got the package. His blip's headed north. He's up to Fifty-third now. Maybe you can head him off." He pulled over to the side of the street into a vacant parking place. "I'll hold position here until we see which side of Central Park he takes."

As Joe stared at the screen, he saw Lightfoot's marker moving steadily north. Two blocks later, Lightfoot's marker turned west.

Joe picked up the mike. "Frank, turn north."

"Roger. North it is."

Joe started the van, made a quick left, checked the screen again, and grinned.

Lightfoot was caught right between the two brothers.

Frank scanned the traffic moving west. Sure enough, there was Lightfoot, a half-block ahead. He was pedaling fast, his bulging messenger bag slung over his shoulder. Frank saw the flash of spokes as Lightfoot banked steeply to the right, just in front of him.

"Joe, he's turning into the park—going the wrong way on a one-way drive," Frank said. He strained to see as he followed Lightfoot into the park.

"I'll cut up Central Park West and parallel you," Joe said promptly. "Better save your breath for your footwork."

"Roger," Frank said as he strained to close the gap between Lightfoot and him. There were other bikes now, as well as the usual fast-moving traffic, and once Frank thought he'd lost him. But then he spotted him again, crossing the bridge over Transverse Road. Lightfoot stepped off his bike and disappeared down the embankment on the far side.

Frank slammed on his brakes in the middle of the bridge. "Joe!" he barked. "The bridge over Transverse Drive!" Without waiting to hear Joe's response, he pulled off his headset, leapt off the bike, and ran to the rail. Directly below, he could see Lightfoot scrambling down to the road.

This is it, Frank thought. Without his bike we can't tail him. If I try running down the bank, I'll probably lose him. He backed up a step or two, gauged the angle of Lightfoot's descent, and vaulted far out over the rail.

But the instant he jumped, he saw it.

Nearly hidden beneath the arch of the bridge was the cream-colored van!

Chapter

11

LIGHTFOOT WAS HALFWAY down the brushy slope when Frank crashed heavily onto his back. Lightfoot exploded with a loud *hunh* as the wind was knocked out of him. Frank's arm locked in a stranglehold around his neck. His heavy messenger bag dragging from his shoulders, Lightfoot began to thrash wildly as the pair slid down the steep slope.

At the foot of the slope, almost on the road, Lightfoot landed on his hands and knees. "Get away, man!" he yelled. He gave a mighty heave and threw Frank off.

Frank fell with a thud, and his head whacked against the curb at the edge of the roadway. For a second a starburst of pain hammered at him, and he slumped over, almost blacking out. Head swimming, he rolled over and pushed himself up. He stood, swaying, fighting the blackness that threatened to swallow him.

A couple of yards away Lightfoot was reeling to his feet. He appeared dazed and confused, and an ugly scrape on his forehead was welling blood. He turned, fumbling in his messenger bag as he staggered toward the cream-colored van, still parked under the bridge, two wheels on the curb, its hazard lights flashing, the passengers inside making no move to help.

"I've got it," he shouted frantically. "Open up and let me in! I've got what you want!"

Suddenly the van's rear door opened a crack. Through the door Frank could see a face covered with a navy-blue ski mask—and the wicked-looking muzzle of a silencer. The gun was aimed at Lightfoot!

Lightfoot saw the gun, too. For a split second, he stared at it, body frozen. Then, just as the finger tightened on the trigger, Frank summoned all his strength and launched himself forward.

Frank hit Lightfoot with a flying tackle just above the knees, knocking him out of the line of fire. The two of them landed beside the bridge footing, Frank astride Lightfoot's chest.

Frank heard a *pop!* and flattened himself on top of Lightfoot. An arm's length away a three-inch hole appeared in the ground, the shot kicking damp dirt in their faces.

"Don't shoot, man!" Lightfoot shouted toward the van. He pushed against Frank, trying to shove him off, trying to get up.

Then Frank heard the roar of the van's engine and the gritty spin of tires on gravel. A black cloud of rubber and exhaust fumes billowed out from under the arch as the cream-colored van pulled away, heading west.

Lightfoot collapsed, sobbing with fear and rage. "What're they shooting at me for?" he moaned. "I brought 'em what they wanted."

Before Frank could answer, the Hardys' black van, which had appeared under the bridge and frightened off the gunmen, pulled over across the road. Joe jumped out. Lightfoot, struggling to get up, saw Joe and recognition spread across his face. He stumbled backward, holding up both hands as if to ward off a blow.

"What's going on?" Lightfoot said. Then the realization settled on his face. "The investigation. It was you!" he said as though trying to convince himself it was true.

"You got to listen, Hot Dog," Lightfoot cried pleadingly. "Gus made me do it! I only did what he said so I wouldn't lose my job!"

"Give us the bag," Frank said, advancing menacingly on Lightfoot.

With a grunt, Lightfoot threw the bag on the ground. "Take it, man," he said. "It's yours."

He hesitated, then turned and scrambled up the bank.

"You okay?" Joe asked Frank. "You look a little banged up."

"I'm fine," Frank assured him, handing Joe the bag. "I'll go get the bike."

"What about Lightfoot?" Joe called as Frank ran up the hill to retrieve his bike and the headset he'd pulled off when he jumped.

"Let him go," Frank called over his shoulder. "He's small potatoes. We've got what we want."

When Frank returned, Joe helped him load the bike into the back of the van. "Where to?" he asked, as he slid into the driver's seat.

"South, back to SpeedWay," Frank said, slamming the door. "On the double." As Joe turned on the ignition, he opened Lightfoot's bag and lifted out a wrapped package the size of a loaf of bread. He began tearing at the paper.

Joe slammed the van into gear and whipped it onto the drive directly in front of a yellow taxi. The taxi driver leaned on his horn and shook his fist furiously at Joe. Muttering under his breath, Joe pushed the accelerator to the floor and the van surged ahead, leaving the taxi far behind.

"Did you get a look at the driver of the cream-colored van?" Frank asked, still pulling at the paper.

"Yeah. He was definitely Asian," Joe said.

"He looked a lot like the guy who signed for the package in the phony MUX office."

The light in front of them turned yellow. "Run," Frank commanded brusquely.

Joe floored the accelerator and dodged through an intersection ahead of a bus that was coming from the right. He glanced at Frank. "What's the big hurry to get down to SpeedWay?"

Frank frowned. "There was a character in a ski mask with a silencer in that van," he said, "trying to gun Lightfoot down. Now that their scheme's beginning to unravel, they're probably trying to cover their tracks by eliminating the people who've worked for them." He looked at Joe sideways. "They tried to blow *you* away this afternoon."

"That's right," Joe said, catching on. "And Gus is probably the only one who can identify the spy at World-Wide! So it stands to reason that they'd go after him next!"

At the next stoplight, he picked up the mobile phone, dialed his father, and briefly filled him in, trying to play down the part with the gun so they wouldn't get jerked off the case. "We're headed to SpeedWay now," Joe said. He listened a minute, then nodded. "Yeah, we'll be careful," he said, and hung up.

Frank had the wrapping off now and was staring at an instrument on his lap.

"What is it?" Joe asked.

99

"Some type of receiver," Frank said, studying the instrument carefully. "The reception range appears to be for the bands used in satellite transmission. It may also have an unscrambler."

"You think it could have military applications?" asked Joe.

"That's possible," Frank replied. "Anyway, it's a serious piece of equipment."

They were stalled behind a delivery truck unloading vegetables at a corner grocery. Joe leaned forward and switched on the van's AM radio. An announcer was reading a newscast.

"A New York City neighborhood was rocked this afternoon by a violent explosion," the announcer said. "According to an eyewitness, the bomb planted on a bicycle was set off by a blond young man in his teens, wearing a fatigue jacket. The young man, believed to be a bicycle messenger, was taken into custody by police. An official police spokesperson refused to comment. However, there was speculation that there may be a connection between this incident and the mayor's get-tough stand on bicycle messengers. The mayor is considering a plan for strictly curtailing the use of bicycles by messengers in Midtown Manhattan. In other news . . ."

Joe turned the radio off. "That's all we need," he said disgustedly. "Talk about a cover being blown. Now the whole world knows."

"At least they didn't give your real name or

say they'd turned you loose," Frank said. "That's something." He put the confiscated radio carefully behind the seat. "Let's just hope we can get to Gus before it's too late."

Half a block from SpeedWay, on Front Street, Joe spotted a parking spot. "Let's leg it from here," he said, pulling the van against the curb.

Frank was on Joe's heels as they dashed down the block and through the front door of the dispatch office. Everybody was clustered at the far end of the room, listening to the radio.

Apollo looked up and brightened as he saw Joe. "Hey, here's Hot Dog!" he exclaimed. "So it wasn't you who got blown up, after all!"

"Yeah, it was," Joe said. Bruce was sitting at the dispatcher's desk. "Where's Gus?"

"He's not here," Bruce said.

"Where can we find Gus?" Frank snapped.

Bruce's mouth dropped open as he heard the tone in Frank's voice. "He got a phone call and left. If you hurry, you might be able to catch him in the parking garage down the block." Puzzled, he looked from Frank to Joe. "What's going on here, anyway?"

He received no reply. The brothers turned and dashed out the door and down the street.

"There he goes," Frank cried as they rounded the corner by the parking garage. He pointed at a hobbling figure who was just entering the garage.

Seconds later Frank and Joe were inside the garage, too. But there was no sign of Gus.

"The elevator!" Joe shouted, pointing to a pair of elevator doors in the wall. The numbers above the door were lighting up in succession—1, 2, 3. At the third floor, the elevator stopped.

"Upstairs," Frank yelled, racing to the stairway beside the elevator. "Let's hit it!"

They were almost to the second floor when they heard a heavy door slam and the sounds of a violent struggle. Gus's panicked voice echoed in the concrete stairwell.

"Get away from me! Get your hands off!"

There was a resounding whack that Joe recognized immediately. It was the sound of Gus's cane hitting flesh. Then a thud, and a short, gurgling scream. And then a loud clatter, as Gus's cane slid down the stairs and came to rest on the second-floor landing.

Chapter

12

"COME ON!" FRANK yelled as the door slammed again, the echo reverberating through the stairwell. "We've got to help!"

But they were too late. A limp body tumbled down the stairs, arms and legs windmilling.

It was Gus. He lay at their feet, a bloody gash ripped across his face, one leg twisted grotesquely under him.

He wasn't moving.

Without a second's hesitation, Joe dashed for the third floor landing. As he bolted through the door, he watched as the elevator door slid shut. He ran over and slammed his hand against it in frustration. Over his head, the 2 flashed on.

Joe lunged back through the stairwell door and took the stairs down three or four at a time. On the second-floor landing, Frank was kneeling beside Gus, feeling for a pulse. "Get help!" Frank ordered. Without a word, Joe ran down the stairs.

At the far end of the ground floor opposite the exit, Joe saw a dark figure run through the shadows toward the cream-colored van. The van's door was slammed and its engine roared to life.

Joe started to dash toward it but realized he'd never reach it before it pulled away. He'd be an easy target, silhouetted against the exit. He ducked down behind the cars. Let them come to me, he thought. There's only one way out of this place. He felt in his pocket. Yes, it was there—the last transmitter.

The van charged down the center lane. Just beyond Joe was the exit. The van would have to slow down for the right turn that would take it out onto the street.

As the vehicle surged past him, Joe saw the brake lights come on. Hit 'em low, he thought. That's what his football coach always said. He lunged for the back bumper, catching it with both hands.

As the van skidded around the turn, Joe slammed the transmitter onto the bumper. It clamped fast. Joe released his grip. The van's springs crashed against their stops as the vehicle cleared the exit and disappeared into the street.

Bugging the van was enough for now. With Gus injured they'd have to let the gunmen go for the time being. They could pick up the trail later after Gus was in the hospital.

Painfully, Joe picked himself up. His jeans were dusty and badly scuffed where he'd been dragged. The left arm of his field jacket was ripped and he'd lost a considerable patch of skin on his elbow. Other than that, he didn't feel much worse than he felt after a tough scrimmage.

There was a pay phone near the garage entrance. Joe ran for it and dialed the emergency number.

By the time Joe returned to the second floor, Frank had pulled off his turtleneck sweater and was covering Gus with it. "Is he going to make it?" Joe asked worriedly.

"I don't know," Frank said. "He's unconscious. He's in shock and probably has head injuries." He motioned quickly. "Give me your field jacket. About all I can do here is keep him warm."

Joe pulled off his jacket and tossed it to Frank. He covered Gus with Joe's jacket and checked the pulse in his neck again. It was weak and rapid, and his breathing was shallow and fluttery.

The minutes dragged by while Frank and Joe crouched there, watching the injured man. If Gus died without revealing his contact at World-Wide, they might never get to the bottom of this case.

The Hardys heard the wail of a siren on the street below, then footsteps racing up the stairs.

Two white-jacketed paramedics rounded the landing. They were lugging a first-aid case and a metal gurney.

The paramedics worked on Gus briefly. One of them turned to Frank and Joe, stethoscope in hand.

"This is going to be touch and go," he said. "There may be spinal damage. We slid a backboard under him, but we need your help in loading him. He's got to be perfectly level."

Frank nodded. The four of them knelt beside Gus.

"Ready? On three," the medic said. "One, two, three."

Smoothly, they lifted Gus's motionless body onto the gurney's soft white pad. Quickly, the medics strapped him in. They each grabbed a corner of the metal stretcher and carried Gus down the stairs. On the ground floor, the medics unfolded the undercarriage and wheels and pushed Gus to the waiting ambulance.

"You're welcome to come along," the medic said as they hoisted the gurney through the open back doors and slid it inside.

"Thanks," Frank said. There was a chance—a slim one, but a chance—that Gus might come to and reveal the name of his attacker. Besides, if the assailant found out Gus was still alive, he might try to finish the job. He and Joe climbed in and swung the doors shut behind them. The siren wailed and they were off.

"Ooh." Gus gave a soft moan. Frank was instantly attentive.

"Who did this?" Frank asked urgently. "Who was it, Gus?"

Gus's eyelids fluttered. "Oh, it's you, Doc." He coughed painfully, and his chest heaved. Then his eyes flew wide open. Frank nodded in answer to his unspoken question. "That's right," he said. "I've been on the case from the start. If I were you, I'd talk. We're on the same side now."

"It was a setup," Gus wheezed. "Chung was . . . waiting for me." His eyes fluttered closed again.

"Who's Chung?" Joe demanded. But he got no response. Gus had lapsed into unconsciousness again.

The ambulance pulled up to the emergency room doors. As the Hardys swung the back doors open, several orderlies dashed up, unloaded Gus, and pushed him into the emergency room. The brothers tried to follow the gurney, but a stern-faced orderly blocked their way.

"You'll have to wait here," he said.

"But you don't understand," Joe protested angrily. "He's in danger. Somebody tried to kill him, and they might be back to finish the job."

"Then you'd better alert hospital security,"

the orderly said, indicating the reception desk. "They'll have to handle it."

Frank started to argue, then forced himself to relax. "I guess that's all we can do," he told Joe.

"At least until Dad gets here." Joe frowned. "He still carries some weight with his old buddies in the police department."

"Dad?"

"Sure. I called him right after I called nine one one. He's on his way."

Minutes later, Fenton Hardy entered the emergency room. He listened while his sons recounted the events in the garage. This time there was no way to hide the danger.

"I agree that we need to keep Gus under police protection," he said at last, and went to look for a phone.

At that moment a masked surgeon came down the hall toward them.

"Are you the ones who brought in the patient with the head injury?" he asked, removing his surgical mask.

"We are," Frank said. "How is he?"

"He's in a deep coma," the surgeon said. "I don't expect him to be conscious for several hours—he may never regain consciousness. We're moving him to intensive care. I'm sorry."

As the surgeon left, Mr. Hardy returned from the phone. "We're all set. The police will post a guard outside the room."

"The doctor says that we won't be able to talk with Gus until later," Frank said. His voice was grim. "If at all."

Mr. Hardy nodded. "We've got to meet with Mr. Chilton," he said. "He was at a meeting when I tried to get him earlier, but he ought to be back by now. He needs to know what he's up against."

It was almost nine when the three Hardys were finally walking into the president's office at World-Wide Technologies.

"We've got a serious situation," Mr. Hardy told Mr. Chilton. "Whoever is responsible for stealing your designs has attempted three murders in one afternoon."

Mr. Chilton stared at them in disbelief. "Three?"

"Joe was the first," Mr. Hardy said.

Joe's jaw tightened. "While I was downstairs talking to Tiffany somebody packed my bicycle seat with plastic explosive. It blew up."

"Talking to Tiffany?" Mr. Chilton repeated. "You mean, my daughter? Why?"

The three Hardys looked at one another.

"Well," Frank responded finally, "you remember that prime suspect we didn't want to tell you about? It was Tiffany."

"You mean my *daughter* is involved in this thing?" Mr. Chilton's face was a picture of astonishment and outrage. Was he hurt or angry? Joe couldn't tell.

"Not in the way we thought at first," Frank said. "It turns out that she was framed, and now she's being blackmailed. She helped us intercept another delivery to help get herself off the hook. That's when Lightfoot, one of the messengers, was nearly—"

"Then Tiffany's in danger as well," Mr. Chilton said, looking hard at Frank.

Joe gasped. "Tiffany!" he exclaimed remorsefully. "We were so busy with Lightfoot and Gus that we forgot—"

"She should be at home. Listen, maybe you'd better keep her there for a couple of days until—" Frank started to say.

"No!" Joe broke in. How could he have forgotten? "She said she was going to work late, getting out some kind of mailing."

Without a word, Mr. Chilton punched the speaker button on his phone console, then hit three buttons. The Hardys heard two rings. Then there was a sound like a switch hook being depressed—and then a different ring.

"That's funny," Joe said with a puzzled look. "Sounds like the call's being transferred."

"Dad, I'm sorry about all this. Really I am," they heard Tiffany say at last. Joe leaned closer to the speaker. It was Tiffany's voice, but it sounded flat and distant, as if it were recorded.

Then suddenly another voice came on the line, a flat, mechanical-sounding voice distorted by an echo.

"WWeee haavve yyourr ddaughtterr," the voice said. "Listen closely, Charles Chilton. We're calling the shots from now on. You will stop your investigation—

"Or you will never see Tiffany again—alive!"

Chapter

13

THE CLICK AS the phone was disconnected was momentarily loud in the silence, then it was replaced by the hum of the dial tone. Mr. Chilton switched the speaker off and leaned forward, elbows on his desk, face buried in his hands.

"So now they've got Tiffany," he said in a resigned voice, his shoulders slumped in despair.

Joe rose from his chair and pounded his fist on Mr. Chilton's desk so hard that the pen set rattled. "You can't give in like that!" he said desperately. "We've got to find her!"

Mr. Chilton dropped his hands and looked up. His eyes were haunted. "I'm not giving in," he said. "I know the only way to deal with these people—and to get my daughter back—is to fight. It's just that this thing is all my fault! If I hadn't insisted that she work in the mailroom of my company, and then work late tonight to get that mailing out, she'd be safe at home.''

"You had no way of knowing this would happen," Frank said. "We should have kept you better informed of the situation. It's just that things broke so fast, with Lightfoot and Gus—"

His father looked at him. "It would be a good idea to check on Gus. Now that they've got Tiffany, they won't stop at anything to make sure Gus is taken care of too."

"Gus?" Mr. Chilton asked, looking bewildered. "Lightfoot?"

While Mr. Hardy told Mr. Chilton about the afternoon's events, Frank dialed the hospital. "I need to speak to the nurse in charge of intensive care," he said. A moment later he said, "This is Frank Hardy. I need to know the condition of Gus Ireland, the head injury patient who was admitted late this afternoon."

Seconds later a different voice came on the line, and Frank turned up the speaker phone. "This is Dr. Thompson, the attending physician," the voice said. "Mr. Ireland regained consciousness a few minutes ago, but he's extremely disoriented."

"Has he said anything?" Frank asked urgently.

"He keeps asking for a doctor. I told him I was a doctor, but he just shakes his head and calls, 'Doc, Doc.' "

113

"Doc?" Frank exclaimed. "That's me! I'm on my way!"

Frank hung up the phone and stood up. "I'm going to see what I can find out from Gus."

Mr. Hardy stood up, too. "I'll make a search of this building," he said. "And I'll check the answering machine in the mailroom. Maybe I can figure out which office the recording came from." He turned to Mr. Chilton. "I'll join you back here as soon as I'm finished. If the kidnappers call, you may need help with the negotiating."

Joe closed his eyes. Negotiating! Negotiating for Tiffany's life! The whole thing was unbelievable. He'd just met her. And now her life was in danger. It was too much like Iola.

He jumped up. He couldn't sit there, wondering what was happening to her. It would drive him crazy.

"I'm going to make a sweep of the city in the van," he said. "Maybe I can pick up the transmitter's signal." He brightened. "Maybe the guys in the van have Tiffany!"

"That's a possibility," Mr. Hardy said, looking at both boys. "Good luck—but watch out for yourselves."

Frank arrived by cab at the hospital just before ten. As he was passing through the outer doors of the emergency room wing, he collided with a white-coated doctor hurrying out.

"Excuse me," the man muttered, avoiding Frank's gaze.

Something about the doctor's appearance bothered Frank. He turned back just in time to see the Asian doctor slide into the passenger side of a cream-colored van that had just pulled up at the curb. The van had hardly come to a stop before the engine revved and the vehicle pulled quickly away.

Frank slammed through the door and out to the curb, but he realized that he had no chance of catching the van. He wheeled and dashed back inside and down the hall to the intensive care ward. The officer posted outside the door looked up in surprise.

"Frank Hardy," Frank snapped as the officer stood up. "Come with me."

"Trouble?" the officer asked.

"We'll find out," Frank tossed over his shoulder, striding toward Gus's bed. A nurse was bending over Gus with a stethoscope to his chest. The EKG next to the bed was whining, its display tracing a flat wave.

The nurse hit an alarm button at the head of the bed, and running footsteps sounded down the hall. "I don't know what happened," the nurse said, shaking her head. "The doctor was just here and gave him a sedative to help him relax—"

"What doctor?" Frank demanded.

"It was a Doctor Chung," the officer said. "I

heard them page him to intensive care on the P.A. system, so I let him in."

In helpless frustration, Frank slammed his fist against the head of the bed, looking down at Gus's lined gray face. "It was a fake," he muttered. "They must have tapped into the P.A. system from somewhere outside."

The physician who had worked on Gus in the emergency room burst through the doors. He checked Gus's pulse and shook his head. The nurse pulled the sheet over Gus's face.

Frank took a deep breath and walked out the door. Gus hadn't been the nicest guy, but he didn't deserve to die. Besides, now, with Gus gone, their only hope of finding the criminals—and Tiffany—was the transmitter Joe had attached to the van.

Outside, he pulled his earphones out of his pocket and put them on, lowering his chin to his chest and the mike that was still taped there.

"Joe, do you read me?" he asked.

"Roger, Frank!" Joe's voice was charged with excitement. "I've just located the transmitter," he said. "The signal was weak when I first picked it up, but it looked like it was coming from the area of the hospital, where you are. Have you seen anything of it?"

"I have," Frank said gravely. "Listen, Joe. They got Gus. One of them—an Asian going by the name of Chung—masqueraded as a doctor.

He got past security and gave Gus a shot of something that put him out permanently."

"Nice guys," Joe said, his voice hard. "We've got to get them, Frank, before they do the same to Tiffany."

"Where's the van now?"

"They're driving close to the docks—no, they've stopped near Pier Thirty on the Hudson River." There was a pause.

Frank waited in the cool night air. Somewhere in the distance there was a siren, coming closer, then Joe's voice again, vibrating with suppressed energy. "I've just spotted the van. It's parked beside a warehouse across from Pier Thirty-two. I'm going to check it out."

"Joe," Frank warned, "better wait until I can get there. This is a job for both of us."

Joe chuckled. "What's the matter? Afraid I can't handle this?" Frank heard Joe put down the mike, then open the van door. There was silence for a moment or two, and then an eerie, remote *thunk*.

"Joe?" Frank spoke quickly into the mike. "Joe, what's wrong?"

But there was no response. Frank waited, the uneasiness mounting into fear. Then there was a sharp burst of static in the earphones, and the transmission ceased.

Someone had switched off the set.

Chapter

14

"JOE!"

In the semidarkness, Joe stirred painfully, his head throbbing. What time was it? Where was he?

"Joe?" the voice came again, more urgent this time. It was a girl's voice. The girl was bending over him, and the faint, flowery scent of her perfume washed over him.

"Iola?" Joe said, dazed. He reached up to touch her face. "Iola!"

"No, it's Tiffany," the voice said.

"Tiffany!" Joe shook his head and sat up, relief flooding through him with the discovery that she was still alive. But the relief immediately chilled to icy apprehension. "How long have I been out? Where are we?"

"You've been out for about ten minutes," Tiffany said. Her voice was very small and frightened. "And I don't have any idea where we are. It's a warehouse, somewhere close to a river, I'd guess, from the sound of the boats."

Joe looked at Tiffany. She was sitting on a pile of dirty canvas tarps, her face pale and tear-streaked, her dark hair mussed, the sleeve of her blouse torn. Over her head, a single bare bulb in a porcelain fixture cast a stark light over unpainted cinder-block walls. There was something that looked like a heavy fire door in one wall.

As Joe watched, the door opened, and he saw the cruel, menacing face of the Asian man. The man was carrying an ugly-looking assault rifle, with an overhead gas port, a large curved magazine, a pistol grip, and a folding metal stock and butt-plate. The face vanished, and the door closed.

"Wow," Joe muttered. "I'd hate to meet that character in a dark alley." He felt the bump on the back of his head. "On the other hand, maybe I just did," he reflected, with a forced laugh.

"He's the same one who jumped me in the elevator," Tiffany said. Her voice shook.

"That's some heavy artillery he's carrying," Joe remarked. "It has to be a Kalashnikov—an AK-forty-seven."

"Kalashnikov?" Tiffany repeated doubtfully. "That sounds Russian."

"It is," Joe said. He stood up unsteadily and flexed his stiff muscles. "The Russians have turned out some great weapons. That model is a real beauty. It was designed for Soviet paratroopers." He chuckled grimly. "It's also a favorite of terrorists everywhere."

Her pale face turned even whiter.

"Does that mean that the people who are holding us are *terrorists?*" Tiffany gasped. Then she began to cry soundlessly, her shoulders shaking.

Joe felt a chill. Maybe Tiffany was right. The case that had started out as a simple matter of stealing secrets for profit now seemed to have turned into something much more sinister. Gus dead, Tiffany kidnapped, now both of them held captive—

"Hey," he said gently, kneeling beside her, "that's not going to help." He put a finger under her chin and tipped it up, kissing her pale lips. "We've got to think of a way to get out of here."

"Believe me, I've been thinking," Tiffany said mournfully, gulping back the sobs, "and I can't come up with anything. The door is locked and there's no other way out—except back there." She pointed into the shadows.

Joe rose to his feet and began to look around. Besides the fire door, there was a fold-up garage door at one end of the dark room, but it was tightly locked. In the back of the room, behind a tarp pile, was a heap of junk—including an an-

120

cient pickup truck. The bare bulb overhead was the only light. There was no light switch in view.

"Our friend must be on guard right outside," Joe said, indicating the fire door. He dropped down next to Tiffany again and reached for her hand.

"I wonder where the other one is?" Tiffany asked.

Joe turned to face her. Her eyes were dark wells of fear in the pale ivory of her face. "What other one?"

"There was only one in the elevator," Tiffany said. "He jumped me and took me to a locked, unused office, where another guy was waiting. They made me record a telephone message to my father." She shook her head, looking away. "As if my father cares whether I live or die," she said.

"Hey," Joe said gently, "stop that. He cares."

Tiffany stared at him for a minute and then went on. "The second man was tall and thin. He was wearing coveralls and a ski mask. I got the impression that he was the one in charge. He didn't say anything, though. He just pointed."

Joe frowned. It sounded like the same guy who had taken the shot at Lightfoot and Frank through the rear of the van. "How did they get you out of the building?" he asked Tiffany.

"I don't know," she said. "After I made the telephone tape, they knocked me out with something—something on a pad they held over my

121

mouth and nose." She shuddered. "It smelled awful. I got dizzy, and then I blacked out, and when I woke up, I was here. All alone, for hours and hours, before you came."

Joe put his arm around her shoulders. She buried her face in his shirt and sobbed while he gently stroked her hair. But his mind was rapidly sorting alternatives, as he went through a mental checklist.

"Listen, Tiffany," he said after a minute, "it's going to be tough getting out of here. There aren't any windows we can force. Even if we had the tools to try to get through that concrete-block wall, they'd be bound to hear us. Besides, we don't know what's on the other side." He shook his head. "For the moment, I guess we just sit tight and see what happens."

Tiffany sat up and wiped her eyes. "What if they decide we know too much?" she asked.

"Well, the fact that the key man kept his face covered is a good sign," Joe said, trying to sound confident. "As long as we don't know who he is, he can afford to turn us loose—eventually."

Joe was doing his best to reassure Tiffany, but he wasn't all that confident about their chances. He chewed on his lower lip. He should have waited for Frank before he came barreling in after the crooks. It wouldn't have been so likely that they'd jump *both* of them. He rubbed the back of his head ruefully. He couldn't believe he'd been dumb enough to put his head down to check the transmitter on the van's bumper—*without* looking behind him first. That had made him a sitting duck.

But there wasn't any use sharing his regrets with Tiffany. He had to keep her confidence up, even if his was at a low ebb.

"Don't worry, Tiff," he said quietly. "My brother Frank is on the way. He'll get us out of this."

"How can he?" Tiffany asked. "He doesn't even know where we are."

Joe bent closer, so they wouldn't be overheard, and whispered in her ear, "I radioed him just before they jumped me. They had no way to know I was coming, or that I was in contact with Frank. So it's a safe bet that I was right outside their hideout—here—when it happened."

There was a pause. "I hope you're right," Tiffany said, but she didn't sound very hopeful. She tilted her head to look up at him. "I'm praying these goons don't find out that my dad doesn't care what happens to me. If they do, it'll be too bad for both of us."

"He cares about you," Joe protested, looking down at her. He swallowed. When Tiffany tilted her head that way, she reminded him so much of Iola. "He—felt very much responsible for your kidnapping."

He closed his eyes briefly. When he opened them, Tiffany was regarding him with curiosity.

"Why do you look at me that way?" she asked.

"What—what way?" Joe stammered.

"It's like you know me from somewhere," Tiffany replied. Her voice softened. "And there's so much hurt in your eyes." She paused. "Who's Iola?"

"A girl I was very close to once." He picked up Tiffany's hand and held it. "She's dead now."

"Dead?" Tiffany asked wonderingly. "How did she die?"

"She was killed by a bomb that was meant for me," Joe replied. "She was in my car when it blew up. We never found even a trace of her body. For a long time, I hoped that she was still alive—that somehow the Assassins had her. But I've given up that hope now. I—I guess I'm still trying to come to terms with the fact that she's dead."

"The Assassins?" Tiffany asked. "Who are they?"

"They're a group of international terrorists Frank and I were trying to expose. Our dad is Fenton Hardy, a private investigator. Your father hired him to stop the loss of World-Wide's design secrets."

"So *that's* how you got involved with my father!" Tiffany exclaimed. "Your real name is Joe Hardy?"

Joe grinned a little. "I'm sorry I had to lie to you. Sometimes it's part of the job."

Tiffany smiled back. "I have to admit that I was pretty ticked off at you, Joe Hardy. I felt you were using me for something I didn't understand." She paused and looked down at their hands. "But something about you told me that you were an okay guy. You seemed to really want to help me."

A sharp pang of guilt stung Joe. Help her? Sure! He helped her all right—that was why she was in this mess.

At that moment Joe heard a noise outside the fire door. They both scrambled to their feet, and he instinctively stood in front of Tiffany, shielding her. The door opened slowly. A tall, tight-faced woman in a business suit stepped into the room, and the light from the bare bulb fell across her face. She was smiling slightly, and she had something in her hand, something dark blue.

"Louise Trent!" Tiffany exclaimed, behind Joe's shoulder.

Chung stepped through the doorway behind the electronics designer, his AK-47 carelessly slung over one shoulder, a silenced 9mm Browning automatic in his hand.

Joe looked at the designer uneasily. Something about the situation troubled him. "So," he said, "they got you, too."

Louise Trent's smile widened just a little.

"No," she said, with a hint of wry amusement. "In fact, it's the other way around. You see, *I* have *them*."

"What?" Tiffany gasped, with a sharp intake of breath.

"You didn't guess?" Louise Trent tossed Joe the object she held in her hand. "Actually, *I'm* the one who's running this operation!"

Joe looked down at what he'd caught.

It was a navy-blue ski mask.

Chapter
15

"THAT'S ALL FOR now, Chung," Louise said to her companion. "But you can leave me the Browning." With a cold, hard glance at Joe and Tiffany, Chung handed her the pistol, its bulky silencer pulling the barrel down in her hands. Then he left.

"Chung considers you an annoyance," Louise observed. "He deals with annoyances by eliminating them as soon as possible. As you may have noticed," she added, nodding toward the ski mask, "I tend to agree with him."

"Who is he?" Joe asked.

"Chung Lei," Louise answered. "He's on loan, from some of my business associates. A very interesting fellow, actually. He worked for the American Special Forces in Southeast Asia.

After they pulled out, he looked for other suitable employment. That's when my associates picked him up."

"I'm sure he came highly recommended," Joe said sarcastically.

Louise nodded. "He speaks Chinese better than he speaks English. His specialty was prisoner interrogation." She smiled again, and tossed her head. "I've suggested that he use a more civilized weapon than that assault rifle, but he's stubborn."

"So you use him to tie up your loose ends," Joe said. He frowned thoughtfully. It was important to keep Louise talking. The longer they talked, the better the chance that Frank would find them before . . . He looked away from the Browning that Louise held in her hand. "I still don't understand," he said, "why you got involved in espionage."

"That's right," Tiffany put in. "My father always speaks highly of your work. He says that you're his top designer."

"Talk is cheap," Louise said bitterly. She straightened. "Yes, I *am* one of the best. But I haven't been promoted to a position of any real responsibility."

"So you decided to set up MUX," Joe mused.

"Hardly," Louise remarked. "MUX was well on the way to success in the world market before

I came along. You might say that I just helped them open a new division."

"What *is* MUX?" Tiffany asked.

"So many questions." Louise hesitated. "Oh, well, we have a few minutes to wait. I don't suppose it will hurt to tell you a little more.

"Naturally, your father and my colleagues at World-Wide aren't the only ones who know about my ability. There is a group of—shall we say—international businessmen who are constantly on the lookout for design talent. They snap up new product ideas, once the products are out of the expensive design and development stage. Then they tap the enormous Third-World labor pool. You see, it's a very cost-efficient business strategy."

"You mean," Joe said, "they steal other companys' designs and exploit cheap foreign labor."

" 'Steal' is a relative term," Louise snapped. "What would you call it when Chilton takes my designs without giving me the proper recognition? Isn't that theft?"

Joe decided that he'd pushed the point far enough. "How did you manage to set up your system with SpeedWay?" he asked.

Louise looked pleased with herself. "It was a matter of putting together the right people," she said. "Gus needed money. Lightfoot needed his job. Both of them did what they were told."

"But how did you know who Joe was?" Tiffany asked. "And why did you frame me?"

"Good questions," Louise said approvingly. "Actually, all we knew was that Chilton had ordered an investigation. Gus was suspicious of Joe when he applied—we expected some kind of investigation, and there was something about Joe's attitude. So we decided to test him by arranging the delivery of the prototype board."

"And it worked, too, didn't it?" Joe said in a congratulatory tone. "You not only identified me, but you also identified Frank and my father. And you managed to implicate Tiffany as well, so we'd concentrate on her."

"True." Louise nodded. "But you had already penetrated our spy network. Lightfoot didn't matter, but Gus could identify me, and I wasn't about to be compromised. So he had to be eliminated." She looked at them. "And of course, we have to deal with you two, for the same reason."

Tiffany took Joe's hand. "What are you planning to do with us?" Her voice was quavering and Joe could feel her tremble.

"Why, keep you here until Joe's brother arrives," Louise said, with some surprise. "What did you think we were waiting for?"

Joe tried to grin. "Frank? What makes you think Frank's coming here?" His mouth had suddenly gone dry.

"Joe, Joe," Louise chided softly, shaking her

head. Her voice suddenly got harder. "You don't take me for a fool, do you? Of course I know Frank's coming. You see, we've got a band scanner here at the warehouse. We picked up your transmission to him."

"Uh-oh," Joe said, under his breath.

At that moment there was a low tweet from Louise's wristwatch. "I believe that's Frank now," Louise said. She gestured toward the door with her automatic. "If you'll excuse me—"

When she'd gone, Joe pounded angrily at the cinder-block wall. "We played right into her hands," he said, "just like a bunch of amateurs."

Tiffany came up behind him and put her arms around him. Her voice was soft, comforting. "But you couldn't have known—"

There was a loud scuffling outside, and then the crash of something hard against the steel door and a loud cry. Tiffany screamed and clutched Joe, pressing herself against him.

A split second later, the door swung open. A body was pitched through it and landed, motionless, on the floor at their feet.

It was Frank!

Chapter
16

FRANK LAY ON the floor. He could feel the cement cold and rough against his cheek. Waves of blackness sucked at him like an angry surf as he tried to push himself up. He opened his eyes to see Joe lunge furiously at Chung, standing in the open doorway.

"No, Joe!" Somewhere close to him, a girl screamed. It must be Tiffany, Frank thought blearily. Through the haze, he saw Chung slowly and deliberately raise the muzzle of his assault rifle. Joe froze.

Frank sat up, his face twisting with pain. He raised his fingers to his forehead. A trickle of blood was oozing out of a deep cut.

Louise Trent appeared behind Chung. "I trust there will be no more heroics," she said with a pointed look at Joe. Her eyes were gray and hard. "Now that you're all three here, you won't have long to wait. There's a ship coming in tonight. The captain offers a disposal service for hazardous wastes—at a very reasonable rate."

"Hazardous wastes!" Tiffany whispered. She looked at Joe, her face pale. "She means us!"

Louise chuckled. "Until the ship arrives, I suggest that you simply sit tight and enjoy one another's company. Remember, Chung will be just outside, waiting for any excuse to use his Kalashnikov."

With that, she disappeared. Chung stepped back and the door closed firmly behind him. Frank heard the lock click.

"Are you okay?" Joe asked, kneeling beside his brother.

Frank shook his head, trying to clear it. "Yeah, I guess," he said, feeling like a fool. "But I really blew it this time. I walked right into them."

"You and me both," Joe replied.

Tiffany pulled a tissue out of her pocket and began to blot the trickle of blood on Frank's temple. "This doesn't look bad," she said, "but you've got a huge lump on your head."

"They were waiting for me," Frank said. "I spotted the van, and when I stepped around the corner to check it out—wham!"

"Well, the good news is that there're two of us against two of them," Joe said with a wry grin.

"Three of us," Tiffany corrected him firmly. "I can help, too, you know."

"Okay, okay," Joe said, with a glance at Tiffany. "Three of us. Tiffany, meet my brother, Frank Hardy."

Tiffany smiled and Frank tried to smile back. He could see why Joe was attracted to her. When she looked at Joe, her face softened and there was a light in her eyes. But there wasn't time for that right now.

"The bad news," Frank said wearily, "is that there're three of us against a nine-millimeter Browning automatic and an AK-forty-seven assault rifle."

"Spoilsport," Joe said. "What I want to know is where we are."

"I think we're in a warehouse," Tiffany said. "I got a glimpse of it outside when they opened the door. It looks like this is some kind of storage place inside a bigger building, filled with boxes and things." She looked glum. "So even if we could get out of this room we'd still have to get out of the building."

Somewhere outside the room Frank heard the sound of a big door being raised, and then the noise of a motor. "Sounds like the van," he said. "Maybe they're moving it into the warehouse to hide it."

Joe got up and began to wander restlessly around the room. "Isn't this great?" he said angrily, kicking at the back bumper of the rusty old pickup. "Here we are, in the middle of the biggest city in the country. There must be three or four patrol cars within a quarter of a mile, and we've got no way of letting them know where we are. We've got no way out of here."

"Maybe we do," Frank said, in a low voice. He rubbed his throbbing head, a plan beginning to come to him. "Have you looked under the hood of that junker you're slamming your foot into?"

Joe looked at Frank as if the blow to his head had knocked a couple of screws loose. "Sure, sure," he said sarcastically. "We all hop into this wreck, drive out that back door, and make our escape. Just like in the movies, huh?" His eyes glinted. "You want to drive, or you want me to?"

Frank frowned. "Keep your voice down. Is there anything under that hood?"

Joe looked at Frank. "I believe you're serious," he said.

"Absolutely," Frank replied. "Do you want to see how it feels to be labeled Hazardous Waste?"

Without another word, Joe pushed aside a couple of cardboard boxes full of old auto parts and edged around to the front of the truck's cab. He felt under the grille and found the latch. There was a rusty squeak as he opened the hood. Then he put it down again and made his way back to Frank.

"No go," he reported regretfully. "The block's still there, but the head's gone. That old baby has driven its last mile."

"Are the spark coil and the battery still there?" Frank asked.

Joe looked at Frank, a glimmer of understanding in his eyes. "Yeah, I think so," he said. "Hey, what are you—"

Unsteadily, Frank got up. "Pull them, and as much of the wire harness as you can," he said. He looked up and began to study the roof trusses overhead. "But be quiet. We don't want our friend to crash the party."

"Come on, Tiffany," Joe said, and scrambled back to the truck. He raised the hood and began to poke around. "Why don't you see if you can find some tools?"

Tiffany climbed inside the cab and emerged a minute or two later with a smear of dust on her face. She handed Joe a pair of rusty pliers and a stubby screwdriver.

Frank began to search through the piles of junk as Joe cut loose a section of wire and worked the two ends in the front, over the battery. Then Joe looked up at Frank and shook his head, whispering something to Tiffany and motioning her toward Frank. In a moment, she was at Frank's side.

"Joe says the battery's shot," she whispered.

"He jumped the two posts and there wasn't any spark."

"I was afraid of that," Frank said. He opened another box and began to search through it.

"What are you looking for?" Tiffany asked.

"A good battery," Frank answered, without looking up. "Or a battery charger."

"What does a battery charger look like?" Tiffany asked, picking through another pile of debris.

"It's a box with a gauge on the front, with an electrical cord at the back and two electrical clamps on another cord." He made a lobster-claw gesture with his thumb and fingers. "Like this."

"You mean, like this?" Tiffany asked. She held up a clamp with a red grip in one hand and another with a black grip in the other.

Frank grabbed her and gave her a quick hug. "Good job," he exclaimed.

Joe climbed over the boxes toward them, carrying a black metal cylinder—the spark coil—and several long strands of cable were draped over his shoulder.

"Looks like we're in business," Frank told him, holding up the battery charger. "At least, we are if this thing still works."

"But we don't have time to charge the battery," Joe protested. "Anyway, there's nowhere to plug it in."

"Oh, yes, there is," Frank said, nodding toward the porcelain light fixture in the roof. "And we're not going to charge the battery—we're going to use the charger directly." He pointed to a big empty drum. "Give me a hand."

Together, they very slowly rolled the fifty-five gallon oil drum under the fixture, taking care not to make any noise.

"Cut the plug off the charger and strip the two wires down about an inch," Frank instructed Joe. "I'll tie it in up here."

"What do I do?" Tiffany asked.

"Pray," Frank told her grimly. He climbed up on the barrel and unscrewed the fixture from the junction box, leaving the bulb and the fixture dangling from one black and one white wire. Sitting cross-legged on the floor, Joe had worked the insulation off the charger's power cord. He held up the cord, showing two shiny strands of copper.

"Okay, good," Frank said. "Now connect the charger clamps to the two posts on the spark coil." Still standing on the drum, he took the pliers and stripped off a foot of insulation. He lashed the bare wire to the middle of the coil case, leaving one end dangling free. Then he cut and stripped the loose end and bent it so that it reached within a quarter-inch of the coil's pointed tip.

Tiffany watched wide-eyed. "Would you two

138

guys mind telling me what you're up to?" she asked.

Joe grinned. "I think my brother, world-famous electronics genius, is about to create a new type of transmitter," he said.

Frank ignored Joe's teasing and measured off another piece of wire. "I think this is about the right length," he said. With a click of the pliers he cut the wire.

"Right length for what?" Tiffany persisted.

"To jam every police receiver within a quarter of a mile," he said. He forced the end of the wire into the top of the spark coil. "This is our antenna."

Tiffany stared at him. "Isn't that against the law?" she asked curiously.

"You bet it is," Frank said emphatically. "I'm banking that as soon as we start disrupting their frequency, the dispatchers will train all their radio direction finders on us until they've plotted our position. Then they'll send about nine million cops to come looking for us."

"Marconi would be proud," Joe told him. "*If* it works."

"Hand me that crate," Frank said.

Joe handed him an empty wooden crate, which Frank positioned beside him on top of the drum.

"Okay. Now the charger and the coil." He put both on top of the crate and tested the length of the power cord. It easily reached the light fixture.

"Well, we're almost ready," Frank said, satisfied. He jumped down from the barrel. "But before we get this party going, let's see if we can jam our front door. We don't want any uninvited guests if we can help it."

Together, the three of them searched for odd lengths of wood. Frank found a short triangular piece which he pushed under the door, and Joe stuck a length of two-by-four under the doorknob and wedged another in front of the door.

Frank climbed back up on the barrel. "I'm going to use the bulb as a switch," he said. "So I've got to fire in the charger."

"Won't you get shocked?" Tiffany asked worriedly.

"Not if I'm careful," Frank told her. "But I'll have to do it by touch. Here go the lights." And with that, he unscrewed the bulb. The room went dark.

Tiffany pressed close to Joe. He put his arm around her shoulders.

"I've got the white wire loose and one wire of the power cord connected to it," Frank whispered. "I'm connecting the other end to the fixture now. There! That should do it."

The light flickered back on. The battery charger made a low humming noise, and there was a sharp crackle as a blue spark arced between the tip of the wire and the top of the coil.

"That's it?" Joe asked in disbelief, staring at Frank's crazy-looking rig. "Will it work?"

"It should be working right now," Frank said, with a triumphant smile. "Every police receiver in the neighborhood ought to be getting a nasty blast of static."

Tiffany looked bewildered. "But how does it work?" she asked.

Frank pointed to the light fixture. "That's the power source for the battery charger. The charger's connected to the spark coil, which generates a high voltage charge. We're discharging that high voltage to the coil case. That blue spark creates static in the antenna. And the antenna—I hope—is exactly the right length to broadcast on the police frequencies." He grinned. "Just to be sure they figure it out, we'll send them a little message."

He grabbed the bulb and began turning it in and out. The light flickered on and off: three quick flashes, three slow, three quick. He repeated the sequence once, and then twice.

"What's he doing that for?" Tiffany whispered to Joe.

"That's Morse code for SOS," Joe said. "It's the international distress call."

Minutes passed. Patiently, Frank kept sending the signal, while Joe paced up and down, glancing at his wristwatch and feeling more and more

141

apprehensive. Frank climbed down off the barrel, looking dejected.

"Well, we gave it our best shot," he said.

Joe nodded. "It was a nice try," he replied. "But what do we do now? Start sending smoke signals?"

"Wait!" Tiffany cried. "Listen!"

In the distance, they heard the wail of a police siren. It seemed to be growing louder. Then there was the sound of a second siren, coming from a different direction. Seconds later, a third, much closer.

Tiffany hugged Joe and Frank, jumping up and down. "They're coming!" she whispered.

Frank pushed them back in the corner. "The bad guys will get here first," he said. "Get ready!"

Just then they heard the sound of a key in the door lock. Somebody—Chung?—struggled with the door, pounding on it. Joe's two-by-four bent under the strain, but it held. Then there was a brief silence, broken only by the sound of running feet.

"He's coming around the back," Joe exclaimed. "The fold-up door!"

"Everybody down!" Frank shouted, diving for the floor. Joe pushed Tiffany down and flattened himself beside her.

Seconds later, there was a blast of automatic weapons fire. The thin metal door was stitched with holes from left to right, then from right to left. Bullets and pieces of flying shrapnel ricocheted viciously off the rusty pickup and whizzed over their heads. One hit the single light bulb, and there was a bright blue flash as it exploded into a thousand shards.

Then the room went black.

Chapter
17

THE BURST OF fire stopped. Joe's ears were ringing so loudly that he thought he'd gone deaf. He heard an empty magazine clatter onto the cement floor, then the gun bolt slam shut as a new round was chambered.

The hinges of the door groaned loudly. It lifted with a rusty screech. In the dim light of the warehouse Joe could see Chung in the doorway, his assault rifle leveled on them.

Chung glared ferociously at the remains of their transmitter. With something that sounded like a muttered Chinese curse, he stalked into the room. Still keeping the rifle trained on them, he jerked the wires out of the fixture. Then he kicked over the oil drum. The crate, the coil, and the charger crashed to the floor.

"Hey," Joe said mildly. "That's a great scientific experiment you're fooling with there."

Chung's face twisted. "Out!" he screamed, motioning toward the door with the muzzle of his weapon. "Get out!"

Slowly Joe, Frank, and Tiffany raised their hands and stood up.

"Go! Go! Go quick!" Chung shouted. He grabbed Tiffany and pushed her toward the door and into the larger warehouse area. Joe and Frank followed.

"Looks like he's going to take us through the warehouse and down to the river," Frank whispered to Joe.

"Yeah. Our last little stroll," Joe muttered.

"Get ready," he heard Tiffany whisper.

"Shut up! No talking!" Chung shouted.

At that instant Tiffany let out a scream and started running. "Let's go!" she yelled.

Instantly Chung swung the muzzle of his gun toward Tiffany. His finger tightened on the trigger as he fired. But the burst was short and high, for at that second, a well-placed karate kick from Frank caught him in the chin and the rifle flew out of his hands.

As Chung fell backward, Joe hit him in the gut with a head-first tackle. The wind exploded from him in a loud "oomph," and they crashed to the floor. His head hit the cement with a sickening *thwack*, and he lay motionless.

Joe stood up, not taking his eyes off Chung. Quickly, Frank picked up the assault rifle.

Suddenly there was the pop of a silencer and the hiss of an angry bullet passing inches from Joe's head. He and Frank rolled to cover on the floor. From behind a pile of packing crates, the brothers surveyed the place. They were in a long, narrow building, dimly lit, with boxes stacked high on either side of a wide center aisle. At the far end, a big door had been slid open. Through it Joe could see the lights along an empty pier.

Overhead, Joe heard a whistling whirr. He looked up to see an old long-necked bottle sailing end-over-end across the room. It hit the far wall and shattered, raining fragments of glass behind some cardboard boxes.

"She's back there," Tiffany hissed, from the corner. "Where I threw the bottle."

A bent-over figure ducked cautiously along the wall behind the boxes. Joe noticed the cream-colored van just as the figure reached it.

"The van!" he shouted. "She's getting into the van!"

The engine roared to life. With a screech of tires, the van raced down the center aisle toward the open doors.

Joe grabbed the rifle from Frank and ran into the center aisle with the metal stock tucked under his arm, his right hand on the pistol grip, his left on the front hand guard. He aimed low, just under the fleeing van. "Let's try a warning," he muttered, squeezing the trigger.

Bullets ricocheted from the pavement behind the van. Half a dozen holes spider-webbed the rear windows. The van didn't slow. It was almost to the doorway!

Joe took careful aim at the van's rear right tire and squeezed off a long burst. The tire disintegrated. The van lurched to the right and smashed into a stack of packing crates, splintering them. It careened back to the left and crashed into a huge metal container, where it finally came to a rest.

"Stop!" Louise Trent's voice cried from inside the van as Joe and Frank ran up. "Don't shoot!"

Joe and Frank looked at each other. They remained standing in the center aisle, halfway to the van, Joe's rifle ready in his arms. "Come out with your hands up," Frank called cautiously.

Slowly the driver's door opened. Frank and Joe waited tensely for Louise to climb out and surrender. The silence stretched almost too long to bear, and Joe stepped forward to see what was wrong. That's when Louise Trent stepped out of the van, aiming her Browning at the boys and blasting away.

"Dive!" yelled Joe as they leapt to avoid flying bullets. The warehouse was filled with the sinister pop of the silencer, coming closer to where the boys crouched behind some boxes.

Another pop, then a crash, and from somewhere behind them, Tiffany screamed.

"Tiffany!" Joe yelled, starting to run toward her. Frank went to pull him back—too late. Louise whirled, snapping off two shots to force Joe farther into the open. She grinned coldly, aiming the Browning right between his eyes.

"Say a prayer," she murmured triumphantly. "I'm afraid it'll be your last."

Under the insistent gaze of the Browning, Joe had no choice but to let the rifle clatter to the cement floor. Tiffany sobbed as Louise's finger tightened on the trigger.

"Give me the gun, Louise." Frank calmly walked up to her, his hand held out.

Louise Trent didn't take her eyes off Joe. "Don't be impatient, Frank. You'll get your turn."

She squeezed the trigger. Tiffany screamed. Then—nothing. Nothing but a faint click.

Frank's hand closed on the gun. "It's jammed," he said quietly. "I could see it from across the room." A gleaming brass cartridge was caught in the ejection port, looking like a little stovepipe.

Joe, still half in shock, scooped up his rifle and approached Louise Trent. All arrogance had fled from her now. She trembled like a small, cornered animal.

"Don't shoot," she whispered, letting go of the

Browning. Tears began to stream down her face. "I—I give up!"

Outside, a police car with its roof light flashing skidded to a stop on the pier.

Two days later the three Hardys arrived in the reception room of Chief Peterson's spacious office. Joe wasn't prepared to see the person who was waiting for them. There, seated in an overstuffed chair, looking very uncomfortable, was Lightfoot. He wore a good suit and dark shoes. His shapeless felt hat was nowhere in sight. Behind him stood a security officer.

Lightfoot jumped up when he saw Joe. "Hey man," he said, "do *you* know what I'm doing here?"

"Beats me," Joe said. "I figured you were still on the run." He grinned. "But I'm glad to see you." It was true.

"I turned myself in when I heard about Gus," Lightfoot said. "I had no part in that."

"I know," Joe said.

The intercom buzzed and the chief's secretary looked up. "Chief Peterson will see you now," she said with a smile.

They all filed through the double doors and into the chief's office, with Lightfoot hanging back. Samuel Peterson was seated behind a cluttered desk. Across from him sat Mr. Chilton and Tiffany.

Peterson rose and greeted Mr. Hardy warmly. "Good to see you again, Fenton!"

Then he turned to Frank and Joe. There was a stern look on his face. "I suppose you know that interfering with police communications is a most serious matter."

The two boys nodded.

"That contraption of yours nearly deafened the officers in every unit within half a mile of that warehouse, not to mention all the dispatchers on duty."

They nodded again.

"Do I have your word that you'll never do anything like that again?"

They nodded once more.

"Unless it's a matter of life and death."

The boys grinned.

Tiffany got up and put her hand on Joe's arm. Then she stood up on tiptoe and kissed him quickly on the cheek. Joe grinned in surprise.

"And now you, Mr. Wimberley," the chief said, turning to Lightfoot. "You know the D.A. has considered having you named as an accessory to the crime of industrial espionage."

The black youth looked at the black chief of police. Then he dropped his eyes. "Yes, sir," he said.

"However," Chief Peterson said, "since you turned yourself in, and since you were not entirely a willing participant, I've convinced them to give you another chance. Especially since one of our more upstanding citizens has offered you a job that should keep you out of trouble."

"Who? What job?" Lightfoot asked in obvious surprise.

"Mr. Chilton has an opening in his mailroom," the chief replied, his eyes twinkling. "There's room there for advancement. And with your experience with deliveries, you ought to do fine."

Mr. Chilton looked down at Tiffany, where she stood holding Joe's hand. "Our former mail clerk is being enrolled in our management training program," he said proudly.

Tiffany smiled up at Joe. "I was surprised," she whispered. "We had a good talk last night. He's not so bad, after all!"

Lightfoot was staring unbelievingly at Mr. Chilton. "You're offering me a job?" he asked.

Mr. Chilton nodded.

Lightfoot stepped forward. "All right!" he said. He offered his hand palm up to Mr. Chilton.

Mr. Chilton stared at the outstretched palm for a second. Then, grinning self-consciously, he slapped it. Lightfoot laughed happily and returned the slap.

"I guess that's it for now," Chief Peterson said. "Thank you all very much. And, Fenton, don't wait for another crisis to look me up, okay?"

In the hall outside, the Hardys said goodbye to

151

Lightfoot and wished him luck in his new job. Then Mr. Chilton turned to the two brothers. "Thanks again for your help."

"It's good to have a satisfied client," Joe said. Frank and Mr. Hardy nodded.

"What's going to happen to Louise and Chung?" Tiffany asked.

"Their lawyer is working out a plea bargain with the district attorney. But it will probably be a long time before they're out free," Frank said. "Actually I think they're happy to be safely behind bars."

"What do you mean?" Tiffany asked.

"If they get out any time soon," Mr. Hardy told her, "their associates will probably do the same thing to them that they did to Gus."

"Then MUX is still in business!" Tiffany exclaimed.

Joe frowned. "Yes, they're all safely out of the country right now, and there's no way to get at them. But I have a feeling we'll cross paths with those guys again—some other time, some other place, under a different name."

Tiffany put her arm through his. "Give me a call when it happens," she kidded. "I was kind of getting into this cops-and-robbers stuff."

Her father frowned. "I thought you wanted to be in corporate management."

Joe grinned down at Tiffany. "Well, if corporate management doesn't work out, you could always get a job as a messenger.'' He tossed her the key to Frank's bike lock. "Why don't you practice by delivering us an economy-size pizza?''

Tiffany tossed the key back to him. "Future corporate presidents know how to delegate authority,'' she said firmly.

"Well, Madam President," Joe said as he bowed low, "as long as you have the budget, I'm ready to roll.''

The five of them burst out laughing.

DOUBLE EXPOSURE

Chapter

1

"BACON CHEESEBURGERS—they're the best,"
Joe Hardy said, licking a drop of sauce off his
fingers.

Frank Hardy shook his head at his younger
brother. "I don't see how you can eat that glop,
Joe. Do you have a clue as to what that sauce is
made of?" He pulled his own burger from the
box on the car seat between them. "At least you
know where you stand with a plain burger." He
took a bite.

"Plain is dull," Joe said. "Like bland Mexican
food."

"Plain meat"—Frank took another bite, waving his burger in front of Joe's hungry eyes—
"and a plain bun." After downing the last of it,
he swallowed contentedly and brushed crumbs
off his jeans. "That's how the hamburger was
made to be eaten."

"I'll only agree that it was made to be eaten,"

1

Joe said, leaning over the steering wheel. "Even if this guy never shows up, finding that burger joint made the trip worth it. Let's hit it again tomorrow night."

Frank checked his watch. Their contact was almost half an hour late. "Maybe I'll cook tomorrow night," he said. With their parents away on a fishing trip in Canada, and their Aunt Gertrude off visiting a friend, he and Joe had been eating out—and more often than not, they'd had junk food. Frank was beginning to feel unhealthy and bloated, but his lean, six-foot-one frame didn't show the effects of the past week's "diet." And Joe, though a lot broader than Frank, could hardly be called chunky.

"You? Cook? Please," Joe said, holding his hand over his mouth. "I just ate."

"Very funny," Frank said.

"Why can't Callie come over and cook for us?" Joe teased with a grin. "I think it's the least your girlfriend could do."

"I can't believe you said that, Joe," Frank told him. "Just because Callie's a girl doesn't mean she cooks."

"True," Joe said good-naturedly. "But she *is* a good cook."

"Hopeless," Frank muttered. "I'll throw this stuff out." He picked up the trash and stepped out of the van to look for a basket.

The street was empty and quiet, save for the slap of waves from the nearby bay. Frank shivered involuntarily, wishing that he'd worn something heavier than his windbreaker. The day had been sunny and warm, but fog and clouds had rolled in at dusk and the temperature had dropped.

They were parked in Bayport's old port section. Seventy years ago it had been a thriving waterfront district—but now, many buildings facing the piers were run-down and abandoned, the streets covered with litter, the sidewalks cracked with weeds pushing up through them, the docks themselves silent and bare.

Their father often told them this part of town was dangerous. And it looked it. But because of its reputation no one ventured there after dark, making it a perfect place for a secret meeting. Which is why our contact suggested it, Frank supposed. He caught sight of a dumpster about ten feet behind them and started toward it.

"Hey!" Joe called.

Frank turned at the sound. His brother was leaning out the side of the van, waving frantically. "Someone's coming!"

Frank looked. Sure enough, far up the street, he could see the headlights of a car cutting a dull yellow tunnel through the light fog. He threw up the lid of the dumpster, tossed his trash inside, and dashed back to the van.

"Action at last," Joe said as Frank slid into the passenger seat.

"Don't be so eager," Frank said. "I would

3

have thought that after our last escapade, you might want a bit of a rest."

Joe smiled wickedly. "Not on your life."

Frank shook his head. Both he and Joe had nearly gotten killed in their last case, *Street Spies,* working undercover in New York City. But it hadn't stopped either of them from coming to this meeting. Like it or not, adventure was a way of life for the Hardy brothers.

"What could this guy possibly have that could clear Janosik?" Joe asked. "From what the papers are saying, it's an open-and-shut case."

"Don't believe everything you read," Frank said. Like everyone else, he'd followed the meteoric rise of Alexander Janosik, the Czechoslovakian dissident now living in the United States whom the papers had dubbed "the conscience of the Eastern Bloc countries." Now those same papers were saying Janosik had been paid by the CIA to make trouble for his native land. But Frank was standing by his original opinion of the man.

"You've seen him make those speeches, Joe," Frank said. "Do you think he said those things for money?"

"If it was a lot of money," Joe pointed out.

"Money isn't everything," Frank said. "What I'm wondering is why our contact wants to keep this meeting secret—and why he insisted on seeing Dad alone." The boys had been monitoring their dad's answering machine while he was away and decided this call was urgent and demanded their immediate attention.

"Well, we'll know in a second," Joe said. "Here he comes."

The headlights were inching toward them slowly—maybe ten miles an hour, Frank guessed, although he could barely see the car because of the fog and the glare of the headlights.

"Wow," Joe said, raising a hand to just above his eyes. He wanted to shield them from the glare. "Is that—yeah, it is." He nodded to himself. "A fifty-six Mercedes SL. You don't usually see one of those outside a museum." Joe was always fascinated by cars, especially expensive ones.

"Tinted glass," Frank noticed as the car nosed up next to them on Joe's side. The driver's window slid slowly down—and Frank and Joe found themselves face-to-face with one of the most formidable-looking men they'd ever seen.

Just sitting there, the guy gave off an aura of strength. Joe guessed he had to be over six feet, probably closer to six-six. Of course he could have short legs. But he had to weigh two hundred and fifty, judging by his beefy hands and the way his turtleneck strained across the muscles in his arms. His dark hair was clipped close in a way usually seen at army bases or prisons. But what truly made the man remarkable were his eyes.

His glance flicked over everything, but he seemed to look right through what he saw—as if the Hardys weren't any different from the Dumpster behind them. Those eyes turned people into things.

"Hi," Joe said hesitantly. Could this be their contact?

The man glanced at Joe, then Frank, then half turned his head to the back seat.

"Kids," he said in an accent Frank couldn't place.

The reply from the back seat was muffled, but its meaning was clear. Not even giving the Hardys a second look, the driver slid his window up and the Mercedes pulled away.

The brothers stared at each other. "Wow," Joe said. "Who was that?"

"Well, he wasn't our contact," Frank said, exhaling a breath he hadn't even known he was holding.

"I'm glad," Joe replied. "Talk about creepy."

"You can say that again," Frank said, leaning back. "Still—"

"What was he doing here?" Joe asked, anticipating Frank's question. "I hope we never find out."

Frank grinned and checked his watch again. "I don't think we're going to find out anything tonight. It doesn't look like our mysterious caller is going to show."

"Let's get back home then," Joe said, starting up the van. "We can rent a movie for the VCR, Callie can come over and make us some nachos—" He turned to Frank and smiled. "Just kidding."

Frank shook his head. "Hopeless."

Joe fastened his seat belt and checked the view in the van's mirrors. He reached out the window to adjust the sideview mirror.

A hand grasped his wrist.

"Don't be alarmed." A man had emerged out of the fog, leaning in through Joe's window. The upturned collar of his coat didn't give him much protection from the breeze that had come up. His sandy-colored hair was blowing across his forehead as he stared at Joe with gray, intelligent eyes. "You have blond hair." He spoke quietly, with the slightest trace of an English accent. "You must be Joe Hardy."

The man peered into the van. "And you have dark hair—so you're Frank." He shook his head. "I expected your father."

"He's away and we've been answering his messages," Joe said, his heart still racing from being startled by the man's sudden appearance. "How'd you know who we were?" he demanded.

"I asked Fenton to come, and two young men who resemble him have been parked here for an hour. I can add two and two."

Frank stepped out of the van and crossed around the front of it. Now that he was closer, he saw the man was younger than he'd first thought—twenty-five, maybe twenty-six. Though his manners were formal, there was a sparkle in his eyes as he studied Frank—almost as if he were looking at an old friend, instead of someone he'd just met.

"You said on Dad's machine that you have information that will prove Janosik is being framed," Frank said.

The stranger stared at him silently for a moment. "Yes," he finally said. "I suppose I should trust you, too." He smiled. "After all, we're family."

Frank raised an eyebrow. "What do you mean by that?" he asked. "Who are you?"

"Call me Chris," the man said. "I'm—"

Just then the van, the Hardys, and their contact were bathed in a blinding light.

"What?" The stranger turned, raising an arm to shield his face from the glare.

Blinded himself, Frank heard a car roaring toward them.

"The Mercedes!" Joe yelled.

Whatever it was—it was coming *fast*. It had to be doing sixty, Frank realized.

"What the—" Joe began.

A figure was leaning out the car window. As the Mercedes drove past, Frank saw that the person was holding a gun.

"Duck!" Joe yelled.

Gunshots rang out—a half dozen in quick succession.

Their contact spun around, then collapsed on the street.

Chapter

2

As soon as he heard gunfire, Frank flung himself down and rolled under the van. Another shot rang out, followed by the sound of glass shattering. Then the Mercedes roared past.

"Joe!" Frank yelled, scrambling to his feet.

The window on the driver's side had disintegrated. Joe, who had been looking out at Frank and their contact when the shots were fired, was nowhere to be seen.

Frank's heart was racing. Had his brother been hit? "Joe! You all right?"

Joe's head popped up in the shattered window as he brushed pieces of glass off himself. "I'm fine. But what's—" His words were cut off when he saw the contact sprawled on the ground.

"Oh, no!" Frank knelt beside Chris and reached inside his overcoat to check the wound. He pulled out an oblong plastic box, about the size of a hardcover book. It was completely shat-

9

tered—though it still held the remnants of what had obviously been a videocassette.

Chris's eyes cracked open, and he moaned.

"You are one lucky guy," Frank said, opening Chris's overcoat all the way. The bullet had been deflected by the videocassette and had just creased the inside of his arm. It probably stung like mad—but he was alive. "He's okay!" he called to Joe.

Joe looked down the road. The Mercedes' taillights had been swallowed up by the dark and fog. "Well, I'm going to see if I can catch up with those guys," he said, revving the engine. "Nobody takes potshots at us and gets away with it!"

"Don't be a hero!" Frank yelled after him. "We'll call the police, and—"

He might have saved his voice. Joe had put his foot to the floor, and the van had already disappeared.

"No police," Chris said weakly, grabbing onto Frank's shoulder. His face was white; he was still in shock from the impact of the bullet. "Police—they can't handle—your brother will be killed."

"Take it easy," Frank said. "Joe can take care of himself." But remembering the Mercedes' driver, he had to admit he was a little worried.

Joe wasn't worried—he was mad. That was half the reason he was driving faster than usual down the two-lane winding coast road. The other reason was that there were no exits on the road until the next town. He wanted to get the Mercedes in sight before it turned off.

Swinging out of a sharp curve, he found the Mercedes—parked directly across the road, blocking his path!

Joe slammed on his brakes and the van fishtailed to a screeching stop inches short of a collision.

"Dumb, dumb, dumb," he told himself. "I should have guessed they'd know I'd follow them."

"Out of the van." Joe turned and saw the driver of the Mercedes advancing toward him, holding out a gun aimed directly at him. Out of the car, he looked even bigger than Joe had guessed.

"Now!" The man waved the barrel of his gun.

Joe stepped cautiously out of the van.

"Put your hands behind your back."

He did as he was told, keeping one eye on the man.

"Now," the driver said. "I don't know why you're following us, but I want you to remember one thing—I could have just killed you, very easily." He stared at Joe, his eyes cold and unblinking, seeing through him again. "I want you to remember just how easily."

He walked forward till the barrel was less than an inch from Joe's head. Then he cocked the trigger. "And now I want you to remember how important it is to stay out of other people's affairs, affairs that don't concern you. Will you remember?"

"I have an excellent memory." Joe met the guy's gaze coolly, waiting for an opening, any chance to disarm the man. "I certainly couldn't forget a face like yours, for instance."

The man's eyes narrowed. "I see that you may need a further lesson."

Joe smiled. "You may be right. But who is going to teach me?" He deepened his voice, mimicking the man's accent.

The guy's eyes flashed. "I would be happy to."

Joe nodded toward the gun. "And do you need that to do it?"

Tightening his lips into a straight line, the man rammed his weapon into its shoulder holster.

"Gregor, no!" A small, balding man with wire-rim glasses and a loose-fitting suit burst from the back of the Mercedes. "I forbid it," he said, stepping toward them. "We cannot afford to—"

"Security is my department, Doctor," the man-mountain said. "Besides, this will only take a moment." He turned back to Joe. "Now," he said, balling his hands into fists. "Let's begin your lesson, shall we?"

Joe feinted quickly, then stepped back. He was pleased he'd gotten the driver—Gregor, that was what the other man had called him—to put away his gun. Now if he could just hold them there till Frank came with the police—

"Don't run away, my friend," Gregor said, moving toward him again. "How can I give you your lesson if you run away?" He took a half-hearted swing at Joe, trying to draw him closer.

He's big, all right, Joe thought, but he doesn't seem fast. Joe usually depended on his strength, not his speed, but Gregor was so much bigger than he was that Joe would have to use whatever advantages he had.

Seeing an opening, Joe darted left, tagging Gregor in the stomach with a hard right. Perfect!

But Gregor just stood there, smiling. "That is your best punch?"

Joe had a sudden sinking feeling in his stomach. That punch would have had anybody else doubled over, gasping for breath. Gregor didn't seem affected by it at all.

"Now let me show you my best," Gregor said. With that, he swung—much faster than he'd moved before, much faster than Joe would have believed possible for a man his size. He caught Joe square on the jaw. The force of the blow spun Joe around, and he pitched face forward onto the ground. He lay there, stunned.

Gregor stood over Joe, hands on his hips, staring down. "You are strong," he said. "But it seems you cannot take a punch. Perhaps you will need lessons in that as well."

Joe struggled to his hands and knees, trying to

clear his head. Suckered, he thought. He shouldn't have assumed that Gregor was slow just because he was big.

Gregor grabbed him by the neck of his sweatshirt and hauled him to his feet.

"Let us finish this lesson first, though," he said, drawing back his arm.

Joe saw Gregor's fist, about the size of the moon, hurtling toward him till it filled his field of vision.

Then the world went black.

Someone was shaking his shoulder.

"Joe! Wake up!" It was a woman's voice. It must be his mother, trying to wake him up.

"I don't think I can go to school today, Mom," Joe mumbled. "I have a terrible headache." He turned onto his side. His mattress felt awfully hard. "Maybe I should go back to sleep."

"Do that, and you're likely to get run over." That was his brother's voice. "Frank?" Joe asked out loud. He opened his eyes.

He was lying by the side of the road. Frank was kneeling on one side of him, and Callie Shaw on the other.

"Oh, yeah," Joe said, rubbing his jaw. "Now I remember."

"Are you okay? What happened?" Frank asked, helping him sit up.

"The driver of that Mercedes had a hard right.

That's what happened." He looked at Callie. "How'd you get here?"

"He wouldn't let me call the police." Frank nodded toward Callie's car, which was parked by the side of the road. Chris sat in the back seat. "He said he'd tell us everything he knew, as long as we didn't bring the cops in. I asked Callie to come and get us, and we went looking for you."

Joe shook his head, trying to clear his thoughts.

"Did you get a license number?" Frank asked.

"No, it all happened too fast. But that shouldn't matter—that guy in the back of Callie's car has to know who they were." Joe wobbled to his feet.

"Take it easy, Joe," Frank said. "Give him a chance to catch his breath before you start interrogating him."

Joe waved his brother's concerns aside. "Relax—I have just a few simple questions for him."

He walked over to Callie's car. Chris looked up at him through the window.

Joe slammed his hand on the roof—hard. "All right, friend," he said, glaring at Chris. "Start talking. Who were those two guys in the Mercedes—the little man with the glasses and his king-size friend. And why were they shooting at you?"

"Easy, Joe," Frank said, laying a hand on his brother's arm. "He's hurt."

Chris climbed out of the car, rubbing a hand over his face. "I never meant for anyone to be hurt—especially you two." He set his jaw, and a muscle just above the bone moved in and out. "It's too dangerous—I should never have come here. I can't—I *won't* tell you who they are. They'll kill you!"

"They may do that, anyway," Frank pointed out. He laid a hand gently on Chris's shoulder. "You have to tell us who those men were."

Chris sighed and leaned back against Callie's car. He seemed to be deep in thought.

"All right," he said slowly, reluctantly. "Those men—I used to work with them. The man with the glasses is Dr. Finn Liehm. A scientist—and very brilliant."

"And the other?" Joe asked.

"That must have been Gregor Krc." He pronounced it *Kirk*. "They are both members of the Czechoslovakian secret police—what is called the STB."

"The STB," Joe said, smacking his fist into the palm of his hand. That explained the man's training at least. "But what're they doing here?"

"I think I can guess," Frank said. "It's something to do with Alexander Janosik, isn't it?"

Chris nodded but said nothing.

"Why'd you call our father for help? Who are you?" Frank said.

"Who am I?" Chris said slowly. He looked up and met Frank's questioning gaze. "My name is Chris Hardy."

Frank and Joe looked at each other. "Chris

Hardy?'' Frank asked. Joe just stared at him. ''Is that what you meant before—about us all being family? Are you related to us?''

''To your family—to you two especially,'' Chris said. ''You see, I'm your brother.''

Chapter
3

FRANK STARED at the computer screen in stunned silence. "I don't believe it," he said, shaking his head. "I just don't believe it."

He leaned back in his chair and rubbed his eyes. He'd been up since six that morning, trying to make sense of Chris's story. Now it was almost ten o'clock, and the only way things did make sense seemed as impossible now as it had the past night.

"Our long-lost brother," Joe had said when Chris first made his incredible claim, unable to keep the sarcasm out of his voice. "Come to claim the family fortune, I suppose?"

But Chris had ignored Joe's mocking comment and hadn't backed down. Without a word, he'd handed Joe his driver's license.

It was for one Chris Hardy, of 112 Smith Street, Northampton, Massachusetts. According to the license, Chris was twenty-six years old, stood

5'10" tall, and weighed 165 pounds. He had light brown hair and brown eyes. It was all there in living color in a smiling photo.

"So what if you have a license?" Joe asked, after they'd driven back to the Hardys' house and were standing on the walk before going in. "Do you really expect us to believe that you're our brother? I mean, why would our parents keep a secret like that?"

"I see they remodeled the front porch," Chris said, looking at the house.

Joe's mouth dropped open.

"How'd you know that?"

Chris smiled sadly. "I used to live here, too, you know." Then he'd reached into his wallet and handed Joe a yellowed, square snapshot—a shape not printed anymore. It was a picture of a young couple and a boy of not more than five or six, standing together on the Hardys' front porch—before it had been redone.

Frank had peered over his brother's shoulder to get a closer look. He recognized the couple immediately. Although they were a lot younger than he could remember ever seeing them, Frank knew it was a picture of his parents. And the boy? Although Frank couldn't swear to it, he did look a lot like Chris would have at that age.

"Photos can be faked," Joe had said. Of course, he was right. But after Callie had left, Chris told Frank and Joe things about their parents and relatives that he couldn't possibly have known, unless . . .

Unless he really was their brother.

He knew about Aunt Gertrude's secret passion of reading old mystery novels.

"And I'll bet she really loves this, too," Chris had said, pointing to the Hardys' VCR. "She can watch spy movies whenever she wants to now, right?"

Frank had smiled at that—Aunt Gertrude loved nothing better than to settle back in the couch, shut out the lights, close the door, and put a movie on the VCR. In fact, the more he talked to Chris and watched him walk around his house, the more he liked him.

Especially when he'd proven to be a computer buff as well.

"Nice," Chris had said, studying Frank's system. "Small, but very well thought out." Then he smiled. "I've got a different setup—a lot bigger. You're more than welcome to have a look at it."

"I'd like that," Frank said, smiling slowly.

"I'd like it better if you answered some of our questions now," Joe said, cutting in. "Like—"

"Can't they wait until morning?" Chris asked. "It's past two now."

Frank had been shocked to discover Chris was right—the time had passed very quickly. They'd all gone to bed, putting Chris in the guest room upstairs. Yet even though he liked Chris, Frank still didn't believe his story. So he'd gotten up early this morning, and, using access codes a hacker friend had given him, he'd logged on to the Bayport City Hall computer. He had expected the records to prove, beyond a shadow of a doubt, that Chris's story was false.

He'd gotten the surprise of his life.

Chris Hardy was real. But Frank couldn't call his mom and dad to verify it—they were deep in the wilderness.

"I don't believe it," Frank said again, shaking his head at the computer screen. "I just don't believe it."

He was looking at a notice of birth for one Christopher Edward Hardy, parents Fenton and Laura.

Frank pulled Chris's social security number and found a grade-school transcript for him—from the same school that both he and Joe had gone to. Chris had gone there until he was six and a half years old, at which point all trace of him disappeared.

About the time I was born, Frank realized.

He picked up Chris's driver's license for the umpteenth time and stared at it. All the details matched their contact perfectly. If it was a forgery, Frank had to admit it was the best he'd ever seen.

At eight-thirty this morning he'd even asked a contact of his at the Department of Motor Vehicles to check out the Massachusetts license.

21

She'd called back an hour later to verify that it was real.

He put the license down. None of this made any sense. He was getting a headache. And he was getting hungry.

The doorbell rang. It was Callie.

"Morning." Frank gave her a quick kiss at the doorway. "You look wide-awake and ready to face the day." She was wearing a pair of khakis and a bright green sweater underneath her jacket.

Callie looked him over and shook her head. "I hate to say what you look like."

"That bad, huh?" Frank tried to stifle a yawn. "I've been awake for a while—checking up on my new brother."

"Oh, Frank, come on," Callie said, hanging up her coat. "You don't really think—"

"Hey, what's all the racket?" Joe stood at the top of the stairs in his gym shorts and T-shirt, his wavy hair tousled into curls from sleep. "Don't you know there are people trying to sleep up here?"

"You're right—we'll try and keep it down," Frank said. "Chris's first night back home should be a restful one."

Joe and Callie both looked at him as if he'd gone crazy.

"What have you found out, Frank?" Callie asked.

He yawned again and stretched. "I'll explain over breakfast."

22

Joe came downstairs then and somehow convinced Callie to cook.

"Well, I'm still not ready to accept him into the family," Joe said, swirling his pancakes in a small stream of syrup.

Callie nodded. "Neither am I." She was sitting next to Frank on one side of the breakfast table, with Joe directly across from them.

"And I don't understand why you let him stay here last night instead of going to the cops," she continued. "You don't know anything about him."

"He knows a lot about us." Frank put his elbows on the table and rested his chin on his hands.

"Too much, I say." Joe grabbed the last of the pancakes off the platter set between them on the table. "Look, Frank—instead of proving who he isn't, let's just find out who he is."

"Has he told you anything else—about himself, his connection with those guys in the Mercedes, with Janosik?" Callie asked.

"We didn't find out much more about his connections with anyone. We got a little sidetracked last night with family history," Frank admitted.

"Well, I think it's time we got back on track," Joe said. "I owe that driver a thing or two—and they owe us for one new window on the van!" He carried his dishes to the sink. "I'll get dressed, and then we can have a little brotherly chat with our visitor." He smiled at Callie. "Thanks for the breakfast, Callie. You're a great cook."

Frank shook his head. How Joe had managed to talk Callie into making breakfast . . .

Callie turned and punched him playfully on the arm. "How come you never say anything nice about my cooking, Frank?"

Joe winked at him.

Maybe Chris *will* turn out to be my brother, Frank thought, watching Joe head for his bedroom. It's about time for a new one.

When Joe came back downstairs, he found Frank, Callie, and their friend Phil Cohen huddled around the breakfast table. The dishes had been cleared and put away, and what remained of the videocassette Frank had taken out of Chris's jacket the night before was spread across the table.

"The tape itself looks fine—all I have to do is splice it back together and put it in a new case," Phil was saying. He was slightly built with longish, dark curly hair and quick, deft hands. Phil was also Bayport's resident electronics genius. "Then it should be as good as new."

"We'll be really interested to see what's on it," Frank said.

"You think it might prove Janosik's innocence?" Callie asked.

"I hope so."

"Maybe it's an old home movie," Joe said, breaking into their conversation. "Hey, Phil."

24

"Hey, Joe," Phil returned the greeting. He swept up the pieces of the videocassette into a small case he'd brought with him. "Heard you had a little excitement last night."

Joe smiled. "A little," he said.

"So when do I get to meet this new brother of yours?"

Frank stood. "You'd both better let Joe and me talk to him first. He may be a little nervous."

The two brothers went upstairs to the guest room. "I don't care how nervous he is," Joe said, knocking heavily on the door. "We need to start getting some answers."

There was no answer from inside.

"Chris? You in there?" Frank called.

He turned the knob slowly. The door swung open.

"I don't believe it," Frank groaned.

Joe slammed his hand against the wall.

The blankets lay on the floor. The sheets had been rolled tight and tied together. One end was knotted around the bedpost. The other hung out of sight—out the window.

Chris was gone.

Chapter

4

"SO MUCH FOR ANSWERING all our questions in the morning," Frank said, surveying the room.

Callie and Phil joined them after hearing Joe's outburst. "So what are you going to do now?" Callie asked. Frank pulled the sheets back into the room, untied them, and bundled them up in his arms.

"I think Joe had the right idea before," he said, leading them all downstairs and dropping the sheets in the laundry. "Find out who Chris really is."

"And how are we going to do that? We still don't know anything about him!" Joe protested.

"We do know one thing—where he lives."

"Right—if the address on his license isn't a fake," Phil pointed out.

"We can check with the phone company to see if he's listed there," Callie said. She picked up the phone.

"You could also try to find out more about Krc and Liehm," Phil suggested. "Maybe the Czech embassy knows something about them."

"About the STB?" Joe shook his head. "Not very likely."

"And they wouldn't tell us if they did," Frank said. "Especially if those two are involved in a plot to smear Janosik."

Callie hung up the phone. "There is someone named Hardy in Northampton on Smith Street," she said. "But the number's unlisted."

"Which leaves us with only one way to find out if it's Chris," Frank said. He turned to Joe. "Can we take the van?"

Joe frowned. "I had to take the window on the driver's side off completely."

"You'd better get it replaced if we're going to drive all the way to Massachusetts," Callie said. "The weather report said it might rain."

"What do you mean, 'we'?" Joe asked. "This case may be too dangerous for you."

Frank nodded. "I'm afraid Joe's right, Callie."

Callie glared at both of them. "Forget what I said about getting that window replaced. You're both all wet already!"

"Ouch," Joe said, shaking his head. "I'll check the repair shops."

It took them almost an hour to find a shop that could replace the window, and another five hours of steady driving before they reached the out-

27

skirts of Northampton. They had stayed off the big interstate highways and stuck to smaller roads, which made for a more scenic drive if a longer one. By the time they drove into North-ampton, both of them were anxious to get out and stretch.

"Hey," Joe said, pointing ahead. A huge shop-ping mall sprawled on both sides of the road. "Let's stop and get something to eat before we look for Chris."

Frank yawned. His lack of sleep was beginning to catch up to him. "I guess I could use a cup of coffee."

They locked the van and entered the mall.

"All right!" Joe pointed to a sign ahead that said, "Humongous Hamburgers." He grinned. "I see what I want!"

"You go ahead," Frank said, catching sight of a coffee shop. "I'll meet you back here."

He strolled over and stood in the entrance for a moment. The coffee shop was empty, except for a waitress who sat on a stool at the far end of the counter. Her back to the door, she was count-ing out change and watching a small black-and-white television set.

Frank walked in. "Excuse me," he called.

The clatter of a fresh handful of change from her apron drowned out his voice.

Frank walked toward the counter. He was about to tap her on the shoulder when he noticed a newspaper lying in the last booth. It was a

Boston paper—the *Tribune*—and it was opened to the international page. The headline had caught Frank's eye: "Bum Czech?" The byline was Jean Eykis's. He read on.

"Alexander Janosik, the noted Czechoslovakian dissident, will deliver the keynote address at a special Harvard symposium on Saturday. Janosik, whose vigorous opposition to the repressive policies of the Czech government has made him a hero here and in Europe, has recently been accused of accepting money from the CIA in exchange for his anti-Czech speeches. Exclusive sources have promised to provide this reporter with proof of Janosik's guilt before he addresses the symposium on Saturday."

The waitress looked up. "Sorry, hon, I didn't see you there. Did you want something?"

"Never mind," Frank said, bolting out the door.

He found Joe talking to a tall, pretty, dark-haired girl outside the hamburger shop.

"I don't get up here too often," Joe was saying, "but maybe if you give me your number, we could—"

The girl laughed.

"Excuse me," Frank said. He grabbed Joe by the arm. "We're leaving."

"Hey, wait a minute," Joe said, trying to plant his feet. "What's the big rush?"

"Duty calls," Frank said.

"You'll have to excuse my brother," Joe said. "But look, if you're ever in Bayport—"

"I'll know who to avoid," she said, turning around and flouncing off.

Joe watched her walk off and sighed heavily. "You're ruining my life, Frank."

Frank ignored Joe's comment and told him what he'd just read.

"But Chris promised us that Janosik was being framed." Joe shook his head. "Where is this reporter going to get proof of his guilt? From Liehm and Krc?"

"Maybe," Frank said. "What we need right now is information. Let's try Chris first. Come on."

"Smith Street," Joe said, turning off the main road onto a quiet, residential block. The houses lining the street were old and small, but they looked well kept. Children were playing in one of the front yards.

"A nice enough neighborhood," Frank said. "There's number one-twelve." He pointed to a brick house with a postage-stamp garden about halfway down the block on the right side.

They drove past it slowly. "That's the one," Frank said. "The mailbox says C. Hardy."

"Our first lucky break," said Joe, parking the van. "Let's see if he's home."

They crossed the lawn to the front door, and

Joe rang the bell. Frank peered in through the front window. "I don't see anyone," he said.

"And nobody's answering the bell." Joe pushed the buzzer again and then pressed his ear against the door. "I can't hear anything, either. It must be broken." He knocked heavily on the front door—and it swung open.

Frank knelt down beside the door and examined it. "The lock's been smashed."

Joe stepped past him into the house. He groped around for a light switch, found one, and flipped it on. Frank heard him breathe in sharply. "That's not all that's been smashed around here. Take a look at this!"

Frank followed him in. They stood in a small entranceway. Directly ahead of them was a staircase. To their right was the living room, which now looked like a disaster area.

Furniture had been overturned and thrown around the room, papers and books strewn across the floor, and the carpet had been ripped up from the floor in several spots.

"Wow," Joe said quietly. "Someone wanted something pretty bad."

"Here's something they didn't want—something that proves this is Chris's place, anyway," Frank whispered, picking a picture up off the floor and showing it to Joe. It was the same photo Chris had shown them last night, the picture of himself and their parents.

Joe tapped Frank on the shoulder and pointed

down the hall under the staircase. A light shone from beneath a door at the end of the hallway. "I think somebody's in there!" he mouthed.

They tiptoed down the hall runner, and Frank put an ear to the door.

"Someone's in there, all right," he said directly into Joe's ear. "I can hear papers rustling."

"What are we waiting for, then?" Joe whispered back. "Maybe it's Chris."

"It's probably whoever wrecked the house," Frank replied. "Let's do this carefully. We'll go in one at a time."

Joe nodded. Without waiting for Frank, he burst into the room.

Someone was standing in front of a desk with his back to the doorway, going through some papers. He turned when he heard Joe enter.

"You!" the man said, looking astonished.

Joe was almost as startled as he was. It was the guy from the back seat of the Mercedes.

"You know him, Joe?" Frank asked, stepping in behind his brother.

The man reached into his jacket, yanked out an automatic, and pointed it at the Hardys. "I don't know what you two are doing here, but I will most certainly call the police if—"

"Good idea," Joe said, stepping to the left side of him. Frank moved to the right, circling the man. They both began to move closer.

"Yes, why don't you?" Frank chimed in. The

man's gaze darted back and forth between them.

"Stay where you are, or I'll shoot!" he said nervously.

Joe smiled at him. "Just take it easy, Doctor," he said soothingly. "No one's going to shoot anyone. Why don't you just put the gun down, and—"

In one swift motion, Frank's foot lashed out, striking the man's hand. The gun went skittering under the desk.

"Now," Joe said, putting a hand on the man's chest and pushing him back until he sat in the desk chair. "This is the guy who was in the back seat of the Mercedes," he said to Frank. "The driver called him Doctor—Doctor Liehm, Chris said."

Frank stared down at the man. "Maybe you can help us by answering a few questions."

"There is nothing I can tell you," Liehm said.

"Would you rather that *we* call the police?" Frank asked. "I'm sure they'd be interested in talking to you about that mess out there and the broken lock, to say nothing of the shooting last night, and—"

A wide smile spread across the doctor's face. "Talk to *him*," he said, lifting his chin and looking behind the Hardys.

Joe turned and saw Gregor filling the doorway behind them.

"Perhaps I can help you find what you're looking for," he said, advancing on the brothers.

Chapter
5

AS FRANK TURNED to face Gregor, Liehm grabbed the phone from the desk and slammed him over the head with the handset. Frank dropped to his knees.

"Frank!" Joe cried out. He turned on the doctor, who shrank back into the corner, then back toward Gregor.

Gregor raised his fists. "This time, I will make sure you do not wake up."

Gregor feinted with his left, then threw a hard right at Joe, but now Joe knew how fast he was. He dodged back and to the right, letting his left leg follow through and slam Gregor in the side. The man grunted in surprise and pain.

Joe followed with a hard right that caught Gregor full in the face. Blood begin trickling from Gregor's nose. Joe stepped back.

Out of the corner of his eye, he saw Frank struggling to his feet.

Gregor wiped his face and saw the blood on his hand. He looked at Joe with equal amounts of amazement and fury. "No one ever—" he began, his teeth clenched. "For this, you will die!"

"No, Gregor!" Joe turned to see Liehm had retrieved his gun and was holding it on both him and Frank. "Enough—the last thing we need is another murder."

Gregor ignored him. "They know too much," he said, advancing on Joe. "We must make sure they tell none of it—ever."

"Stop!" Liehm pleaded, gesturing wildly with his gun. For a minute Joe thought he might shoot Gregor. "You'll ruin the entire plan!"

Gregor halted and was silent for a moment, as he considered what Liehm had said. Finally he spoke. "All right, Doctor. We do not kill them—this time."

Joe helped Frank to his feet. He could see his brother was still dazed.

"But we will have to ensure they do not follow us," Gregor said, assuming control of the situation again. "There is no evidence here of our presence?" he asked.

"None," Liehm said.

"Good. Hand me the gun, please."

Liehm did so, slowly and uncertainly. He was terrified of what Gregor might do, Joe realized.

"Good," Gregor said, smiling. "Now—there is some rope in the kitchen. Please bring it to me."

Liehm seemed about to protest, then marched off.

"You get along well with everybody, don't you?" Joe asked.

Gregor ignored the taunt. "A very messy weapon, a gun," Gregor said, studying the barrel. "I usually prefer other ways of dealing with my problems." He smiled, revealing large white, even teeth. But the glint in his eye made him look anything but friendly. "I promise you this, though: if I see you again, I will not hesitate to use this gun."

Joe wanted to reply, but the edge in Gregor's voice and the intensity on his face kept him silent. There was no sense in goading Gregor just now.

Joe promised himself he'd find a time to settle matters between the two of them—when there was no gun separating them.

Liehm returned with the rope. Gregor took it, and tied the Hardys' hands and feet—quickly, efficiently, and very tightly. When he was done, Frank and Joe were sitting back to back in the middle of the floor, securely bound.

"Better." Gregor nodded, admiring his work. "Much better." He smiled down at them. Then he calmly kicked Joe very hard in the side. Joe gasped. Gregor kicked him again—harder—then knelt at Joe's side, staring directly at his face.

"Who are you, boy? Why do you follow me?"

Joe gritted his teeth and said nothing. He stared straight ahead, ignoring Gregor's gaze.

36

"No smart words now, eh?" Gregor asked. He pulled Joe's wallet from his pocket, flipped through it, and frowned. "Joe Hardy."

"Hardy?" Liehm echoed, surprise in his voice. "Are you related to Chris?"

Joe started to say no, but Frank's voice stopped him.

"He's our brother—I'm Frank Hardy," he added.

"What has he told you about us? He never mentioned any brothers to me."

"Shut up, Doctor," Gregor said, tossing Joe's wallet on the floor next to them. He ripped one piece of cloth off an overturned couch, then another, and used them to gag the Hardys.

He knelt down beside them again. "You follow us to avenge your brother—admirable." He shook his head. "But stupid. Don't do it anymore." He stood and turned to go, but stopped at the door.

"Remember what I said." He met Joe's eyes. "Because the next time I see you, I *will* kill you."

The door slammed shut behind him.

It took Frank and Joe almost an hour before they were free.

"That's another one I owe that Gregor," Joe said, gingerly touching the spot on his side where Gregor had kicked him. He felt the bruise starting to form already.

"Did you notice Gregor said 'avenge your brother'?" Frank asked, getting to his feet and stretching. His head still hurt where he'd been slugged with the phone. "They think they killed Chris."

"Well, that's an advantage for him," Joe said. "I only wish it was one for us."

"So what were they looking for here?" Frank asked.

"The videotape Chris had with him?"

"That's a good guess," Frank said. "But I don't see a VCR. Or a computer, for that matter. Remember when Chris told me I should see his system, because it was so big?"

Joe nodded. "Yeah. So where is it?"

"Maybe he keeps it somewhere else." Frank went to the desk they'd found Liehm rifling through and began looking through some papers. "Here's a stack of printouts—and an electric bill from a few months ago for over a hundred dollars! You don't pay that kind of money to keep your refrigerator running. That equipment's here somewhere."

They searched the house from top to bottom but found nothing. Finally, they retraced their steps to the front hall and surveyed the wreckage in the living room.

"Maybe Gregor and Liehm found his equipment and took it," Joe said.

"I don't think so," Frank said. "I think they decided there wasn't anything here." He walked through the living room slowly, studying the over-turned furniture, the scattered papers, the ripped carpet. Finally, he stopped by a section of bare wood floor the torn carpet had exposed. He knelt down, staring intently.

"What is it?"

"Am I crazy, or does the wood here have a lighter varnish than that in the hall?" Frank asked, pulling up more of the carpet. He looked at Joe. "Give me a hand with this, will you?"

They peeled back the entire carpet to the right of the staircase till an area about ten feet square had been exposed.

Joe nodded. "This whole section of the floor is new—but so what?"

"I'm not sure." Frank paced back and forth several times between the living room and the front hall, stopping to gaze up the staircase and then back at the exposed floor.

He snapped his fingers.

"A basement," he said.

Joe looked at him. "A basement?"

Frank nodded. "That's where Chris's equipment is."

Joe scrutinized the floor carefully. "You mean a trap door? I don't see anything."

"Maybe not," Frank said. "I think they moved the whole staircase to cover it."

"Sure," Joe said, shaking his head. "I think you've been watching too many spy movies."

"No, look." Frank stood squarely in the center

of the brighter section of floor. "The stairs used to start here, and took a ninety-degree turn halfway up. All they had to do was knock out the old basement entrance, and swing that bottom half of the staircase around to cover it."

" 'All they had to do.' " Joe shook his head and stared at Frank dubiously for a minute. "All right," he said. "So there's a hidden basement. How do we get down there?"

"Simple enough," Frank said. "There ought to be a hidden entrance." He walked around in front of the staircase again and reached below the edge of the first step. "Aha!" he said, lifting up. The first six steps were hinged; they raised up to reveal a set of stairs leading down.

Frank grinned up at Joe's frowning face. "Just like in the spy movies." He held the entranceway up for his brother. "See if you can find a light down there."

Joe took several tentative steps down the dark stairway. "Got it," he said. Frank lowered the hinged steps, and followed him. Joe stopped on the bottom step.

"You're not going to believe this till you see it," Joe called up.

Frank joined his brother on the bottom step and caught his breath.

The basement was filled with electronic gear. There were five separate computers, two large-screen televisions, four videotape recorders, and several machines he barely recognized at all.

"This is incredible," Frank said. "There's more computer memory down here than in our entire school." He moved to one of the unfamiliar machines and hesitantly touched it.

"One of the new laser imagers," he said wonderingly. "I didn't even know they were on the market yet." He touched another next to it. "And this modem—it's even more advanced than the one we have at home."

Joe stared. The modem on their computer system didn't just let them use telephone lines to communicate with other computers. It was a highly sophisticated piece of gear, to keep them in contact with the Network, a supersecret government agency.

"I think this is what Gregor and Liehm were looking for."

"But what's it all for?"

"Beats me." Frank took another look around the room. "It's not your standard business computing setup, or anything like that. No one would need all this video equipment." He walked around and finally sat down in front of one of the computers with a keyboard. "Let's try asking the machine what it's doing here."

He switched the machine on and began typing commands into the computer. Joe came and stood behind his shoulder.

Frank shook his head. "He's got the whole system keyed to a password."

"Are you trying to guess it?"

"That would take forever. No, I'm trying to bypass his program and talk to the machine directly." He typed instructions too fast for Joe to understand. Suddenly the screen lit up.

Frank grinned. "We're in," he said. Joe clapped him on the shoulder. "Now let's find out what he's got on file here."

He called up a directory and let the names of the files scroll by. Nothing looked familiar, until—

"Hold it!" Joe said. "What's that one say?"

"I see it," Frank replied. " 'Janosik'—and it's not just one file, it's a whole directory of them." He called up one of the files onscreen. A whole array of symbols appeared.

"This is weird," Frank said, studying the monitor. "I don't know what this is—looks like a very complicated series of printing commands."

"What does it mean?" Joe asked.

"I don't know," Frank said. "Let's try another file." He called up one called "Itinerary."

"At least this one's in English," Joe said. The screen showed a listing of place names and times.

"Yeah," Frank said, reading off the screen. " 'Arrive Hotel Charles—' " He shook his head. "Let's look at the other one again for a second." He called up the directory again and stared at it for a moment.

"Hey!" Joe exclaimed. "What's going on? What are you doing?

Double Exposure

The list of files in the directory was shrinking, disappearing one by one.

"I'm not doing anything," Frank said. "Someone else is in the system—and destroying all the files!"

Chapter

6

"Do something! Stop it!" Joe yelled.

"I'm trying to!" Frank frantically typed in new instructions to the computer. Before his eyes, the files were disappearing.

"What's happening?"

"I don't know—maybe I triggered some kind of self-destruct program, or—" He glanced up quickly and looked across the basement. "No! It's got to be the modem! Somebody must be tying in by phone and telling the computer to erase these files!" He dashed across the room, Joe a step behind him.

"Can we stop it?" Joe asked.

"That's what I'm trying to do," Frank said, staring intently at the modem. He knelt behind it and found the wire connecting it to the main system.

"Here it is," he said, holding the wire in his

hand. "If I disconnect this, we should be able to cut off whoever's on the modem."

Joe stared at him. "Well, what are you waiting for?"

Frank hesitated. "We may not only disconnect the modem, we may crash the whole system. That way, we'll lose all the files."

Joe yanked the wire out of Frank's hand. "We're definitely going to lose them if we don't."

Frank nodded.

Joe pulled the wire free.

Across the room, the monitor went suddenly dark. The computer made a soft humming noise that gradually faded away, like a car running out of gas. Then the basement was completely silent.

Joe cleared his throat and looked at Frank questioningly. Frank shook his head. "I think—"

"Don't say it," Joe said, leaning back against a wall of equipment.

Frank sighed. Whatever had been in the computer, whatever Chris had known about Janosik—all that information was gone.

"There's nothing more we can get here," Frank said. Joe nodded reluctantly.

They went upstairs again, carefully lowering the stairs on the secret entrance to Chris's basement.

In spite of all the equipment in the basement, they'd found nothing—no computer disks, no videocassettes, no records of any kind—to indicate what had gone on there. Erasing the computer's files was apparently the last step in a very thorough housecleaning operation.

"Nothing is what we've got," Joe said in disgust.

"Not quite," Frank said. He picked up the phone and dialed. "Yes. I'd like the number of the Charles. It's a hotel in Cambridge." He covered the mouthpiece with one hand. "Let's check and see if that little bit of itinerary we saw was really Janosik's."

Lifting his hand, he spoke into the receiver again. "I see—yes, thank you, operator." He hung up quickly and looked at his watch. 10:00. Not too late to call.

"I'm going to see if he's there," he told Joe, dialing the number the operator had given him.

"This is the Charles, Bonnie speaking. How may I help you this evening?" The woman who answered had a distinct Boston accent and the efficient, practiced voice of a well-trained receptionist. The Charles was clearly a classy hotel.

"May I have Mr. Janosik's room?"

"Ah—yes, one minute please." A note of uncertainty crept into her voice. "I'll connect you." Frank recognized the hesitation and covered the receiver again. "Something's going on," he told Joe. "They put me on hold."

Joe moved in closer and stood by his side, leaning over his shoulder to listen in on the conversation.

The next voice that came on the phone was not

the receptionist's, but a man's—deep, powerful, and authoritative.

"This is Lieutenant Considine—to whom am I speaking, please?"

"I'm sorry. I was looking for Alexander Janosik." Frank mouthed the word *police* to Joe.

"How did you know Mr. Janosik was staying here? Who is this?"

Frank replaced the receiver quietly. He didn't have anything he could tell the police—yet.

"He's there, all right."

Joe nodded. "We ought to be there, too."

"I think you're right, but we have to take care of a few loose ends first."

They phoned the local police anonymously to let them know that Chris's house had been broken into, and climbed in the van to start the long drive back to Bayport.

No sooner had they gotten onto the highway than it started to rain—lightly at first, then harder. The rhythm of the raindrops beating on the windshield and the swish of the wipers as they cleared the glass quickly lulled Frank to sleep, and he didn't wake up until they were almost home.

"How are you doing?" he asked Joe, peering out through the windshield. He could barely see the road, it was raining so heavily. "Want me to drive?"

"No, it's all right," Joe said. "I'm fine." He

paused for a moment. "Who do you think was on the other end of that modem? Chris?"

"Probably," Frank said, stifling a yawn. "But why would he destroy his own information?"

"Because there was something in there he didn't want anyone to see," Joe replied. "Something that connected him with Gregor and Liehm—maybe what they were going to use to frame Janosik. Maybe after he ran away from us, Chris got cold feet about turning them in."

Frank was silent for a moment. What his brother was saying made sense. He wanted to like Chris, but more and more, it was impossible to see his role in this as innocent.

"Frank?" Joe asked quietly. "You don't really think he's our brother, do you?"

"Of course not," he said, trying to hide the lingering doubts in his voice. Watching the road ahead of them flash by, he thought of the birth certificate he'd seen that morning and the smiling young man who had seemed so comfortable in their house.

He shook his head. "It's impossible."

They finally got home at three in the morning and found a small package waiting for them in the mailbox.

"I'll bet I know what this is," Frank said, holding it in his hand. "Chris's videotape, in a brand-new case, courtesy of Phil Cohen."

He unlocked the front door and stepped inside,

turning on the hall light. Joe rushed in behind him, running to escape the downpour.

"Whew—that's the hardest it's rained in a long time!" Joe said, taking off his coat and kicking off his wet shoes.

"It'll be good for Mom's garden," Frank said, hanging up his own coat.

"If you like vegetables." Joe blew on his hands and walked toward the kitchen. "How about some hot chocolate?"

"Sounds good." Frank ripped the package open. It was the videotape, with a brief note from Phil.

"Frank/Joe," it read. "Here's the tape. Part did get damaged—about two seconds, total. I watched it. Call me tomorrow after you do. Phil."

Frank smiled. "It's the tape, all right. I'll go slip it in the VCR."

"Be there in a minute," Joe called back.

Frank went into the den and turned on the TV, then the VCR. He checked that the tape was rewound to the beginning and inserted it in the machine.

A minute later Joe walked into the room carrying two steaming mugs of cocoa and handed one to Frank.

"Thanks," he said, sitting back on the couch and taking a sip of the hot chocolate. Joe sat down next to him.

"Now," Frank said, picking up the remote

control and setting the VCR to Play. "Let's see what's on this tape."

At first they saw nothing but snow—no signal at all. Then the screen turned black and some letters appeared.

" 'Janosik Project—DD Insertion'?" Joe read aloud.

"Beats me," Frank said, shaking his head.

The letters cleared, and for a moment there was static again. Then a picture appeared.

On the screen, it was winter—outdoors, in a rural area. Two men, one old, one young, both wearing army uniforms, stood on the steps before a large white frame house. They were talking, but the tape had no sound.

"Those are Russian uniforms!" Joe exclaimed.

Frank nodded. Something about the scene seemed terribly familiar. "The older one's a colonel, but the picture quality is really terrible. I'm surprised. With all that video equipment Chris had . . ." His voice trailed off.

On the screen the two men were arguing now. The older man's face betrayed confusion and surprise. He gestured angrily.

The younger man's face became frozen, an expressionless mask. Without betraying what he was about to do, he raised a gun. The older man fell backward down the steps of the building, his blood staining the snow.

Frank turned white and leaned forward, spilling his hot chocolate on the couch.

Joe's eyes widened. "Frank—that soldier . . ."

Frank nodded, his mouth suddenly dry. He rewound the tape till he reached a single closeup of the young soldier, then pressed Freeze-Frame on the remote control.

The face on the screen, the man who had shot the older officer—

It was Chris.

Chapter

7

"YOU'LL GO to the police now, right?" Callie asked Frank. It was the next morning, and she was sitting in the Hardys' den, facing Frank.

"Wrong." Frank released the Freeze-Frame button on the remote control and rewound the videotape. He'd watched the shooting too many times since last night.

"Yeah," Joe said, walking out of the room and returning with two suitcases. "We're not going anywhere—except where we're going." He smiled.

"Which is Boston and Cambridge," Frank said. He took Callie's hand and smiled reassuringly. "We don't have anything to tell the police. What would we say? We may have witnessed a tape of a murder in Russia? If we go to Boston, we'll be near Janosik, we'll be able to talk to that newspaper reporter, and we'll—"

"Be right in the line of fire if Chris decides to shoot Janosik, too!" Callie said angrily.

She leapt up and began to pace the room. "Frank, he's *not* what he pretended to be. He's a killer—a member of the Russian army, maybe even the KGB! What if those two guys from the Czech secret police—whatever their names are—"

"Krc and Liehm," Joe said.

"Right—what if they're trying to stop Chris from killing Janosik? Did you think of that? What if they're the good guys?"

"If they're good guys, I'll never eat a burger again," Joe said. He stood in front of Callie. "Take a look at this." He lifted his shirt, revealing an ugly bruise that practically covered one whole side of his body. "Good guys don't kick you when you're tied up."

"I don't think they're on Janosik's side," Frank added. "And we don't know whose side Chris is on. But I think you're right about one thing—Alexander Janosik's life could be in danger."

"So we're flying to Boston," Joe said. "We want to make sure that Janosik is safe."

"And how are you going to do that?" Callie asked. "You told me the police wouldn't even let you talk to him on the phone. Once that symposium begins, you won't be able to get near him."

"We'll manage," Frank said. The doorbell rang. "Come on in—it's open!" he yelled.

"Hi, everybody," Phil Cohen said, walking

53

into the room. "You're all set." He handed Joe a piece of paper. "Go to this address and ask for the Beast. He'll get you into Janosik's symposium."

Callie threw up her hands in defeat.

"The Beast?" Joe asked, his eyes widening as he studied the note. "What kind of name is that?"

"He's a friend of mine," Phil said defensively. "I don't know his real name—I just exchange messages with him on a computer network. He goes to Harvard and knows how to do things with computers I'd never even think of trying."

"How's he going to get us into the symposium?" Frank asked.

Phil shrugged. "I didn't ask. And I don't want to know."

Joe grinned. "Good enough for me." He picked up the suitcases. "Come on, Frank, we've got a plane to catch."

Frank turned to Callie. "We'll be staying at the Charles."

"You're going to stay *there?* Frank, that's the most exclusive hotel in Cambridge! How are you going to afford it?"

"Oh, we'll figure out a way."

"Maybe the Beast can help you," Callie suggested wryly.

"He probably could," Phil offered. "Once he told me about the time that he—"

Frank smothered a laugh. "We'd better catch that plane."

The plane ride was uneventful. They arrived at Boston's Logan Airport in late morning and took a cab to Cambridge, emerging into an early-September afternoon.

"This is Harvard," Frank said as they walked through an open gate in the fence that surrounded the "Yard," the old part of Harvard's campus. "That's the Quad, where all the dorms are." He pointed straight ahead, then stopped to take a jacket out of his bag and slip it on. It had been unseasonably cool the past week.

"Wow," Joe said, studying the beautiful old campus and ivy-covered buildings. "This is really great."

Frank smiled and took a long look around. Everyone walking by seemed to be a student— not much older than they were.

But they were at Harvard for reasons other than sightseeing. "Come on," he said to Joe. "What's that dorm where Phil's friend is?"

"The Beast." Joe shook his head and pulled the note out of his pocket. "Columbus—building F."

They stopped a campus security guard and asked him for directions. He pointed off to the left. "Columbus," he said. "It's a whole new set of buildings back that way. You can't miss it."

"Thanks," said Frank. He and Joe followed

the instructions. The buildings they passed were all hundreds of years old, four- and five-story brick dorms, classroom halls, a Greek-looking building with the single word *Philosophy* carved above its door.

For a second Frank felt as if he and Joe had traveled in time—perhaps to some ancient English university like Cambridge or Oxford. But when they came to a group of squat, modern three-story buildings, they were definitely back in the present.

"There," Joe said, pointing to a building in the middle. The door was locked, so Joe rapped loudly on it.

A girl opened it. "Yes? Can I help you?" she said. She was beautiful, and when her eyes met Joe's, she gave him a dazzling smile.

Joe gulped but said nothing. Frank gave him a quick poke with his elbow.

"Oh—ah, yes, we're looking for someone named—the Beast," Joe said, clearing his throat.

The girl's face fell. "Corner room all the way down the hall." She held the door open to let them pass. "Just follow your nose."

"Phil's friends are loved everywhere," Joe said, watching her walk away. They found the corner room. Frank set down his suitcase and knocked on the door.

It opened a crack. This time, it wasn't a beautiful girl who answered, but a slight young man. He looked about fourteen, and had short blond hair and wire-rim glasses. His T-shirt said Computers Are People, Too. And drifting out of his room came the odor of stale popcorn. "Who are you?" he asked, peering at them suspiciously.

Frank exchanged a glance with Joe. "We're looking for the Beast. Phil Cohen sent us—we're Frank and Joe Hardy."

"Oh." The little blond student squinted up at them and nodded. "That's me—I'm the Beast."

Joe did a double take. "You? The Beast? You don't look like a beast." In fact, he added silently, you don't look old enough to be in high school, much less college.

"I know, I know," he said, pushing his glasses back up on his nose. "My real name is Larry— Larry Biester—so they call me the Beast. Hold on a minute." He shut the door.

Joe looked at the pages of computer printout that were plastered across the face of the door, and then looked at Frank. "The Beast."

Frank nodded. "The Beast."

When the door reopened, Larry emerged and handed Joe an envelope. "These'll get you into the government symposium—it's over at the JFK Center, across campus."

"Thanks," Joe said. Beyond the Beast's shoulder, he could see a dark room, dominated by a flashing computer terminal and to the side of it a pyramid of empty soda cans.

"Okay," the little guy said and shut the door so fast it almost slammed.

"Wow," Joe said. "And I thought high school was strange."

"Yeah," Frank nodded. "Maybe college isn't such a good idea after all."

The guard they'd gotten directions from before told them where the JFK Center was, and they found it without much trouble. It was an entire group of buildings, combining classrooms, offices, and a research library. They also found something else.

"The Charles," Joe said, pointing to a building on the hill behind the JFK complex.

"Where Janosik is now," Frank said. He stared at the large, fenced-off construction area that spread between the campus and the hotel. "Looks like they're building a parking garage here."

"When does the symposium start?" Joe asked.

Frank studied the announcement schedule on the center's bulletin board. "According to this, today—continuing over the next three days. Janosik doesn't speak till Saturday, though."

Joe continued to stare up the hill at the Charles. "You know what I'm thinking? Maybe we should go to the hotel, register, dump these bags, and find Janosik. Tell him what we know."

"Good idea," Frank said. "We can also call that reporter—Eykis—and see what she's got that proves Janosik was being paid by the CIA."

They followed the sidewalk up the hill to the

Charles. It was a huge building, sprawled across the top of the hill and down one side, all the way to the Charles River. Its ground floor was a series of restaurants and shops, tailored for Harvard's visitors.

The lobby itself was so overcrowded that at first Frank had trouble spotting the registration desk. Finally he saw it at the far end of a long corridor lined with stores. He and Joe made their way to the desk.

"Hi," Joe said to one of the six or seven women behind the long desk. "We'd like a room for tonight, please."

She didn't even bother to look down. "I'm sorry, sir, we're totally booked through the weekend."

"Oh, no!" Joe leaned over the counter and tried to look horrified. "Couldn't you please double-check—isn't there anything?"

The girl leaned over her computer terminal. "I'll see if there are any last-minute cancellations," she said doubtfully. Joe waved Frank over to the desk, not so much because he thought she might find them a room, but so that Frank could see what she was doing on the computer.

"No, nothing," she said. She smiled at them. "There's a motel down the street you might try."

"Thanks," Joe said. "Could we leave our bags here for a couple of hours?"

The girl started to say no. But Joe smiled his most winning white-toothed smile, and she nodded and pointed to a spot beside the desk. Then Joe and Frank walked out of the lobby.

"There was an office around back," Frank said. "I'll bet there's another computer in there. All I have to do is get on that reservations systems for a minute, and I'll have the best suite in the house."

"It'll have to be later," Joe said, studying the crowd. "When this place clears out." He brightened. "Let's go down to the river and check it out."

He stopped suddenly as he realized Frank was no longer walking beside him. His older brother had halted a few paces back, staring to the left.

"What is it, Frank? What's the matter?"

"There," Frank pointed. An elderly man sat on one of the benches in the courtyard in front of the hotel, engrossed in reading a book. "That's Janosik!"

He and Joe walked toward the benches and sat down next to him.

"Alexander Janosik?" Frank asked.

The man looked up from his book slowly, staring at Frank. His hair was almost entirely white, and his deep-set eyes were friendly. Heavy bags under them made him look as if he hadn't slept in years.

"Yes, I am Alexander Janosik. Who are you?" Unlike Gregor or Liehm, his English was almost entirely unaccented.

"My name is Frank Hardy, sir. This is my

brother, Joe—but we're not important right now," he began. "Mr. Janosik, I have reason to believe your life could be in danger. Have you ever heard of two men named Krc and Liehm?"

To Frank's surprise, the man began to laugh. "Heard of them? Yes, I have, young man—but I'm quite safe. I have some very qualified people watching over me."

"Really?" Joe, amazed at Janosik's disregard for his safety, moved forward. "Like who?"

"Like me." Suddenly a large black man towered over them. "Move away from him—now!"

Chapter

8

FRANK AND JOE STOOD CAUTIOUSLY.

"Please, Lieutenant," Janosik said. "These young men are harmless enough, surely."

"Let's see some ID," the man said, ignoring Janosik.

Frank tried desperately to think of what to do—and then remembered the envelope that the Beast had given them. He handed it to the man.

That should buy them some time to think of a story, at least.

"What's this?" The security man tore the envelope open and pulled out two cards, scrutinized them and then looked at Frank and Joe.

It was over, Frank realized. He started to look for a way to explain that they only wanted to help Janosik, but the man interrupted him.

"Why didn't you say you were grad students?" he asked, handing them back their cards.

Frank looked at his. There was his picture—on

a Harvard graduate student ID. He looked at Joe, who was studying his card with the same apparent confusion.

"Oh, ah—yes. The program today was particularly interesting," Frank said. "That's all we wanted to tell Mr. Janosik."

"I thought I heard you say something about his life being in danger." The security man stared hard at Frank. "Your voice is very familiar—and the name Hardy rings a bell, too."

"Please, Lieutenant Considine," Janosik said. "They are merely students—and it is young people that I am most interested in talking to."

Considine! Frank thought. He answered the phone last night when I called. He tried not to look nervous as the lieutenant studied him.

"All right," Considine said finally.

"Thank you." Janosik carefully marked his place in the book he was reading and stood. "Perhaps you two young men would like to accompany me on a walk through the park down there?" He pointed past the hotel in the direction of the river.

"We'd be honored," Frank said.

Joe nodded. "You bet."

"All right, then." Janosik smiled.

"My men will stay close behind you." Considine motioned, and two men who had been inconspicuously studying hotel shop windows moved forward. "Have a nice walk, Mr. Janosik."

Frank and Joe flanked Janosik as he started down the hill, the two men following.

"So," Janosik began. "You know Liehm and Krc. I am surprised. You seem a little young to be traveling in their circles."

Frank smiled. "We sort of stumbled in."

"Let me give you some advice, young man—stumble back out. They are dangerous men."

"It's you we're worried about," Joe said.

Janosik laughed again, more harshly. "Me? Liehm, Krc—they cannot hurt me." He shook his head. "I am dead already."

Frank and Joe exchanged startled glances, but Janosik offered no explanation.

They came to the end of the hotel grounds. Two marble pillars stood flanking the entranceway to a small park. Each was engraved with quotations.

"These are the words of your President Kennedy," Janosik said. "You are too young to remember him—but he was a great man."

Frank nodded and said nothing.

"The world was full of great men in those days," Janosik said, staring at the words on the pillar. "Kennedy, his brother Robert, Martin Luther King, Dubcek, Svoboda—" He shook his head as if to clear it and smiled at the Hardys. "Those last two names mean nothing to you."

"No," Frank admitted. "I'm afraid they don't."

Janosik slowly traced the outline of the engraved quote with his hand. When he finally spoke, his voice was strained and harsh.

"They were the leaders of my country in 1968, the year King and Kennedy's brother were assassinated. Now they have been erased from our history books." He turned to the two young men at his side. "Alexander Dubcek tried to reform our government, to give the people a voice in their own affairs, to give socialism a human face, as your western press said."

"What happened?" Joe asked.

"He failed," Janosik said curtly, striding past the pillars and into the park. There was a fountain in the center, with benches carved into the marble around it. More quotations from President Kennedy were engraved on the marble surrounding the fountain.

Janosik sat on one of the benches and continued his story. "The Russians invaded my country. On the night of August twentieth, 1968, their tanks crossed our borders." He shuddered. "Their troops filled our streets. They kidnapped our leaders and dragged them back to Moscow, tried to force them to submit to the Kremlin's will, make them renounce the changes they had begun.

"They held them for seven days, but Dubcek would not yield." His voice shook with remembered anger. "He would not yield! And the country stood firmly behind him. We gave the Russians nothing!" He was silent for a moment, then pointed at the quotation carved into the marble in front of them, and began reading from it.

" 'When at some future date the high court of history sits in judgment on us . . . our success or failure in whatever office we hold will be measured by the answers to these four questions: Were we truly men of courage? Were we truly men of integrity? Were we truly men of judgment? Were we truly men of dedication?' "

Frank watched Janosik read those words, and it was as if the old man were somewhere else, reliving the most important moments of his life.

"For seven days—and several months beyond—the people of Czechoslovakia were all those things, and more. Then it ended. The reforms were repealed. Husak"—he spat the name—"came to power. And men like Liehm and Krc emerged from the sewers they'd been hiding in to frighten my country into silence once again."

He sighed heavily. "I sometimes wonder what would have happened if John Kennedy, or his brother, had been president in 1968. Maybe they would have stopped the Russians. Maybe I—and my country—would still be alive."

He turned to Frank again. "It does not matter what they do to me—I am as one dead and have been for more than twenty years. I continue to speak out so the words of men like Dubcek are not forever lost. So that what happened to Czechoslovakia never happens again."

Janosik gave them a tired smile. "But you two are young, you have your whole lives ahead of you. Don't risk them trying to save me." He nodded at Considine's men, who stood at the edge of the fountain. "That is their job."

He stood. "Now if you'll excuse me, I must return to my room. I grow tired." He nodded in farewell and shuffled slowly out of the park. Considine's two men followed him out.

Frank watched him go. "Still think he's being paid by the CIA?" he asked Joe.

Joe shook his head slowly. "Forget I ever said that."

"I don't care what he said—I'm not letting anything happen to that old man."

"Me, either," Joe said.

The boys were suddenly famished and went in search of lunch. They found a pizza place, which made Joe happy, although he did end up having to pay for the whole thing.

"Didn't I buy dinner the other night, too?" Joe asked.

"You did," said Frank. "And don't think I don't appreciate it."

"Very funny," Joe said. "I'm keeping track, you can bet on that."

Frank didn't bother to point out that Joe had already spent most of the money they had for the entire week on hamburgers.

When they returned to the Charles, it was

midafternoon, and the lobby was much less crowded. The same young woman was on duty at the registration desk and smiled sadly when she saw them approaching.

"I'm afraid we're still all booked up," she said.

"I thought you might be," Joe said. "But I really came back to ask you about that motel, I couldn't find it anywhere. Do you think you could show me where it is?" He gave her his most charming smile.

"I'm sorry—I can't leave the desk," she said.

"I could watch it for you," Frank volunteered. "If anyone comes, I'll direct them to one of the other registration clerks." Frank smiled at the long line of women identically dressed in blue suits. They all seemed to be enjoying a joke and weren't paying any attention to the boys.

The young woman studied their faces carefully. "All right," she said finally. "Come on," she said to Joe. "I'll point it out for you."

Her place was at the end of the counter, and Frank stood and watched them walk out of the lobby. It was easier than he'd expected. He reached over with his left hand and idly logged on to the terminal. The women were still occupied with their stories, and Frank just appeared to be waiting for someone. First he found Janosik's room, and then he quickly discovered that the suites adjoining it on either side were being held empty. He logged on a reservation for himself and Joe in one of them.

He finished in just a couple of seconds. "It really is just up the road—I don't know how we could have missed it," Joe said.

"Then we're set," Frank said, nodding at Joe and picking up his bag.

When they got outside, Joe turned to Frank. "So?"

"We're in," Frank said. He smiled. "But we'll have to be very quiet."

When their reservation clerk went on break, they simply approached one of the others and checked in.

"Easy enough," Joe said, tossing his bag on one of the two beds in their room. "Now what?"

"Now we try that reporter—the one who said she was going to get proof of Janosik's guilt."

"Jean Eykis, you said."

"Right," Frank said, picking up the phone. They put him through quickly when he called the newspaper, and he made an appointment to see her in an hour.

Joe frowned. "Shouldn't one of us stay, and keep an eye on Janosik?"

"He really made an impression on you, didn't he?"

"No," Joe said defensively. "I just don't like the idea of leaving him alone here, without one of us watching him. I'm not too impressed with his police protection."

"Okay," Frank said, checking his watch. "I'd

better get going. You stay here—I'll go talk to Jean Eykis." He opened the door and checked the hall for any sign of Lieutenant Considine or his men. The coast was clear.

"And remember," he told Joe. "Be quiet."

Their room had a TV, so Joe spent the next couple of hours switching back and forth between various programs. But there wasn't anything worth watching, so he eventually got bored and shut it off.

He stood and crossed to the window. Outside it was still bright daylight. He had a view of the courtyard in front of the hotel and the street beyond.

Cambridge, like every other city he'd ever been in, had at least one problem in common with all other big cities—too many cars, and not enough parking spaces. Right now, on the street below, Joe could see some kind of fight taking place over a space.

A man stepped out of one car and leaned through the window of the other. Whatever he said to the driver made that car give up the fight for the space and speed away.

Joe smiled—then he looked closer.

The car now pulling into the parking spot was the silver Mercedes that had shot at them two nights before!

Chapter

9

JOE REALIZED THE DRIVER had to be Gregor, and he watched the Mercedes for a moment, his mind racing. Should he warn Janosik? Or Considine? Where was Liehm?

Then he heard the sound of loud, angry voices coming from the room next door. He leaned up to the wall and pressed his ear against it.

"What threats you make! I will not be silenced!" That was Janosik's voice—more passionate than it had sounded earlier in the park. Joe had to smile. Maybe Janosik thought he was dead to the world, but he sounded very much alive.

"Come, Alexander, be sensible." Joe knew that voice, too. Liehm. "We do not require you to stop speaking entirely. All we ask is that you stop making these foolish speeches against our government, and our friends, the Soviets."

"Nothing you can do will make me stop speaking against those invaders!" Janosik said.

"Oh?" Liehm asked. "Let me show you this." There was the sound of furniture, or something heavy, being moved in the next room.

"Watch closely, Alexander."

Joe strained to hear but was unable to make out what was happening. They had stopped talking completely.

Then Janosik spoke again. "This is not how it happened—not at all. I met with them, yes—but I never took money."

Liehm laughed—a cruel, barking sound. "Who is to say how it really happened? All that is important is that the television stations will have this tomorrow—unless you change your speech."

Janosik's reply, when it came, was quiet and subdued. "I need to think."

"Fine. I give you until this evening at ten. If I do not hear from you by then, I will release the tape to the TV stations." The sound of moving furniture came again. "Goodbye, Alexander." Liehm's voice was mocking. Joe heard Janosik's door open, then shut again.

The tape? What was going on here? Joe moved from the wall to his door. He cracked it open to watch Liehm walk slowly down the hall to the elevators, carrying a large suitcase.

What could Liehm have shown Janosik that would make him think about changing his speech? Joe had to find out. He had to follow Liehm.

Grabbing his coat off the bed, Joe dashed into the hall. He raced down the three flights of stairs and outside into the courtyard. There was the Mercedes—and Gregor. He itched for a chance to confront him, but Liehm would be coming out of the elevator in a minute. He had to find a way to follow them. If only he had a car . . .

Just then a young boy raced past on a skateboard, and Joe barreled after him.

"Hey, kid!" Joe yelled.

The boy turned.

"I need to borrow your skateboard," he said.

"Borrow?" the boy asked. He looked Joe up and down. "Get real. I don't even know you."

"All right, all right," Joe said. He saw Liehm moving through the hotel lobby and turned his face away. "I'll buy it from you. How much?"

The boy sized Joe up. "I paid a hundred bucks for this skateboard, mister."

"A hundred bucks?" Joe's eyes widened. He didn't have that much on him. "For a skateboard?"

The boy smiled at Joe. "A hundred bucks— take it or leave it."

Joe glanced around. Gregor had gotten out of the car to put Liehm's bag in the trunk. Liehm was sliding into the back seat.

"All I have is a twenty," Joe said desperately. "Twenty to rent it—how about it?"

"Rent it?" the boy shouted indignantly. "You trying to cheat me or something?"

At the curb Gregor turned to see what was happening. His eyes met Joe's, just before he reached into his coat.

"Duck!" Joe yelled, throwing his arm across the kid and dropping to the sidewalk, putting himself between Gregor and the boy.

Gregor pulled out his gun and fired. The bullet clanged off one of the courtyard benches. He'd used a silencer—a couple of people looked up but saw no cause for alarm.

Gregor fired again. Joe rolled behind a bench, still shielding the boy. The bullet slammed into the walkway, spraying them with chips of cement.

This time someone saw. "He's got a gun," a woman screamed. Gregory holstered it and climbed into the Mercedes. The car screeched off down the street.

The boy looked up at Joe with wonder in his eyes. He wasn't even scared, Joe saw. None of this was real to him.

"Wow," the boy said. "Are you a secret agent, or something?"

"Or something," Joe said, brushing himself off. Gregory was getting away, and he couldn't follow.

"Well, why didn't you say so?" the boy asked. He pointed at his skateboard. "Take it."

Joe smiled at the boy. "Thanks—I'll return it."

He climbed on the skateboard and started to roll uncertainly down the sidewalk, slowly at first, then picking up speed. He hadn't been on a skateboard in a couple of years.

"Go get 'em!" the boy cheered, raising his fists and shouting.

"Gangway," Joe yelled as he wobbled down the hill.

People dodged from the path of the obvious maniac, letting Joe keep the Mercedes in sight. The car came to the bottom of the hill and turned right—into heavy traffic. Joe knew he'd be able to keep up with a car caught in traffic.

Then he saw the sidewalk ended at the bottom of the hill. Joe gulped. Taking a deep breath, he jumped the curb and landed smack in the middle of traffic.

Joe leaned wildly to his left, then right. He was going to fall. He was going to get run over.

Desperate, he grabbed onto a truck in front of him to steady himself. He clung to it like a drowning swimmer to a life preserver, until he'd regained his balance.

Joe looked up and smiled. He'd managed to latch onto a vehicle two cars behind the Mercedes. If they stayed off the highway, he'd be able to follow it wherever it went.

Of course all that depended on how long he could keep his balance and whether the truck turned off.

*　　*　　*

Frank held out his hand. "Jean Eykis?"

"That's right." The woman in front of him smiled and shook hands firmly. She looked in her midthirties, with long dark hair and a square, pleasant face. "And you are—"

"Frank Hardy," he said. "I was hoping to talk to you about Alexander Janosik."

The woman nodded. "I have very little time, but you said you had some information for me?"

Frank pulled up a chair next to her desk. They were in the middle of the newspaper's city room. Dozens of people occupied the single room, some dropping off copy on the many desks around him, while others were typing in front of small computer monitors attached to all the desktops.

"What do you have for me?"

Frank decided to take the direct approach. "What makes you so certain that"—he tried to remember her exact words—"Alexander Janosik has been accepting money from the CIA for his anti-Czech speeches?"

She frowned. "Why are you so concerned?"

Frank leaned forward. "I think he's being smeared—and I think you're being used."

Her lips tightened. "A strong accusation."

Frank nodded. "I realize that. Who are your sources for this information?"

"You know I can't tell you that," she said.

"A man named Liehm—or Krc, perhaps?"

Her eyes widened, and she stared at Frank, surprised by his knowledge.

"They're with the STB—the Czech secret police. How I know this isn't important," Frank quickly continued. "But I have to know if they gave you anything—you said that you were promised proof positive of Janosik's guilt."

Eykis continued to stare at Frank—then shook her head. "You're either on the level, or . . ." Her voice trailed off. "They promised me something tomorrow morning. And that's all you get."

Frank smiled.

"With the STB, you said?" Eykis repeated. "You're sure?"

"As sure as I am of anything right now," Frank said. "Do you have a way to get in touch with them?"

"Why should I give away that information?"

"Because your story's not true," Frank said simply.

She laughed. "All right. I may kick myself in the morning for doing this, but—Liehm did give me a number." She rummaged around her desk. "Let's see—here it is."

She copied it onto a piece of note paper and handed it to Frank. "If they really are STB, that would explain why they're so anxious to see me announce Janosik's guilt." Jean Eykis gave Frank a concerned stare. "And if they really are STB, you shouldn't be fooling around with them."

Frank stood. "I'll be careful."

"All right, Frank," she said, getting up as well. "And I'll have some of my sources check on

77

Liehm. I'm not anxious to print this story unless it's true—I've been an admirer of Janosik's for years.''

"Thanks," Frank said. "And good luck—you can reach me at the Charles if you need to.''

"Good luck to you, too.''

He went downstairs to a phone booth and called Joe. No answer. Maybe Janosik went out, and Joe followed him. In that case, he was on his own for a while. He decided to dig a little more, dialing the number Eykis had just given him.

No answer there, either.

If only he had a way to find the address to go with that number—he'd have something. If he were home, he'd be able to tie in to the telephone company's computer. . . .

But he didn't need his computer at home to do that. Not when there was someone here in Boston who could supposedly do anything with a computer.

The trip back to the dorms took only a few minutes.

"Beast!" Frank banged on the door loudly. "Open up!"

A rustling noise came from inside the room.

Frank hit the door again. "Come on, Beast.''

The door creaked open slowly. The little blond guy, in a long nightshirt and slippers, appeared at the door, staring at Frank. "Who are you?''

"Frank Hardy—don't you remember? Phil Cohen's friend.''

"Oh." The Beast nodded. "Need some more ID?"

Frank shook his head. "No—I'm sorry to bother you, but it's important." He handed him the phone number. "Can you get me an address to go with this?"

Beast yawned and took the slip of paper back into his room, shutting the door behind him. A moment later he emerged and handed Frank another slip of paper.

"This is it?"

"That's it," the Beast said, yawning. "I'm going back to bed now."

Frank started to say good-night, but the door closed in his face.

Going back to bed. Frank looked at his watch. At five o'clock?

He shook his head.

College was going to be weird.

Joe was lucky—not only did the Mercedes stay off the highway, but the truck that he'd attached himself to stayed with the Mercedes till it pulled off the road and into a parking garage near the center of Cambridge.

He let go of the truck and glided silently to a halt across the street from the garage. Gregor and Liehm left the garage and entered the lobby of the building next door. As they entered, a uniformed guard waved a hand in greeting, and all three crossed to the back of the lobby and disappeared into an elevator.

Joe tucked the skateboard under his arm, crossed the street, and entered the building. While waiting for the elevator and its operator to return, he studied the building directory.

Apparently there were few tenants. One whole floor was occupied by Rehearsal Systems, Inc. Another floor belonged to a firm named Video Imaging. There was a copying firm, a collection agency, and an exercise studio as well.

"Hello? Can I help you?"

Joe turned and found himself facing the elevator operator, a young man not much older than he was. He smiled.

"Yes—maybe you can. The two men you just took up—I saw one of them drop his wallet in the garage next door. I'd like to return it."

"Sure, come on in." He let Joe enter the elevator first, then followed and shut the door. "That's very nice of you. Not many people would turn in a wallet."

Joe shrugged. "No big deal."

"Oh, but it is," the operator said. "I'm sure there are some important papers in that wallet. Their company does a lot of important work."

"Oh?" Joe asked, trying to appear casual. "What kind of work?"

"I think it's something to do with television—they're called Video Imaging."

"Video Imaging," Joe repeated, keeping his

voice calm. Their first real break! Now maybe he'd be able to start figuring out how Janosik, Liehm, Gregor, and the mysterious disappearing Chris Hardy tied together.

All he had to do was find a phone—Frank should be back from his meeting by now—and they were in business.

"Here you go," the operator said, opening the door. "They're at the end of the hall."

"Thanks," he said, stepping out of the elevator. "I can take it from here."

"Oh, no, Mr. Hardy."

Joe turned, and saw the elevator operator holding an automatic on him.

"Dr. Liehm and Mr. Krc would never forgive me if you got lost on the way." He smiled. "They're waiting for you."

Chapter

10

FRANK HUNG UP the phone again, concerned and puzzled. There was still no answer at their hotel room. What had happened to Joe? Where had he gone?

He stood by the phone booth on the corner and looked down the block. The address the Beast had given him was for an office building. It seemed ordinary enough. But somehow he felt the answers to a lot of the questions he and Joe had been facing these last few days were in there.

He was dying to check it out—but he wasn't going in alone. That's the kind of stunt Joe would pull. He always leapt before he looked.

This part of Cambridge was almost entirely commercial and almost entirely deserted now that it was after five o'clock.

The ground-floor stationery stores were all locked up, and the delicatessens and restaurants were closing up.

At that moment a flicker of movement in the alleyway between the building and the parking garage caught his attention. He pressed back against the wall and looked closer.

There was a man at the service entrance of the building, trying to force his way in!

Frank crossed the street quietly and made his way toward that alleyway, sticking close to the storefronts and staying out of sight. He reached the end of the last building and peered around the corner.

Apparently, the intruder was having no luck. The service door was resisting all his efforts to force it open.

There was something familiar about the man, about the way he moved. Then he turned slightly, giving Frank a quick look at his face.

Frank stepped out into the open, unconcerned about the noise he made now. The man spun around, startled, and almost dropped the tools he'd been using.

For a moment they stared at each other. It was hard to tell who was more surprised.

Then Frank spoke. "Hello—brother."

Chris Hardy said nothing.

"Hardy? Me?" Joe asked, studying the man's face and the way he held his gun. He was a professional, too—probably STB. Definitely not an elevator operator. "I'm afraid you have the wrong guy, mister. And what's with the gun?"

"Please." The operator shook his head tolerantly. "Don't insult my intelligence. Mr. Krc saw you following them on that ridiculous toy"—he indicated the skateboard—"and told me to make sure you didn't get lost on your way up to see them." He motioned Joe forward with his gun.

"All right, but you're making a mistake." Joe threw up his hands, as if he were going along quietly, then suddenly he flung the skateboard at the man's gun hand. The gun went off with a loud crack and flew halfway down the hall. He followed the skateboard with a left that caught the STB man square on the jaw and sent him reeling backward.

He had to get out of there and fast. That gunshot would bring everyone else on the floor running. He started for the elevator, but the operator grabbed his arm and spun him around.

Joe threw a quick right, but the man ducked and circled behind Joe to block his path to the elevator. Then the STB man pivoted swiftly on his right foot and aimed a karate kick at Joe's head.

Joe ducked under it and grabbed the man's foot as it passed over him. He intended to use it as a lever to swing him around. But the agent kept his balance, and swung his other leg under Joe, cutting his knees out from under him. Both fell to the floor.

They rolled over and over, each trying to get on top of the other. There was a flurry of blows—

and then the STB man had his hands tight around Joe's throat and was forcing the breath out of his body.

With his last bit of strength, Joe rammed his knees into the man's chest, lifting him up and over and slamming him into the far wall with a loud crack.

"Whew." Joe struggled to his knees, gasping for breath. The other man didn't move.

Someone clapped. "Very nicely done, Mr. Hardy."

Joe groaned. He recognized that voice.

Liehm stood over him, two other men flanking him. Both were holding guns on Joe.

"And now, if you would please accompany us"—he smiled—"Mr. Krc is very anxious to see you."

Slowly Chris let his hands drop to his sides. "I shouldn't be so surprised you managed to find this place." He forced a smile. "Actually, I'm glad you're here."

"I didn't think I'd ever see you again," Frank said. He studied the tools Chris had dropped. Now that he was closer, he could see that they were electronic gadgets. It seemed as if Chris wasn't using force to get into the building at all. "What are you doing?"

"I'm disarming the building's—Liehm's—security system," Chris said. "It's quite sophisticated." He picked up his tools again. "I can stop them, here, tonight—with your help."

"Not so fast," Frank said, grabbing Chris's shoulder and turning him so he was looking directly into his eyes. "A friend of mine pieced together that videotape you were carrying. We watched it last night. Who was that man you shot?"

Chris shook his head slowly but said nothing.

"And who are you? What country do you work for?" Frank asked.

Again, Chris shook his head, avoiding Frank's eyes.

Frank exploded. "Why don't you tell us what's going on? First you come to us to help you prove Janosik is being framed—then you run away before we can help you!"

"I didn't come to you for help!" Chris yelled back. "I came to your father!"

"Well, you got us," Frank said angrily. "And you'll find that once Joe and I start something, we like to finish it. Now, what's this all about?"

Chris took a deep breath. "I've been waiting across the street all day for the chance to disarm and get inside this building," Chris said. "Earlier Liehm and Krc went out. I thought the others would leave soon."

"Others?"

"The other employees of Liehm's company— the other STB agents here. But they haven't left yet—and now Liehm and Krc have returned."

He looked Frank directly in the eye. "Joe followed them in half an hour ago. He hasn't come out yet."

Frank turned white. "Joe followed them in—alone?" He was too concerned for his brother to be angry at him.

"I didn't see him until it was too late to stop him," Chris said. "Now, are we going to disarm this system and go in there, or do you want to ask me any more questions?"

In answer, Frank picked up one of the electronic gadgets and carried it over to Chris. "Okay," he said, grim determination in his voice. "Show me how to use this."

"I said I would kill you, and I will—make no mistake about that." In contrast to the last time Joe had seen him, Gregor was calm and in complete control of himself. He paced slowly back and forth in front of Joe, who was sitting in a chair with armed guards standing on either side.

They were in the company's security center. A long console covered with television screens split the room in half. The screens were tied in to cameras hidden throughout the building. Joe hadn't expected to find this level of technical sophistication—but that wasn't the only surprise he'd gotten at Video Imaging.

The first had come after Liehm led him through dozens of offices to this room. The equipment around him exactly duplicated that which he and Frank had found in Chris's basement.

He hadn't been able to put all these pieces of the puzzle together yet—but the picture was getting clearer.

"I will not have you interfering in our plans again. I want to know everything you and your brother know." Gregor stopped pacing directly in front of him and rested his palms on the arms of the chair Joe sat in. He leaned forward until their faces were barely six inches apart. "Tell me, and I promise you a painless death."

Joe shook his head. "That doesn't sound like much of a bargain to me."

"Where is your brother now?" Gregor asked.

Joe stifled the urge to ask which one and merely smiled.

Gregor shrugged as if to turn away—and backhanded Joe hard across the face.

"I do not like you, boy," he said. "I do not like looking over my shoulder and finding you there." He snapped his fingers. One of the guards handed him a gun. He pointed it at Joe. "Answer my question—where is your brother?"

Joe shook his head. He tasted blood running from a cut in his lip. "I honestly don't know."

Gregor studied the gun in his hand. "I said before I didn't like using this as a weapon." He smiled and cocked the trigger. "Perhaps in your case I will make an exception. . . ."

Joe shut his eyes.

"No, I forbid it!"

Joe cracked an eye open. Liehm had entered the room and stood beside Gregor, one hand on his arm.

"We cannot keep committing murders, Gregor—not in this country."

The taller man removed his finger from the trigger and pressed his lips tightly together, trying to control himself. "Yes, Doctor," he said, lowering the gun slightly. "What would you have me do?"

Liehm smiled. "Be patient, my friend. All our plans will triumph, very soon." He reached for the gun in Gregor's hand.

Gregor swung his arm around viciously, catching Liehm full in the face with the butt of his gun. The doctor fell to the ground as if he'd been struck by lightning.

"Patience?" Gregor roared. "Patience is for weaklings, Doctor."

Liehm stirred slightly. Gregor reached down and hauled him to his feet. "I will let you continue with your ridiculous, expensive scheme because Prague has ordered me to. But it is I who am in control here, I who will deal with this intruder. Is that clear?"

Liehm nodded feebly.

"Now do what ever you need to do!" He shoved Liehm, and the doctor stumbled out the door.

Gregor turned his attention back to Joe.

"Wait a minute, I thought you were on the same side."

"We are," Gregor said. "But I disagree with the doctor's methods. He will be satisfied to ruin Janosik's name—as if that would silence the traitor forever. But there is only one way to make sure one's enemies are truly silenced." He smiled at Joe and raised the gun, pressing it to Joe's head.

"This way."

Chapter

11

JOE SHUT HIS EYES.

He heard a loud, almost deafening noise.

Then another. And another.

He opened his eyes.

The security center was in a state of frenzied activity. Alarms were going off everywhere.

"What—?" Gregor said, turning away from Joe. "What is happening?"

"A break-in, sir—downstairs!" One of the men who had been guarding Joe was now hunched over a security monitor. "Unable to isolate the location!"

"Doctor!" Gregor yelled, striding out of the room. He turned back and pointed at Joe. "Keep an eye on him!"

The guard not watching the monitor leveled his gun at Joe. Gregor returned with Liehm. The whole right side of the doctor's face was swollen.

Gregor motioned him over to the security monitor. "What is this taking place? Why don't we see anything on the cameras?" he asked.

Liehm's fingers ranged over the controls expertly, and the cameras began moving, their view changing on all the screens.

"There!" Gregor pointed. "Downstairs, at the service entrance." He turned to Joe and smiled. "It looks as if your brother has decided to join us."

Joe sat up. Sure enough, there was Frank, apparently trying to force a door downstairs.

Liehm shut off the alarms, but continued to work the console. "This is strange," he said. "I can't get the cameras to move any farther."

"What is the matter?" Gregor asked. He pointed to the two guards. "You! And you! Go downstairs, escort our friend back here. He'll want to see his brother."

The two guards left, and the man Joe had met earlier, who had been posing as the elevator operator, walked in.

"What is it, Ludvik?" Gregor asked.

"The tapes—should I send them now, Doctor?" Ludvik asked Liehm. "Or do we wait till morning?"

Liehm shrugged and said nothing.

"Doctor?" Ludvik pressed.

"Send them now—it doesn't matter," Gregor said, smiling. "One newspaper and two television stations—and they all think they have an 'exclusive.' Yes—send it."

Ludvik nodded and left.

"Something is wrong with this monitor, Krc!" Liehm insisted. "Someone has tampered with it!"

"Nonsense, Doctor." Gregor came and stood by his side. "I have been here the whole time."

While they were talking, Joe made a move as if to stand up—and Gregor, still talking to Liehm, shook his head.

"I wouldn't do that, Mr. Hardy," he said, pulling out his own gun again. "You'll miss your last chance to see your brother—breathing."

Joe sat down, disgusted. How had Frank managed to find this place? And why was he breaking in alone? Why hadn't he brought along any backup? He shook his head. It didn't sound like Frank. It sounded like him.

Gregor called his attention back to the monitor. "I want you to watch this."

On the screen, Frank, who had been attaching something to a cable running along the outside of the building, suddenly looked up from what he was doing. The two guards moved into the picture, guns held high. Frank raised his hands, and for a minute, he looked directly into the camera.

Then the screen went dark.

"What has happened, Doctor?"

"I don't know!" Liehm's voice was both angry and frustrated. "I tell you, something is the matter with this machine!"

Gregor frowned. "Perhaps," he said. "We will

wait till the guards return, and run a check on the system.''

Gregor paced the floor anxiously, while Liehm stood silently by the security console. Five minutes had gone by.

"I do not understand this!" Gregor said. "Where are they? They should have been back long ago!"

Joe shrugged and said nothing, but inside he felt a tiny spark of hope flicker. "Maybe somebody offered them a better job," Joe suggested.

Gregor shot him an angry look and was about to say something.

Then the alarms went off again.

"Another break-in!" Liehm said, studying the console, confusion in his voice. "In two places at once!" If his run-in with Gregor had punctured his self-confidence, his inability to make the security system work had clearly shattered it.

"Calm yourself, Doctor!" Gregor said. "Shut off the alarms, and isolate the break-ins." He frowned at Joe. "Clearly, your brother is a lot cleverer than you are. Somehow, he has managed to turn our security system against us."

Liehm complied with Gregor's orders. "The break-in is again at the service entrance and our private staircase," he said.

"I will go myself, this time," Gregor said. He handed Liehm his gun. "Watch him. Do not leave this room. His brother may be leading us all on a wild goose chase. If I do not find him, I will return in five minutes."

"Wait!" Liehm said. "What if you don't come back?"

"Then you will be in charge again, Doctor." Gregor smiled. "You can do what you like."

As soon as Gregor left the room, Joe leaned forward in his chair. "He's going to kill Janosik," Joe began.

"Shut up!" Liehm yelled. "Do you think I don't know that?"

He raised his gun. "Bring that chair over here—that's it." He positioned Joe against the wall, keeping the console with its rows of TV monitors between the two of them, so he could watch both. "Now sit down, and be quiet!"

Joe decided not to test Liehm any further. Clearly, the man was on the verge of cracking up.

Now that he couldn't see the monitor screen he had no way of judging what was happening downstairs. He remained still in his chair, listening intently for any sound.

Five minutes passed quickly, and Liehm grew more agitated, more concerned. "What's happening out there?" He slammed his hand down on the console. He turned to Joe. "Where is everyone?" he demanded.

"Here I am, Doctor."

Both of them turned to see who had spoken. Chris stood framed in the doorway.

"You!" Liehm said.

"I'll bet you never thought you'd see me again," Chris said, walking into the room. "Hello, Joe."

Joe nodded but said nothing. He was as confused as Liehm was upset.

"But you're dead!" Liehm shouted hysterically, all his self-control gone now. "I saw Gregor shoot you!"

Chris shrugged and circled slowly around the room, maintaining his distance from Liehm till he was standing beside Joe. "Here I am," he said, spreading his arms. "Alive and kicking."

A wicked grin split the doctor's bruised face. "Not for long," he said, raising his gun.

Joe looked up at Chris, horrified. What was he doing?

Why was he offering Liehm such a perfect target?

Chapter

12

A SECOND LATER JOE had his answer.

A hand fell on Liehm's shoulder.

"Ah, Gregor," Liehm said excitedly, without turning. "See who I have found here? Now we can take care of all these Hardys at once."

"Sorry to disappoint you, Doctor."

Liehm turned. He barely had enough time to be surprised before a fist caught him hard on the chin, and he crumpled to the floor.

Frank stood over him, rubbing his knuckles. "That's for slugging me with that phone."

Chris picked up Liehm's fallen gun.

Joe clapped Frank on the back. "Nice work." He looked behind Frank. "Anybody else coming?"

Frank shook his head. "Just us—the two guards that came after us are downstairs, out of it."

"How'd you do it?"

"He did it." Frank nodded toward Chris. "He was planning to break in here and take on all of them single-handedly before I showed up. We triggered a few alarms, ambushed the guards that came . . ." Frank shrugged.

"You saved my life," Joe said to Chris.

"I'm the one who put it in danger in the first place," Chris said.

Joe grinned. "Nobody's responsible for what I do but me." He aimed an accusing finger at Chris. "But I still have a lot of questions for you!"

Chris smiled faintly and nodded. "I know I haven't been completely honest with you, but I'm ready to give you the answers you need."

"Good," Joe said.

"Hey!" Frank interrupted. "Where's Gregor?"

Joe's face dropped. "Gregor? He left after you set off the alarms the second time." He stared at Frank. "He didn't go past you?"

Frank shook his head.

"Then where *did* he go?" Chris asked.

"If you didn't pass him coming up from the service entrance, then he must have gone to the private staircase."

"I know where it is," Chris said. "Come on."

Frank and Joe followed him on a dead run back through the office till they came to a closed door. Chris tried the knob.

"He locked it behind him."

Joe tightened his lips in frustration. He thought of Gregor on the other side of the door. Then he pushed Chris aside. "Watch it."

Chris turned to him. "What are you doing?"

"I said, watch it."

Joe put his shoulder down and charged the door. The hinges groaned, and the wood around them cracked.

"Come on," Chris said, putting his hand on Joe's arm. "Let's go around the other way. That door's solid—it's not going to give."

"Give me Liehm's gun. I'll try shooting out the lock," Frank said, holding out his hand to Chris.

Joe pushed Frank's hand down. "One more time," he said. He charged the door again.

The wood split on one side. Joe kicked hard, and the door fell to the floor with a loud crash.

"Let's go," he said, stepping over it.

Behind the door was a short hallway leading to a set of stairs. Joe took the steps two at a time, expecting at any moment to find Gregor standing on one of the landings below him. But he reached the bottom of the staircase without an incident, Frank a step behind him.

Now another door stood in front of him. Without breaking step, Joe kicked it open—and found himself outside, looking into the parking garage.

The space where the Mercedes had been was empty.

"He got away." Joe shook his head and looked at Chris and Frank. "He's going to kill Janosik!"

"Kill him?" Frank grabbed his shoulders.

"Gregor and Liehm had some kind of fight," Joe said. "Gregor said Liehm could continue with his plan, but the only sure way to keep Janosik quiet was to kill him." He turned to Frank again. "And that's what he's going to do!"

"Easy," Frank said. "Lieutenant Considine is out at the hotel, with a lot of other cops. Nothing's going to happen to Janosik." He thought for a moment. "How did Liehm plan to keep Janosik from speaking?"

"I don't know," Joe said. "Liehm came to the hotel and showed Janosik something. Whatever it was really shook him. Wait a minute! It must've been that tape they said they were sending."

"And I bet I know where they're sending it," Frank said.

Joe nodded. "Jean Eykis. Has to be."

Frank turned. "Chris, what do you know about—"

But Chris wasn't there.

"He's got a real bad habit of disappearing," Joe said.

"I don't believe this!" Frank shook his head. "Come on, he must still be inside."

He and Joe raced back upstairs. At the entrance to the stairway, where Joe had knocked down the door, Frank stopped and picked something up off the floor.

"Liehm's gun," he said and frowned.

"What?" Joe asked.

"Why would he leave this?"

"I don't know!" Joe said angrily. "Nothing he's done so far has made any sense!"

Frank shook his head slowly. "I really thought Chris was going to level with us this time. Whose side is he on?"

"His own, apparently," Joe said.

Frank looked around the offices. "Liehm's gone!" he said. "We should have tied him up. How could we be so dumb? You know, this place has even more computer equipment than Chris's basement."

"That's obviously the link between Chris and Gregor and Liehm—but what's it all mean?"

"I don't know," Frank said. "If we could get a look at that tape they sent Eykis, that might help us."

Joe nodded, then slapped his forehead. "Whoa. Hold on a minute." He ducked into another room.

When he came out, he grinned at Frank. "Almost forgot my skateboard."

Eykis seemed surprised to see Frank again so soon. After he introduced Joe, he told her why they'd come.

"We think whatever they sent you is the key to this whole case we're working on," he said.

"It might be some kind of set-up, or a frame," Joe added.

She shook her head sadly. "I don't think so." She put her hands on her desk and stood up, leaning on her fingertips. "Well—you might as well watch it. You'll see it sometime soon."

She led them down the hall into a small room that was empty except for a desk with a TV set and VCR and a few chairs.

"This came about an hour ago," she said, unlocking the top drawer and taking out a video-cassette. "The man who gave it to me asked me to call Liehm if I had any questions."

She inserted the cassette into the machine and turned back to them.

"Before I play this, I want you to know something. I've been writing for the *Tribune* for five years—and I've admired nobody in the world as much as I've admired Alexander Janosik." She sighed heavily. "This tape broke my heart."

Frank met her eyes and nodded but said nothing.

"That's the only reason I'm showing it to you—because I think it will break yours too. And because if there's any chance you can help prove it is a fake or a setup"—she managed a tired smile—"well, I'll take that chance. Otherwise, I'm stuck with a story that I really don't want to write."

She started the tape and sat down with them to watch.

It looked like the kind of film a bank's security camera would take, only with sound. The camera showed two men sitting at a table in an otherwise empty room. Frank didn't recognize either of them. Then Alexander Janosik entered.

Frank sat up and watched closely as the two men on screen rose to greet Janosik. They obviously knew one another, though their greetings were more courteous than friendly.

Janosik sat down at the table, facing the two men. They handed him a sheaf of notes and an envelope. Janosik glanced over the paper and opened the envelope.

It was full of hundred-dollar bills. Smiling at the two men, Janosik stood, shook hands again, and left the room.

The reporter stopped the tape.

"I assume you recognize Janosik—the two men you saw with him are Roger Douglas and David McCormick. They're both CIA."

Frank shook his head, unable to believe what he'd seen.

"Still think he's being framed?" Eykis asked bitterly. "Or are we the patsies in this picture?"

The Hardys said nothing. There was nothing they could say.

"Well, then, you'd better show yourselves out." Eykis stood and turned to go. "I have to get busy. I have a story to write."

* * *

Frank and Joe took the subway back to the Charles. Both were silent for most of the ride. Earlier that day, when he had listened to Janosik talk about what had happened to his country, Joe had thought of him as a patriot and hero. Now he didn't know what to think. How could he doubt the evidence of his own eyes?

"Frank," he asked. "Do you believe what we just saw?"

His brother took a long time answering. "I have to," he said finally. "But it doesn't make sense. Why would Janosik take a payoff? He doesn't seem like the kind of man who needs—or wants—a lot of money." He shook his head. "It just doesn't make sense."

"Nothing about this case makes sense," Joe agreed.

Frank knotted his hands together, frustrated. "I can't help the feeling that the clue we need is right in front of us, and we're just missing it. Maybe we ought to call in the police."

"The police? You mean Considine?" Joe asked, opening the door to their hotel room. "I don't think he wants to hear anything more from us."

He walked in the room and stopped suddenly.

"Oh, I wouldn't say that," a familiar voice said. "There's a whole lot more I want to hear from you. Only I'd rather not talk here."

The lights came on. Lieutenant Considine was

sitting on one of the beds. Two uniformed police officers stood by the window.

Considine motioned the two officers forward. "Let's take a little trip to headquarters, shall we?"

Chapter

13

"I DON'T KNOW WHAT kind of police force you have in Bayport," Considine said, pacing back and forth in front of the small table where the Hardys sat—where they'd been sitting for the past four hours. "But here we don't look kindly on kids who fake graduate student IDs and break into hotels. I could throw the book at both of you!"

Joe glared at the lieutenant but held his tongue.

"Lieutenant, did you check those names we gave you—Gregor Krc, Finn Liehm?" Frank asked, taking another sip of the coffee in front of him. He'd almost nodded off twice during Considine's interrogation.

"I'm not interested in fantastic conspiracy stories, or how the Czech secret police is invading Boston Common." Considine tossed their phony ID cards on the table. "Let's start with where you got these!"

"Look," Frank began. "I told you—what's important here is that this Gregor Krc is on the loose and he intends to kill Janosik. Lieutenant, that's what you ought to be focusing on—"

"Don't you tell me what my job is!" Considine roared, slamming his hand down on the table right in front of Frank. Coffee sloshed from the cup onto the table.

His partner laid a restraining hand on Considine's arm.

"I'm going to walk out of this room for five minutes," the lieutenant continued softly, stabbing a finger in Frank's face. "When I come back, you boys had better be ready to give me some answers." He stalked out of the room, slamming the door behind him.

"The lieutenant gets a little intense sometimes." His partner, a detective named Mitchell, pulled up a chair and sat in front of them. "But he's an all-right guy." He smiled at Frank and Joe.

"Maybe before he comes back, you could tell me a little bit more about why you checked into the Charles—in the room right next door to Janosik's."

The brothers exchanged a knowing glance. They knew this game too well, having pulled it a few times themselves—the good cop–bad cop routine.

"Like we said," Joe began, "we felt Janosik's life might be in danger. We knew that they—

Gregor and Liehm, that is—were going to try to frame him somehow, so—"

"Please," the detective said, holding up his hand. "No more talk about Janosik being framed—we've all seen the film on the local newscasts tonight."

Joe glowered at him. "That's not the point, is it? This guy Gregor was crazy enough to shoot at me—and now he's after Janosik! It doesn't matter whether or not he took money from the CIA; his life's in danger!"

"So *you* say." Mitchell stood and began pacing.

"What about the kid whose skateboard I borrowed?" Joe asked. "His name's on it. Why don't you call and ask him about the shooting at the hotel?"

The detective smiled faintly, as if to let Joe know he didn't believe that part of his story, either. "We'll try that in the morning. For now, I'd like to go back to where you got these IDs—"

"Hold it." Considine walked back into the room, madder than he'd been before. Joe braced himself for another round of questions.

"Let 'em go," Considine said flatly.

Joe swiveled around to stare first at Frank, then at Considine.

"Let us go?" Joe asked.

"Let them go?" Mitchell repeated.

"You heard me!" Considine roared. "Let them go! FBI says the guys they're talking about—

Gregor and Liehm—really are Czech agents. We've got orders to arrest them on sight. And those two guys we picked up unconscious at that Video Imaging place—they're STB, too."

He turned to Frank and Joe. "You must have some heavy friends in Washington, because they told us to let you walk—no questions asked."

Frank tried to hide a smile. "Friends in Washington" meant one thing to him: the Gray Man and the Network. Despite the trouble they often had working with America's most secret intelligence network, sometimes the connection proved useful.

"We'd be glad to stay and help you look for Liehm and Gregor, Lieutenant," Frank said. "We've seen them close up—"

"Their pictures will be coming over the wire. I think we can manage without your help." Considine motioned behind them through the open door, and a uniformed officer brought in two suitcases. "I took the liberty of having your bags packed and brought here." Considine looked at his watch. "The first plane leaves Logan at seven this morning. Catch it. And I don't want to see you guys playing detective in my town again, is that clear?"

Frank and Joe stood but said nothing.

Considine pulled the IDs the Beast had given them out of their wallets. "I'll keep these, if you don't mind—even if you're not involved in the phony ID ring, like Washington says. I'd like them as little souvenirs."

His grin vanished. "Make sure these boys get on that plane," he told Mitchell. "And then come see me—we have to beef up security for Janosik." He stalked out of the room.

As Frank and Joe reached the airport, a newspaper truck was just pulling up. Frank watched bale after bale of newspapers hit the sidewalk. "Hold on a minute," he said. Setting his suitcase down, he walked over and studied the headlines. "Janosik Took Money from CIA," they screamed. Janosik's picture ran next to the article, a shot the paper must have had on file. He was speaking in front of a crowd somewhere, and the photographer had caught him in midsentence, his mouth open, his hand waving as he strove to make some point. He looked exactly as he had the day before in the park, when he'd been speaking of freedom and great men.

"It says he's speaking anyway." Mitchell read the article over Frank's shoulder. "You have to admire his guts."

Frank took a deep breath. "I do," he said. He turned away and picked up his suitcase again. "Come on—let's board."

"I don't like running away from a case like this, Frank," Joe grumbled.

"We're not running, Joe," Frank said. "The police know about Gregor and Liehm now, and you heard Considine say they're beefing up security for Janosik's speech. We've done everything we can. We do anything else, and Considine'll lock us up and throw away the key—never mind what our friend in Washington says."

Joe still wasn't convinced. "What about Chris?" he asked quietly.

Frank shook his head. "What about him? He's disappeared again—along with whatever proof he promised us of Janosik's innocence. If he wants to contact us, he knows where we are."

He was tired, he was disillusioned, and he was hungry—and all he wanted to do right then was sleep. "Wake me when we get to New York," he said, leaning back in his seat.

The Hardys took a cab to their house from the airport—and found a surprise waiting for them at home.

"Mom! Dad! You're home early!" Frank said as he walked into the living room.

"And so are you, from what Callie told us," Fenton Hardy said. "Fill me in on this Alexander Janosik case. I can't believe what the papers and TV stations are saying."

"It's even weirder than you've heard." Joe flopped down on the couch. He and Frank hadn't slept yet.

"Well?" their father asked.

Frank looked at Joe. "Chris?" Frank asked him.

Joe nodded. "Ask them."

"Chris?" Their mother looked puzzled. "Who's he?"

"*This* is Chris." Frank took out the driver's license he'd been carrying around and handed it to his mother. "Do you know him?"

She shook her head and passed it on to Fenton, who looked at it a little more closely.

"No, I don't know him," he said, reading the license. "Hardy? Is he related to us?"

"That's what we were going to ask you," Joe said.

Their parents stared at him. "Go ahead, we're listening."

Joe opened his mouth, then shut it. "You tell them," he said to Frank.

"He told us——" He stopped and tried to start again, unsure of how to ask the question without seeming ridiculous. He looked at Joe, who nodded vigorously, silently urging him on.

Frank decided there was no way to handle it without being ridiculous, so he just came out with it.

"He told us he's our older brother."

Frank and Laura Hardy stared at him, then Joe; then they turned to each other.

"Well?" Joe asked. "Is it true?"

His parents began to laugh.

"What kind of a question is that?" his father asked, shaking his head.

"Boys," his mother said, still trying to stop

laughing. "I can assure you you don't have an older brother! Whatever or whoever gave you that idea?"

"It has to do with this case," Frank said. He told them how he and Joe had met Chris down by the waterfront, how Chris had made his shocking claim, and how he'd known so much about their family.

"I saw his birth certificate—it's on file at City Hall. I also saw a school transcript."

"Frank," his father interrupted. "All those things can be faked. You ought to know that better than anyone else."

"But how could he get onto the City Hall computer system?"

"If you could, so could he," his father said firmly. "It interests me, though, that he knew so much about us. I think it's important we find out who this young man really is."

"We've been trying to do that," Joe said. "Only we haven't had much luck."

"There's something else about him, too," Frank said. "The videotape."

"Right," Joe said, grabbing his father by the arm. "Come watch this. If nothing else, at least you'll get a better look at him."

They all followed Joe into the den, where their Aunt Gertrude, who had returned from her visit, was sitting quietly, reading. She glanced up from her book. "What's all the fuss?"

"Just a little confusion, Aunt Gertrude," Joe said. "It has to do with our older brother."

"Oh." Aunt Gertrude began to read her book again. Then she frowned and looked up. "What did you say?"

Frank inserted the videotape and started it up. "He brought this with him when he came to meet us at the waterfront—said it would help prove Janosik was innocent."

They all settled down to watch the tape.

"What does it mean—'DD insertion'?" their father asked as the words appeared on the screen.

"We don't know," Frank said, shaking his head.

When they came to the close-up of the young soldier, Frank froze the tape, and turned to his parents.

"Does this help—does he look at all familiar?"

Both shook their heads.

"I don't understand." Aunt Gertrude spoke up from her chair in the corner. "Are you trying to identify that actor?"

"Actor?" Frank echoed.

"That's right, Frank." She shook her finger. "Don't you recognize this film?"

Frank shook his head. "Tell me."

She stood and walked to the screen. "This is a scene from *Deadly Deception*—that big suspense movie from a couple of years ago. This is the scene where they kill General Voroloff." She pointed at Chris's face and frowned. "This man's

114

face doesn't look familiar. I was quite sure that another actor played this part. Oh, well," she said, sitting back down. "I must have been wrong."

"No, Aunt Gertrude," Frank said, as understanding dawned on him at last. "No, you weren't wrong!" He turned to Joe. "Get it? DD insertion—"

"*Deadly Deception* insertion!" Joe said excitedly. "Somehow, Chris's face has been inserted on top of the original actor's!"

"Right." Frank nodded. "So he never killed anybody."

Joe balled his right hand into a fist and smacked it into his left palm. "And that could mean Janosik never took that money, either! The whole thing's a fake!"

Chapter

14

"A FAKE?" LAURA HARDY ASKED. "How can you fake a film?"

"We're not talking about film, Mom," Frank said. "We're talking about videotape. It doesn't record pictures, it records data magnetically—like audio cassettes, or computer disks."

"So Chris used all those computers to help Krc and Liehm make this phony videotape?" Joe asked.

"Right," Frank said.

"I'm afraid I still don't understand," their mother said.

Frank sat down next to her. "There's a piece of equipment called a photo imager. It breaks up any photo into little dots—"

"Like on a TV set," his mother said.

"Exactly," Frank nodded. "Once you have an image broken and recorded, you can use a computer to move it around any way you want. It's

how they colorize old black-and-white movies."
He shook his head. "The company was called
Video Imaging," he said to himself. "I should
have seen it!"

"Easy, Frank." His father put a hand on his
shoulder. "What you're talking about doesn't
sound quite as simple as colorizing film. I didn't
know things like this were possible."

"They sure are, Dad," he said. "In a few years
this'll seem like kid stuff. The *Deadly Deception*
tape must have just been a test. Making the videotape of Janosik taking the bribe, that was the
real project."

He shook his head. "It must have taken them
months—maybe even a year. They probably began with a real tape of Janosik meeting those two
CIA guys—then changed it to smear him."

"And that must be where Chris came in. He
worked with them to develop that tape," Joe said.
"So his 'proof' of Janosik's innocence—"

"Was the tape that he brought with him, showing what kind of image manipulation was possible." Frank was still angry at himself. "I should
have seen it—they've been doing this kind of
thing on commercials for the last year or so."

"I'm starting to get lost," Fenton said. "I want
this whole story from the beginning. Come on."

Frank and Joe followed their father into his
study and laid out the whole story for him. When
his sons had finished talking, Fenton Hardy
stood. "This Chris sounds like a very mixed-up

young man," he said. "He can't seem to make up his mind whose side he's on."

Frank nodded. "Once he found out the tape he'd helped put together was going to the press and TV stations, he just took off, I guess."

"Sounds like you don't really believe that, Frank."

"I don't know, Dad." Frank smiled for a second. "I kind of liked the guy. And last night, I thought he was going to stick with us."

"He may surprise you yet," Fenton Hardy frowned as he concentrated. "Well, the first thing we have to do is get Janosik's name cleared."

"We can't just tell everyone the tape's a fake, though," Frank said. "It will take some proof—probably even beyond the phony *Deadly Deception* tape."

"From what you told me, I'd say the best place to get that proof is in Boston—at that place you broke into, Video Imaging," his father said.

Frank cleared his throat, glancing at Joe. "Uh, Dad, we're not supposed to go back there. We had a sort of run-in with a police lieutenant. . . ."

"You left that part out of your story." Fenton Hardy raised an eyebrow. "Never mind. One of the people I worked with on the force in New York is pretty important up there now. He should be able to smooth the way for us."

Joe and Frank exchanged sheepish grins.

Their father picked up the phone and dialed. "Yes, I'll hold." He picked up a pencil and started tapping it absentmindedly on his desk. "We'll take the next shuttle up."

"Right, Dad," said Joe. He turned to Frank, whispering, "I'd love to see the look on Considine's face when he sees us again."

Frank nodded, grinning.

"They're putting me through. We'll have this cleared up in a minute," their father said, leaning back in his chair. "Ah, yes—can you get me Ben Considine's office, please?"

Joe's mouth dropped open.

"Ben, Fenton Hardy here. . . . Yes, it has been a long time. I wonder if—"

As one, Joe and Frank got up quietly and headed for the door.

"Hold on a minute, Ben." Fenton covered the receiver. "What's the matter with you two? Don't you want to tell Lieutenant Considine what you've found out?" he asked.

They both shook their heads.

"We're kind of tired of talking to the police, dad." Frank smiled weakly. "You do it."

The plane ride to Boston was just long enough to be uncomfortable for Frank and Joe. They'd had to explain to their father why they hadn't been entirely truthful with Lieutenant Considine. By the time they reached Cambridge again, though, they had cleared that up.

Considine met them at the precinct house.

"Fenton!" he said. The two men shook hands. Then he stared at Frank and Joe.

"I knew that name was familiar," he said, scowling at them. Then he broke into a smile. "You kids remind me of myself, when I was younger—real troublemakers," he said, turning to Fenton Hardy. "Like when we were on the force in New York, Fenton, right?"

"Not quite," Fenton Hardy said. "We always worked with our superior officers—not against them." Frank and Joe knew those words were meant for them—a not-so-subtle reminder that if they wanted to be detectives, they had to learn to cooperate with the law.

Frank moved the subject to more comfortable territory. "I think the thing to do—with your help, Lieutenant," he added, "is to check out Video Imaging again. That's where we'll find proof of how they made these tapes."

"Yeah," Joe said. "We didn't exactly give it a thorough going-over before."

Fenton nodded. "Seems like a good idea to me. Can you spare a few men to help?"

Considine shook his head. "I haven't had a chance to check the place out at all—the new 'proof' about Janosik has the campus up in arms. Demonstrations are starting already—"

He frowned. "And we're still waiting for the FBI to get us pictures of those two—Krc and Liehm. With all the VIPs in town for Janosik's speech, I need everyone I have on campus."

120

Frank thought for a moment. "I know who could help us, Lieutenant. There's a student on campus who's a real computer expert."

"Get him down here," Considine said, glancing at his watch. He pointed Frank to an empty desk. "Use that phone." He turned to Fenton. "I'll count on you to keep everything under control. I've got to get back to the JFK Center."

Fenton nodded.

Frank called the Beast and explained why they needed his help.

"Wow," he said when they were finished. "They must really have some hardware to pull that trick. I'll be there in five minutes."

He was, and a few minutes later the four of them were in a borrowed police car on their way to downtown Cambridge. Fenton drove, with Joe in the front seat next to him and Frank and the Beast—who introduced himself as Larry—in back.

"Right here?" their father asked, pulling into the parking garage next door.

"This is it," Frank said.

"I never thought I'd see this place again." Joe shook his head, thinking of how close he'd come to dying in that building.

"I've been here before—only at night, though," the Beast said, getting out of the car. "We're going to Video Imaging—right?"

The three Hardys stared at him.

"My friend Chris works here," the Beast explained.

"Hold it," Frank said, pulling him back into the car. "Chris? Chris Hardy?"

"Nah," the Beast said. "Chris Bayer."

Fenton smacked the steering wheel. "Chris Bayer," he said. "Of course."

"You know him, Dad?"

"I did." He turned and faced his sons. "Chris is the son of a man I knew years back. Walter Bayer, a key witness in a mob case we were prosecuting in New York. His testimony helped put a big mob boss behind bars—"

"Tom Luther?" Joe asked. He remembered his father talking about the case a long time ago.

"Tom Luther." Fenton nodded. "His people killed Walter and his wife. Chris was about five or six at the time, but he'd seen the murder, so the mob was after him."

He shook his head. "When Laura and I heard about it, we took Chris in. It was only for half a year, and we had to keep it quiet. We were always afraid they'd track Chris down and kill him, too."

"No wonder you didn't recognize his picture," Joe said.

"It's been a long time," Fenton said. "Then the FBI decided he'd be safer if they moved him to another city, under the witness protection program." He took a deep breath. "It really shook your mother up when they took him away. Such a little boy being sent somewhere to new parents where he didn't know anyone.''

Frank dug Chris's license out of his pocket and showed it to the Beast. "Is this the guy?"

"That's him," the Beast said. He took the license from Frank and looked at it. "Excellent forgery—Chris really is much better at this than I am.''

Frank took the license back. "What else can you tell us about him?"

The Beast frowned. "Not much. We used to meet here, or at his place.''

"All the way out in Northampton?" Joe asked. "That's at least a two-hour drive from here."

"Northampton?" the Beast shook his head. "No, his apartment's here in Cambridge, right on Windham Street.''

"It might be worth taking a look at that apartment, Dad," Frank said.

Fenton Hardy nodded, starting up the car again. "Let's try there first.''

They found Windham easily enough. Except for the motel on the corner, it was a street of quiet frame houses. The one they pulled up at had been a bright yellow. Now it needed a fresh coat of paint.

"This is it," the Beast said.

"Looks like student housing to me," Fenton Hardy said.

Larry nodded. "Most of the block is. Chris has

been here for a while, though. He's really got the basement fixed up.''

''Let's check it out,'' Joe said.

They went down a short flight of steps to a separate basement entrance, with its own bell. They rang it.

No answer.

Frank wasn't too surprised. He hadn't expected it to be this easy to find Chris—not after the wild goose chase he'd led them on.

''Dad! Frank! Come here!''

Joe knelt at one of the basement windows. ''There's somebody in there, but he's not moving!''

Fenton Hardy gently pushed his son aside. ''Let me see, Joe.'' Frank peered over his father's shoulder. ''Dad, it looks like Chris!''

Fenton nodded. ''Let's get in there.'' He took off his jacket, wrapped it around his fist, then smashed the window. Joe reached through the broken glass, unlatched the window, climbed inside, and gasped.

''What's that smell?''

''Gas.'' Fenton was right behind his son. ''Don't touch a light switch, or do anything to cause a spark. You could turn the whole place into an inferno. Let's get Chris and get out of here.''

He turned to the Beast, who peered nervously through the window. ''Larry, ring doorbells—get anybody who's in the house out on the street.''

The Beast left. Fenton and Joe moved forward.

Chris lay sprawled in the middle of the living room floor. Joe knelt down, feeling for a pulse. "He's not dead, just unconscious. And he has a very nasty lump on the head."

"All right," Fenton said. He glanced around. "Let's pick him up—and get out of here."

"Dad, wait!" Joe had caught sight of something around the corner, in the next room.

He stepped back and found himself in the kitchen. The oven door was open, and on the floor lay another body, that of a woman.

Joe bent down to look closer. Then he heard a noise behind him.

Ludvik—the man who'd posed as the elevator operator the night before at Video Imaging—was tapping on the back window. He smiled when he saw he'd gotten Joe's attention.

"What the—" Joe began.

Then he saw the cigarette lighter in Ludvik's right hand. The STB man flicked it, sending a small flame shooting up into the air.

Still smiling, he kicked in the window, tossing the lighter into the kitchen.

Joe threw his hands over his face.

But that didn't stop the explosion that followed.

Chapter

15

FRANK SAW JOE HURTLING toward him—then a ball of hot air slammed him against the wall.

A split second later the entire room erupted into fire.

He struggled to his feet.

Joe was sprawled against one wall.

Fenton Hardy lay on the floor, pinned under a huge bookcase that had toppled over. Chris had been thrown clear. Flames were already licking at the bookcase.

Joe's eyes flickered open, and he began to cough. "Frank, what—"

"Help me!" Frank cried. "We've got to get this bookcase off Dad!"

Joe staggered to his feet.

"Mr. Hardy! Frank! Joe!" The Beast was at the window. "Are you all right?"

"Larry—get in here! We need your help!" Frank yelled. He knelt beside his father. Fenton

Hardy's eyes were shut, and blood trickled from a small gash on his forehead.

Larry climbed gingerly in through the window.

"Come on, come on," Frank called impatiently. The room was already starting to fill with smoke.

Joe and the Beast knelt beside him.

"Don't try to pick this thing up," Frank said. "Let's just lift it a little, and roll him out from under it. Together—one, two, three, lift!"

The bookcase didn't move.

"Too heavy," the Beast said, coughing. It was getting hard to breathe in the room.

"Take some of these books out!" Frank frantically began scooping books from the shelves and throwing them to the side.

"Again!" Frank yelled. They lifted the bookcase up a few inches.

Frank rolled his father out from underneath.

"Joe—take Chris." Frank's voice was raw as he picked up his father, slinging him over his shoulder. He opened the front door and staggered out onto the front lawn.

Fenton Hardy began coughing.

"Easy, Dad," Frank said. "You'll be all right." A group of students who must have been in the other apartments in the building crowded around.

"Don't just stand there!" Frank yelled. "Get the fire department!"

"Frank!" Joe and the Beast came out of the

apartment, carrying Chris. They lay him on the ground next to Fenton Hardy. Joe collapsed to his knees, gasping for breath. "Frank, there's a woman in the kitchen, unconscious!"

Frank glanced back at Chris's apartment. Smoke was billowing out through the front window.

Frank stood. "Keep the crowd back—I'm going in after her."

"Be careful!" Joe called out, struggling to his feet.

Frank nodded, bent low, and went in the front door.

He could barely see two feet ahead of him now—the fire was everywhere. He dropped to the floor to avoid the smoke and began slithering on his stomach in the direction of the kitchen.

How could the woman have survived? he asked himself.

And who was she, anyway?

Pushing that question to the back of his mind—there'd be time enough to answer it later, assuming there was a later—he moved forward. The heat grew more intense. He expected at any moment to feel the hot flames actually singe his hand.

Then he touched something so unexpected that he almost jumped to his feet.

Water!

He squinted and peered into the smoke.

The explosion had ripped some water pipes

loose. Water was spraying everywere around the kitchen, and a small shower of it had formed a puddle around—Jean Eykis!

He pulled her to him, and turned back toward the front door.

"What's taking him so long?" Joe asked, sitting on the front lawn beside his father. Chris had yet to stir, but his father had come around a few seconds ago and immediately started coughing. Larry had run off to look for some water for him.

"Shouldn't have let him go in there, Joe," his father said.

"Could you have stopped him, Dad?" Joe asked. "You know how hard it is to get Frank to change his mind once he's got it set on something." Joe spoke lightly, but he was worried. Frank had been gone almost a minute. The whole house was on fire now, flames and smoke billowing out of every window.

"I'm going in there after him, Dad," Joe said.

"No, wait," his father said, holding up his hand. They heard sirens in the distance, and a few seconds later a fire engine roared to a stop in front of the house.

"About time," Joe said. "Come on!" he yelled, rushing up to the firemen. "My brother's still in there!"

"All right," one said. He waved to the men behind him. "Let's go!"

Suddenly there was a huge roar behind them, like a clap of thunder. Joe turned. The building shuddered and leaned to one side.

"The crossbeams are giving way!" the fireman in charge shouted. The house shuddered again and collapsed forward. "Everybody back!"

"Frank!" Joe yelled and started toward the house.

"Easy, kid," the fireman grabbed his shoulder. "Nobody could have survived that."

"No!" Joe shouted, struggling free of the fireman's grasp. "Let me go!"

He shoved the fireman aside and moved forward.

"I appreciate the thought, but there's no one in there to save, Joe."

He turned. Frank stood behind him, holding Eykis in his arms.

"We had to go out the back," Frank said. "The flames cut us off." He smiled. "It's nice to know you care, though."

"It's not just that," Joe replied, trying hard not to let his relief show through. "You still owe me for the pizza."

"I thought you were headed for Video Imaging," Considine said, handing Fenton Hardy a bandage. The lieutenant had come as soon as he'd heard the report of the fire—and who was involved—over his radio.

"We were," Fenton said, wrapping it around his hand. "But something else came up." He filled Considine in.

"So now we've got to look out for this Ludvik guy, too," he said. He turned back to Frank and Joe. They were sitting on the street curb beside Chris, who had finally come around. An ambulance crew had arrived and had passed out bandages and oxygen to those who had been in the fire. They were still attending to Eykis—but it looked as if she was going to be all right, too.

"How's your friend, boys?"

"I'm all right, Lieutenant," Chris said.

"He's been filling in some of the missing pieces to the story," Frank explained.

"Last night at Video Imaging," Chris continued. "I started to follow you down the stairs—then someone smashed something over my head. The next thing I knew, I was in my own apartment with Gregor bending over me."

Frank smiled. "I knew you didn't run out on us."

Their father came and stood over the three of them.

"Hello, Chris," he said.

"Hello, Mr. Hardy," Chris replied. "It's been a long time."

Fenton nodded.

"I guess I've made an awful mess of things,

131

haven't I?" Chris stared at the street in front of him.

"Nothing we can't fix, I hope," Fenton replied. "But how did you get mixed up with Krc and Liehm in the first place?"

"They came to me," Chris said, finally raising his gaze to meet Fenton Hardy's. "You see, I was doing some—things—for some friends of mine at school." He glanced over quickly at the Beast, who glanced quickly at Frank and Joe.

"The phony ID ring," Considine grumbled. "I'll want to talk to you some more about this, young man. You have a lot of people on campus very upset. I hear there may be someone else involved in this as well, Larry," he said to the Beast.

Larry gulped.

Chris continued his story. "Liehm heard about what I was doing with the imager, I guess, and came to me to help him with this project he was starting. It was an incredible opportunity, they had a lot of money backing them up. I worked for almost a year with that crazy spy film—"

"Deadly Deception," Joe said.

"Right, and when that came out so well, Liehm said they were going to do something else using the techniques I'd developed, and if I didn't help they'd turn me in to the police for the phony ID stuff I'd done!"

"What made you decide to stop them?" Frank asked.

"Seeing Janosik speak," Chris said. "I know it sounds corny, but—"

Joe smiled. "It doesn't sound corny at all."

"Why were you pretending to be our brother?" Frank asked.

Chris shrugged. "That's an ID I've been using for a while. I did up the driver's license, the City Hall documents to show how much could be done. I guess I'd always had a secret wish that"—he looked up at Fenton Hardy—"well, that . . ."

"I understand," Fenton said, laying a hand on his shoulder.

"But why'd you run away that first night?" Frank asked.

"Because I didn't want to see you get killed! Your parents . . ." He swallowed. "The time I spent with them—I just couldn't bear to be responsible if anything happened to you, for what it would have done to them." He smiled weakly. "So that's it—the whole story."

"All right, Chris," Fenton said. "You'd better rest now." He turned to Considine. "Where's Janosik now?"

"He's speaking with a group of reporters—just the local press and TV people."

"Wait a minute," Frank said. "Jean Eykis is with the *Tribune*."

"Yeah, that's right," Considine said. "Gene Eykis. I checked his credentials myself before we allowed him to enter the room with Janosik."

"No," Frank said, a sudden chill running down his back. "You don't understand."

He pointed at the woman who lay unconscious on the stretcher.

"*That's* Jean Eykis!"

Chapter

16

CONSIDINE STARED FOR A MOMENT.

"Then who's with—oh, no." His eyes widened.

"Oh, yes," Frank said. "Gregor. It has to be." He described the man.

"That's him," Considine agreed. "But how could—"

Joe jerked a thumb at Chris. Considine snapped his fingers.

"That's why he brought me here," Chris realized. "He must have used the equipment in my other apartment to fake her press card."

"And that's why she was here," Frank said. "So she'd be out of the way." He looked up at Considine. "He means to kill Janosik, Lieutenant."

Considine got on the police radio. "Get me Mitchell—he's at the JFK Center symposium. And I mean now!"

He turned back to the Hardys. "All of you—Chris, Frank, Joe, that includes you—get in my car. I'll want you there to help us identify him and the other men."

The three nodded and hopped in the back seat. Their father got in the front on the passenger side. Larry was sent home in a squad car.

"Mitchell, this is Considine. Don't talk, just listen. Stay close to Janosik—got that? One of the reporters there is the guy we want. He's going by the name Gene Eykis. I'll be there in five minutes."

He replaced the handset and climbed in the front seat.

"Fasten your seat belts, boys," he said, switching on the siren. Considine slammed the car into gear, leaving behind the firemen to fight the still-smoldering blaze.

When they arrived, the JFK Center was chaos. Demonstrators surrounded the entire complex, brought there by the news that Janosik was a CIA plant.

"If only they knew the truth," Joe said as they pulled up across the street.

"They'll find out soon enough," Considine said, getting out of the car. "That isn't going to help us right now, unfortunately. We're going to have to go through them to get to Janosik."

He forced a path through the demonstrators—and they followed in his wake. Frank hoped the walls of the lecture hall inside were thick enough so that Janosik couldn't hear what the demonstrators were saying about him.

Finally, they reached the door to the library-lecture hall complex. A guard waved them in, holding back the fringes of the crowd. "They're in the reception hall upstairs. Second door on your left, Lieutenant."

"Thanks, Johnson." Considine clapped the man on the shoulder and led them up the stairs. Inside the hall they found Janosik mingling with reporters and other members of the symposium. Considine's partner Mitchell stood quietly at his side. There was a small podium set up at the far end of the room, where Janosik would take questions from the press later.

"I don't see Krc," Considine said, frowning. "Are any of the others here?"

Frank looked the room over. It was almost as crowded in there as it had been outside. He shook his head, as did Joe and Chris.

"No sign of them, Lieutenant," Frank said, speaking for all three of them.

"Stick close to Janosik, then." He motioned to Fenton Hardy, and the two of them went off to check the hall.

Janosik smiled when he caught sight of the Hardys.

"Frank and Joe," he said, shaking hands with each of them enthusiastically. "I'm very glad to see you again."

137

"And we're glad to see you, too, sir," Frank put in.

Just then the catcalls of the demonstrators outside got very loud. They were saying some very cruel things about Alexander Janosik.

"Free speech," Janosik said ruefully, trying to make light of the moment. "It is a wonderful thing to see in action—no matter what the cause."

"We know you haven't done anything wrong, sir," Frank began. Joe nodded his agreement. "That's partially why we're here."

Janosik's eyes glistened. "I am glad you believe me." He frowned. "This tape—Liehm showed it to me. I do not understand how he did it, but it is preposterous! Never would I take money from the CIA."

Chris spoke up for the first time. "I'm afraid that it's my fault you're in all this trouble."

"Oh?" Janosik raised an eyebrow. "And who are you?"

"This is Chris Bayer, Mr. Janosik," Frank said.

Janosik bowed his head slightly. "I am pleased to meet you, Mr. Bayer."

Chris explained what he had done. When he was through, Janosik shook his head gently. "That is not your fault, Chris." He smiled. "You were weak, when you perhaps should have been strong, but to say this is your fault is nonsense. I know whose fault this is."

A bearded man motioned to Janosik.

"I believe it is time for me to talk to the press," Janosik said, nodding in the direction of the podium. "You'll excuse me."

He strode off, but before he could reach his place at the podium, Considine reentered the room and pulled him aside to whisper a few words in his ear. Janosik nodded. Considine walked behind the lectern and began to speak.

"I'm Lieutenant Ben Considine of the Cambridge Police Force," he began. "If I could just have your attention for a moment—"

The crowd gathered in a semicircle facing the podium. The press, Frank could see, shoved closer to the front. I guess they have a lot of questions for Janosik, Frank thought. He could hardly blame them.

"We've all seen the stories in this morning's papers," Considine continued, "and on TV. Some of you have even written them." The audience gave a few appreciative snickers.

Considine leaned forward at the lectern. "I want you all to know that based on information we have recently uncovered, I can tell you that these stories—and the videotape they are based on—are absolute lies. Alexander Janosik is not now, nor has he ever been, an agent of our government." He smiled. "Though we're very glad to have him in this country."

Considine held out his hand. "Mr. Janosik,"

he said calmly, indicating the lectern. "The stage is yours."

Janosik smiled and moved forward.

The room erupted into bedlam.

Frank exchanged a knowing glance with his brother. He began to think things were going to work out after all.

Just then Frank saw Gregor enter the room and reach into his jacket pocket while heading for Janosik.

"Joe!" Frank said. His brother turned, and at that instant Gregor caught sight of them as well. He cursed and disappeared into the hallway.

"Let's go! Chris, stay with Janosik!" He and Frank began moving as fast as they could through the crowd. They reached the hallway. Gregor was nowhere in sight.

"This way!" Joe said, pointing off to his right, back toward the staircase they had come up.

With Frank a step behind, Joe leapt down the stairs, taking them two at a time. This time, he swore, Gregor wasn't going to get away. He'd chase him down on foot if he had to.

They bounded past the guard at the entrance and out into the crowd of demonstrators.

"There he is! And Liehm's with him!" Joe yelled. He pointed down a path that led into JFK Park, the same path they'd taken with Janosik the day before. Gregor and Liehm were on that path, running past the pillars engraved with the late president's speeches.

The STB agents cut across the park diagonally, heading for the far corner near the river. Frank and Joe set off in pursuit, steadily closing the gap.

A few hundred feet in front of them, the park ended at an intersection where two busy roads crossed, one running parallel to the river, the other back over it into downtown Boston.

Gregor and Liehm reached the intersection and started through it. A car screeched to a halt, barely missing them. As they got to the other side, another car plowed into the one that had stopped. In seconds the entire intersection was jammed with cars. Drivers began honking their horns and screaming at one another.

"Great." Joe stopped at the corner, breathing heavily. "How are we going to get across that—"

Frank never missed a step. He scrambled onto the hood of one car, and jumped from that one onto the hood of the next, leap-frogging his way across the intersection. Joe followed him. They left behind many angry drivers.

Directly across the intersection, an old brick building, covered with ivy, stood on the river's edge—one of the many boathouses that dotted the banks of the Charles. There was a small motorboat tied to the dock at the back of it. Gregor and Liehm had apparently seen it, too, for they were already splashing through the water toward it.

Joe waded in after them, the shock of the cold river water sending chills up his back.

"Hey, what are you doing? You can't take that boat!" Two students stood on the sloping wooden launch platform next to the dock, about to launch a two-man scull. One of them gestured angrily at Gregor. "That's not—"

The STB man raised a gun.

The student backed off, dropping his oars. His friend did likewise. Both turned and ran, disappearing around the far side of the boathouse.

Gregor and Liehm clambered into the boat. Liehm started the engine.

"Oh, no!" Joe yelled, watching the motorboat pull out onto the river. "They're getting away!"

"MAYBE NOT," FRANK SAID. He picked up the scull the students had set down and dragged it to the water. "Come on!"

Joe shook his head. "Are you crazy? We'll never catch them in that!"

"At least we can keep them in sight," Frank said. Joe shrugged and picked up a single set of oars. Frank settled himself in the back of the boat, and Joe took the front.

Slowly at first, then picking up speed as they synchronized their rowing motion, they moved out on the river.

But their best speed was nowhere near fast enough. The motorboat was rapidly pulling away.

"They won't get far!" one of the students who had dropped the small scull shouted from the dock. "The gas tank's almost empty!"

Sure enough, up ahead on the river the motorboat had slowed, and as they watched, stopped.

Frank and Joe resumed their own efforts with redoubled speed, and rapidly closed on them.

Gregor raised his gun when he saw them coming. Taking careful aim, he squeezed off a shot.

The bullet buried itself in the hull of the Hardys' boat.

Their scull shot past the stopped STB men. Joe raised his oar and swung it, knocking the gun out of Gregor's hands. It went spinning into the river.

Liehm sat motionless in the small motorboat, holding another gun on his lap.

"What are you waiting for, fool?" Gregor shouted. "Shoot them! Shoot!"

"No, Gregor." Liehm dropped his gun into the bottom of the boat. He raised his hands. "The time for running, for fighting, is over."

With an inarticulate cry, Gregor bent over and snatched the gun Liehm had dropped. Joe leapt across the water into the motorboat and onto Gregor. As the two wrestled for control of the gun, they pitched into the water.

Wading into the water had been a bracing shock, but diving in was as if a cold fist had suddenly clenched tight around his heart, driving the breath from his body. Joe surfaced, gasping for air.

Gregor was swimming for shore.

Thrusting aside any exhaustion he felt, Joe set out after him.

He'd sworn it—this time Gregor wasn't getting away.

Behind him, Frank struggled to get the scull moving again with one oar. Joe heard him yelling something, but it didn't matter.

He had to catch Gregor.

He reached the riverbank and dragged himself onto the shore. Gregor was barely fifty feet ahead of him.

He put on a burst of speed. Gregor turned and saw him coming. There was a hint of fear in the man's eyes.

At that instant Joe knew he was going to catch him.

Gregor stopped running halfway up the hill between the JFK Center and the Hotel Charles, right beside the construction pit. He turned to face Joe.

"Hardy," he said, breathing heavily. Joe approached to within ten feet of him and stopped. "You have been a source of great annoyance to me."

"My pleasure," Joe said.

Gregor shook his head. "Still you make jokes. Good." He reached down and pulled a knife out of his boot. "You will die laughing then."

He moved forward, brandishing the knife like an expert. Joe stepped back quickly, his eyes tracking Gregor's wrist. If his concentration slipped for even a second, the knife would be in him.

"No jokes now, eh?" Gregor taunted, circling him.

"What kind would you like to hear?" Joe asked warily.

Gregor lunged forward. At the last possible second, Joe dodged. As Gregor passed him, he pushed the STB man into the wooden fence around the construction pit. With a loud crack, the flimsy wood gave way. Gregor went tumbling down into the construction area itself.

Joe jumped down after him, tumbling head-over-heels. He came to a stop and scrambled to his feet.

A two-by-four missed his head by inches.

Gregor must have lost his knife when he fell into the pit, but he'd found something to replace it quickly enough. Building materials littered the floor of the pit—many of them lethal looking. Gregor had wasted no time in choosing another weapon.

The STB man laughed and swung the beam around again. This time it caught Joe full in the chest, and he was slammed to the ground. He lay there stunned, unable for a moment to breathe, or even to think.

"Hah!" Gregor hovered over him, raising his improvised club high over his head, his face twisted with anger and pleasure.

"Now, Hardy, I am rid of you forever!"

He brought the beam crashing down.

Chapter

18

JOE ROLLED TO HIS SIDE. The beam missed him by inches, raising a cloud of dust as it smashed into the ground. Gregor raised it again and brought it down—and again Joe rolled out of harm's way.

This time, as he rolled over, Joe snatched up a handful of dirt and flung it in Gregor's eyes.

"Arrgh!" Blinded, Gregor staggered backward. Joe scrambled to his feet and kicked out, knocking the beam from the agent's hand. He followed through with a right to the jaw that sent the STB man stumbling into a pile of cinder blocks.

Gregor wiped dirt from his eyes. He grabbed a cinder block off the pile next to him, hurling it at Joe, who barely managed to dodge.

"Don't play caveman!" Joe taunted him. "Show me some secret agent tricks!"

147

Gregor snarled and picked up another cinder block. He threw this one even harder.

Joe stepped quickly to his right. The block whistled by and grazed him lightly on the side of the leg.

He fell to the ground as if he'd been shot.

With an awful smile, Gregor picked up another cinder block and moved toward him.

Joe scrambled backward—until he felt something hard at his back.

A cement wall. The foundation of the building being built there. He dragged himself to his feet.

"You can't run any more, Hardy," Gregor said. "Now—"

Springing off the wall, Joe shot forward to drop-kick Gregor in the stomach with both feet. Gregor grunted heavily and dropped the cinder block.

"It is not over yet, Hardy," Gregor said, swaying on his feet, his breath coming in harsh, ragged gulps.

"Isn't it?" Joe asked, wiping the dirt off his face. "Janosik's safe—and you're dead on your feet."

"Not yet," Gregor said. With the last of his strength, he half swung, half fell at Joe. Joe dodged the blow.

Now it was his turn. He balled his right hand into a fist and swung with all his might.

His knuckles connected with Gregor's jaw with

a satisfying *crack*—and Gregor toppled to the ground like a fallen tree.

Joe stood over him, breathing heavily. He was covered with dirt. His jacket was torn, and his body ached all over, but he felt pretty good.

"Joe!" He turned. Frank was standing above him, looking down into the construction pit.

"Everything all right down there?" his brother called down.

"Under control," Joe called back.

"You could have waited for me, you know," Frank said accusingly.

"Oh, no," Joe replied, rubbing his hand and staring down at Gregor. "This one was all mine."

"We caught Ludvik at the airport. He'll be sharing that cell with Gregor and Liehm—for a long, long time," Considine said. "In this country. Prague has officially denied any connection with Liehm's project, and any of the people we've taken into custody."

"I find that hard to believe," Frank said. He and Joe, in dry clothes they'd borrowed from one of the Beast's dorm neighbors, sat at a table back in the Cambridge precinct house, their father and Considine across from them.

"So do I," Considine said. "But we're not going to complain. By the way," he added, "we finally turned up that kid you borrowed the skateboard from. He'll be testifying about Krc attacking you from his car. He also asked if the 'government agent' was done with his board."

Joe laughed. "Well, I guess you can tell us where to return it."

A uniformed officer opened the door. "Excuse me, Lieutenant, those two young men you wanted to see are here."

Considine nodded. "Show them in."

The officer stepped aside, and Chris and Larry walked into the room. They sat down nervously next to Frank.

Fenton Hardy smiled. "Now, Ben, what we were talking about before—"

"Yes," Considine had a grim stare for the newcomers. Both shifted in their seats, looking uncomfortable. "I've talked with the authorities here at Harvard, and based on both your records, and the good words of Mr. Hardy here"—he nodded at Fenton—"the university people and the district attorney's office are willing to drop all charges against you two. Under one condition."

Chris looked up unbelievingly. "Name it."

The Beast nodded his assent.

Considine smiled. "You are both directed to report to the superintendent of continuing education, for teaching assignments in computer education. You'll each be required to teach five hundred hours of classes."

Larry gulped. "I've never been very good at communicating with other people."

"Well, here's your chance to learn," Considine

said. "Their equipment may not be as fancy as what you're used to—"

"I know where they can get more—if they want it," Chris said. "A whole basement full."

Considine nodded. "I'm sure they'd be delighted to accept."

Frank and Joe exchanged smiles.

The door to the room opened again, and Alexander Janosik walked in.

"Mr. Janosik!" Joe exclaimed, standing. "What brings you here?"

The old man was wearing a Harvard sweatshirt that made him look like a grandfatherly undergraduate. "I came to thank you all for everything, and to ask you to attend my closing speech tomorrow at the symposium."

"We really should be getting back home," Fenton Hardy said regretfully, looking at his watch.

"Dad," Joe pleaded. "Can't we stay and hear the speech?"

"Well, wrapping this case up is a good excuse for a celebration, isn't it?" Fenton smiled. "All right, we'll stay in Cambridge tonight."

"Now you're talking. I'll even treat you and the boys to dinner," Considine said.

"No, no." Fenton shook his head. "My treat."

"Maybe Mr. Janosik would like to join us, too," Frank suggested.

Janosik bowed. "I would be honored."

Fenton smiled at his sons. "I'll call your mother and tell her not to expect us home." He turned to Chris. "And there's something else I'd like to tell her about, too."

"Where should we eat?" Frank asked.

"I know this pizza joint right around the corner," Chris suggested.

"I think something a little nicer," Fenton said. "Maybe an Italian restaurant, or—"

"Hamburgers!" Janosik proudly proclaimed. "Very American. Especially with the cheese and bacon—excellent."

Joe clapped him on the back.

"How about it, Frank?" Chris asked. "Bacon cheeseburgers all right with you?"

"Frank likes his burgers plain—don't you, Frank?" Joe teased.

Frank shook his head, knowing when he was beaten. "Bacon cheeseburgers sound fine."